Little Deaths

Little Deaths

A Novel

EMMA FLINT

hachette
BOOKS

New York   Boston

Hachette Books
Hachette Book Group
1290 Avenue of the Americas
New York, NY 10104
HachetteBookGroup.com

First U.S. Edition: January 2017

Hachette Books is a division of Hachette Book Group, Inc.
The Hachette Books name and logo is a trademark of Hachette Book Group, Inc.

The publisher is not responsible for websites (or their content) that are not owned by the publisher.

The Hachette Speakers Bureau provides a wide range of authors for speaking events. To find out more, go to www.hachettespeakersbureau.com or call (866) 376-6591.

Library of Congress Cataloging-in-Publication Data has been applied for.

ISBNs: 978-0316272476 (hardcover), 978-0-316-27248-3 (trade paperback), 978-0316272490 (ebook)

Printed in the United States of America

LSC-C

10 9 8 7 6 5 4 3

For everyone who believed in me when I didn't believe in myself.

Especially for Janet and Rebecca, who have been with me through everything.

And for Alfie, who is always with me, and who I miss every day.

1

On the rare nights that she sleeps, she is back in the skin of the woman from before.

Then: she rarely slept neat in a nightgown, pillows plumped, face shining with cold cream. She sometimes woke in a rumpled bed with a snoring figure beside her; more often she woke alone on the sofa with near-empty bottles and near-full ashtrays, her skin clogged with stale smoke and yesterday's makeup, her body tender, her mind empty. She would sit up, wincing, aware of the ache in her neck and of the sad, sour taste in her mouth.

Now she wakes, not with the thickness of a headache or the softness of a blurred night behind her, but with forced clarity. Her days begin with a bell, with harsh voices, clanging metal, yelling. With the throat-scraping smells of bleach and urine. There's no room in these mornings for memories.

Then, she would make her way across the hallway each morning, and into the kitchen to put coffee on the stove. She would light her first cigarette of the day, and listen to the morning come alive around her: to the blast of Gina's radio overhead, Tony Bonelli's heavy tread on the stairs. Doors slamming, cars starting up. Nina Lombardo yelling at her kids next door.

She would go into the bathroom at the end of the hallway and lock the door behind her. More than a year since Frank moved out, and she still didn't take her privacy for granted. She would strip off yesterday's clothes, and wash in the tiny basin: her hands, her face, under her arms, under her breasts, between her legs. Sometimes she could smell herself—that ripe, yellow odor that she still thinks of as peculiarly her, and that embarrassed her on those days she woke up with company.

Like a bitch in heat ain't ya, honey?

She would scrub between her legs with the rough blue wash-cloth, hard, so that it hurt, and then harder still. Would rub herself dry, pushing along her thigh with the heel of her hand, making it look firm for a moment before letting it fall back into the familiar dimples. Hang up the towel, shrug into her robe, back down the hallway into the kitchen where she poured coffee, thought about the sugar in the jar, never tipped a spoonful into her cup.

Into the bedroom, where she pulled on slacks and a shirt. If she was working a shift at Callaghan's later, she would take out her uniform, hang it on the outside of her closet, check for loose threads and spots. A crisp blouse ironed on Sunday evening. A skirt, just a shade too tight. Shoes lined up, toes together, the heels too high to be practical for a cocktail waitress on her feet all night. But the eyes on her gave her a certain glow that made the tips increase, that made the hours go by faster.

Then she lit another cigarette, slipped her feet into her house slippers, and took her coffee back to the bathroom. Only then, awake and alert, her clothes protecting her, could she look in the mirror.

Skin first—always skin first. On a good day, it was as pale and smooth as a black-and-white photograph. On a bad one, blemishes and old scars speckled the surface and needed to be hidden. She set her cup on the edge of the basin, took another drag on her cigarette, and balanced it in the ashtray that sat on the shelf.

Each morning she smeared on foundation with fingers that trembled depending on how much the view in the mirror had upset her, or on what kind of night she'd had. There were days when her hands were shaking and sweating so that her makeup was patchy, or when her skin was so marked that two layers of foundation seemed to make little difference. On those days, she slapped her face as she applied it. Punishing. She watched her eyes in the mirror as she did it. Hard enough to hurt, not hard enough to mark.

Then the powder, patted into the familiar mask. She pursed her lips, stroked blush into the hollows made beneath her cheekbones, squinted until the face in the mirror became a blurred oval, and she could see that the stripes of color were even. Enough. She blinked, took up her pencil, focused. The eyebrows first: high, surprised arches framing her long eyes. Shadow, liquid liner, three coats of mascara. She worked like an artist: blending, smudging, deepening colors. Occasionally she took a drag on her cigarette, a mouthful of coffee. A final dusting of powder; a coat of lipstick, blotted; a comb through her hair, teasing it taller; a silver spiral of hairspray. And it was done. For the first time that day, she could look at her face as a whole.

She was Ruth, then.

Now she is one of twenty shivering women in a tiled room, huddled beneath thin trickles of lukewarm water. Twenty slivers of cheap green soap. Twenty thin towels on twenty rusty hooks.

In here, she closes her eyes, blocks out the echoing shouts, the singing, the cursing. Tries to pretend she's alone, and concentrates on getting clean. She never feels clean enough. In her first week, she asked for a nail brush, and she digs the bristles into the soap, focuses on picking up the shards of slimy green, on working it into a thin lather between her palm and the brush. And then she scrubs, the way they used to scour her face at the convent school until her skin burned. She closes her eyes and sees herself as she was then—thirteen and tiny; flat-chested; lank-haired; her face a film of oil, covered in red and white pimples. She feels the water sting her skin in the same way, inhales the same smells of bleach and steam, and she isn't sure where she is any longer and she knows that it hardly matters.

And when the guards shout at her to move it along, she opens her eyes and takes her rough towel and rubs her skin until it smarts.

Later she will take the tiny mirror they have allowed her, and look at a fragment of her face and see the shine, the oil, the pimples and know that she is still being punished.

Just occasionally she will lift the mirror to her eyes—quickly, so as not to see the worst—and smooth out her eyebrows, lick her finger and curl it up her lashes, wipe away some of the shine, and try to see herself in her reflection. Tiny vanities are all she has left of herself.

She dresses quickly in the graying underwear and cotton dress they have given her, and pulls on a sweater because she is never warm enough. She waits for the inspection—of her bunk, her cell, herself—and then it's time for breakfast.

At one time, *breakfast* meant magazine-perfect thoughts of coffee pots and warm toast and sunshiny pats of butter. Of a mommy and a daddy and tousle-headed children with milky mouths. Of smiles and kisses and the start of an ordinary day. She thought pictures like these would help lift her out of here, until she learned that the sunshine images would return at night, and the brightness of those breakfast smiles would make her sob into the darkness. Now she concentrates on one moment at a time. On the echoing sounds of the stairwells. The cold metallic handrails. Then the feel of the tray and the plastic cutlery. The smell of eggs and grits and grease. The taste of bitter coffee and the noises that three hundred and twenty-four women make when they chew.

There is a long line of these moments, one after another, like beads on a rosary. She need only hold one at a time, and then they are over, and she can walk to the library and say good morning to Christine. Christine is the librarian and a lifer, and therefore has certain privileges. She was a schoolteacher in Port Washington until she killed her husband with an ice pick and a kitchen knife.

Christine is almost sixty: slender, dark-haired, unfailingly courteous and serene. Her husband wanted to leave her for his twenty-two-year-old secretary, and she had to use the kitchen knife to finish it when the ice pick stuck in his shoulder. She skips breakfast because she is always watching her weight, so the books will often be piled ready by the time Ruth arrives.

Ruth's job is to load the books onto the cart, spines facing outward, giving a little thought to the order of her route and to who might want to read what. Then she sets off on her rounds, collects the books she distributed on previous days and gives out new ones, making a note of who has read what, which books are returned and which are so dog-eared and tattered they will need to be taped up or pulped.

And every day, as she pushes the cart along each landing, and peers into each doorway and says hello to the women she knows will answer, she thinks of that last morning. She has learned not to think of *breakfast* but she cannot help remembering this. The figures curled up on their beds napping or reading, keeping pace with the words using their fingers, never fail to remind her.

On that last day, she finished putting on her face and closed the bathroom door behind her. Minnie circled in the hallway, whining softly. Ruth clicked her tongue and cooed at her, fumbled for her shoes and keys, and headed out into the morning. The air was bright with the promise of another hot day in Queens. They walked for fifteen minutes, past neat, sun-bleached lawns, past rows of identical apartment buildings, Minnie tugging at the leash, Ruth smiling at the men they passed, nodding to one or two women from behind her sunglasses.

Back at the apartment, Ruth drank a tall cold glass of water, reheated the coffee and poured another cup, watched Minnie eat for a moment. Then she decided it was time to wake the kids.

Only they were always awake already. She knew before she lifted the hook-and-eye latch each morning and opened the door to their room what she was going to see. If it was wintertime, they would

be snuggled together in one bed under the blue blanket, Frankie's
arm around Cindy as he read to her. His eyes would be fixed on the
page, the book balanced on his raised knees, his other hand following the letters. When he reached a word he couldn't pronounce, he
would skip over it or look at the pictures and make it up. Cindy
would be holding her doll, her thumb in her mouth, eyes flickering between the book and her brother's serious face. When he read
something funny or did one of his special voices, she would clap
her hands and laugh.

But on hot days like that July morning, they were always up,
standing on Cindy's bed, looking out of their first-floor window,
waving at everyone who passed by. Even the faces they didn't
know would smile back at those wide toothy grins, those soft baby
cheeks. Ruth knew she should be proud of these kids. She should
be proud of herself, bringing them up practically alone. They had
toys and books, their clothes were neat and clean, they ate vegetables for dinner every night. They were safe here. It was a friendly
neighborhood: when they climbed out of their window back in the
spring, an old lady brought them home before Ruth even knew
they were gone. She had to hide her surprise. The woman looked
a little crazy—bright red hair and a shapeless flowered dress—but
she hugged and kissed the kids good-bye before they ran inside.
She clearly wanted to come in after them, but Ruth held the door
and stood in the gap.

"It's hard, Mrs. Malone. I know. I am alone a lot of the time too.
It's hard."

Her voice was harsh, heavily accented. German or maybe Polish. She looked at Ruth and there was judgment in her eyes.

Ruth smiled tightly at her and opened her mouth to say
good-bye.

"I want to say, Mrs. Malone, if you need help, you must only
ask. We are just living over there"—pointing—"number forty-four.
Come by any time."

Ruth stopped smiling and looked her right in the face.

"We don't need help. We're fine."

And she slammed the door and walked into the kitchen where she took down the bottle that was never opened before six at night, and took a long swallow. Then she went into the kids' bedroom where they were waiting for her and she laid into them both with her tiny hands. Because they'd made her take a drink. Because of the way the old woman had looked at her. Because she was so tired of all this.

On that last day, she heard a faint giggling as she approached their room. She lifted the hook-and-eye and there was a thud as they jumped down from Cindy's bed and pattered toward the door. When she opened it, Frankie scooted past her, turned right to go to the bathroom. He wouldn't use Cindy's potty any more. He was a big boy, he said, almost six. Cindy was only four—still her baby. Ruth bent and picked her up, buried her face in the soft golden hair, headed left down the hallway. Cindy's legs circled her waist; one plump arm curled around her neck. She felt her daughter's eyes on her, stroking her powdered cheeks, her sooty lashes, the sticky cupid's bow of her lips. Felt those tiny fingers like kisses, patting her skin, tugging and twisting her hair. Sometimes Cindy told her, "You look like a princess-lady," and she drew pink mouths and round pink cheeks on her dolls, colored their hair red with her finger paints.

Princess Mommy.

Ruth reached the kitchen, let Cindy slide to the floor. Frankie came in, his hands wet, took his seat, frowned at his cereal.

"Can we have eggs?"

Inwardly, she sighed. Nine in the morning and she was already exhausted.

"No. Eat your cereal."

He pouted. "I want eggs."

"For Chrissakes, Frankie, we don't have any fucking eggs! Eat your cereal!"

As she walked out of the room, she saw Cindy's face crumple, heard the start of a wail. She opened the screen door, let it slam behind her, breathed deeply.

She was aware of the crying behind her, of Minnie barking, of the eyes on her from the surrounding windows. Carla Bonelli up on the third floor. Sally Burke's nosy bitch of a mother in the next building. Nina Lombardo looking out from next door. Fuck them. They weren't bringing up two kids single-handed, trying to hold down a job, trying to make a living, dealing with a crazy ex-husband. They didn't understand what her life was like.

It wasn't supposed to be this way. Everything about Frank that had once made her heart race—his way of saying her name, the way he looked at her—after nine years and two kids together, all of that had become like the throb of a familiar headache.

Her eyes were suddenly full of tears and she blinked her way down a couple of steps and sat heavily, took her cigarettes and lighter out of her pocket.

For a moment, she was back outside another apartment building in another summer. She was sitting on the stoop, her hand cradling the swell of her stomach. The door opened and her husband was there beside her, crouching low. She turned to him, and he kissed her cheek, put his hand over hers, felt the baby kick.

"How you doing, honey?"

"I'm okay. Tired." She stretched, yawned. She was always tired. It had been the same when she was carrying Frankie: the last two months, all she'd wanted to do was sleep.

He reached into his jacket pocket. "Got you a present."

She took the small package, tugged at the paper. There was something soft inside: not jewelry, then. Maybe stockings? A nightdress?

It was a toy rabbit: soft plush fur, glassy eyes staring up at her.

"It's for the baby."

She nodded, struggled to her feet, saying something about dinner. Left the rabbit on the step, only noticing later that he'd brought it inside and put it in the nursery, up on the shelf where Frankie couldn't grab it.

She wonders sometimes if that's when she started to resent him.

On that last day it took her a moment to come back to herself. She blinked again, realized her cigarette had burned down to the filter. Stood and turned to go back inside, nodding toward Maria Burke's window. The curtain twitched and Ruth smiled to herself.

Now, as she pushes the library cart from cell to cell, this is what she remembers. She remembers that she went back inside, into the kitchen, poured more coffee, looked at the kids over the rim of the cup.

Cindy was chewing on her cereal, her blue eyes on her brother. Frankie was staring down into his half-empty bowl, his face sullen, his lip sticking out. Just like his father.

She took another mouthful, asked, "Did you have fun with Daddy yesterday?"

They looked up at her. She could see they didn't know what was the right thing to say.

"What did you do?"

Cindy dropped her spoon with a clatter. "He took us to his new house. It was nice."

"Yeah? I didn't know Daddy had moved out of Grandma's place."

She was surprised his mother had let him go again. Surprised he'd had the balls to do it.

She asked, "Does Daddy live by himself now?"

Cindy shook her head, her mouth full again. Ruth waited and it was Frankie who answered.

"He's got a room in a big ol' house. He shares a bathroom with three other men. An' a kitchen. They got one cupboard each for their stuff. The cupboards have *padlocks*."

She nodded, took another sip of her coffee to hide her broadening grin. How the hell did Frank expect to get custody when he didn't even have a house for his kids? She put her cup down.

"Okay, Mommy doesn't have to go to work today. What do you want to do?"

Cindy stopped chewing, her spoon dangling from her hand. Frankie looked up, sulk forgotten.

"Really?"

"Really. Do you want to go to the park?"

Cindy started to whoop, dropped her spoon again, did a wiggling dance in her chair.

"The park! The park!"

Frankie looked at Ruth from under his long eyelashes. "Can Daddy come too?"

There was a stillness, like breath drawn in. She took a last drag on her cigarette, turned away, and crushed it in a saucer. Still with her back to them, she said, "You saw Daddy yesterday, Frankie."

She turned back. "Do you want to go to the park or not?"

Frankie nodded and Cindy beamed again. "Can I wear my dress with daisies, Mommy?"

She smiled at her daughter. Her easy, angelic daughter. "Sure. Finish your cereal and we'll go get you washed and dressed. Frankie, you want to wear your Giants shirt?"

He shrugged, staring down at his bowl.

"Frankie, I asked you a question."

"Yes, Mommy." Still not looking up.

"Okay. Mommy's going to finish getting ready. Frankie, put the dishes in the sink when you're done, then you can watch cartoons with your sister."

He nodded. She decided to let it go this time, took her coffee into the bathroom. Checked her face. Reapplied her lipstick.

She did not know that this was the last morning she would be able to do this freely. That it was the last morning her face would be hers alone.

2

It is easier to think of the rest of that day through the filter of her retelling.

She remembers a windowless room. Wooden chairs.

Then a click. The hiss of static. A man clearing his throat, giving the time and date.

And then the questions. Her hesitant, faltering replies.

"We went for a picnic in Kissena Park."

"I guess...about two-thirty."

"Uh...meatball subs and soda. Pepsi."

"We drove there. The kids were in the front seat with me."

Frankie, rushing down the slide toward her, bolt upright, legs out, chin up. Jumping off the end, running straight back up the steps. Cindy on one of the baby swings with the safety bars, despite her protests, because she always forgot to hold on.

"Higher, Mommy, higher!"

Pushing harder. "Higher, Mommy!"

Her laughter like bubbling water. Dimpled hands clapping. Blond hair flying.

"Again! Again!"

She pushed until she was tired. Then they went to sit in the shade, a little way apart from the other mothers. Ruth spread out the blue blanket she had taken from Frankie's bed and they watched Frankie on the slide. One of Norma's kids kicked a ball wild and it bounced close to

Cindy's face, making her squeal. Frankie ran over, squared up to him: the boy was two years older and four inches taller.

"Hey! Don't you hurt my Cindy! Don't you hurt her!"

The kid looked like he might laugh, so Ruth called Frankie back, showed him that Cindy was fine. They shared the last of the soda between them.

Within five minutes it was forgotten and Frankie trotted over to the jungle gym. Ruth leaned against the rough bark of a tree, holding Cindy against her, soothing her, half-listening to the voices around them.

"I said to him, I said, for Chrissakes, Phil, she's your mother, you need to tell her, and he said yeah yeah, but I know he won't say anything, he's such a..."

"...so his boss came over for dinner on Saturday. I made that turkey roll thing, Joanie's recipe. You know. And my lemon pie. He had three helpings. Three! I never saw..."

She felt Cindy's head droop, felt her limbs grow heavy. She let her own eyes close.

"He says he's working late, but I know what that means. I call the office and there's no reply. And when he gets home, I tell him straight, I say, I know what you're up to, Bob, but he just..."

Ruth came to with a start. Her arms were empty. She sat up, heart thudding. Angela saw her face and laughed. "They're over there, with Norma. Don't worry!" Ruth breathed out, nodded her thanks. Checked her watch and got to her feet.

"You leaving already?"

She brushed down the back of her slacks, folded the blanket. "Got to go. Got to make a call and get dinner for the kids. See you, Angie. See you, Norma."

She walked toward the playground, called Cindy and Frankie to her, put an arm around each of them. They left the park together, the three of them. For the last time.

*   *   *

"We left at four."

"Because I made sure to leave by then. I had to make a call before five."

"Arnold Green. My lawyer."

"He told me to call back. Normally he finished work at five, but he told me he'd be working late."

"Well, we came home. Oh, I picked some food up first. From Walsh's Deli. On Main Street. There was nothing in the apartment for dinner."

"Uh…meat. Veal. And a can of string beans. Milk."

"No, we drove straight home. The kids went outside to play, and I called Mr. Green again. We talked for…I don't know, maybe fifteen, twenty minutes."

"Well, about the custody case. Look, why is all this necessary? What has this got to do with anything?"

"Okay, Okay. I'm sorry. I'm just upset, I guess. I understand. I'm sorry."

"Do you have another cigarette?"

"He told me that my former sitter is going to testify against me."

"No—*not* about the kids! She's claiming that I owe her money. Six hundred dollars. It's bullshit. She says that if I pay her, she won't testify for Frank. He wants the kids to live with him and she's threatening to help him get custody."

"I told you, it's not true. She's trying to blackmail me into giving her money I don't owe her."

"Like hell I will."

A pause. The click of a lighter.

"It's just another problem I have to deal with. That Frank left me to deal with."

"Christ, Arnold, she's lying!…I told you before, she's a mean bitch and she's just bitter because I fired her."

"Okay, Ruth, okay. Calm down."

"I am calm! Jesus. What does this mean? What does it mean for the case?"

"It depends. I need to hear what she has to say first. I'm going to talk to her again before the hearing."

"He can't win, Arnold. He can't."

"Don't worry, okay? She doesn't make a good impression. The judge won't like her. We'll talk about it tomorrow."

"He can't get the kids. I won't let him take them. I won't."

"He won't win, Ruth. No judge is going to take two young kids away from their mother unless . . . well, he won't get custody. It'll be okay."

"Are you sure? You don't sound as sure as you did last week."

"Ruth, don't worry. It'll be fine, you'll see."

"You better be right. He can't have the kids. He can't have them. I'd rather see them dead than with Frank."

"Yeah, then I started dinner. No, wait—first I made another call."

"A friend. He told me he'd call back."

"Just a friend."

"Okay, Christ—okay! His name is Lou Gallagher."

"Yeah. That Lou Gallagher. The construction guy."

Another pause. The murmur of voices, just low enough that the tape couldn't catch them.

"Lou said he'd call me back. So I started dinner. The kids were out front with Sally. Sally Burke."

"I gave them half an orange each and she was helping peel them. I could hear her talking to them and they were giggling. They were . . . oh hell, I just . . ."

The noise of water being poured, a glass being set down.

"Thank you . . . I . . . then I called them inside."

Setting the table, standing over the stove, she thought about her conversation with Arnold Green. About Frank, pushing his way into the apartment last month, telling her he was going for custody of the kids. And why. His sneering face, as he'd listed all the nights she'd been out late, all the men she'd spoken to. Danced with. Flirted with.

"You're not fit to be a mom."

"They need someone reliable taking care of them."

"Your own mother agrees with me."

She watched the kids eat, all the while brooding and prodding that tender spot his words had left. Then she said: "Wanna go for a ride?"

Frankie and Cindy, both holding their plastic cups up to their mouths, finishing their milk.

"Come on, let's go, before it gets dark."

The kids in the backseat, covered by the blue blanket, giggling at the adventure, Ruth alone in the front. Jaw clenched, hands tight on the steering wheel. That son-of-a-bitch thinks he can take my kids away? He can think again. I know Frank. I know he can't manage alone. He must have a woman. And I'm going to find her.

"Let's play a game, okay? Look out for Daddy's car!"

If I can find your car, I can find your place, and who knows what I'll find there, Frank? All about your new life and your new girlfriend. How dare you talk to me about the men in my life! There ain't no way you're living like a monk, you goddamn hypocrite.

You call me a bad mother? You got a big shock coming, and you're too dumb to realize it.

Driving for an hour, the kids in the back growing quieter until she heard Cindy snoring gently and Frankie mutter something in his sleep. Still no sign of Frank's car.

She yawned. Shook herself. Realized she was too tired to keep driving. Turned and headed for home, stopping for gas on the way.

"I undressed the kids, washed them—they had grass stains on their knees from playing in the park and they made a mess when they were eating dinner. I put fresh T-shirts and underwear on them, and I put them to bed."

"Nine-thirty."

"Yeah, I'm sure. You think I let my kids stay up all night? It was nine-thirty."

"Then I started cleaning the apartment. Mr. Green told me that the court would inspect it and it would have to be reported as a good home for the kids. So I was in the middle of a big cleaning project—you know, painting the hallway, clearing out closets, replacing the broken screen in the kids' window."

"What? No, I had a spare one—I got an air-conditioner in my room, so I had a spare screen—my old one."

"Well, I took the screen into their room earlier in the week but I noticed some...some dried dog mess on it. We used it to fence in Minnie's puppies when they were just born and I guess it was never cleaned right. So I put theirs back—the broken one—but I couldn't bolt it in. I'm going to...I was going to clean mine and replace it as soon as I could."

"No, I closed the window. To keep the bugs out."

"Then I collected all the empty bottles around the apartment and put them out for the garbage. I made a pile of old clothes. Mostly Frank's stuff that he'd left behind when he moved out. I washed the dishes. Then I was tired, so I sat on the couch and watched some TV."

"Um... *The Fugitive.* On CBS."

"Until about eleven-thirty. Then I called Lou again."

"No, not at home. He was at Santini's. On Williamsbridge Road."

The phone rang out ten, twelve times before one of the hostesses picked up. Ruth asked for Mr. Gallagher and the girl asked who was calling. When she heard it wasn't Mrs. Gallagher, her voice became less refined.

"Gimme a minute. I'll see if he's around."

She put the receiver down and Ruth listened to her heels clicking into the distance. Music, laughter, the clink of glasses. She wondered what Lou was doing. Who he was with. Why he was taking so long.

Finally she heard footsteps, a change in the air as he picked up.

"Hello?"

"Lou, it's me. You didn't call me back."

"I was busy, sweetheart."

Her legs were tucked beneath her on the sofa. She tapped ash into an overflowing saucer.

"You could come over." She hated the pleading note in her voice.

"Where are you?"

"Home."

"I'm tired, Ruth. I'm just gonna have a drink and go home."

He wasn't alone. She knew he wasn't, just as she knew he wasn't going home. He was with the bowling girls again. The women who said they were going bowling to get away from their husbands. When she'd had a husband, she had been one of them.

After she hung up, she felt like she had an itch she couldn't reach. She fell back on the couch, smoking and thinking.

The phone rang. She snatched it up, her voice breathy, but it was only Johnny.

"Hey, baby, guess who's here?"

He was drunk. He'd probably been drinking all day again.

"Meyer's here, and Dick. Remember Dick, baby? Dick Patmore. He wants to see you. Hell, I wanna see you, baby. I miss you. I ain't seen you in weeks. Why don't you come over?"

"I don't have a sitter, Johnny."

"Can't you get one? I'll give you the money. You know I'm good for the money, baby."

"It's late and I've got this custody thing coming up—I have to see my lawyer tomorrow."

She listened to his heavy, ragged breathing.

"Johnny? I'm going to go now..."

"There was a time you would've got a sitter. A time you'd have come down here like a shot."

"Look, this isn't a good time."

"What's changed, baby? I haven't changed. I still love you, baby. Ruthie. I love you, Ruthie."

Then his voice changed.

"Is it that guy? Gallagher? Is he there?"

"No, of course not. That's…"

"Are you with him now? You're always with him, these days."

"Johnny, there's no one here. It's late and I have to go. Call me tomorrow."

She hung up and turned the TV on again. Poured herself a drink.

"I checked on the kids at midnight. Frankie was half-asleep but he needed to use the bathroom. I tried to wake Cindy but she just rolled over, so I let her sleep."

"Yeah, I put the hook back on their door afterward. I always do."

"No, I don't remember doing it, but I always do."

"We put it up a year ago. Frankie got up one morning and ate everything in the refrigerator. He was sick for hours. After that, I got Frank to put a lock on the door."

"Then I took Minnie for a walk. I saw Tony Bonelli—I waved to him. He had his dog with him too. I was gone twenty minutes, and then I sat on the stoop for a while. It was nice out. A little cooler. I could hear people in the distance. And music. I thought maybe it was the World's Fair."

"I think I bolted the front door when I went back inside."

"I think so."

"I don't remember."

"Look, I don't remember, okay? I don't remember! If I'd known I'd need to remember…did you bolt your door last night, huh? Do you remember doing it?"

"Sorry. I'm sorry. I'm just upset."

"No, I'm okay. I can keep going."

"I gave Minnie some water, then I went into my bedroom and

lay down. Just for a minute, but I must have fallen asleep. Something woke me up. I don't think I was out long."

"Uh…two-thirty…two forty-five."

"No, I don't know. Maybe a nightmare. I thought I heard one of the kids crying, but when I listened—nothing."

"I went to the bathroom. Oh, and then the phone rang again. It was Frank."

"He wanted to talk about Linda, my sitter. The one who says I owe her money."

"I just wanted to get him off the phone. Told him to drop dead. Hung up on him."

"Yeah, I was mad. He called me sometimes in the middle of the night, hoping to wake me up. He wanted to make me mad, and it worked."

"I took the dog out again. Around the block. Then I sat outside for ten minutes or so."

"No, I didn't check on the kids. I checked on them at midnight. They were fine then. They were…Christ."

"No, I'm okay."

"I said I'm okay."

"I took a bath. I was still hot and I took a cool bath. Then I went back to bed."

"Around three forty-five I guess. Maybe four."

She woke when the alarm went off at eight, sticky with sweat. The memory of a dream: a crying child, a dark sky, a white face.

She struggled to sit up, ran her hands through her hair, yawned. Another hot day. She heard Gina coughing upstairs, and then Bill Lombardo yelling at his wife through the wall. A door slammed.

She put coffee on the stove and headed to the bathroom where she stripped and washed. Pulled on her robe and back into the kitchen where she poured a cup of coffee and lit her first cigarette of the day.

She was supposed to be seeing her lawyer later, but for now, she put on
pale Capri pants, a pink shirt. Barefoot, she took her cup into the bath-
room. Started the routine that would bring Ruth to life in the mirror.

"I came out of the bathroom and I took the dog for a walk."

"Eight forty-five. Maybe a little later—I couldn't find my shoes."

"Fifteen minutes. Probably less."

"Um . . . a couple of people. No one I knew."

"We got back and I fed Minnie. Refilled her water bowl. Drank
another cup of coffee."

"Yeah, about ten after nine. No later."

"Nothing unusual. I could smell something burning. Toast, I
think. And I could hear Gina's radio. Oh, and I heard a phone
ringing somewhere. Distant."

"No, nothing else. Except . . . well, the silence. The apartment
was quiet."

"Yeah, I remember noticing the quiet. Wondering if they were
still asleep. And I . . . then I opened the door."

But none of that tells how it was.

Minnie whining, restless. Ruth's hurried, self-conscious walk, tug-
ging at the hem of her shirt, feeling the heat seep through her layers of
makeup. Thinking about her meeting with Arnold Green that after-
noon, about Frank, about the rent due at the end of the week.

Back at the apartment: the taste of lukewarm coffee. The crack in
the ceiling she'd noticed the week before and forgotten about. The smell
of hairspray through the half-open bathroom door. Her headache and
her clumsy rummaging for aspirin.

And then the silence. Not just the fact of it, but how loud it was.
How the space that would normally be filled with voices and giggling
and the pad of their feet was just that: space.

And the sight of her hand in front of her, lifting the latch, pushing the door. And again, and again, and again, every moment since: the slow sweep of the white-painted wood, and the widening expanse of light, and her hand falling to her side through the weight of the still air, and her voice catching in her dry throat. And the room beyond. Empty.

3

So that was how it began. With a locked door to an empty room. With her running out into the street, a set of sweat-slick keys held tightly in her hand, pressed hard into her palm. With her circling the block calling their names.

It began with anger. *If they've climbed out the damn window again, they'll be in a whole heap of trouble.*

And then the anger faded to a gradual awareness of her uneven breathing, of the sickness in her stomach. A realization, as she came back to the corner of 72nd Drive, that her skin, her hair, were wet.

She turned both ways, unable to decide which direction to go.

The wrong choice could mean.

It could.

She bit her lip to kill that thought. Turned left.

So many kids. Every gleam of fair hair was a jolt to her heart. Then she saw a little boy ahead of her, and there was something about his walk. She grabbed his arm and spun him around.

"Frankie! What the fuck..."

She looked into the face of a stranger and dropped his arm, saw his mouth open. Barely registered his rosebud mouth breaking into a howl. Barely heard his mother.

"Hey! Hey lady! What the hell do you think..."

She walked on, faster, until she lost sight of where she was going. Kept her eyes fixed on the faces that passed her, on the sidewalk ahead. She walked unevenly, avoiding the cracks.

Step on a crack and break your back
Step on a crack, kids ain't coming back

She pressed her hand against her mouth to stop anything escaping, began to run. She ran with no sense of where she was, then took another turn and she was back on 72nd Drive. She saw a figure hurrying toward her. Realized it was Carla Bonelli. Saw the woman's lips move, managed to get out:

"Frankie and Cindy are...they're...I can't find them...help me find them..."

Carla went to take her arm but Ruth shook her off angrily, stared wide-eyed around her, and then back. "Find them. Please."

And she moved on, stumbling, her arms wrapped around herself. Carla stood staring after her.

Back home, Ruth picked up the phone with shaking fingers and dialed. Pressed the receiver hard against her ear, clenched her other hand, nails digging into her palm. Listened to the phone ring.

Waiting.

Waiting.

And then:

"Frank? Have you got the kids?"

"Don't fool around! Where are the kids?"

"They're not here. They're..."

"Of course I checked their room! I've been all around the block."

"Twenty, thirty minutes—I don't know! I've looked everywhere and I...I can't find them."

"Please. If you have the kids, tell me. Don't do this, Frankie. Please."

It was the last time she called him Frankie.

He said something, but she couldn't take it in, just heard the words "coming over" and when he hung up, she clung to this. She went to the window to look for his car, and put a cigarette in her mouth. It took her three attempts to light it.

*　　*　　*

Frank arrived. She opened the door and he took her in his arms. Ruth stood stiffly for a moment and then patted his shoulder. He let her go and then he just stood in the hallway.

"You need to . . ." she gestured toward the kitchen and finally he began to take charge.

He picked up the phone and she heard:

"I want to report . . . my kids are missing. I want to report my kids missing."

"An hour ago."

"Malone."

"My address or the address the kids live at?"

"No, we're . . . they live with their mother at present."

He brewed more coffee, made her sit down. Poured a glug of brandy in and watched while she drank. It was the last of the bottle that Gina had brought down on New Year's. It burned and Ruth shuddered, but the sick feeling disappeared. She looked at him, saw his lips slide back over his clenched teeth in an imitation of a smile.

"Okay, honey. Okay. The cops are on their way. We have to stay calm. We have to think."

Minnie trotted in and pressed her nose against Ruth's knee until she pushed her away. She couldn't bear to be touched.

It took Ruth a moment to get to her feet. She had to pee, and then she looked at herself in the bathroom mirror. Her face was covered in a film of perspiration, and her eye makeup had smudged.

She repaired the damage as best she could, lifted her arm to comb her hair and smelled sweat. She looked in the mirror again. Beneath that layer of makeup, her body, her face, were all wrong. She looked wrong. Smelled wrong.

You smell like a bitch in heat.

She went into the bedroom and changed her clothes. Put on a clean blouse that flattered her figure. She knew that there would be men, strangers, looking at her, asking questions. Their eyes all over her like hands. She had to be ready for them. She had to look right.

As she walked back into the kitchen, there was a knock at the front door.

There were two of them. Two cops, in her home. One of them, the younger one, said, "I understand that you're separated, Mr. and Mizz Malone?" That's the first thing he said. Then he said, "Is this about custody?" She had no idea what he meant, what to say.

They sat in the kitchen. Ruth put a clean ashtray on the table, and one of them got on the phone to someone. He came back, and there was a look between them, then he took Frank off into the living room. She was left with the younger one. He told her his name but she forgot it.

He just sat there, asking questions. What were the kids' full names? Their ages? Had they gone missing before? Did she have a recent photograph?

Then he asked, "How long have you been separated from your husband, Mizz Malone?"

"I don't...what does this have to do with the kids?"

He said nothing, just waited.

"Since last spring. Frank moved out in April last year."

"Why did you split up?"

She looked at him, sitting there in his cheap suit and his scuffed shoes, and she knew she couldn't make him understand. None of her reasons had been enough for Frank, for her mother, for most other women she knew. It wouldn't be enough for this cop, this kid.

"We weren't getting along. We were arguing a lot."

"And now he's suing for full custody of the children? On what grounds?"

"He says I'm...he's claiming the children would be better off with him."

He wrote that down and then his voice got stern.

"If this is some kind of game, Mizz Malone, if you're doing this to get back at your husband, you better stop before it goes too far."

She looked at him. A game? Her face grew warm and she could feel a prickling at her hairline, and she couldn't hold it in any longer.

"What the hell is all this? Why aren't you out there looking for my children? You need to find my children!"

He cleared his throat. Ignored her. "Have you hidden the kids somewhere?"

Something in her eyes made him raise his hands. "Okay, okay," he said. His face was flushed. He looked like he should have been in high school.

She swallowed hard, then took a long drag on her cigarette. Shook her head, although by then he'd left the room.

It burned down to her fingers and she threw the butt in the sink, ran cold water over her hand. The icy spattering on her skin woke her: she became aware of the sourness in her mouth, the sick feeling in her stomach.

Time passed. Frank came in, asked if she'd eaten that morning. She made a gesture with her shoulder, pushing him away. Drank more coffee. All she could hear was Frank's harsh breathing as he smoked, occasionally the murmur of the other cop's voice on the phone.

Frank left the room and she heard water running in the bathroom. Then there was a knock at the door and she heard Carla Bonelli's voice. There was a low murmur and she heard "...to help. Can I see her?" Another low rumble, then the door closed. Frank came in and said, "Carla wanted to come in. I told her it was best not to."

She didn't understand, but she nodded.

He said, "I asked her to take the dog too. Just until...for now."

She nodded again, lit another cigarette, stared at the clock on the wall until she remembered it had stopped the week before. It had made them late for Frankie's dentist appointment.

Another knock at the door and footsteps in the hall. She looked at Frank and he looked back at her. Voices. Two men stood in the doorway: one was the kid cop with the pink face.

The other man was older. There was a stillness about him that let her mind rest for a moment. He was big, square-shouldered, wearing a loose-fitting suit that hung from his large frame. His skin was yellowish, waxy, with large pores, his face sagging above his thick neck, heavy eyes drooping above a scowl. His nose twitched as he looked at her, like she smelled bad. She smoothed her skirt. Patted her hair.

He reminded her a little of an actor she'd seen somewhere. In a film, maybe with Ingrid Bergman. Something that was on the TV one afternoon.

He was still looking at her and she realized he'd said something. She had to get him to repeat it.

"I'm Sergeant Devlin, ma'am. I'm in charge here."

His voice was pure Bronx.

Jerry, that was the actor's name. Jerry something.

She nodded, began to turn away. And then, "We ran your name through our files, Mrs. Malone. Seems like our officers have been here before. Several times."

He took a piece of paper out of his pocket.

"Noise complaints in April and June last year. And March 5 and May 19 this year."

"I don't..."

"And one count of public intoxication. November 12, 1964."

She smoothed her hair. Cleared her throat. "What does this have to do with my children?"

He just kept looking at her. Then suddenly, "We need to search the apartment. Might need to take some things away with us. That a problem, Mrs. Malone?"

She shook her head. What else could she do?

She and Frank sat silently. She chewed the skin around her nails, stared at the clock again. Every noise made her jump. Then Devlin was back in the doorway.

"We need you to come with us for a moment."

She looked at his face. "Did you find them? Did you find Frankie and Cindy?"

He looked her straight in the eye. "Just come with us, please."

She stood. "Both of us?"

His eyes flickered to Frank. "Yeah."

She expected him to lead them to the kids' room, but instead, they went outside and around to the trash cans. She almost laughed when she saw what they'd done. The cans were empty, their contents all over the ground. Two more cops in uniform were raking through piles of garbage: empty milk cartons, food packaging, cans of dog food, pieces of orange peel, papers, coffee grounds. The smell turned her stomach. Devlin pointed to a plastic sack, the top untied. "Is this yours, ma'am?"

She looked at him, looked at the bag. She walked over and looked inside. There were nine or ten empty bottles. Gin. Bourbon. Wine. She looked back at him. Was he serious?

"I don't know. I can't remember what I threw out recently. Maybe."

His face didn't change. Frozen, just like an actor in a still. He nodded at one of the uniforms, who came over holding an envelope. He thrust it into her face and she recoiled; it had been lying under old food.

"It has your name on it, Mrs. Malone."

She saw it had contained a bill for something, she couldn't remember what. But she remembered opening it and throwing the envelope away and putting the bill in the drawer. Wondering when she'd be able to pay it.

"That was in the same bag."

"Oh. Then . . . yeah, I guess it's mine."

"And the bottles?"

She looked again. "Well, yeah, I guess they're mine too. If the bill was in this bag with them."

"All of them?" He did something with his mouth.

"What does this have to do with the kids? Why aren't you looking for Frankie and Cindy?"

"Just trying to establish some background, ma'am."

"I was cleaning up the apartment. My lawyer told me...there's going to be an inspection by the court. He told me to clean the place. Paint it. Make it look nice." She didn't look at Frank.

Devlin looked at her for a long time and then, without taking his eyes off her, spoke to the cop in uniform standing behind him. "Make a note, Officer. Related to the custody case." He made them sound like dirty words.

She turned, but Frank was avoiding her eyes.

"I was just cleaning up."

He nodded, but he still didn't look at her.

More time passed. Ruth drifted into the hallway, paced the living room, chewing her nails, smoking past the lump in her throat. There was a man with a brush and a pot kneeling by the coffee table, dusting it with powder. He was working his way through all the rooms, leaving a white trail behind him. He glanced up at her but didn't speak.

Back in the hallway, she noticed that the door to the kids' room was ajar, the light spreading over the worn carpet. She took a step toward it, saw three men bending over the bureau by the window: Devlin, the pink-faced cop, a guy with a camera.

"Make sure you get it all." Devlin's voice was low, his tone intense, focused. It made her stop and lean against the doorframe.

The shouts from the searchers outside were a hundred miles away, distant and distorted through the hot, shimmering afternoon.

There was nothing on the bureau: a couple of Frankie's books, a lamp, a tube of cream for Cindy's eczema. Ruth had cleaned up a couple of days before, put away a pile of laundry that had been on the top, some of the kids' toys. She remembered wiping it, rubbing at the rings of a dozen cups. Remembered the smell of beeswax polish.

The photographer looked up at Devlin. He was short, with thin hair and round glasses. There were damp patches under his arms and his tie was crooked. She watched as he bent over, as he lined up his camera. As the sunlight through the window made a cloud of white dust specks dance.

The shutter clicked once. Twice.

Her head ached. She turned away.

More cops arrived. The phone rang often. Devlin was still there. He came into the living room, asked to speak to Ruth, ushered her into her own bedroom. She came in, still clutching Cindy's toy rabbit. He stood with his back against the door. Her legs were shaking and she sat on the bed, pressed them together so that he wouldn't see.

She tried to speak but was afraid that when she opened her mouth, the tears in her throat would spill out. Something inside her, something instinctive and ancient, kept her from letting go. Instead, she hunched over, holding the rabbit against her, holding in the sickness and the fear, bent double with the effort. Her mouth wanted to open and she had to clench her jaw to keep it shut. She had to keep the wrong part of her, the messy part, hidden.

Devlin took out a notebook and started to ask questions. At first she couldn't hear. All she could feel was the soft, worn fur under her hands.

"She doesn't have her rabbit."

Her voice was too quiet.

"Mrs. Malone?"

"Cindy didn't...she doesn't have her rabbit. She'll be scared without him."

She looked up. He was frowning at her.

"Mrs. Malone, I need to ask you some questions. Please try to focus."

She nodded at him to go on, and her voice was flat and rasping when she answered.

"Midnight. I checked them at midnight. I took Frankie to the bathroom. He was half-asleep but he needed to use the bathroom. I tried to wake Cindy but she just rolled over. So I let her sleep."

"I told you, I bolted the door afterward."

"No, I don't remember doing it, but I always do."

Devlin went back to the living room, asked Frank to come into the kids' room. Curious, Ruth moved to the doorway of her own room, watched them cross the hallway.

Heard, "What do you think, Mr. Malone? What do you think happened here?"

There was a pause. She could almost hear Frank thinking, could see him looking around the room, wondering what to say.

"I don't know. How would I know?"

"Mr. Malone, I've got five kids myself. I understand how you feel. Is there anything you can tell us—anything at all? The smallest thing might be important."

Frank again, slowly. "The window's open. Whoever took the kids...that must be how they got in."

"Why do you say that?" Devlin's voice was sharp.

"Well, Ruth wouldn't leave it open like that without the screen—she was always worrying about bugs. Frank Jr. got stung once—his arm swelled up and we had to take him to the emergency room. Whoever took them, they came in there."

"Mr. Malone—are you sure your wife didn't hide the kids somewhere?"

Another pause. "I don't think so. I don't know."

She was in the living room, lying on the sofa, a blanket over her despite the heat. Frank kept telling her to get some rest. She was holding Cindy's rabbit to her face, stroking the threadbare fur over and over, breathing in the smell of Cindy's skin, Cindy's hair,

Cindy's sleeping breath. When she got up to pee, she saw that the door of her bedroom was ajar. She pushed it, saw the young cop with the pink face kneeling on the floor.

"What the hell are you doing?"

He jumped, turned. He was holding a blue overnight case that he'd found under the bed.

"What are you doing with that?"

He looked down at the case and blushed, and for a moment she thought he was going to apologize. Then he remembered what he was doing and the mask fell back into place.

"It's just routine, ma'am."

"Routine? That's *my* case. That's nothing to do with my kids. Why aren't you out looking for my children?"

There was a shadow behind her and a smell of Players. Devlin.

"What's the problem, Detective Quinn?"

"Mizz Malone was just..."

"I'm sure Mrs. Malone wants to cooperate fully, don't you ma'am?"

She let her hands fall from where they were balled into fists, let her shoulders drop, and took in the wreckage of her privacy: the underwear strewn on the bed, the open drawers, the bags and shoes pulled out of her closet.

"We know what we're doing." Quinn unzipped the case.

A waterfall of postcards, letters, cards. He picked them up one by one and read the signatures. Dozens of them. All from men. Some from Frank, before they were married. A year's worth from Johnny Salcito. A few from Lou Gallagher, going back to March or April. And some from other men, men she could barely remember.

"Jesus Christ," he said. He looked up and his eyes went past her to Devlin.

She lifted her chin and permitted herself a small smile. Then she turned, and Devlin was watching her.

She dropped her eyes. Dropped the smile.

4

It was a Wednesday when the call came into the *Herald*. A Wednesday morning in the hottest week of July, and Pete Wonicke was sitting at a desk that didn't feel like his.

Back in May he'd paid Horowitz twenty bucks to trade and the desk still felt strange to him, although it had been over two months now. His new desk was near enough to the secretaries that he got a heads-up on anything that came through on the main switchboard and needed someone assigned to it. The other reporters, the ones who'd been here a while, all had sources among the local cops or snitches they had on retainer. So occasionally they'd get a call, disappear for a couple of days, and come back with something. Pete knew the only way he'd get a start on a decent story was with luck.

He'd gone for a beer with Terry DeWitt the night before, and they'd ended the night in a dark basement bar in the Bowery. There was a line four deep at the bar, and a layer of blue smoke at head-height that wrapped the room in gauze and made Pete's eyes water. It was the kind of place he would never have gone to if it had been up to him. Terry DeWitt had been at the *Herald* for almost eight years, and six at the *Courier* before that. He'd earned respect. There was even talk of him getting a regular column. He was the kind of guy Pete needed to know.

Terry had left the bar at midnight and Pete wound up taking three games of pool off a guy called Lucky with a missing finger and a wad of tobacco between his cheek and his back teeth. He'd still had a buzz on when he'd woken a few hours later, fully clothed and sticky on top of the sheets. He'd made it to the office feeling remarkably well—first to arrive for the day shift, like always—but now the buzz was fading and it was time to admit the hangover knocking on his skull and tell it to take a good slug at him and then leave him in peace.

Pete stretched out his legs and kept sifting through the overnight bulletins in search of the start of a story, kept one eye on what was going on around him. Head throbbing, he was struggling to focus over the clatter of typewriter keys, ringing phones, the rise and fall of voices, and, above it all, the hum of the stark fluorescent lighting. He pushed his hair off his forehead and fanned himself with a notebook. The newsroom smelled, as it always did, like a cross between a locker room and a cheap diner: the smell of men who didn't bathe too often mingled with the odor of stale clothes, cigarettes, and fried food. Today it was making him nauseous.

He wondered if he could talk one of the girls in the typing pool into running down to Brooke's and getting him a root beer float. He reached into his jacket for his wallet and felt the crackle of his mother's latest letter, and sickness rose in his belly and daubed his skin with sweat.

Janine kept walking back and forth between the boss's office and the copy machine, and he could feel her glances against his neck. Pete kept his head bowed over his bundle of papers, his mind drifting to something sweet and cold and fresh. To the clink of a long spoon against an old-fashioned sundae glass, the thick yellow foam where ice cream meets soda.

He continued flicking through the bulletins and made occasional notes. His mind kept drifting to the folded white square in his pocket. Overlaying the familiar feeling of suffocation was a more recent sensation of relief at the distance between the world his mother's letters brought back and his own life here in New York.

She wrote every week on flimsy white paper that she bought at the stationery store in town. Every time he felt the thinness, the cheapness, of the paper she used, he thought he should buy her a box of something *nice*. Thick paper the yellow color of fresh cream. Or something with a watermark and a wash of faint lilac, or pale blue notecards with a border of flowers. Something from a store in Manhattan: he could ask them to wrap it and send it to her, and he could reward himself for spending money he didn't have by imagining her face when she opened it.

And then he would think of how her letters made him feel. And he hated himself every time he thought of how he knew, he *knew*, he wouldn't be able to bear reading his mother's words written in her neat, careful hand on paper meant for rich city women.

He would dash off a formulaic reply to each letter within hours of its arrival, and then guilt would compel him to carry it around for days afterward, like a security blanket. He'd told her to write him at the paper: he wanted her to see, to acknowledge each time she wrote out the address, that he'd made it. He'd done what he'd set out to do: he had a real job, in the city, at the kind of place where mail was delivered to his desk.

But as much as he tried to focus on that feeling, as much as he wanted to believe he was a success, there was always a nagging worry at the back of his mind about how much longer he might have this job. The circulation numbers were dropping every week, and there were always rumors about cutbacks. He couldn't afford to lose his place here, and not just because he was barely making the rent each month. He'd done his time here—typing up weather reports and traffic accidents and summaries of college football games—and they owed him. He'd been waiting a long time for a break—and when the call came in, *that* call, he'd be ready.

And on that hot July morning, the call came in.

Janine took it, listened for a moment, chewing gum and scribbling, mumbling the occasional "uh-huh." He kept his eyes on her face, and noticed that the stem of her cat's-eye glasses was cracked, that her lipstick had begun to bleed into the lines around her mouth.

Then she said, "How old?" and "What's the address?"

Just a missing kid, then. A teenager who'd stayed out past curfew, or a preschooler who'd wandered away in the street while his mom's back was turned. It happened. There'd be a panicked couple of hours, then someone would notice him crying on a sidewalk and call the cops, and there'd be a happy ending and a nice photo of the kid and the mom, tearful and smiling through a mixture of shock and relief.

Predictable. Dull.

Still, it was a story and he might be able to work it up into something—a piece about rising crime stats or working mothers and latchkey kids, maybe. Something with a little human interest. So Pete put the bulletins to one side, swung his feet down, and straightened his tie.

Janine hung up, finished writing something, and tore a sheet off her notepad, then stood and headed for the metro desk. Pete was in front of her before she'd taken half a dozen steps.

"Hey there, Janine."

She blushed. Snapped her gum. Took off her glasses and fiddled with the chain they hung from.

"Hey, Pete."

"You're looking awful nice today. I tell you that yet?"

Her blush deepened and she tucked a strand of hair behind her ear.

"Uh...no..."

"Well, you are. That husband of yours is a lucky guy. I hope he knows it."

She giggled, one hand over her mouth, hiding her crooked teeth, and looked up at him, shifting her weight onto one hip.

"So what was that?" He nodded at the paper in her hand.

"Oh, it's just a kid. A kid gone missing in Queens. In...um... between Queens College and Kissena Park."

"And where might you be taking this missing kid?"

She giggled again.

"Oh...well, Mr. Friedmann told me to give the next call to Jack Lamont."

Jack Lamont, who had picked up the murdered hooker story last month. Who'd somehow gotten an interview with the star witness at the Mendoza trial in March.

Out of the corner of his eye, Pete saw Jack getting to his feet, heading for the bathroom or the coffee machine.

He leaned forward, inhaled the smells of cigarettes and perfume and the face powder she wore. Lightly stroked the sleeve of her blouse.

"That's a real pretty color on you, Janine."

Her eyes widened and she blushed again. He risked a glance sideways and sure enough, Jack was gone. Pete straightened up.

"I don't think Jack's in today."

She blinked.

"He isn't? Oh I could have sworn I saw him earlier..." She turned and they both looked over at Jack's empty desk. Then she looked back at Pete, a little helpless.

"It's okay. I'll take it for you."

"Oh, well, I don't know. Mr. Friedmann said..."

"C'mon, Janine. I bet Friedmann would rather have someone else take it than leave a message lying around while the *Star* or the *Courier* pick up the story."

He plucked the paper out of her hand and tucked it in his pocket. Then he winked at her.

"Oh," she said again. "But Mr. Friedmann said... I mean..."

"Don't worry about it. I've got it now."

Pete drove slowly, looking for a parking spot. He might have thought he had the wrong street—this was a quiet neighborhood, not the kind of place where kids went missing—except for the women. Ten or fifteen of them, clustered in small groups on a patch of yellow grass outside an apartment building. Teased hair, low voices, faces glistening in the heat. Then he noticed a guy who worked at the *Courier*: Anderson, maybe. Something Swedish-sounding.

Pete had seen him at a press conference: his shaggy blond hair and faded corduroy jacket standing out among the suits and ties. He was leaning on the hood of his car, doodling in his notebook.

Pete strolled up to him as casually as he could.

"Pete Wonicke from the *Herald*. You're Anderson, right?"

The guy barely glanced up from his drawing. "It's Anders."

"Right. Sorry."

Pete stood beside him for a moment, then took his notebook out of his pocket, needing something to do with his hands. He saw a cop walking around the corner of the building with an evidence bag and another standing at the edge of the women, frowning up at the windows of the building.

They were taking this seriously, then.

He asked, "Anything happen yet?"

Anders shrugged. "It's just a kid who wandered off. No big deal."

His voice was clipped. Bored. He looked Pete up and down. "Why? You expecting something more interesting?"

Pete felt his face flush and looked away, pretending to fiddle with his camera. He turned away from Anders, snapped two or three pictures of the building, then approached the nearest group of women. They noticed the notebook and then the camera, and their hands went to their hair; they began smoothing, primping.

He pasted a smile onto his face and stepped forward.

"Good morning, ladies. I'm Peter Wonicke from the *Herald*. I'm here because my editor's very concerned about the missing child. I wonder if any of you can tell me..."

"Children."

She wasn't looking at him, but he knew she was the one who had spoken. Stocky legs, wide hips, a tight print dress, and house slippers. Brassy blond hair scraped up to hide the roots. A round face, heavy on the rouge. No wedding ring. She was smoking and watching the cop flick through his notebook.

"Excuse me, Miss...?"

"Eissen. Gina Eissen." She turned toward him. "Double S."

She blew a plume of smoke into the space between them. "You said 'child.' There are two children missing. Frankie and Cindy Malone."

She looked at him now and under her stare, he felt his inexperience like a thick wool coat. His skin prickled and his armpits were damp.

He noticed a girl hovering nervously on the edges of the group. Maybe fourteen, fifteen. Then another woman stepped forward. Tall, with piled curls and a long nose, she wore a pale blue cardigan draped loosely around her shoulders, a white handbag over her arm. She held out a manicured hand.

"Maria Burke. What did you say your name was?"

"Wonicke. Peter Wonicke from the *Herald*."

"I see. Well, it's very nice that your newspaper has sent someone out to cover this, Mr. Wonicke, and I'm glad you're at least wearing a tie, unlike that other reporter—but I'm afraid you're wasting your time."

She was looking at his face, but her eyes didn't meet his.

"Ma'am?"

"The Malone children aren't *missing*. Mrs. Malone is sometimes a little . . . distracted, and they've just gotten out somehow when her back was turned. That's all. There's no story here. Children don't go missing in this neighborhood."

This he could deal with.

"Did you say Malone, Mrs. Burke?"

"I did."

"And how old are the children?"

He got the full names and ages of the kids and the parents, how long they had lived on the street, and Mrs. Burke's opinions on everything from Mrs. Malone's clothes to the *Herald*'s coverage of the last presidential election to the slackness of municipal officials in Queens. He even took a picture of the women. All the time he was aware of the girl nearby. Finally she stepped forward and looked at Maria Burke.

"Uh . . . Mom?"

Mrs. Burke was in the middle of a tirade about garbage collection and scarcely paused for breath.

"Not now, dear. Mommy's busy."

"Mom, I have to..."

"Sally, I've told you before. It's rude to interrupt adults when they're having a conversation."

"But it's about Frankie and Cindy."

That got all of their attention.

"What do you mean?"

"Well, it's just..." She was twisting her hands, looking from Mrs. Burke to Gina Eissen to Pete. "I don't know what to do. I tried to tell the policeman and he said he was busy too."

"Tell him what, dear?"

"The stroller over there?" They all looked. It was a sturdy baby carriage with a box on top, standing a couple of feet from a window that was open to seventy-five degrees. Pete raised his camera, got off a couple of shots.

"What about it?"

"Last night, it was way over past Mrs. Rossi's building. It's been moved."

She looked at Pete. "The open window? That's their bedroom. That's Frankie and Cindy's bedroom."

Mrs. Burke still looked impatient. "And?"

"Well, I just thought...maybe someone moved the baby carriage to...you know, to get them out that way. Or maybe they used it to climb out by themselves."

"Sally, don't be ridiculous. Two small children couldn't move that great thing on their own—they could hardly reach the handle. Stop trying to draw attention to yourself, dear, and let the policemen do their job."

Pete felt Gina Eissen's eyes on him and turned his head to meet them.

"What do you think, Miss Eissen? What do you think happened to the children?"

No hesitation. "Someone took them."

There was a gasp from a small, dark woman who had been silent until then. She turned to face them, her olive skin flushed. "Don't say that, Gina! Don't you say it!"

Gina dropped her cigarette and ground it out with her toe, slowly, deliberately.

"Why not? He asked me what I thought."

She looked directly at Pete.

"Ruth Malone wouldn't let those kids out of her sight, Mr. Wonicke. They're everything to her. She isn't *distracted*"—a venomous look at the pursed mouth of Mrs. Burke—"she's *busy*. She works long hours and she's bringing the kids up by herself. She's busy and she's tired, but she'd know if they wandered away. Someone took 'em. You'll see."

She bit her lip. Swallowed.

"Someone, some crazy, came in the night and took 'em, and she'll"—a nod toward the open window—"she'll be going nuts in there."

All at once Pete felt the story swell to fill the fears of the women around him. Gina Eissen at least believed something bad had happened to those kids. He was suddenly aware of the pounding of his heart, of his dry mouth. This could be the start of something big.

In here, during the long black nights or the still, slow hours pacing the yard, Ruth has tried to pinpoint the moment that everything changed. If there was even a moment.

Perhaps it was when Devlin found the bottles in her garbage that first morning. Or perhaps it was that afternoon, when the call came in.

She was standing in her living room holding a glass of cold ginger ale, looking out of the window at the cops on the lawn and at the women on the sidewalk. She watched the women through the slats of the blinds: their darting eyes, shiny beneath teased hair, their glossy mouths opening and closing. Their elbows nudged out from beneath folded arms whenever one of the cops moved.

And then the phone rang. She turned, but the young pink-faced cop got there before her. He picked up the receiver, then moved away from her, muttering something that she couldn't hear. She thought it was just another of those calls between cops. Nothing to do with her.

Then he cupped his hand over the receiver and shouted, "Sergeant Devlin! You need to take this call, sir!"

Her mouth was already open to ask the questions she somehow knew he wouldn't answer, when Devlin came through the door, moving quickly despite that solid square bulk. He took the phone and ran a hand over his forehead, through his slick hair.

"Devlin." A pause. "When?...Are you sure?"

His eyes slid around the room as he talked, his mind elsewhere. And then his gaze cleared and came to rest on Ruth. She has imagined what he must have seen in that moment: the shape of her body against the bright window, her hair a fiery halo around her white face, her eyes wide and afraid and fixed on his.

For a long moment they looked at each other through the clear golden light. She took a step forward.

"Have they...what's..."

Then the person on the other end of the phone said something, and the question died on her lips. Devlin hung up, turned his whole body to face her.

"I need you to come with me, Mrs. Malone."

"Did they find them? Did they find Frankie and Cindy? Have they...are they okay?"

She could almost feel their tiny hands in hers. She imagined their tears. Their stained shirts. The candy she would buy them.

He looked at her and his expression was unreadable.

"Just come with us, ma'am."

"Where to? Are they okay?"

He didn't answer, just opened the door for her. She put her glass down and walked ahead of him into the hallway. She was trembling.

As she stepped out of the building, Devlin half a pace behind her, Ruth saw again the group of women on the sidewalk. Women she knew, women whose kids played with hers. Some had tears in their eyes or sad, blurred faces. Some were whispering behind their hands. She saw frowns, pursed mouths. She saw pity. She saw faces white with fear, curiosity, and something else, something harder, that she shied away from naming.

Ruth caught Maria Burke's eye, before the other woman looked away. As though it was contagious, Nina Lombardo looked down too.

Ruth moved on until she came to the cops. A dark cluster of uniforms and suits and there, at the edge, watching her: Johnny Salcito. She stopped short, startled, unable to take her eyes from his face. That lovely, strong face, which had begun to change in the last year or so; the jowls grown heavier, looser, the broken veins on his nose more prominent. Those sad brown eyes that had gazed at her over countless tables in countless bars and restaurants, that had stared, hot and unfocused, as he thrust above her. Now those eyes were empty.

Johnny stepped back into the crowd and folded his arms and said something to one of the other cops to make him laugh. He stared expressionlessly at her and she stared back until her eyes watered and his figure blurred into the group of hostile figures. All watching her.

The women drifted back inside to fix lunch; some of them reappeared. More cops arrived and milled around on the grass, murmuring. Pete approached a couple of them, asked if they had any comment to make; they all said the same thing: there was no news and the search for the Malone kids was ongoing.

Pete looked around for Anders, but his car was gone. He took a few more shots, tried to capture the sense of waiting. The low voices, the tense stances, the drawn faces.

The small dark woman brought out sandwiches, blushed when

Pete thanked her, introduced herself as Carla Bonelli. She stood with him while he ate, chattered about Mr. Bonelli's job, brought him a glass of milk.

Pete asked if she had any photos of the kids who were missing and she went inside, reappeared with an album neatly covered in leftover floral wallpaper. She leafed through pages of round-faced Italians at weddings and parties—and then she stopped, lifted the cellophane, and took out two photographs.

One was of a group of children playing in the street—this street? There wasn't enough detail to tell—a fire hydrant open, the silver spray of the water filling the background. Pete noticed the patterns of light first; the arc of rainbow drops as a little girl spun around and her wet hair spread behind her. He noticed the detail of her frilled bathing suit against her plump arms and legs, and next to her, the skinny frame of a boy in shorts. He was maybe a year or two older than her, but a head and a half taller, all long brown limbs and white teeth.

The other photo showed the same two children on a sofa with a woman between them. Her arm was around the girl and the little boy leaned into her. All three were laughing into the camera. They had the same wide mouths, the same high foreheads, but where the kids were all innocence and open grins, the woman's glossy smile didn't quite reach her eyes.

Mrs. Bonelli touched the photo gently. "That's them. Frankie and Cindy. And their mom. That's Ruth."

Then she said, "I saw her, you know. This morning. I can't believe it was just this morning."

"You saw Mrs. Malone? Where?"

"She was over there"—she pointed toward the corner of the street. "She was looking for the children. She told me they were missing."

"What did you do?"

"I didn't know what to do. I didn't even know if what she was saying was real. God forgive me, I thought"—tears came into her eyes—"I thought she might be drunk."

She sniffed. "I'll never forgive myself for that."

Pete tried to think of something to say. Could only come up with, "Mrs. Bonelli, I'm sure…well, let's just wait for some news."

She nodded. Wiped her eyes on her apron. Took the plate and glass and went back inside.

Pete glanced around and slid the photos into his notebook, quickly closed the album, and left it on the stoop. He got back in the car. There wasn't much else he could do here: he had the names, the background details. From what he had seen and overheard, the cops seemed to know as little as he did.

He turned the engine over and decided to find a phone to call the office, head back, and type up his notes.

Then the door to the apartment building opened and a murmur passed through the small crowd like a breeze in a cornfield.

A cop in uniform emerged from the doorway. Blushing at the eyes on him, he hurried to a police car parked at the end of the path, got into the driver's seat.

A second guy appeared in the doorway, squinting against the afternoon sun. He was big, broad-shouldered, with slicked-back hair and a square sallow face.

Although he wore a suit, he was a cop too. He walked like a cop, and the uniforms stood at attention as he came out.

Pete raised his camera and clicked the shutter.

Click.

He held the door, and a woman appeared behind him.

She wasn't what he'd expected. And as soon as he became aware of that, he asked himself what he had expected; what the women had led him to expect. Someone wild, he thought. Tangled hair, disordered clothes. Hysterics.

Instead, she was easily recognizable as the glossy woman in the photograph. Her outline was as neat as a doll's. She was slim, wearing pale pants that came halfway down her calves, a tight shirt. And she was tiny, or seemed so, dwarfed as she was by the men around her: the cop ahead of her, a guy behind her holding a cigarette. Her hair was short, dark in the doorway, bursting into a red-gold flame as she came into the sunlight.

Click.

She lifted her head and looked first at the women, then at the cops. Her mouth formed a surprised O. But before he could figure out what she was looking at, she turned away and followed the cop in the suit to the waiting car.

Pete looked again at the doorway and saw the third man emerge. He was still holding the cigarette, but loosely, as though he'd forgotten about it. He was big, like the plainclothes cop, but where the cop was all business and purpose, this one seemed lost. His shirt was wrinkled, his jaw blue where he hadn't shaved. He stared toward Mrs. Malone as she got into the car and as he watched her, his face changed. From the dazed look of a man who'd just woken up, his expression set into something like fear.

Click.

The car started up and moved away. Pete started his own engine, and followed as closely as he could.

Ruth sat in the back of the car, still, silent, holding her breath for long, tense moments. Devlin was in front, in the passenger seat. She couldn't look at him, but felt his eyes on her in the mirror now and again, the weight of his stare, the relief as he slid his gaze away.

She wanted to ask again where they were going but she knew they wouldn't answer. She forced herself to be silent. To wait. They must be taking her to the kids. She should focus on that. On Frankie and Cindy.

The hot leather seat stuck to her legs through her cotton pants: her palms were damp. The siren was blaring and as they sped through lunchtime traffic, Ruth felt a thin current of warm air from the front windows drift back to her as she sat, stifled, trapped. The driver muttered something at an old station wagon that was slow to get out of his way.

She watched his impatience as though from a distance. Stared at the pink freckled skin emerging from his stiff collar, at the freshly cut hair, shaved too short at the back. She realized that it was the cop from the apartment. The one called Quinn. She remembered her anger at the sight of him on his knees by her bed and felt it fade, replaced by an unexpected dart of tenderness, by a desire to protect him. He was too young for all of this: to have a boss like Devlin, to be a cop in the first place.

She leaned back against the ripped headrest and closed her eyes. Wished she was somewhere cool. Somewhere with space and silence. Then came an unexpected memory of summers at her uncle's farm in Nebraska, and an intense longing for the rippling shadows of the prairie grass in the evening, and the wide skies bleached by the fading light. She remembered the uneven creak of her Aunt Shauna's rocking chair, the ice cracking in her glass of lemonade, wheat chaff dusting her skinny, tanned legs, and she wished herself there now: rocking gently on the porch, looking out over the darkening stretch of land, listening to the whispering breeze and the crickets and the hush of night in a town that was a thousand miles from New York in July.

The car stopped abruptly and she was brought back and jerked forward and had to put her hand on the seat in front to get her balance. The pink freckled neck did not turn.

She saw that they were in an empty lot in a neighborhood she didn't know. Confused and suddenly panicked, Ruth looked at Devlin, but he was already out of the car and opening her door. To anyone watching, it might have seemed like courtesy, but these doors only opened from the outside. He bent and reached in and she flinched in horror as he fitted his wide palm into her armpit. She tried to move back, to shrug him off: she couldn't bear that he should feel the dampness of her, that he should smell her on his hand—but he pulled hard and she found herself halfway out of the car and slipping on the rough ground, and then walking with him, his hand still tucked in that shameful place.

They stumbled on, Ruth's blouse sticking to her and her ankles aching where the straps of her shoes cut into her heat-swollen flesh. She could feel that her face was flushed: partly heat and partly humiliation at what this walk—this *man*—was forcing her to reveal.

A fly buzzed around her face and she slapped at it, then another, and another. She waved her hand, fanned herself, tried desperately to hold on to some sliver of poise. So many flies. Could they smell her: that yellow, female stink of her? Her groin, her armpits, even the sweat running in dirty trickles down her neck and back. Staining her.

She was breathing hard through her mouth when she realized that it wasn't herself that she was smelling and tasting. This was a new smell. A smell like meat that had lain too long in the sun. Something sweetish.

She saw a dark swarm of gathering flies ahead, heard their impatient buzzing as they jostled to get closer to that smell.

Devlin dragged her on and she kept stumbling, but this time it wasn't the stones or her heels: she was pushing at him, fighting him, biting her lip to keep the tears back, determined not to let him see her cry, no matter what lay under that pulsing black cloud.

He pulled her on and now she really did fight because the smell was stronger, and she could no longer pretend she didn't know. The truth was in his set lips and his unflinching face and even in the starched set of his shoulders. She twisted and moaned and pleaded with him in whispers to stop, and finally he stopped. He did not take his hand off her arm, and she did not take her eyes off his face. She would not look. He could not make her look.

He tried. He shouted at her to look, and his spit landed on her cheek, but she was past disgust. Then he grabbed her shoulder and spun her around. She turned her head away, but he took hold of her chin and pushed and finally, she had to look.

There was dirt everywhere. Dirt and trash: cans and bottles glinting in the sunshine, garbage bags, some split by rats, a bike missing a wheel. And in the middle of this stinking pile, soft pink cotton. A pattern of flowers. A glimpse of something mottled like purple and white marble. And a fall of blond hair. She stretched out a hand but Devlin was suddenly there, pulling her back. Forbidding her to touch. She opened her mouth, but the flies and the heat and the smell and the sudden awareness that this was the hair she had shampooed and combed and braided for four years made everything go dark for a moment. Devlin caught her, and his touch felt almost gentle. He set her straight, then turned her away and for a second she felt grateful for this unexpected tenderness.

Then she saw the crowd across the street. Saw the line of faces he had turned her toward, the hands shading eyes, the moving mouths. Saw the cameras, felt the heat of their curiosity.

There was a flash and then, as a single raindrop heralds a shower, there were scores of flashes.

And behind it all, his bruising grip on her arm, his voice against her ear, low and hissing.

"Is it her? Is that your daughter?"

She looked down at the crumpled thing at her feet, and then the world turned faster and she fell again into the kind darkness.

5

No matter how she views the events after that first day, the day itself is always a long one in her mind. There were hours of waiting: in the morning, at home, before Cindy. And afterward at the police station, in anonymous rooms with plastic chairs where she was left alone with her grief and with the horror of it all. With no one to answer her worst fears about Frankie. And then hours of questions from them, and still no one would answer her, reassure her. They just kept asking the same questions again and again.

Devlin and another cop took turns. She answered mechanically. What did these questions matter, now? What did any of it matter now?

Finally, they let her go. Frank was in the foyer, pacing, his hand in his hair, waiting for her.

"Ruthie...oh God, Ruth."

She couldn't look at his soft, leaking face, so she let him fold her in his arms and sank against him, exhausted.

It was after eleven when they reached the apartment. He wanted to come in, to rehash all the questions they'd been asked, the answers they'd given. She sighed and told him she was tired. He frowned and then he just nodded and cleared his throat, and then he drove away.

The door of the apartment opened before she had time to raise her key and her mother was there. Ruth looked at her, at her hard, lined face, at her hollow eyes, felt the memory of a thousand grievances and arguments rise inside her like vomit.

Ruth shut the door carefully and quietly, and then leaned her head back against it and let her shoulders drop, and closed her eyes. Finally she could weep. Even now she remembers the sweet relief of being able to let go in front of a woman who had seen the worst of her all her life. How it felt like cool water after the heat of the day.

Her mouth opened and she sobbed and the tears dripped from her face, and her sobs became wails. She howled like a dog until her throat was raw and a strand of saliva trailed from her lip. She wiped at it savagely and thought how she must look: smudged and blotched and swollen. *Drooling.* And for a while she did not care.

Her mother took her in her arms for the first time since she was a child, rubbed her back and shushed her in a way she hadn't done in twenty years. And then Ruth let her own arms creep around that thin, bent body.

Her mother guided her to the sofa. "Hush, now. Hush, Ruthie. Hush. It will be all right. It's God's will, is all. Cindy's with Jesus now. Hush, Ruthie. Shush now. Shush."

The noises that her mother made were empty, meaningless, but somehow Ruth understood that she had to make them, and she let her. It was her way of giving back a little comfort in return. It was all she had.

After a while, her mother let go. Ruth lifted her own hand to her face to wipe away the tears, and then to rub away the beginning of a headache. She felt the warm, oily skin of her forehead and drew her arm back with a breath of disgust. She wiped her hand almost absently on her pants, stared without seeing at a crayon scribble on the wall, at Minnie, curled in the corner with one ear cocked.

And as she stared, her eyes gradually closed, her chin sank onto her chest. She slept tucked in like a bird, floating with the tides of her dreams, her feet scrabbling frantically to reach the bottom of a cold, dark lake.

She was woken what felt like seconds later by a clatter of crockery, heard the slap-slosh of the mop in the kitchen, and, for a brief soft moment, wondered why her mother was cleaning at that hour, how she hadn't disturbed the kids. Her brain groped for clarity and was hit by the shock of memory.

The kids.

Her babies.

And she opened her swollen eyes on the horror of that quiet room.

She was shivering, feverish, her skin burning and her chest aching. She sat up, wrapped her arms around her body, trying not to think of her body, because that would mean thinking of the children it had carried and borne and fed and comforted and nursed and held and slapped and stroked and soothed and loved. It would mean thinking of where Frankie might be, and of something other than that present moment and the effort of breathing, and she was not capable.

Then the door opened and her mother was there and the soft shushing was gone. That harsh, dry voice was back between them, pecking, pecking, her beak rubbing the salty sting into the wound that was Ruth's head and Ruth's thin skin.

And as her mother spoke and pecked and jabbed, she hovered and flapped: cushions were plumped and straightened, magazines lined up with the edges of the table, and shoes picked up in pairs. Two-by-two by baby-pink and big-boy-blue. And her mother swiveled her head, her sharp eyes missing nothing. Then a pat of the neat gray hair, a sweep of that apron and those respectable tan stockings, and a final pat-a-cake of Max Factor no. 23 to hide any shameful trace of tears.

And it was done, and the room was tidy and ordered and neat. Her mother was tidy and ordered and neat. And in the middle of everything sat Ruth. Slumped on the sofa like a sack of old clothes. Her hair awry, her skin damp, her blouse wrinkled.

Her mother was silent but her eyes, those flat gray stones, were on her and in her, all the way inside her head where the sharp voice still pecked, insisted that it was all Ruth's fault. The dirt in the apartment was *her* dirt, it was *her* sweat, *her* smell, *her* looseness,

her leaking wet body that had betrayed her. It was her fault that
someone had taken the children, her fault that Frankie was missing, that Cindy was . . . gone.

The voice followed Ruth to the bathroom, where she washed
and redid her face, scarcely looking at her reflection, trying not to
think of Frankie, trying not to let the waves of terror come, trying
to concentrate on the temperature of the water, on reaching for the
soap, on the lather in her hands, on getting the right amount of
powder on the brush.

The voice followed her into the kitchen where she made tea.
Where the marks of the mop were still visible on the floor, where
it had pushed the dirt into brown corners. Her mother had lined
up the jars and canisters at the back of the counter and she noticed
that the jelly jar Cindy had stuck with shells and glitter was gone—
hidden away or thrown out with the garbage.

The voice followed her into the bedroom where she changed her
clothes slowly, as though her body was bruised. She combed her hair
in front of the mirror, still avoiding her own eyes, sprayed a sticky
spiraling web around her head, walked back to the kitchen and
past the closed door of the other bedroom, past Minnie, scratching
and whining to be let inside, anxious because she couldn't find the
kids. Ruth snapped at her, watched her sink to the floor.

In the kitchen, she poured the tea, reached past her mother
for the mop and bucket, for the bleach, took them back into the
bathroom. And as she rubbed and scratched at stains, the voice
grew quieter. As the sky paled into another hot blue dawn, she was
scrubbing the sink, scouring the bathtub, polishing floors. She
refilled the bucket again and again, breathed in the steam and the
bleach, focused on her red, raw hands and on the ache in her back,
knowing that if she stopped, the voice would start again.

Home was a one-room apartment in the hippest neighborhood
that Pete could afford. He'd taken it knowing he'd prefer bars and

bohemian types to tree-lined sidewalks and baby strollers. In a neighborhood like the one his mother thought he was living in, he could have been in any decent-sized town. Here he could make out the music and laughter from St. Mark's Place and see the glow of the city, and know he'd made it to New York.

Coming in that night, he threw his jacket over the back of the chair and loosened his tie, turned on the lamp, rinsed a mug, and filled it with cold water. Drank deep, wrinkling his nose at the faint taste of coffee. He wanted to like coffee because it was what the other guys at the paper drank. It was what everyone drank.

He sat on the bed and finally the day was over. He untied his shoes and removed his pants and socks and shirt and folded them over the chair and lay down wondering if there was anything in the refrigerator for the morning. If he would call the girl with the green eyes he'd met in a bar off Union Square. How he was going to begin writing up the Malone case. And that got him thinking of her and there he stopped, his mind coming to rest on the image of her slim figure. Her raised hand. Her open mouth.

He thought again of the photograph and of her watchful eyes. He wondered what color they were up close. How her voice sounded.

And he wondered if he would dream of her, but then he didn't remember his dreams at all.

The next morning, Frank arrived and suggested they go to church. Ruth just nodded; it was easier than arguing, and she needed to get out of the apartment. She thought of the cool shadows inside the church, of the familiar scenes on the stained-glass windows, of the smell of incense.

Mass was ending as they arrived. Ruth slipped into one of the pews while Frank walked heavily toward the confessional. She bowed her head and closed her eyes but she did not pray. She wanted the comfort she had seen prayer bring to others, wanted the relief of confession and absolution, but she had lost her faith when her father died.

She remembered her mother's prayers at his bedside, her father's shuddering breaths, her own anger. She remembered sneaking out of the house one night, drinking rum in the backseat of someone's car as they drove to North Point, needing to forget the scenes at home, laughing as Charlie Houston kissed her neck, laughing as he spilled sweet liquor on her arm and laughing as he licked it up, her heart racing as her father's stopped as Charlie slid his hand up her skirt as her father died.

She remembered coming home at dawn to her mother's fury. Refusing to feel ashamed. Refusing to feel. She remembered facing down her grief at the graveside, knowing herself as white and still while her mother raged red and wet and that voice shrieked blame: "You killed him! Running around and drinking and all the way you do—you killed him!"

There had been no room for her grief then. No one had wanted to see the madness or the ugliness of it. No one had wanted it, just as no one wanted it now. She remembered digging her nails into her palms to keep it down inside, and then looking up and seeing the crucified figure with nails in His, and laughing and shaking and gasping, and then walking away not knowing if she was laughing or crying any more.

And that was the last time she had been in a church, apart from her wedding day. Five months after her father's death, her mother pink and tense with the haste of it all, with what people might think. The week before the wedding, Ruth had said almost absently, "Let them think what they like. They'll soon know the truth when there's no baby," and had been shocked by her mother's slap, by that sharp voice telling her not to be so vulgar.

She remembered running to her room and burying her face in her pillow, determined not to give her mother the satisfaction of hearing her tears. And even more determined to get married and to get out.

Now the idea of confessing to a priest made her feel afraid. The thought of shutting up her vulnerability in that tiny box, being unable to breathe or think, invisible to the man in front of her—his calm voice, his face scattered in the grille, his absolute possession of himself, his confidence in his God, his strength—those thoughts and images were unbearable. If she let herself open up, it would break the dam she had spent years building. And once released, she knew she would not be able to stem the rush of emotion. Far better to keep it under control, to keep herself safe and hidden.

And so when Frank came back from the confessional, she simply stood and walked toward the daylight at the back of the church, knowing he would follow.

In the car she smoothed out her white skirt and said to him, "I need to stop at the store."

He turned to look at her, then back to the road. "We should get back, honey. Sergeant Devlin said he'd come by later. He has more questions for us."

She stared straight ahead of her and thought of the backseat of the squad car the day before. Of the dirty windshield, the driver's neck, of Devlin's set profile as he took her to see the dead body of her child.

"I need to go shopping, Frank. I have to buy a new dress."

6

Pete filed his first article on the Malone case and waited while Friedmann read it over, pacing the strip of carpet between the metro and crime desks until Jack Lamont told him to knock it off. He poured a cup of stale coffee from the pot in the hallway and took two sips before giving up and asking Janine to get him a Coke from the drugstore. Checked his reflection in the men's room mirror and tried a smile to hide his apprehension. And then Friedmann bellowed from his office.

"VO-NICK-EE! In here, now!"

Friedmann had the piece in front of him. Every line was scored with blue pencil. He nodded at Pete to sit and then tapped the pages on the desk.

"This"—*tap, tap*—"is a piece of shit. It reads like a fucking college assignment. I don't give a fuck about the weather, what it felt like to be on the scene, who else was there. I just want the fucking story, and so do the readers. *What?*"

This last was to Jeff White, who was standing in the doorway holding a couple of sheets of paper. He put them on Friedmann's desk, waited while he skimmed them. Pete looked around him: at the stacks of files, the shelves of reference books, and then at the huge fish tank on the wall behind Friedmann. Rumor had it that they'd had to double the thickness of the wall, reinforce it so it was strong enough to hold the tank. Pete looked at the fish collecting at the glass, felt they were gathering to watch him. He stared back at their round, unblinking eyes, their open mouths, and shuddered.

Friedmann gave the pages back to White. "Get confirmation. A quote, anything—but something we can print. Then run with it."

White dismissed, Friedmann leaned back in his chair, pushed Pete's article aside, steepled his fingers.

"You know what sells papers, kid?"

Pete opened his mouth and Friedmann shook his head.

"Don't fucking talk when I'm talking. You'll know when it's your turn."

He took a gulp of something from a mug on his desk.

"Stories. Stories sell papers. Stories about shit that happened. Not shit that you're describing in a fucking essay. *Shit. That. Happened.* Got that?"

Pete nodded.

"Readers want three things, Wonicke." He ticked them off on his fingers. "They want to see the money. Or the lack of it. To feel envious, or superior."

Another finger, bent back. "They want sex. There's always a hot dame. Or a dame we can work up into hot. There's always an angle we can use."

A third finger. "And every story needs a bad guy. Every story needs fear."

Another swig.

"I'm guessing there ain't much money on...uh...72nd Drive, so you got to play up the sex and the fear. Where's the sex appeal? Is it the mother? The babysitter? I want a sexy broad. The readers want a sexy broad."

Pete nodded.

"And the fear: What should they be scared of? What are the neighbors scared of? Is there a maniac out there targeting kids? What did he do to them? Where's the other one, the boy?"

Pete nodded again and Friedmann leaned forward. "*Is* there a nut job out there?"

"I...uh..."

"What do the cops think?"

"I don't…"

"Of course you don't fucking know. So you find out. Your job is to find out."

"Right."

"How you plan on doing that?"

"I asked the cops at the apartment. They weren't talking."

Friedmann sighed.

"Who's the lead detective on this?"

Pete flipped through his notes.

"A Sergeant Devlin."

"Okay. The—Jesus Christ, *what*?"

This time it was one of the secretaries who needed him to sign a check. Pete stared again at the fish. At the slow, languid movements, the flickering colors. And then at Friedmann—the wiry gray hair, the glasses with the square black frames. Suddenly the eyes behind them met Pete's.

"Where were we? The cops. Okay. So your job is to stick with this…"

"Devlin."

"Devlin, right. You find him and you get on his ass. You stick closer to him than his own wife until this case is done. Where does this guy live? What time does he get to work? Where does he park? Where does he get his fucking coffee? Mr. Devlin don't do shit without you knowing about it. Every place he goes, every conversation he has, you're half a step behind and you get everything down. Okay?"

Pete nodded, but Friedmann was looking at the report again.

"And the photos. Jesus. The fucking photos are terrible."

He shoved half a dozen prints across the desk and Pete flipped through them. They were all close-ups of Ruth Malone. His eyes roamed over her long lashes, her thick soft hair, her pouting lips.

Pete looked up, puzzled. Friedmann jabbed the pile with a wide forefinger.

"*This* is a grieving mother? Where's the fucking grief? Huh?

Where's the tears? Take Reilly out with you. Tell him to get a shot of her crying, whatever it takes."

He leaned back, and when Pete didn't immediately stand to leave, he raised an eyebrow.

"Something you want to ask me?"

"Yeah...it's just—all this that you're saying about sex appeal and tears and all that...don't you want me just to write the truth? That's my job, right?"

Friedmann barked a laugh. "Your job is to write what I tell you to write. And I'm telling you how to turn a dead kid into a story. You don't want to lead on this, I got five good reporters out there I could give it to."

"I'm leading with this? I'm...this is mine?"

Friedmann stood then, took a jar of fish food from a shelf, and sprinkled a pinch on the surface of the tank.

"You like fish, Wonicke?"

Without waiting for a reply, watching the fish pushing up to the surface to feed, he said, "I find them soothing. I look at them and I think—life must be so quiet in there. Everything muffled by the water."

Still in the same even tone, he said, "Looks like this is your lucky day, Wonicke. Horowitz is on the fraud trial in Manhattan and I just put Lamont on that serial rapist case. And O'Connor has two weeks of his vacation left. You can stay on this story until he's back."

Fifteen minutes in the archives got Pete a few clippings about three of Devlin's previous cases. One of them came with a photo: it was the big guy with the jowls who'd taken Mrs. Malone to see her daughter's body. As he headed for the door, Pete stared down at him, wondering what went on in the mind of a guy who could do something like that to a woman, wondering why he'd done it. And as he stared, he ran into Horowitz and dropped the clippings.

"Shit...sorry man, I didn't see you..."

They bent down at the same time. Horowitz got there first, glanced at the picture before handing it back.

"You got something interesting there?" Nodding at the clippings. "Sure hope so."

Pete made to move away, but Horowitz patted his pockets and asked, "Got a smoke, kid?"

Horowitz smoked Camels; heavy, unfiltered, and eye-watering. And now he wanted one of Pete's skinny-ass filter tips.

Pete pulled out the pack, angled it toward him, took one for himself. Stifled a laugh when he saw the face the other guy pulled.

Then Horowitz nodded at the clippings again.

"So what's the story?"

Suspicion slithered to the top of Pete's spine. He'd worked and waited for this break, and now Horowitz wanted in? Well, too fucking bad. The old guy had his white-collar fraud case, and Friedmann had gift-wrapped this one and labeled it his. He was as short with Horowitz as he knew how to be.

"Murder in Queens. Yesterday. One kid dead, another missing."

Horowitz's head came up fast and he looked Pete right in the eye for the first time since they collided in the doorway.

"Murder!" He grinned at the clippings. "Well, now. Ain't that a thing. Your first one, huh?"

Pete smiled back uncertainly, nodded.

Horowitz clapped him on the shoulder.

"Your first big story. Congratulations, kid."

He gave a quick glance downward and said casually, "That the lead detective?"

Pete nodded again and Horowitz straightened up and walked on. Pete was halfway to the parking lot before he thought to wonder how Horowitz knew that the grainy close-up of a guy in a suit was a picture of a cop.

Pete spent a couple of hours in the Malones' neighborhood: knocking on doors, fishing for quotes about the kids, the parents. Then he made his way to the station house. Five bucks and a pack of smokes to the desk sergeant got him the name of the coffee shop where the senior detectives ate lunch.

Tony's Diner turned out to be a noisy brightly lit place on Queens Boulevard. Pete gave the waitress his full college-boy grin and asked her to seat him in back and leave him alone for a while. She rolled her eyes but brought him a chocolate malt and a slice of pie and left him to it.

The photos first. Most of the pictures of Ruth Malone were still on Friedmann's desk and Pete was left with one shot of her walking to the car, her head turned toward the line of cops. There was a guy in the middle who was listening to the cop next to him but watching Ruth. His mouth was set in a thin line and he looked oddly satisfied. Pete made a note.

Then the shots of the building. The women. The baby carriage with the box on top that Mrs. Burke's daughter had pointed out. Pete spent a moment longer looking at that, made another note, then spread out the rest of his papers.

He didn't have much: the discovery of the girl's body, his impressions of the street where the mother lived with her kids, and interviews with the neighbors—the three from yesterday, and two more this morning. That was it.

The kids were angels. That was the word everyone used. He wondered if that was the word that was always used in cases like this.

But their mother wasn't too popular, even with the other mothers. She'd separated from the husband: the consensus was that she'd kicked him out, but no one knew why. He was a nice guy, apparently—better liked than her, anyway. He had a good job—worked nights as a mechanic at the airport. Didn't drink, didn't knock her around, didn't even raise his voice. This last from a lady with a bruise on her cheek that her makeup didn't quite hide.

Pete looked at the photograph he'd taken of Frank Malone as he'd emerged from the doorway behind his wife. He studied the fleshy, set face. Saw again the fear he'd noticed the day before.

Then Pete heard voices and looked up to see two men

approaching. He recognized one of them right away and stuffed the photographs back into their folder just as the men took a seat in a booth across from him.

Devlin walked like he was on parade, and then sat straight with his hands clasped in front of him. The other guy was younger, with sandy hair and pink freckled skin, like he'd been out in the sun for too long.

The diner was half-full and there was a buzz of voices in the background, but Pete was close enough to overhear. The men ordered and when the waitress left, Devlin was silent for a moment, lining up the cutlery, the salt shaker, the sugar bowl. Then he looked up, pointed a thick forefinger at the other man's wrinkled shirt.

"That's sloppy, Quinn. I want to see an improvement tomorrow. Don't let me catch you showing up for a shift like that again."

"Yes, sir. Sorry, sir. The case . . ."

Devlin's eyes flickered sideways. Pete tried to look invisible in his booth.

"We don't talk about the case, Quinn. Not here. Not anywhere public. Got that?"

"Sir."

"And the case ain't no excuse anyhow. The public, the chief, they see a guy in a wrinkled shirt or a guy who can't be bothered to shave, they lose faith. Wife or mom not taking care of him right? That's a sloppy household, right there. Cop can't even keep order at home, how will he keep the case together, how will he solve this? That's what people think. All the time"—he tapped his temple—"you gotta think the way other people do."

The waitress reappeared with two plates of spaghetti and meat-balls. It smelled good. Devlin tucked his napkin into his collar, and Quinn followed suit.

Pete watched, fascinated, as Devlin shoveled in forkfuls of food, as he chewed openmouthed, the mass of brown and red churning and glistening on his tongue before he swallowed. They ate in silence. Then Devlin dabbed his mouth with a napkin, reached for a toothpick, and worked at his teeth.

He leaned back and the waitress returned and took their plates. She dropped a fork as she did so, and Pete saw a flush spread over her neck as she bent to pick it up, heard her murmured apology. Devlin just looked at her, frowning, until she scurried away, head down.

Then he turned his attention back to Quinn and she was forgotten, like she'd never existed.

"Okay, I gotta go. Got a meeting at two-thirty with the chief. He wants a quick result on this. So I want you to go over the statements again. The husband's. The wife's. There's something there… something not right."

He got to his feet and headed for the door, leaving Quinn with the check.

Pete studied Quinn as he signaled to the girl to bring him some coffee. He didn't look like the type to welcome an afternoon of paperwork. He slouched in his seat, head bent, picking at the skin around his thumbnail. His lip stuck out, giving him the look of a sullen teenager.

Quinn seemed to become aware of Pete's eyes on him, and looked up to meet them. Before he could speak, Pete nodded at him.

"Your boss sounds like mine. Pain in the ass, am I right?" Grinned at him.

Quinn narrowed his eyes. "Huh?"

"I couldn't help overhearing. What's his problem, anyway?"

Quinn shrugged. "You want something?"

Pete slid into the seat opposite him.

"Pete Wonicke. I'm with the *Herald.* I'd like to talk to you about the Malone case."

Quinn was shaking his head before he'd even finished speaking.

"Oh, no. I ain't talking to the press. No way."

His coffee arrived, and Pete ordered one too. When the girl had left, he asked: "Coffee any good here?"

Quinn shrugged. "It's hot and strong, that's about all you can say."

Then he frowned. "Look, I can't talk to you about the case. My sergeant would tear me a new one."

Pete nodded. "I understand. That's okay."

The girl brought Pete's coffee and he poured in a good amount of sugar, added creamer, stirred. He sipped for a moment and then he said casually, "He seems like a tough guy to work for."

Quinn shot him a suspicious look and Pete raised his hands, leaned back. "Nothing about the case, okay? Just making conversation. How long you been working for him?"

There was a pause, and then: "Three years. A little over. Since I made detective."

Pete nodded. "He reminds me of a guy I used to work for. One time, he gave me a report to proof. Five thousand words, at four-thirty on a Friday afternoon. Told me it had to be done by Monday morning. And I had a camping trip planned that weekend with my buddy."

He sipped his coffee. Shook his head. Waited.

And Quinn said, "So what did you do?"

"Went on the trip. Got back Sunday night with the worst god-damn hangover of my life. Went straight to bed and the next morning, I told him the report was perfect and he was a genius."

That got him a grin and a nod. Pete put down his mug.

"Listen, Detective, I need to ask you a favor."

"I told you, I can't talk about the case."

"I know, I know. What I need is just a few facts. Information I could get from anyone. Most of it I already know—you can just confirm what I have."

"Well, I don't know . . ."

"You won't be mentioned by name."

"Facts? Like what?"

"Like how long the kids have been missing. And the father's job—where does he work?"

"He's a mechanic over at the airport."

"Fixing engines, that kind of thing?"

"I guess."

"Okay—listen, you mind if I take a few notes? Just to remind me. My memory ain't so good sometimes."

Quinn shrugged.

"So does he work shifts? The father?"

"Yeah."

"Was he at work when the kids went missing?"

"No, but he don't live with them. He and the mother are separated."

"Tough on him. Not being with his family."

"Guess so."

Pete shook his head. Exhaled loudly. Then—trying to appear casual—"Say, you want another cup of coffee? Slice of pie? Bet you've been working damn hard recently."

"We've been doing door-to-door interviews for two days straight. We got 'bout three hundred cops searching for that boy. Helicopters, too."

Pete shook his head. "And in this heat."

He ordered more coffee. Two slices of pecan pie with ice cream.

"All those interviews get you anywhere?"

"Well, I can't..."

"Oh, no. I didn't mean specifics. I just meant...you know, generally. Is it going well?"

Quinn shook his head. "Just the usual. A few suspicious wives, couple of stories about the creepy guy in the next building. There's always a lot of that kinda thing. But still, everything's got to be checked, cross-checked, eliminated."

"How are the parents holding up? Got to be real tough for them."

"The father's in pieces. It's hard to see a man like that."

"What's he like?"

"He's a nice guy. Just...normal, you know? Ain't too bright. He wants to believe they just climbed out of the window and ran off. That the girl was...that it was an accident. I don't think he gets it. Maybe it's the shock. Or he's a little slow."

Pete thought about the photograph he'd taken of the stroller beneath the kids' window. Even if someone else had pushed the large baby carriage across the grass with the box on top, two small children couldn't have opened the window and taken the screen off.

Their desserts arrived and they chewed in silence for a few moments. Then Quinn said, "Yeah, the father's a nice guy. But the mother, well, she's something else."

"She was there? That night?"

"Yeah. Says she checked on the kids at midnight, went to sleep at three-thirty, four. Found they were missing in the morning. And there ain't no one to contradict that since she separated from the father."

"How long they been separated?"

"Almost a year and a half. Since last spring. And believe me, she's making the best of it. Makeup, clothes, all that. She don't look how a woman should look when her kids go missing. She works nights. Two little kids and she's a waitress in some goddamn bar."

He shook his head, scooped up another spoonful of ice cream and rolled it around his mouth.

"And the apartment was a mess—a ton of empty liquor bottles in the trash. There was brandy on her breath at eleven in the morning. Turns out she's got a record as well. We've had guys from the station at that address a few times. Noise, drinking, all that."

Pete exhaled slowly. "Jeez. That's not right."

"That ain't all. She had a suitcase in her bedroom full of letters. From men. Not just her husband—lots of men. And they weren't talking about the weather, if you get my drift."

Quinn stared ahead for a moment, drumming his fingers on the table.

"My boss"—he nodded toward the door—"he took her to see her daughter's body yesterday. Wanted to get a straight-up reaction from her, he said. And there was nothing. Nothing till she saw the god-damn reporters. And even then—no tears. She fainted for the cam-eras but she never cried, not when she saw the girl, and not afterward."

He took a gulp of coffee.

"The sergeant wants us to keep an eye on the mother. Dig down some. He thinks there's something there, and if we keep digging, we'll find it."

Pete looked at him, at his narrowed eyes, his set jaw, at his hand on the table. His fist clenching, unclenching.

Quinn finally left to go back to the station house and the state-ments. Pete stayed where he was, stirring his coffee, thinking about Mrs. Malone. About the letters Quinn had mentioned, the liquor bot-tles in the garbage. It seemed pretty clear she was worth investigating. His first big story, and maybe it would be over before it had begun.

Then he shook his head, gathered up his notebook and headed for the door. Even if it fell out that this was an open-and-shut domestic incident—no big mystery, no front-page headlines—he still had a job to do. He could still follow Friedmann's guidelines, could still learn something here. And maybe he could start to carve out a name for himself as a half-decent reporter.

With that in mind he followed Quinn back to the station house. There was a different guy on the front desk from the one who'd given him the name of the coffee shop. This one had mean eyes and a twist to his lip that made it look like a permanent sneer and when Pete asked to see Devlin, he just raised an eyebrow and said, "Who wants him?"

"My name's Wonicke. It's about the Malone case."

The guy yawned and scratched his armpit, then reached for the phone. "You got some information?"

"Uh...yeah. Yeah, I do."

The hand paused and the guy looked him up and down.

"Why don't you tell me and I'll make sure it reaches him."

Unable to think of a lie fast enough, Pete flushed.

"It's...I just need to speak to him."

The hand drew back from the phone and the guy pulled a pile of paperwork toward him.

"Well, Sergeant Devlin is pretty busy right now, what with the case and all. He can't just see everyone who drops by. You change your mind, Mr. Wonicke, or you... *remember* what you wanted to pass on to him, you come back and let me know."

He turned his attention to the papers in front of him. Pete gave up, went outside. He lit a cigarette and looked at his watch. His deadline was coming up: he'd have to work with what he had. Devlin could wait.

HELICOPTERS JOIN SEARCH FOR BOY, 5, IN QUEENS ABDUCTION
By Staff Reporter Peter Wonicke

QUEENS, July 16—A search by hundreds of police officers yesterday failed to turn up any clues to the whereabouts of 5-year-old Frank Malone Jr. The boy disappeared along with his 4-year-old sister, Cindy, from their Queens apartment early on Wednesday morning.

Cindy was found dead in an abandoned lot about one mile from her home at noon on Wednesday. Tests are being carried out to determine the cause of death.

Three police helicopters joined the search for the boy yesterday, hoping to spot from the air the white T-shirt he was wearing when he disappeared.

The children lived with their mother, Mrs. Ruth Malone, a 26-year-old cocktail waitress. Her husband, Frank Malone Sr., an airline mechanic at Kennedy International Airport, has been living apart from the family since the couple separated last year.

A senior police official said yesterday that hope of finding the boy alive was fading. "This hot weather means that dehydration is a real risk, the longer the search goes on."

The children's father spent yesterday with detectives at the 107th Precinct Station in Fresh Meadows, waiting for news of his son.

Mrs. Malone, slim, red-haired, and wearing a fashionable black dress, was escorted to the station house yesterday afternoon by detectives. She was questioned for over two hours and then returned to her home.

Neighbors of Mrs. Malone said they knew very little about her. Her children had played with other children in the neighborhood, but their mother "kept to herself." One neighbor volunteered that Mrs. Malone often worked long hours, especially at night, and that her lifestyle was "chaotic" as a result.

"We certainly never had no trouble like this around here before now," said a mother of three preschool children, who wished to remain anonymous.

The wake for Cindy was held on July 19 at O'Rourke's Funeral Home. On one side of the room, Monsignor Contri presided, his wrinkled brown face placid under a halo of white hair, his voice a soft murmur. Cindy was in Heaven now, her soul was at peace. On the other side, Ruth stood tall wearing her new black dress and half-veil, black heels, and straight-seamed stockings, the best part of an eighth of vodka inside her and a trembling cigarette in one hand. To everyone who came to offer their condolences, she put out her other hand, her amber eyes bright and unblinking through black chiffon, her voice harsh from smoking and from the effort of keeping the tears back.

She wanted to break down. To fall to her knees, to scream, to beg, to bargain.

"They're all I've got. You can't have them both—they're all I've got!"

Instead she lifted her chin and swallowed and said to everyone: "My children are very religious, you know. Every night, they say their prayers before bed. Every night."

An image came to her: Frankie and Cindy kneeling by their beds in the safe glow of the nightlight, their soft voices rising and falling, stumbling over the familiar words. And then an image of Frankie alone, kneeling on a bare floor, eyes squeezed shut in terror, his voice a whispered plea. Begging. Bargaining. *I'll be good. Please God. Please. Please. I won't talk back to Mommy no more. Please.*

Ruth blinked. And then took a long dry suck on the cigarette, and her lips set perfectly, and she moved on to the next guest.

They had to wait ten more days before the cops would release Cindy's body. Ten more days before they could hold the funeral.

For Ruth it was ten days of waiting for her baby to come back to her. Waiting for news of Frankie. Ten days of Devlin's questions.

They blurred together, those days. Each one was stifling. Each was a listless shimmer over slow-moving streets, full of brown and yellow dust, the kind that gets into your eyes and throat and thickens your thoughts.

One morning she woke on the living room floor: her mouth dry, her head pounding. There was a warmth against her back and for a moment she let herself lean against the weight and the softness of the small body beside her. She let herself imagine: even as the tears leaked from her swollen eyelids, she let herself hope.

And then the dog yawned and stretched and grunted beside her and Ruth could no longer pretend, so she gave herself up entirely to weeping. She pressed her fists against her sore eyes and sobbed, hunched into a tight ball against the pain. She heard a gentle snuffling near her face and felt Minnie's wet, curious nose and her rough tongue licking the salt from her skin. She heard her worried whine and reached blindly for the dog's reassuring bulk, and pulled Minnie against her. She buried her face in the warm, familiar smell of her, rubbed her skin against the soft fur. Minnie whined again and she held her tighter and tried to give and take what comfort she could.

*   *   *

One afternoon she started to make coffee, realized the Folgers can was empty. She checked the pantry and saw there was nothing in there except a jar of pickles and half a box of stale graham crackers. The sight of them reminded her that she hadn't eaten that day. She couldn't remember eating the day before. She couldn't imagine wanting to eat again—but some sense of what was right, what was normal, made her slide her feet into her shoes, made her pick up her purse and keys.

As though it were that easy to leave one world behind and enter another, she stepped outside and closed the door behind her.

Dust clung to her sticky skin and lost itself in her strawlike hair and in the creases of her cotton dress. Her white cuffs were stained the color of old blood. Behind her sunglasses, dust scratched her swollen eyes, bringing her close to tears.

She walked, forgetting where she was going, why she had come out. One foot in front of the other, ignoring other feet, voices, flashes of light, car horns.

And all the while, the rhythm of her feet trod out the rhythm of endless stories, endless possibilities, each one a vivid picture of what might have happened to Frankie.

She looked up, realized she was outside the store and remembered that she needed coffee. She took a wire basket, went inside, recoiled from the fluorescent lighting.

Her feet took her down the aisles and she put things in her basket: a blue box, a can with a green label, a white carton.

She kept walking, kept picking things up and putting them in the basket, because this was what people did.

She kept going. She trod away the pictures of Frankie's tearstained face, his terrified voice. And she waited for each new one to rise to the surface.

She reached the checkout and saw the girl's mouth form words that she couldn't hear, and she nodded and reached for a bag. Then she saw what she had put in the basket. Animal crackers. Chocolate milk. Cindy's favorite cereal.

And her hand stopped and her breath stopped and all sound stopped.

She was dimly aware of someone's arm around her, and a chair and the too-loud tick of a clock. Of voices and a phone ringing in the distance, and then of Frank arriving: the familiar smell of him, the hot seat of his car, the quiet of the apartment. He brought her a glass of water and she stared at it and then at him.

"I wanted coffee," she said. "I'm out of coffee."

Finally, Cindy was given back to them. And then it was nine in the morning on another sweltering July day and they were in the chapel of St. Theresa's. Small, intimate, and ninety-three degrees inside. Ruth stood near the coffin: protective, eyes downcast under the veil, Frank so close she could feel the heat coming off him, hear each ragged breath he took before raising his face to a new mourner. He thanked them so that she didn't have to, so that she could keep her head bent, could stay still and perfect. Black dress, white skin, red lips.

Only Gina, slipping in late, found a weak spot and let a little daylight into Ruth's thoughts.

She felt a hand on her arm and a squeeze, a rough friendliness that interrupted the polite press of the others. She stared at the hand, with its bitten cuticles and cheap rings, and she couldn't look up because she knew that the understanding in Gina's face would break her. She felt tears threaten and began to panic and, in her confusion, she turned away from Gina toward the coffin, and was shocked again at how small it was. At how white and smooth and perfect it was, at how pretty the silver handles looked. If Cindy's dollhouse had come with funeral home accessories, this coffin would have been the centerpiece.

A sound escaped Ruth's throat then, and she swallowed down the sob, the lump that was lodged there. That seemed to satisfy

Gina, and she gave a final squeeze and moved on. Ruth kept her head down and watched her feet walk away: thick tan ankles with a gold chain that Mick had given her; dark blue heels scuffed at the back; that familiar heavy wiggling walk.

After the mass, the slow steady drive to the cemetery. Limousines like a caravan of ants bearing a tiny load. Ruth sat in the first car, between Frank and her mother, feeling the dampness of her stockings and the sweat pricking her upper lip.

The grave was still raw—a small hole lined with something bright and green, as though it was going to be a display of oranges in a grocery store. A mound of earth and two men leaning on spades a distance away, standing in the cool shade of a tree, waiting to throw dirt on top of her daughter. She stared down into the hole while Father O'Brien spoke.

As they turned to go, she saw that a space had been left beside the grave and she realized that, if they found him, Frankie would lie beside Cindy. Her daughter had been alone in death for almost two weeks. But if they found him, Frankie would be with her and he could look after her, as he had always done.

7

There were two articles on Pete's desk when he got in the next morning, neither of them related to the Malone case. The copy editor's blue pencil meandered from line to line like snail tracks. He poured himself a cup of coffee, stirred in three packets of sugar, and started typing, but his thoughts kept drifting to Devlin; to Quinn, talking about Mrs. Malone. To Ruth Malone herself.

It had been sixteen days since the kids had been taken and the girl found dead, and there was no real news—about who'd killed her, about her missing brother. The police had released a statement saying that Cindy had been strangled, but giving no other details. All the papers could print was a rehash of names, ages, dates; where she'd been found; a description of Frankie and what he'd been wearing the night they disappeared; speculation about what had happened.

Fluff, Friedmann called it. They were just keeping the kids in the public eye. They were all waiting for the next thing.

And that morning the next thing happened.

The phone rang. Pete looked up automatically and saw that Janine was watching him as she answered. She turned away slightly, cupped her hand around the receiver. He started to pay attention.

Then she put the caller on hold, ignored his hissed *"Hey, what's..."* and trotted over to Friedmann's office. It must be something big: she didn't even want to risk being overheard putting this one through. Her tight skirt meant she could only take small steps, but she was scurrying fast enough that Pete pushed his proofs aside and turned to a blank page in his notebook.

Janine's other line rang and Pete ignored it, but it kept ringing until one of the secretaries covered her own mouthpiece with her hand and hissed at him to pick up. He lifted the receiver, kept his eyes on Friedmann's door.

It was O'Connor. As soon as he heard his voice, Pete thought of Friedmann saying, "O'Connor has two weeks of his vacation left. You can stay on this story until he's back."

He kept his tone light. "Hey, man. I thought you were in Florida."

"Wonicke? What, you're a goddamn receptionist now? Listen, I don't got much time. I *am* in Florida. I'm in the fucking hospital."

"What happened? You okay?"

"No, I'm not *okay*. If I was okay, I wouldn't be in here, dumbass."

Pete was still watching Friedmann's door, but neither of them had come out yet.

"Is Friedmann around?"

"He's got someone with him."

"Listen, I need you to give him a message. I'm due back tomorrow. Tell him I need another week. My idiot brother totaled his truck."

"Shit."

"Shit is right."

"What happened?"

"We were in a bar, playing a little pool, drinking beer. We had a few shots. Only the fucking moron can't hold his liquor. He wouldn't give me the goddamn keys to his truck. Said he was fine, said he could drive. And now he's in here with two broken ribs and a punctured lung, and it's up to me to take care of the goddamn insurance paperwork."

"Jesus, Con. Is he going to be okay?"

"That asshole? He's fine. I'm the one with my neck in a brace. They're telling me I can't get behind a wheel for six weeks."

There was a voice in the background and Con said loudly, "Two more minutes…Jesus, they don't even got a working pay phone in here. I'm at the nurses' station. I got to get out of here, man. This place is a shithole. The heat, the goddamn mosquitoes. My arms are like fucking pincushions. Soon as I'm discharged and the paperwork's done I'm going straight to the nearest car rental and getting on the road…yeah, yeah, I hear you, nurse. I'm just finishing up.

"Anyway, I'll be back in a week or so. Say Monday. The ninth. Okay? Can you tell Friedmann?"

"Sure."

"So what's going on there? Anything interesting turn up? Anything worth rushing back for?"

What would I know, Con? I'm just the goddamn receptionist.

Pete glanced over at the row of secretaries, all busy with their own calls, their typing. He looked down at his desk, at his notes on the Malone case. The interview transcripts, with his scribbles and questions in the margin.

He took a deep breath and tried to sound casual.

"Not really. Just a couple of traffic accidents. The usual. You know."

"Okay. Good. You tell him, anything big comes in, I'll be back on Monday. I can pick it up then. Okay? You got that?"

"Sure. Monday." Pete scribbled it in his notepad, still looking at Friedmann's door. When it opened, Janine emerged and Friedmann appeared behind her, neck swiveling, scanning the room. Pete stood up, caught his eye.

"Gotta go, Con. Take it easy."

He hung up. Friedmann jerked his head and Pete was in.

"I need you to get over to Queens, Wonicke. Toot sweet. 68th Drive. There's been a development on the Malone case, but I don't know what they got."

Pete gave O'Connor's message to Janine and ran to the parking lot. He drove over the Williamsburg Bridge as fast as his ancient Chevy would take him, frantically scanning his street map at every red light. The road was cordoned off, asphalt shimmering in the stifling August heat. It was a dead end, probably a weekend hangout for kids on bikes: there was a built-up embankment, a small cluster of scrubby trees. Like the neighborhood where the Malones lived, this was the kind of place that no one noticed.

But the Malone story was news, and whatever had happened that morning, it had already brought crowds. There were cops everywhere. Huddles of reporters. And groups of watchers two or three deep on the embankment. The mood was different too: there was no grief here. No sympathy. Pete looked at the curious faces of the crowd and realized these weren't friends or neighbors, but most likely strangers caught up in the drama. They stood in silence, arms folded, necks craning to watch the cops coming in and out of the trees. Waiting.

Pete got out of the car, notebook in hand, sweating through his sports coat. Took his place near the veteran reporters who were leaning casually against a van. He recognized a couple from their byline headshots.

This was what he wanted: to be one of these guys. He wanted their confidence at a scene, their loose walk, their way of turning neighbors and shop owners into sources, their trick of pulling the threads of a rumor into a story.

He'd done two years in this job—two years of typing up routine stories, of living in a one-room apartment where trains rumbled underground through the night and where the crazy guy next door shouted in his sleep—and this was his chance. He could feel it. This story was *his*.

Twenty-three tense minutes later, a cop sauntered over to the group of reporters. He took his time, hitching his belt up over his belly, swinging his nightstick, drawing out the wait a little longer. One of the senior men—Miller? Mellor?—nosed his way out of the crowd of reporters to meet him halfway. The cop talked in a low rumble, the other guy bent his head, nodded, remained motionless, looking down, even as the cop clapped him on the shoulder and lumbered back to the perimeter tape. Then the reporter made his way back to the other old hands, who in turn passed back snippets to the guys at the edge of the pack. Pete hung onto his notebook and concentrated on sidling closer to the group. No one spoke to him. He strained to hear the murmured threads of conversation.

There's something in there. In the trees.

It's gotta be the Malone kid.

I heard it was some kinda clue. Clothes or somethin'.

The cops ain't saying nothing.

Naw, there's gonna be a statement in an hour.

"Bitch did it. No doubt." That was a guy with the nose of a drinker and a drooping eyelid that looked like a wink. "You seen how she looks coming in and out of the station—face all made up and hair done. She's never cried for 'em. Not once."

The rest nodded sagely, lit cigarettes, sipped coffee from paper cups. Pete thought about that blaze of hair, those wide eyes. Wondered why she hadn't even pretended to cry, to pull the grieving mother act. Wondered what was going on there, under the surface.

Still thinking, he stuffed his notebook into his pocket and turned away, wiping the sweat basting his forehead, feeling for a breeze. So he was the first one to see the police photographer come out of the trees. The guy's face was white and he was staggering a little, and then Pete knew.

The photographer leaned against a parked cruiser and bent to get his breath, or to be sick. Pete moved quickly, put a hand on his shoulder, and said, "You look like you could use this." Gave him a cigarette. The photographer took it with a shaking hand, waited while Pete lit it for him. As he inhaled, a little color flushed his waxy skin.

He was looking at Pete, but his eyes were wide and glazed and Pete realized he was still seeing some of what he'd left behind in the trees.

"I did two tours in Korea. But this…this…"

Then he lifted his hand to his face for a second and covered his eyes. Pete bowed his head in sympathy but kept watching him.

"That poor fucking kid. Only...well, he ain't a kid anymore. His arms are gone, his neck..." He swallowed hard. "Animals pulled him apart. And the heat, the doc said."

Pete felt the hairs stand up on his neck and arms, and the metallic tang of nausea filled his mouth.

The photographer took another long drag on the cigarette. "He looked like a piece of wood. That's what I thought when I saw him laying there. Just a black shape on the ground. His face...I thought at first he was a fucking log. And the smell. Jesus..."

And then the photographer did throw up, and Pete backed away, feeling his throat constrict. He looked at the cops coming out of the clump of trees with the same greenish pallor as the photographer, the same dazed expression, at the men from the coroner's van conferring in low voices, and at the ambulance men going in, carrying gallon bottles of alcohol—for the maggots, he guessed.

And he wondered how the hell he was going to convey the pity and the horror of this death. And how he was going to make the people of Queens feel his rage and his disgust that a child should become an object of revulsion.

Pete's piece made the morning edition, though with so many changes he couldn't recognize his own style. And the *Courier*, the *Star*, and the *Times* were all leading with the same story. But even so, it was something. It was the first time his byline had been on the front page. It was a start.

He spent the next couple of days around 72nd Drive, working on follow-up pieces. He weaved in and out of the teams of uniformed cops in the neighborhood, keeping one eye out for Devlin. The uniforms were working their way door to door for the second time, looking for witnesses. What had been horrifying just a few weeks before had already become routine.

"Anything suspicious, sir, doesn't matter how insignificant it might seem, please call us…no, you won't be wasting our time, ma'am…yes sir, terrible business. Thanks, folks…"

He watched them show a picture of Frankie and Cindy at each house, watched them wait with patient, tired faces while people stared at those innocent smiles and clicked their tongues and unconsciously touched the heads of their own curious children, peeping around legs and doors at these real policemen. Then they handed back the pictures. Shook their heads and took the cards with the precinct address and the public telephone number. They knew nothing. They'd seen nothing. They'd heard nothing.

Pete was emerging from one apartment a few minutes' walk from 72nd Drive, when he saw two officers knocking at a door across the hallway. The woman who opened it seemed flustered: her plump hands patted her dyed red hair, tugged at her bright pink housecoat, flapped at the air around her face. She gave her name as Mrs. Gobek, and she never met their eyes all the time Pete stood there; shook her head before they even showed her the pictures. *No, we never saw anything. Never heard anything. My husband and I live very quietly, we like to get to bed early.*

The door closed and the two cops looked at each other and shook their heads. They moved on, and Pete went to sit in his car, lit a cigarette, and read over his notes.

The neighbors were keen to talk about the family. About the parents' separation.

"Ten years ago, we didn't get people like the Malones in this neighborhood. Divorces and such. I moved here from the city for some peace and quiet. And now look what happened."

"Can't say I blame him, up and leaving like that. You seen Mrs. Malone? The way she dresses? Ain't no chance she was faithful to Frank."

"Frank Malone? Oh, he's a sweetheart. One morning last winter I came out of my building and the car wouldn't start. I was standing there wondering what to do, who to call—and he came by and asked if he could help. He'd fixed it for me in fifteen minutes. And he wouldn't accept a dime. A real gentleman."

"I think she's a little crazy, the way she acts. Drinking and all. Even though she had those children to take care of. She comes home awful late four or five nights a week—and the way she curses sometimes is just terrible. There's no smoke without fire, isn't that what they say? A woman like that—well, who really knows what she might do?"

The strength of feeling against Mrs. Malone was feeding his curiosity about her. About what had happened to her kids. About why she didn't look the way a grieving mother should. It was time he saw for himself what lay at the root of it. He wanted to hear what she had to say. To form his own judgment about her.

So he straightened up, threw away his cigarette, and approached her building. It was one in a line of redbrick three-story apartment buildings: shabby, with paint peeling on a couple of the windowsills. He could hear music from an open window on the second floor.

He pressed the buzzer to the Malones' apartment. No response. Waited, and tried again. Still nothing.

He scribbled a note for her and put it in her mailbox with his business card. He told her he wanted to hear her side of the story, that he wanted to know what she thought had happened to her children.

He stood by his car for a while, smoked a cigarette, wondering if she'd appear. Nothing.

On Monday morning Pete arrived even earlier than usual. Picked up the latest set of proofs, popped open a Coke, started reading. When he saw Friedmann making his way across the floor, he darted over to meet him.

"You got a minute, Mr. Friedmann?"

Friedmann checked his watch. "Literally one minute."

Pete followed him into his office. Friedmann sank into his chair, waited.

"Thank you, sir. So, Con…O'Connor isn't back. I told Janine…"

"Yeah, yeah, I heard. The accident. The brother. Blah, blah, blah. What about it?"

"I want to stay on the story."

Friedmann sat back, raised an eyebrow.

"I know the case. Even if Con comes back…well, we don't know when he'll be back. I know the neighborhood. I got a feel for it. I want to take a real look at this. Dig around a little and see what I can find."

He thought of Ruth Malone: the makeup, the teased hair, the lack of grief. "I think there's more to this than we're seeing right now."

Friedmann got to his feet, picked up the jar of fish food.

"You been here how long? A year?"

"Two."

"Two. Well." He scattered flakes of food on the water, watched the fish swimming up to the surface, their rhythmic gulping.

He turned back to Pete. "Okay."

"Okay?"

"It's yours. Your byline. You lead."

"Shit. Thank you. Thanks, Mr. Friedmann. Really."

"You fuck it up, I take it away. No argument."

"You won't regret it, Mr. Friedmann."

"Yeah. Yeah, I will. But if the good Lord sees fit to put my senior crime reporter in the hospital and send me you instead, who am I to argue? He giveth, he taketh away. Now get out of here. Go write me something I can print."

Three days later. Twenty-two in total since the kids were reported missing. Three weeks since Quinn had told him Devlin thought Ruth Malone was worth looking at. And yet, despite the details Quinn had given him, despite the apparent determination of the cops to dig down and find evidence against her, they hadn't made an arrest. Pete wondered about that. What they'd found—and what they hadn't.

He stood at the cemetery gates, waiting for the cars. He'd left a bottle of Coke in the car, feeling it would look disrespectful to drink it—and he thought now of the taste of it, sweating through the glass, the sweet jolt of caffeine.

Then he heard the slow approach of a car and turned to see the hearse creeping through the hot afternoon toward him. As it passed, he caught a glimpse of an old woman, rod-straight, lips pursed, looking dead ahead. A priest, with the set expression of someone on his way to a tough day's work.

And that was it. Both parents were still being questioned at the station house. Maybe there was just a little relief that they wouldn't have to watch another small coffin being lowered into the same ground.

Then a cab pulled up and one of the Malones' neighbors got out—the woman who'd told him on the first day that someone had taken the kids. Greta something. No—Gina. Gina Eissen. She was pink-cheeked, perspiring, clutching a handkerchief and a drooping bunch of white daisies. She looked at him and moved to walk past him, but her heel slid on the gravel and she stumbled. Pete caught her elbow to steady her.

"Shit. Shit and damn and fuck these stupid shoes. And fuck…"

And then she was crying—noisy Scotch-soaked tears through her nose, and angry muffled words.

"Shouldn't even fuckin' *be* here…this ain't fuckin' right… shouldn't be burying kids…"

She began to wail and he patted her arm awkwardly, fished out his handkerchief and offered it to her. Stared out at the dusty road and wondered what the hell to say.

She blew her nose, straightened up, ran a finger under each eye to wipe away the worst of the damage. Sighed.

"Jesus. Thanks for…well, thanks."

"Tough day."

"Yeah." She took out a half-empty bottle from her bag. Drank from it. "Anyone else here?"

"Just one car so far. A woman in it."

"Probably Ruth's mom." Another mouthful. "Did she look like she had a poker up her ass?"

She giggled, then stopped as suddenly as she'd started. "Fuck, Gina, shouldn't say things like that."

"Miss Eissen . . . are you sure you're up to this?"

She took a mouthful, then another. "Got to go in. Promised Ruth I'd go. He needs someone who knew him. Not just Christmas cards like *her*"—a scornful jerk of her head at the church—"but someone who knew his favorite toys, and that he din't like carrots." She sniffed. "Someone who knew him."

And she turned and walked toward the church, limping a little on her broken heel, legs as thick as tree trunks below her frayed hem, stuffing the bottle back in her bag.

Pete caught up to her, took her arm. "Let me take you in."

"I'm fine. I just . . ."

"Really, let me help."

And before she could say anything else, they were at the church door and he was holding it open for her.

The service was short: just Pete and Gina in one pew and the old woman across the aisle. Gina nodded toward her and muttered, "That's her. Grandma Kelly."

Pete watched the woman during the service: her dry eyes, her set lips. She ignored them both. The priest approached her afterward, sat down heavily beside her, patted her hand. They began to speak in low voices.

As Pete looked on, she turned, almost as though she felt his gaze. He saw the lines etched into her face. Took in her tight gray curls, the black hollows under her eyes.

He bowed his head, glad they couldn't see his skin flush, and followed Gina out of the church, grateful for the warmth and the heat after the dark chill inside.

"Can I give you a lift home, Miss Eissen?"

She took the bottle out again, drank from it, shrugged. Tottered behind him to the car.

Gina was asleep before they reached the main road. He glanced over at her, slumped sideways and snoring, the tracks of tears still visible through her thick makeup, and he wondered how the hell he was going to get her out of the car.

But she woke when he pulled onto 72nd Drive and turned the engine off. Gazed around her blearily, rubbed her eyes, looked over at him. Then she sighed and stared out through the windshield. There was still a small crowd of reporters out there, buzzing around the apartment building like flies around rotting meat. It was almost five. Still hot.

Without looking at him, she said, "Thanks for bringing me home. And for coming in with me."

"Sure. Listen, can I ask you a few questions? About Mrs. Malone."

"Nope." She took out her cigarettes, lit one.

"I just want to get a..."

"I said no. Thanks for the lift, but Ruth don't need some damn reporter poking and prying into her life. Like the cops ain't bad enough."

Her voice was slurred but her anger was clear.

She exhaled, squinted at him through the smoke. "She got fired, did you know that? Not even three weeks since it happened. She can't go into work, so she lost her job. So *you*"—jabbing her cigarette toward Pete—"you need to give her a fucking break. Leave her alone."

She opened the car door, swung her legs out, and then sagged forward, her cigarette falling to the ground, her head drooping almost gracefully toward her knees.

Pete waited a moment, and then another, and when she

remained still, he reached forward and tapped her lightly on her wide flat back.

Gina nodded. Mumbled something. Flapped her hand without raising her head.

"Just need a moment. Just a little...a moment."

She was quiet again, this time for long enough that he wondered if she'd passed out. And then she gave a long sigh, raised her head, and stood up in one smooth movement.

She paused to stretch, to light another cigarette, and then made her slow, meandering way across the sidewalk, through the crowd of press men, and crossed the lawn. As she reached the steps leading up to the front door of the building, she lifted her hand without turning, and wiggled her fingers back in his direction.

Pete sat for a moment. He could smell her Scotch and cigarettes.

He took out his own pack, slid one out and tapped it against the dash, lit up and sat quietly smoking, watching the light change and the afternoon die around him. He could hear the World's Fair in the distance: music, the rise and fall of a voice calling to customers.

People passed his car: mostly women, in twos and threes, carrying bags or with arms linked or pushing strollers. Groups of children raced along the sidewalk, yelling threats and insults, their faces blurred above bright T-shirts. The children didn't see him. Doubtless they'd been warned since the Malone kids were taken, but the habits of childhood were stronger than the words of their parents. To them, it was just an idea. Just another scary story.

But the women noticed him. They looked right at him and frowned, and kept their eyes fixed on him while they dipped their chins and squared their shoulders and spoke to one another in low tones about the strange man in the car. A couple wrote down his license plate number, ostentatiously, hoping that would be enough to make him go away, and when it was not, they wrote over the letters to make them thicker and darker: an insurance policy against something bad happening again.

Pete thought about the empty refrigerator in his apartment,

reached into his jacket for his wallet, and felt the crinkle of his mother's latest letter.

Usually she wrote about the weather, which was *very warm* or *awful wet* or *dreadful cold*. She wrote about her occasional outings into town and the expense of the bus and the lines in the stores. She wrote about her arthritis, which was always *no worse, thank the Lord*, and as he read he would feel that old creeping sense of boredom and suffocation.

But this letter was different. He took it out of his pocket. Folded inside was a check.

As he reread it, he could see her sitting at the kitchen table in the amber lamplight, the white hair at her temples, the brown age spots on her hands. He could smell the familiar aromas of furniture polish and cooked vegetables.

He heard her thin, hopeful voice in her words.

There's not a lot, you know we never had much. But we kept up the payments and the policy paid out after your father passed. The money is in the bank, waiting for you. You'll surely need it one day. When your time comes to settle down.

He saw the unspoken words, the expectation, as clearly as if she had written them down.

He folded the letter, slipped it back in the envelope. He had a sudden desire to lie down and sleep for a long time. Then something made him look up, and he saw Ruth Malone at the window of her apartment. She wore a dress of some pale, clinging material and she stood with her hands and her forehead pressed against the glass, looking down at the sunlit street. At the world going on without her.

He watched her watching the women and children and thought about the neighbors he'd spoken to. The things they'd said about her. Maybe she felt safe, up there, behind the glass. Perhaps she thought that if she couldn't hear what they were saying, their words couldn't hurt her.

As he gazed up at her, she stretched sideways so that she rested one shoulder and her hip against the window. Her head was arched back so that her thick sheaf of bright hair hung heavy and full at an angle to her neck.

And then she turned, pivoting on the back of her shoulders, which remained in contact with the windowpane. She rolled over as though she was in bed and this was a lazy Sunday morning and everything was normal. She rolled again and came to a stop with her hands pressed against the glass, looking up at the burning sky. Almost as though she were praying.

And suddenly Ruth Malone didn't look safe. She looked like a pale shimmering moth fluttering behind the glass. She looked trapped.

He had the strangest desire to touch her and, as he thought this, as he felt shame flush his skin in response, she stared straight at him. Her eyes widened, and for a long moment, neither moved. Then her lips parted. Slowly.

Pete dropped his gaze, let the letter fall to the floor. He started the car, fumbling with the key. He did not look at her again but he could feel her watching him, all the way back to the highway. He felt naked, as though she'd seen through to the core of him, and it made him afraid.

He drove home and lay on his bed and tried not to think about her. But his mind kept returning to her parted lips. The way she had looked at him.

And then he realized that his hand had found his cock and was rubbing it through his underwear, and that he was thinking of that mouth on his. That lipsticked O around his hardness, his hand in that glowing hair. And he pushed the cotton down around his thighs and came with a groan and wiped his hand on his stomach, and he was asleep before the stickiness had dried in the hot night.

8

This, then, was grief. It came to her as heaviness. It came as a stone in her throat, preventing her from swallowing; as a pressure behind her eyes, forcing out tears; as a weight in her stomach. It meant that she could not breathe. That she could not have a single moment of not remembering.

It was with her every moment and it fed on her pain and it would not be satisfied. Sometimes she sat up at night with it, cradling it, placating it, but it would not be soothed. It was black and hungry and huge like a screaming mouth and it became bigger and deeper the more she focused on it until it filled up her mind and there was no room at the edges for thoughts or for words, for food or faces or whether she was thirsty or tired or needed to take a shower: only this vast, expanding blackness.

And inside it: the loneliness, the loss. She had no means of orienting herself. The only thing she knew was that this would never end.

Everything came to her through the gray haze of grief. She saw her hands reaching for a lipstick, or a pencil, and they were alien and clumsy because she could not see them clearly for grief. She swallowed coffee and the nibbled corners of things and they were bitter through the grief-taste that lay thick on her tongue. Voices were muffled, finding their way down through the weight of her grief, and her throat was choked with it. She had learned simply to shake her head when the voices paused or rose into questions. No, she did not want to eat. She did not want to lie down. She did not want to pray. To be touched. All she could do was hold Cindy's stuffed rabbit in her curled claw hands, her pain wrapped by her curled rocking body. There were no words that could console her. This was her suffering, and her bones and her breath had become grief.

And into this place of grief came Devlin. With his steady voice, which carried no emotion. With his steady gaze, sharp and observant as a bird's. Always watching.

August 10. Twenty-seven days since the children were taken.

Pete was working on other assignments, but the Malone case was always there, like a nagging headache, always at the back of his mind. He read over the bulletins every morning, spoke to the guys on the crime desk, hung around the station house after work. A couple of times he'd buttonholed Quinn at the diner. It all amounted to the same thing: there was no new evidence.

He was heading out of the office, thinking about a bar and a baseball game on the tube and a couple of cold beers, when a figure appeared in front of him.

"Con."

"I want to talk to you, you little shit. You took my story. The dead kids—that should have been mine."

"You weren't here."

"I was away one more week!"

"It was Friedmann's decision."

Con took a couple of steps forward, his fists clenched by his sides. "Sure. Sure it was. And you didn't want it, right? You didn't push it?"

"What do you want me to say? Look, Con, it's too late now. I got the story. That's it. Something else will come up soon, and you'll get that."

"Fuck you."

"You would've done the exact same thing."

That brought Con up short.

"Yeah. Yeah, I would. And you know why? Because I'm good at my job. Because I got experience, and contacts, and I know how to write a fucking story. You? You're just a college kid who's way out of his league. You're a dumb nobody. Fuck you."

Pete watched him walk away and felt the words burrowing under his skin. And so instead of heading out to a bar, he went home and thought about the case. He needed something to justify Friedmann's decision to give him the story: a new angle or a new hook. Just as he was falling asleep, an idea came to him.

He was at the office by seven-thirty the next morning, typing up articles, making calls, checking facts. Waiting. And just before noon, Horowitz came in, his face tired, his jacket slung over his shoulder. Pete hadn't seen him in weeks: he'd been in court following the progress of the fraud trial. Pete stood and cut him off before he reached his desk.

"Busy?"

Horowitz shrugged.

"Want to get lunch?"

"Sure."

They headed out. Halfway across the parking lot, Pete turned to face him.

"You know I've been working on this case about the murdered kids? Frankie and Cindy Malone?"

Horowitz pulled out his smokes.

"I heard, yeah. Read a couple of your pieces."

Pete let himself be sidetracked.

"You did? What did you think?"

"Not bad. Your style could use a little polish. You repeat yourself. But not bad at all."

Pete tried to stop the grin spreading across his face. Focused on the question he wanted to ask.

"The guy leading the investigation—Devlin—you know him, right?"

"Yeah, a little."

Pete stayed quiet, and then Horowitz asked: "How did you know?"

"When I bumped into you in the files, the first day of the case, I dropped a photo of him. It could've been anyone. But you made him for a cop."

Horowitz nodded. Shrugged.

"Yeah, I know him. So what? I've been a crime reporter for thirty years. He's a cop. New York ain't that big."

"Can you get me a meet?"

Horowitz raised an eyebrow and Pete spoke quickly. "I just want to meet him. Get a feel for the guy."

Horowitz could be like gridlock in rush hour.

"It's not gonna happen, kid. He don't talk to reporters."

"He talked to you."

"Yeah, but we're—"

"You're what?"

Horowitz dropped his cigarette and ground it out carefully. Then took out his pack of Camels again, fumbled for a light. Inhaled deeply. All the while avoiding Pete's eyes.

Pete decided to push it. "You're what? Friends? Neighbors? Golf buddies?"

"We go back a long way."

"Okay, so you..."

"Look. I get that you're just starting out, Wonicke. I get that. You're trying to make your name. But Charlie Devlin and I go back. I owe him. So I'm not letting you put so much as one damn question mark over the way he's running this investigation."

Pete kept his eyes on the other man's. Kept his voice steady. Wondered about what seemed like a hell of an overreaction.

"I just want to meet the guy. Just color him in in my mind. Satisfy my curiosity. You say the word and I won't even mention his name in print, not unless he gives me an official statement and says I can use it."

Silence.

Then: "Wait here."

Horowitz made his way back inside, and Pete leaned against the hood of a Ford. For an old guy, Horowitz walked fluidly, from the hips.

He was back within ten minutes. As he approached, he jerked his head, and led the way to a dusty gray sedan parked at the back of the lot.

"Where we going?"

"You wanted to meet him."

"Now?"

"Why not?"

"You called him?"

"Yep."

Horowitz's car was filthy inside: paper coffee cups, sandwich wrappers, cartons of Chinese food. It was like the graveyard of a hundred stakeouts.

Pete took a pile of papers from the passenger seat, tossed them in back. "Thanks, man. Really, I..."

"I'm not doing this for you."

Horowitz backed out, head turned, eyes on the road.

"Then..."

"Devlin's a good cop but he's under a lot of pressure on this one. He's got five kids and he needs this job. He'll be up for retirement in a few years, and he needs to finish out his thirty with a clean record."

He swung onto the highway, checked the mirror.

"He had some...trouble in the past—but he's good at his job. He's focused. He needs a result on this: he'll get there, but he don't need bad press."

Pete fumbled for a cigarette. "So, what, you're telling me... what are you telling me?"

Horowitz sighed. "Charlie Devlin's an ornery sonofabitch. Can be a real bastard. He's a tough guy to like—but I owe him."

He took a hard left and Pete was flung against the door.

"Look, Wonicke. You wanted to speak to him—but it works both ways. I'm not telling you to write anything that isn't true. Just give him a break. That trouble I mentioned? He needs to wipe the slate clean. I can't help him, I'm stuck on this goddamn fraud thing. And I won't be around forever anyway."

"But I don't owe him anything."

"No, you don't. Not yet. But you sure as hell need him. That's why you asked for this, right? He's lead detective on the biggest case I've seen in years."

"It's just a…"

"I know it ain't that big a story yet. But it will be. You got two dead kids, no witnesses, and a hot broad who's slept with half of New York. If it ever goes to trial, it'll be fucking dynamite."

Pete thought about this.

"You need an in. And Devlin needs you. Or someone like you. You don't want to work like this, just say the word and I'll find someone else."

Pete stared out of the window. Kept his mouth shut.

Horowitz pulled into the parking lot of Tony's and they got out. As they headed for the entrance, a car pulled in behind them and the driver sounded his horn. Horowitz raised a hand, then turned to Pete. Spoke through his teeth.

"Let me do the talking. Just act like you agree with me. And no fucking swearing."

They watched Devlin strolling across the parking lot as though it was his own backyard. He reached them, slowly shook Horowitz's outstretched hand.

"Arthur. Been a long while." He turned to Pete and frowned.

Horowitz took half a step forward. "This is Pete Wonicke. He's lead reporter on the Malone case."

Devlin looked him up and down, stuck out his hand and gripped Pete's.

"Wonicke? That a Polack name?"

"My grandfather was Polish. I grew up in Iowa."

"Uh-huh." He raised an eyebrow at Horowitz, who shrugged and opened his arms.

"Let's eat, boys."

They ordered and Horowitz asked, "How's Kate? And the kids?"

Devlin nodded. "Good, good. John and Mike are in college now. Mikey graduates next year. And Tom's still playing football. Hoping for a scholarship."

For a moment he was like any other proud father.

Horowitz laughed. "Jesus. Time goes quick, right?" He turned to Pete. "Last time I saw them, John and Mike were in grade school and Tom—I'm not sure Tom was out of diapers."

Devlin was taking two photographs out of his wallet.

"That's the boys. Taken last year. And that's Kate with the girls at the church picnic."

Pete craned his neck, caught a glimpse of a woman in a faded shirtdress, two girls dressed identically in pink with neat braids, straight white socks.

Devlin smiled at the figures in the pictures, tucked them carefully away.

Then Horowitz leaned back, sipped his beer, looked at Devlin over the rim of his glass.

"So how's the case?"

He barked a laugh. "How's the case? You come out with it just like that, in front of this kid I don't know from Abe Lincoln?"

"Charlie, Charlie. I told you. Trust me. You need to talk to him."

"Yeah, you told me."

There was a long, uncomfortable pause, then Devlin pointed a thick finger at Pete.

"Okay. Here's how it's gonna be. I tell you what goes on the record. Anything else, you assume it ain't for publication. Got that?"

Pete nodded.

Devlin watched him for a moment longer. Then he leaned back, took a gulp of iced tea. Turned to Horowitz.

"It's all garbage. The autopsy reports came back with nothing. The mother ain't talking, the father ain't talking. She checked on the kids at midnight, fell asleep around four. He was home by midnight, didn't wake up till she called him the next morning. That's it. That's all they're saying."

Horowitz waited until their food had arrived and the waitress had left.

"Do you think they're lying?"

Devlin grunted through a mouthful of fries.

"*Someone's* lying. You been to that neighborhood?"

He went on without waiting for an answer.

"When I got assigned to this, I took a good look at the map. I got two missing kids, so I thought I'd try to figure out how to make the search. I saw how close the neighborhood is to the World's Fair and I set myself up for a long job. Thought I'd be interviewing witnesses and suspects and tourists until we put a man on the moon. Then I drove down there."

He bit into his hamburger. "Those apartment buildings: they're packed in so tight no one can squeak in there without the whole neighborhood knowing. If a car came along and parked by the building, or a stranger was there that night, someone would've seen them. Would've heard something. No doubt."

Horowitz waited. He pressed his foot against Pete's, warning him to keep quiet, and sure enough Devlin spoke again.

"There's something wrong with the mother."

"Something wrong with her?" It slipped out before Pete could think about it, and Horowitz winced, but Devlin didn't seem to notice. He chewed slowly, nodding.

"The apartment was a mess. It was full of empty liquor bottles, letters from men. A lot of men."

He shook his head.

"Soon as I saw her, I knew there was something wrong. The way she looked: makeup an inch thick, hair just so, clothes that showed everything the good Lord gave her. That's not a grieving mother. That's a woman who wanted to get rid of her children because they got in the way of her partying and her drinking. Of her men friends.

"And that's not all. Her statement's wrong too. There's discrepancies in her times. We got a couple of witnesses who contradict things she said. She claims she was home all night, other than for twenty minutes when she took the dog out. That was just after midnight. I got a witness who called her at midnight, and then again at two a.m.—the second time he called, no one was home."

His face was flushed.

"I took one look at her and I knew we had a problem, and everything I've found out since just confirms that."

He shook his head, took another gulp of iced tea.

"You know, this job makes me sick sometimes. The dirt you dig up makes you want to go home and take a hot bath before you sit down at the table with your own kids."

The pressure on Pete's foot had eased up, which he guessed meant he could ask questions—but he couldn't think of a single thing to say.

Then Horowitz surprised Pete.

"You sure about this? About her?"

"Arthur, I've been doing this job for over twenty-five years. You get a sense. Ask any cop. You get to know how to smell guilt. And I smell it on her like cheap perfume."

Pete leaned forward. "Are you going to charge her?"

Devlin looked him in the eye for the first time since they'd sat down.

"I want to. Believe me, there ain't nothing I want more than to see that bitch behind bars. I'm under a lot of pressure on this one. But we don't have enough yet. I need a witness."

"To the murders?"

Devlin snorted. "Right. I should be so lucky. No—more like

someone who saw her with the kids after midnight. After she said she put them to bed."

He ate the last of his fries and said, "I need evidence to break her story. We'll get it. We're doing a public appeal for information. I got guys going over every statement that's come in so far. We'll get something."

Then he swallowed the last of his iced tea and stood, bulky against the bright windows. Eyeballed Pete.

"For the record, *Mr.* Wonicke, we have several promising leads and you'll be the first to know when we make an arrest."

He hitched his belt up, straightened his tie.

"And now I'm off to crack that whore," and he was gone, leaving the ring of that final word reverberating around the booth like a slap.

The next morning, Pete woke early. He lay in bed and thought about Ruth Malone. About how she'd appeared trapped behind the window. About how she'd looked at him. He couldn't get the memory of her face out of his mind: her lowered eyelids, her red lips. His skin felt hot and his chest ached as he thought about her.

Then he thought about Devlin's determination to find a witness. He seemed so certain about her. So confident. Pete felt anything but sure about her.

Eventually, he got out of bed, dressed, and drank a glass of milk. Then he went back to 72nd Drive, knocked on Mrs. Malone's door again, and again got no reply. He scribbled another note for her and put it in her mailbox with his business card, then sat in his car and watched her building for over an hour. No one went in or out, and there was no movement at the windows on the first floor. He looked at the drop between the windows and the ground, thought about what Quinn had said: that Frank believed the kids had climbed down themselves.

That got him thinking about Frank. If he couldn't get an interview with Mrs. Malone, maybe he could speak to her husband.

He drove back to the office and called the airport, and after getting passed around between supervisors, learned that Frank's shift finished at four. Pete was in the parking lot by three-forty, waiting for the doors to open. Eventually he saw Frank emerge, and jogged over to intercept him before he could drive away.

"Mr. Malone?"

"Yeah?" Frank put his hand up to his face, to shade his eyes from the sun.

"I'm Pete Wonicke, from the *Herald*. Can I have a few moments of your time?"

Frank dropped his hand, looked around him.

"Here?"

"I'd like to buy you a cup of coffee. How about we head back toward Kew Gardens Hills and stop somewhere on the way?"

"Well...sure. I guess that would be okay."

Frank seemed a little bewildered.

"Great. I appreciate this, Mr. Malone. Is your car over there? I'll follow you. If you see a diner, just pull over. I'll be right behind you."

Frank blinked at him. Cleared his throat.

"There's...uh...Marty's off the expressway. That okay?"

"Perfect. I'm right behind you." Pete was already running back to his car.

Marty's was a big place with chrome trim and a lunch counter running the length of the room. Pete led the way to a corner table, away from the kitchen bell and the bustle of the counter.

A waitress brought over two menus and Frank smiled at her.

"Hey, Lisa. I'll take a cheeseburger and fries. And a Coke."

"Sure, hon. And for you?"

"Just a Coke, thanks."

"Two Cokes, coming up."

She winked at Frank and headed for the kitchen, hips and hair swaying in her wake. Frank didn't seem to notice; he was staring down at the tabletop, picking at a hangnail.

"You a regular here?"

"Huh?"

"You didn't look at the menu. Assumed you must come here a lot."

"Oh. Yeah. I guess. It's on the way home. And I don't... I've never liked eating alone."

His face flushed and he cleared his throat. "So, what did you want to talk to me about?"

Pete leaned forward, keeping eye contact.

"Mr. Malone, we at the *Herald* are truly sorry for your loss. What happened to your children was a tragedy."

Frank nodded. "I appreciate that, Mr...."

"Wonicke. Pete Wonicke. A truly terrible tragedy. And we want to do everything we can to help catch the person who took your kids."

Frank licked dry lips. "Thank you. Do you mean...uh...is your paper offering some kind of reward?"

"That's a very good idea, Mr. Malone, and one I'll certainly mention to my editor. But what I was thinking of was some way that I might help today. Is there a message you'd like to give to our readers? Something you'd like to say to them?"

Frank looked puzzled. "Like what?"

"Well, you could ask for their help. Make a public appeal through the newspaper."

Frank was frowning, and Pete realized Quinn had been right about him: he wasn't too bright.

He made his voice softer. "We can just ask if anyone knows anything, or saw anything that day. I can help you write something."

Frank nodded slowly. "Sure. That would be real nice of you, Mr. Wonicke. Thank you. Thank you very much."

*   *   *

Back at the office, Pete sat down to work on the story he knew he had to write. One that carried Devlin's conviction there was something off about Ruth Malone. One that gave Friedmann the sexy broad that he thought would sell newspapers.

He pulled the sheets from his typewriter and took them into Friedmann's office. Friedmann read the story over, made a couple of corrections, nodded.

As Pete left the office and headed over to the typists, Horowitz winked at him.

No matter what doubts he might have about Ruth's guilt, Pete needed a solid angle to write from. He needed Devlin's certainty. He needed to believe in something.

MALONE MURDERS LATEST: NEW LEADS
By Staff Reporter Peter Wonicke

QUEENS, Aug. 12–Police have several promising leads in the case of the two murdered Malone children, a source said last night.

Little Frank Jr., 5, and Cindy Marie, 4, disappeared from 72nd Drive in the early hours of July 14. They were reported missing from the apartment they shared with their mother, a cocktail waitress who is separated from their father.

At 1:30 p.m. that day, the body of the little girl was found in an empty lot on 162nd Street near 71st Street, about a half-mile from her home. She had been strangled.

On July 25, the decomposing body of her brother was found on an embankment near the New York World's Fair site. No autopsy could be made on the boy due to the condition of the body.

Frank Malone Sr., an airline mechanic who works nights at Kennedy International Airport, yesterday made a fresh appeal for information.

He looked visibly upset as he spoke to this reporter. "There's no need to tell you how we feel," he said. "If anybody in the city or anyplace has any idea what happened to Frankie and Cindy, please call the police."

While her estranged husband was speaking to reporters, Mrs. Malone, a petite strawberry blonde, attended another interview at Fresh Meadows police station. She was freshly made up with lipstick and eyeliner and wore a fashionable blue skirt, matching heels and a low-necked cream-colored blouse. Mrs. Malone left the station house at 4:50 p.m. and was driven away by a male friend.

Pete kept thinking about Horowitz. About the look on his face as he avoided the question of how he knew Devlin. The way he wouldn't meet Pete's eyes.

So one morning, Pete went to the public library and spent some time in the stacks. It took him a while—he had to go back more than eight years—but he found the story that Horowitz hadn't told him.

He used the ancient copy machine to make duplicates of the news articles, and left with the pages folded in his notebook and the facts clear in his mind.

He wasn't sure why it was important to have this. But he decided to hold onto it, just in case.

9

Pete's thoughts kept turning back to what Friedmann had said about every story needing a villain. It seemed to him that the police weren't looking at other suspects. He wondered if they'd even asked Ruth Malone who she thought had done it.

He needed to speak to her.

He told Friedmann he had a lead, and spent a couple of days sitting outside her building, waiting.

And finally she emerged.

She walked to her car, head bent, and didn't notice him.

"Mrs. Malone?"

Her face was drawn and tired beneath the makeup. Her lips were chapped, dry. She didn't smile or ask him what he wanted. Just waited for him to speak.

"Mrs. Malone, I'm Pete Wonicke from the *Herald*. Can I have a few moments of your time?"

"What..." Her voice cracked, and she cleared her throat. "What do you want?"

"Well, I want to hear your side of things. I wondered if you had..."

She didn't raise her voice, or bluster, or avoid his eyes. She simply stood on the sidewalk and said, "No."

"It's important..."

"I'm not interested." And then, like a child, "I don't want to."

"Mrs. Malone, this could be your only chance to tell your side of things."

And now she smiled, but it was a smile without warmth or humor.

"I sincerely doubt that. You people"—and here her lip curled—"you people are always bothering me."

She took a pair of sunglasses from her bag and slipped them on.

"I just want to be left alone, Mr. Whatever-Your-Name-Is. Just leave me alone."

There was a tiny catch in her voice and she pressed her hand to her lips. Then she got in her car and drove away.

He kept watching her, waiting for another opportunity. She didn't go out much during the day. She shopped for food. Looked listlessly in store windows. Once she went to the beauty parlor and had her hair done.

Nights were different. She was out every night: at Callaghan's, at Santini's. Mostly with the same guy: short, thickset, with sallow skin and oiled black hair, expensive suits, cigars. Sometimes she went out with girlfriends and once or twice with other men. She drank too much, laughed too loudly, complained it was early when the others wanted to call it a night.

The cops were trailing her too. There were four of them, working in shifts. Pete would stroll over to their cars, offer around cigarettes, sticks of gum. Then he would stand and smoke with them, lead the conversation to why they were all there. He would ask how the case was going, if they had anything he could run with yet. They talked a lot about Ruth Malone, mostly dirty jokes, but their answers about the case were always the same.

"It won't be long now before we have enough to charge her."

"You'll be the first to know when we do, Wonicke."

"We're bringing her in again tomorrow. She's gonna crack sometime. They always do."

More than once, someone mentioned Devlin's obsession with the case. With Ruth. Pete learned that Devlin had photos of her pinned on the wall over his desk: dozens of them.

"He's like my kid sister with her pictures of the Beatles." This was a skinny Irish cop called O'Shea. "Maybe he just wants to screw her."

They all laughed, and then one of the others, an older guy, shook his head. "Naw. She ain't his type. He wants her put away for this. I heard he got called in to see the chief about the overtime bill. And that he said he'd work late for no pay."

He looked at the others, shrugged. "That's what I heard, anyway. You seen him: he's like a dog worrying at a bone. He ain't gonna give up until she's behind bars."

Every place she went, Ruth was at the center of the room. At first he thought it was because of who she was, because of what had happened to her. Then he realized it was because of who she'd always been. It was how she looked. How she carried herself. In those bars, next to the suburban moms and the tired divorcees heading for forty, she glowed. There was something about her that made it impossible to look away.

When she danced, she moved and stretched and rippled in a way that showed off her body, keeping her eyes on the men in the crowd, making sure their eyes stayed on her.

Friedmann kept telling him: add just enough color to make the story memorable. Ruth had enough color for neon and stained glass and Christmas. Pete didn't need to make her up, all he had to do was follow her and take a picture with his pen and pad and his memory, and there she was: Kodak-bright on the page.

When she had danced enough to sweat out the alcohol, and the flashing lights were showing her strained face and dead eyes, she pushed her way to the bar or waved to a passing waitress and ordered another round of drinks, and another. It was as if she couldn't bear to be sober, even for a moment.

And as it grew late, she chose one guy and fixed all her attention on him so that she didn't have to go home alone.

Same thing the next night. She was never alone.

The hostess at Callaghan's told Pete she'd known Ruth for years, since it was still the Four Seasons, since Kennedy was alive. She was short, heavy, with platinum curls and disappointed lines running from each corner of her mouth. Her eyes flickered from the door to the bar to the register.

"Oh sure, I liked her. She was a good worker. And she had something about her. She could sit down with anyone, a bunch of suits, anyone. And within five minutes, she'd have them laughing, ordering cocktails. She was bright. A real live wire."

She shook her head. "When I first heard about this, I didn't believe she had anything to do with it. I mean, I could never really see her as a mother, the way she was, the way she looked."

She shrugged. "Still."

She stubbed out her cigarette and lit another. And then, "But afterward. Well, she was back here four days after they buried the boy. So drunk she couldn't stand up straight and flirting with every guy in sight. And no tears. Nothing."

She blew out a long plume of smoke, her lips a sticky pink O. "I changed my mind about her after that. The next day I called her, two, three times, to ask when she was coming back to work. I figured—she can go out and enjoy herself, she can come into work. Right? She never called back."

She shrugged. "So the boss told me to send her a check for two weeks' pay, tell her she was being laid off. And now look at her."

She nodded toward Ruth, moving slowly on the dance floor, arms raised, eyes closed. "I mean, what kind of mother behaves like that?"

Ruth's car was in the shop for a week, which made trailing her harder. He got into the habit of parking on the corner around seven each morning, before his shift began, waiting for her to come out. If she turned onto Main Street, she was grocery shopping. If she kept going toward the expressway, it meant she was catching a bus.

One morning she came out dressed in a neat blue suit, low heels. Not shopping, then.

It was August 20. Five weeks since the kids were reported missing.

The bus came and she took a seat in the middle, by the window. Pete sat two rows back, on the other side of the aisle.

She didn't seem to notice him. Didn't seem to notice anyone. She just held her handbag on her lap, a cigarette between her listless fingers, her head turned toward the smeared glass.

Pete could smell stale sweat, hairspray, the damp pantyhose of the woman next to him who had slipped off her shoes.

The bus ground to a sighing halt and the door opened.

And then the girl appeared.

She walked down the aisle and took the seat in front of Ruth. She was young, small, slender, with tiny breasts and hips and round arms and calves. She wore a simple blue blouse, her hair was long and shining and she looked like she should smell of soap and something sweet: cream soda or talcum powder.

Ruth didn't take her eyes off her. Pete watched her watching the girl as she turned to look out of the window, her clear skin flushed, her chin raised. She was on the verge of becoming a woman but she lacked those womanly trappings: lipstick, powder, cigarettes.

Pete looked at the girl and at Ruth's pale face and then he realized she must be thinking of her daughter. This girl was just like Cindy, but Cindy grown older.

Apparently without realizing what she was doing, without any kind of conscious thought, Ruth stretched out an arm and stroked the soft cotton. As gently as falling blossoms. The material was thin and the girl's skin showed through it. Ruth stroked a loose strand of hair that flowed over that shoulder like water, fingered the long, cool smoothness of it, stared at the change in depth and color as the light danced over it, and then as it was jerked up and away.

"Hey," said the girl, her face red. "Hey!"

Ruth's hands flew up, white and tremulous as birds.

"Sorry. I'm so sorry. I thought...I thought you were someone else."

She stumbled into the aisle and pulled the bell again and again until the driver yelled into his rearview mirror and brought the bus to a halt and shook his head at her.

The door hissed shut behind her and the bus moved on and Pete twisted to see her lonely figure grow smaller in the rear window as the long gray road stretched between them.

Pete was on his way back from lunch when Friedmann appeared in the doorway to his office and beckoned him over.

"Take a seat. What you working on right now, Wonicke?"

"Well, the Malone case."

"That's it?" Friedmann shook his head. "I can't afford to leave you on that. We got too many other stories need attention."

"Sir, it's still news. Two unsolved murders."

"*Unsolved* being the key word. Until the cops make an arrest, there's nothing we got to tell readers that they want to hear. They close to pulling somebody in?"

"I don't think so. But..."

"But nothing. You come back with a new angle or new information, we'll talk. Look, you've been doing some good work lately. That piece you wrote about the father's appeal—the contrast with the mother, that was nice. But now I want you on that Panty Burglar case in Jamaica."

"The *what*?"

"I know. The *Star* gave the guy a name, it stuck. Series of burglaries going back a few weeks. Guy only steals women's underwear."

He took off his glasses and polished them on his tie. "It takes all kinds, right?"

"Jesus."

Pete stared down at Friedmann's desk, thinking. As Horowitz had said, this story could be huge—and he wanted to be there when it took off. He wanted to break the story of an arrest, or a conviction. Even—and he felt adrenaline rush through him at the prospect—even be the one to uncover evidence that might prove who the killer was.

"How about I go and talk to the cops again? See if they got anything..."

"You still stuck on this? I told you, we don't have time. Go talk to Gluckstein about this burglar thing. He was talking to one of the victims this morning. He'll give you what you need."

Pete stood. Then with one hand on the door, he said in a rush, "What if I can get an interview with the parents? Mr. and Mrs. Malone. An exclusive."

Friedmann frowned at him. "You really want this? Okay, you get me an exclusive, we'll talk. But make it good. I'll give you twenty-four hours, then I need you back here to pick up whatever comes in."

Pete called the airport and learned that Frank's shift ended at seven. He was in the parking lot by six-thirty, watched Frank leave, and followed him to Marty's.

"Hey, Mr. Malone. How you doing? Can I get you something?"

"Oh, hey, Mr. Wonicke. Uh...I'll take a bacon cheeseburger. Onion rings."

Pete ordered for them both, then glanced over at Frank. He looked like he'd lost weight in the last week or so. There was a patch of stubble by his ear that he'd missed while shaving.

"How you holding up, Mr. Malone?"

"Okay, I guess. It's tough, you know."

Pete nodded. "Sure. I understand. Listen, I've been thinking. I'd like to do an interview with you and Mrs. Malone together. That kind of thing always attracts interest, and it'll keep Cindy and Frank Jr. in everyone's minds. Might jog a few memories—it might even bring out a few more witnesses. I've seen it work before."

"You have?"

"Oh, sure. People often don't realize that what they've seen is important. They don't understand that even seeing nothing may be useful information."

Frank looked confused, so Pete kept talking.

"Would you ask your...would you ask Mrs. Malone to talk to me?"

"Well, I'll try. But she can be awful stubborn."

Pete held out a dime. "Give her a call. Maybe she can come over now."

Frank hesitated.

"If we run something with the both of you, it might make a difference. You never know."

Frank was back from the phone in a couple of minutes. "She's not home."

"Okay. Let's do this without her for now. Why don't we begin by talking about the days leading up to the...to the children's disappearance. Say the twelfth and thirteenth—what did you do on those days?"

Frank sighed. "I went through all of this already. With the cops."

"I know, Mr. Malone. But this is background for our readers. It could help."

"Okay. Well, on the Monday and Tuesday I was off work. Monday, I took the kids to the park. That was the twelfth."

"Did anything unusual happen while you were there?"

"Well, Frankie fell off the jungle gym, cut his knee. That what you mean?"

"Did you talk to anyone while you were there? Did you see anyone acting strange? Anyone hanging around the kids?"

"No. Nothing like that. I saw Nina Lombardo there with her kids. She lives next door to Ruth. We said hello. And I spoke to the guy with the ice-cream cart. I bought popsicles for Frankie and Cin."

"And then you took the kids back to Mrs. Malone's apartment?"

"Well, first we went to my place. I just moved in, wanted the kids to see it. I gave them some milk, let them watch cartoons while I cleaned up. Then I took them over to Ruth's about six, six-thirty."

"How did she seem?"

"What do you mean?"

"Well, was she in a good mood? Did you talk at all?"

"Not really."

He swallowed another mouthful of soda. Crunched on the ice. Looked around the diner, then out of the window.

Pete leaned forward.

"I bet she was mad because the kids got dirty playing in the park, right? I was always coming home with mud on my shoes and my clothes. It used to drive my mom crazy."

Frank gave a sad little smile.

"Ruth hated for the kids to get dirty. I told her, they're just kids, but it made her real mad."

He sighed. "She told Frankie to start running a bath. Said she'd have to wash Cin's hair and clean up Frankie's knee. She sounded pissed. Like it was more chores."

"Does she often get mad?"

"You mean, at the kids?"

"Yeah—did she yell at them? Hit them?"

"Sure, when they were outta line. She's got one of those tempers that flares up, then it's over real quick."

Frank frowned. "But I don't think she'd...she wouldn't hurt them, Mr. Wonicke. I'm sure she wouldn't."

But his voice held a note of doubt. The waitress brought their food and as Frank smiled up at her, Pete watched him, thinking about what he'd said. He couldn't know for sure what Ruth would do.

"And after you left your kids at your wife's place, then what?"

"I drove around for a while. Thought about the kids. About the custody case. I drove to a bar but then I turned back. Went home instead."

"Why didn't you go in?"

"I dunno. I was tired, I guess. Sometimes the kids would tire me out. I drove home, drank a couple of beers, watched the Mets on TV. I fell asleep around eleven."

"What about the next day? The thirteenth. What did you do?"

"I played golf in the morning. I had a tee time at seven, so I got up around six, showered, headed out. It was pretty quiet, I remember. Not much traffic."

He was talking freely now. Maybe it was easier to talk about himself instead of the kids.

"How come you were playing so early? It was your day off. You could've taken it easy."

"I like to get up early, get a head start on the day. My pop always said early was the best part of the day. And it gets too hot later on. I don't like to be out in the sun in the afternoon."

"So you played your round—how was it?"

"It was good to be outside. But the guy I played with, Ed, he said twice my game was shot to hell. Guess he was right."

"Why was that?"

"Well—the custody thing. It was on my mind a lot. Seeing the kids, it got me thinking. Guess I was upset."

"I can understand that. It must have been tough on you—that, and the separation."

Frank nodded. Pushed the food around his plate. Wouldn't meet his eyes.

Pete leaned in again. "The separation, that was Mrs. Malone's idea?"

"Yeah. I guess." He still didn't look up.

Pete pitched his voice low. "That's real hard. Did she ever tell you why?"

He shrugged.

"Was there maybe another woman involved?"

Frank's head whipped around. "You think I was cheating on her? No way. No way! That's not how it was!"

Pete raised his hands in apology. "So how was it?"

"She was...I found her. With someone."

Pete felt adrenaline surging through him. This hadn't been in any of the papers. "You found her with another guy?"

Frank's eyes were wet, his voice was almost a whisper. "I came home early one day. I was sick to my stomach and the boss told me to go home. I walked in and I heard noises. In the bedroom. They were ... they ..."

"I'm sorry, Mr. Malone."

"The guy just picked up his clothes and ran past me. I wanted to grab him. Wanted to hit him so damn hard he'd never go near my wife or anyone's wife ever again. But I was so ... I just ..."

His voice trailed off and he passed a hand over his face. It was as though he'd forgotten Pete was there.

"She was crying. I thought she was sorry. I went to her—and she screamed at me to leave her alone."

Now he looked up. "You know, I would have forgiven her. I never wanted us to split. But she ..."

Tears filled his eyes and he blinked them away. Swallowed.

Pete gave him a moment and then asked, "Is that why you were going for custody? She was seeing other men?"

Frank nodded. "I thought ... the guy I caught her with, I thought it was a one-time thing. But Frankie told me ... he used to tell me that they'd wake up and there'd be men in the apartment. Different men."

He shook his head. "I couldn't have that. Lord knows what it would do to the kids, growing up like that."

Pete pushed aside their plates, took out his cigarettes, and offered one to Frank, watched him inhale a little shakily.

"So what happened then, on the thirteenth? You played golf in the morning—then what?"

"Uh ... I had a drink in the clubhouse with Ed. He left around noon. I had a couple more beers, ate a sandwich, watched the game on TV."

"You see the whole game?"

"No. I left around two."

"Did you go home?"

Frank sighed. "I feel dumb saying this. I didn't tell the cops. But I guess it'll have to come out."

Pete tried to make his voice calm. "What will? What did you do?"

"I drove out to Huntington."

"Huntington?"

"Yeah. To Redwood Drive."

"Why? What's out there?"

Frank drained his soda, waited until the waitress had taken his glass.

"There's a guy who lives out there. Salcito. He's a friend of Ruth's."

He sighed.

"I thought they were...you know. I thought they had something going on. That he was another one who...that she was having an affair with him."

"So what was on your mind when you drove out there?"

Frank leaned forward, his face flushed.

"She's my *wife*. I wanted to...I guess I wanted to teach him a lesson about playing around with another guy's wife."

"So what happened?"

A sudden, harsh laugh. "The bastard wasn't home! I parked on the street, psyched myself up. I walked up the driveway and rang the doorbell. Rang it twice. And no one was home! I could hear a dog barking in back, but no one answered."

"What did you do then?"

"Just turned around. Drove away."

"What were you thinking?"

"I don't know. I was pissed at first. Then I thought maybe it was a good thing he wasn't home. He might've had people with him. A gun, maybe. Anything. Anything could have happened."

"Where did you go next?"

"I drove around the neighborhood for a while."

"Were you looking for him?"

"I guess at first I was looking for Ruth's car. I wanted to be sure she wasn't there. But I didn't see it. There were cars everywhere, but they were mostly new. Station wagons, Chryslers. You know, mom cars. But they were mostly shiny, like they were taken care of. I would've noticed her car there.

"A while later, I realized I wasn't even looking for her anymore. I was just driving. It was a nice neighborhood. Quiet. Green lawns. It seemed like a place you'd want to bring up kids.

"Anyway," Frank cleared his throat. "Anyway, she wasn't there. Then I drove home and took a nap. Then I watched some TV. About eight, I got hungry, so I headed out along Union Street. There's a guy has a stand there, makes good pizzas. I bought a large pepperoni. Went home again to eat."

"Did you stay home the rest of the night?

"Mr. Malone?"

"I drove back to the Union. Went to a bar—the Lakeside. Had a few drinks."

"What time did you leave there?"

"About eleven. Maybe a little before."

"You talk to anyone?"

"The bartender, Al. He knows me, I've been there a coupla times. He'll remember me. I was drinking gin. We talked about the Mets game. He'll remember."

"You normally drink gin?"

"Felt like a change."

"Okay, then what? What did you do when you left the Lakeside?"

"Drove around some more."

"Where did you go?"

Silence. Then: "I went to Ruth's. I drove to her place and parked outside."

"How long were you there?"

"I dunno. Fifteen, twenty minutes. There was a light on in the bedroom and in the living room."

"Did you get out of the car? Speak to her?"

"No."

"Did you see anyone while you were there?"

"No."

"If you didn't go there to see Ruth or the kids, why were you there?"

"Well, to get evidence. For the custody case. I thought she might have another guy there. I wanted to be sure the kids were okay. And..."

"And what?"

Another sigh. "I just went there sometimes. I'd park up and just sit. I wanted to be near her, I guess. Near Ruth. Near my kids. She's my wife. That's...that was my family."

He spread his hands. Looked at Pete.

"I'm living in a shitty boardinghouse with three other guys. The bathroom stinks, the kitchen's a mess. That's why I don't eat dinner at home. No one cleans. Things never get fixed. The lightbulb in the hallway went out nineteen days ago, and nobody's replaced it yet. Nineteen days. I count 'em, every morning.

"That's where I live now, and I miss my home. I miss my wife. I miss my family. Sometimes I used to go to the apartment building to be near them. So what? That's not a crime."

There was another pause, and then Pete asked, "What time did you leave?"

"Eleven-thirty, eleven forty-five maybe."

"Then what did you do?"

"Like I told the cops—I drove home. Went to bed. I didn't wake up until Ruth called in the morning."

Pete was back outside Ruth's building the following night. He watched her get into a cab, and trailed her to Gloria's. It used to be a fancy place, back when it first opened: ropes for the lines, the bouncers young and tough. When the novelty had worn off, the lines died away, the bouncers were replaced by an older guy with glazed eyes and a broken nose, and then even he disappeared.

The night Pete walked in, the sidewalk outside was dead. There was no one on the door, no one lined up outside. No homeless, even, panning for change—there wasn't enough passing traffic to make it worth their while.

He saw Ruth right away. She looked at him, puzzled, like she half-recognized him, then turned back to her drink. She was sitting alone at the bar, but there were two cops at the far end. She kept shooting them filthy glances, checking her nails, looking up from under her lashes whenever someone stood next to her. Pete knew her well enough by now to guess she was on her third Scotch Mist. Almost drunk enough.

She leaned into the bar, beckoned the bartender over.

"Another one, Hud."

Hud and Pete both looked at her and there was a moment where Pete thought the other man might say something. It passed, like all moments, and Hud just shrugged and poured her drink in silence. She raised it to the cops at the end of the bar, threw it back, and turned to face the room.

She leaned her weight on her elbow, resting on the bar, back arched. Her hair was pinned and sprayed, her skin matte and flawless, her eyes huge: what Pete's Irish grandmother used to call "put in with a smutty finger."

As he watched her, Ruth lowered her gaze. Moistened her lip with the tip of her pink tongue. Crossed her legs.

She reminded him of the cat who lived in the apartment building across from him: a tortoiseshell who spent hours staring at the birds that settled on the small plane tree in the front yard. They both circled their space with golden eyes: they owned it.

And then her prey appeared.

A swagger in a suit with slick hair and a dimple in his chin and the laughter of his friends shoving him forward. She took out a cigarette, he produced a lighter. They started the practiced dance: she bent to the flame, his eyes flickered to the V of her breasts, to the way it widened as she leaned back again.

He smiled at her, stepped up to the bar, and raised his chin; the bartender was there, smooth as a long streak of polished wood.

"Whatever the lady's drinking," his gaze on her again, "two of those."

A bill appeared between his fingers, disappeared as the glasses were placed carefully between them. While he raised his to her, her eyes slid sideways to the solemn-faced Hud. Maybe there was just the hint of a comradely wink.

They drank. He told her a name, she told him one in return. She sought out the damp pink faces of his friends over his shoulder, baying like dogs, beating the table, and she turned back, smiled, fluttered.

Next time, it was Ruth who caught the bartender's eye. He asked, "What'll it be, folks?"

She looked at her friend and said, "You choose. Last time we had my drink. I want to know what you like."

He held her gaze, but he wasn't quite drunk enough for a line, or a lie. Not quite. Ruth just sipped and waited.

Pete could tell that the next round of drinks didn't matter so much; it was just something to do with their hands. Ruth raised her eyes to the bartender and ordered two more without speaking, but this time there was no smile and no conspiring with Hud because by then their heads were close, Ruth's and her friend's, and the rest of the bar was just noise and light and figures in the background.

By then she probably knew that his wife didn't understand him, and she had probably told him that her husband was a jerk, and they both knew what would happen, but it still wasn't quite time. Not yet. That was time for sweet anticipation, for delicious teasing, for the rush of confidence, for feeling the blood pumping and knowing that this was what being young and good-looking and alive was for.

He excused himself to go to the bathroom and she turned a little so she wouldn't have to see him pause at his friends' table and see the grins and the backslapping, and Pete saw her hold on tight to the bar and dig her nails in.

When he came back, he sat a little closer and ordered two Scotches, straight up, one for the road, here's mud in your eye, baby, and that made her laugh, hard, but then he put his arm around her and she stopped laughing and looked up at him.

They got up and left and Pete followed. He needed to know what she was like when she thought she wasn't being observed.

So he followed them home, the cops behind him. He let one hand sit lightly on the wheel, his other arm resting on the window, elbow bent, palm curved against the roof. He spread his fingers and let the warm night air trail between them.

When they stopped at the lights, he saw their figures silhouetted against the neon, watched as his arm came up around her, and as she leaned in against him. Watched as their darkness merged and the space between them closed.

When they reached 72nd Drive, Pete rolled up and parked nearby, watched them go inside, Ruth tucked into his arm and her face turned up to his. Pete lit a cigarette and saw the soft pop of light that signaled a lamp being lit, and then Ruth's slender figure against the window as she closed the blinds.

He imagined the dark heat of the room, the golden glow of the lamp. Maybe she'd put a Sinatra album on the record player—surely this was the kind of guy who'd appreciate that husky, easy voice, who'd hear the yearning behind the words.

She'd excuse herself to go freshen up, then mix a couple of drinks, sit close, wait for him because she knew guys liked to make the first move, but she'd tell him she wanted him to make it—with her eyes and her mouth and her slim, dancing finger circling the rim of the glass.

Pete got out of his car and walked toward her building, feeling the eyes of the cops on him and not caring. He walked right up to the ground-floor windows but he heard nothing from inside, so he kept walking, around the side of the building and then to the back. Not knowing what he was doing, just needing to be nearby. There were no other lights on and he had to watch carefully where he was putting his feet. And so, looking down, he saw it.

A window in the basement was partly open. Just an inch or so, but enough to get his fingers through and open it. He climbed inside and pulled it closed behind him. The basement smelled of laundry detergent and Marlboros and dust, and he fumbled his way to the wall and felt for a light switch. Turned it on for a second to orient himself, and noticed an old sofa against one wall, a stack of boxes, piles of magazines, a row of empty beer bottles on the floor.

He turned the light off again, felt his way to the sofa, and lay down. Let his eyes adjust to the darkness. He couldn't hear anything from the apartment above him, only the faint scurrying of an insect and the soft creaks as the building settled in for the night.

And then he heard a louder creak, and something that could have been a groan. He saw them together: Ruth winding her fingers in the man's hair and pushing her body up against his as he moved her back and down into the couch, as she let her moans become incoherent pleas, *please*, as he gazed at her with wild eyes and started to unbuckle his belt.

Pete heard a thud as she let her shoes fall, and then footsteps as she led him into the dark bedroom. Another groan, this time from him, and he saw her smiling in the darkness because she knew she had him now. Silence again: she might be undressing him slowly. Teasing.

Pete imagined her soft voice in the dark, the laughter in it as she whispered. *It's more fun this way, in the darkness, don't you think so, baby? because*—she stroked—*you never know where the next move*—she licked—*will come from, you know?* And she laughed low and husky when he couldn't talk, and removed her dress and panties but left the stockings on because there was nothing like the silver whisper of silk against skin, and if this was going to be the most memorable night of his life, she had to work on all his senses.

Pete heard him gasping, heard him beg and moan and, indistinct, her soft voice asking a question. And then a half-yell from above *yes yes yes fuck yes just do it baby do it* and there was a creak as they came together, and he said *oh Jesus* and he said *God yes fuck* and she raised herself up again and this time he was wise and this time he told her before she had to ask *You are the best baby the best the best goddamn fuck I've ever* and she slammed down onto him and he yelled into her hair and neck and she held him as he shuddered and groaned hot release and was still.

Ruth woke and lay quiet as he dozed with his arm flung over her. She gently scratched the hairs on his arm and leaned into his warmth and thought about what she would say to Gina later, poor Gina who'd probably been on a date with Mick last night, which meant a sad two-dollar steak at Arnie's and afterward, Mick humping away, red-faced and breathless, while Gina sighed and moaned under him. She'd say *I woke up with him but I was thinking about you!* and they would giggle like little kids. Gina would ask *Was he handsome?* and Ruth would say *Yeah, sure, dark like Elvis, with eyes like Paul Newman or someone else*, and she'd think *What does it matter?*

She stretched and smiled now because he'd told her that was the best sex he'd ever had.

She'd worked so hard—at touching him, at guiding his fingers to the parts of her that he wanted to feel, at letting him smell her freshly washed hair, her perfume-dabbed wrists, at letting him taste the mouthwash on her tongue—nothing untoward, nothing *wrong*—until he'd said he wanted her.

She couldn't bear to be alone. Mustn't be alone. And he wanted her so bad, how could he not want to stay?

So she closed her eyes and dreamed of him saying that he loved her, that he'd take care of her, and woke again as he threw back the covers and slid into his clothes and told her in a whisper like he was in church that he had to get home, that the kids would be up soon, that she knew he was married didn't she, so why was she looking like that—and it was just a little fun, and he'd call her, okay?

He left without taking her number and a door slammed and a car started up and she lay in the half-light of the glow from the living room, still and stiff like she could preserve heat by not moving. Then she steeled herself and looked down.

Naked sagging stomach, stretch marks, thighs with telltale dimples, a rash on her calf, a missed penny of hair on her ankle, breasts slumped sideways, and that ripe, yellow smell.

Like a bitch in heat.

Like a whore.

She was disgusting.

She was a monster.

She curled her knees up and fell sideways. She'd guessed by now that the cops had bugged the phone and thought the apartment might be too, so she stayed silent because she wouldn't give any listeners the satisfaction of her tears.

All she could do was hold on tight and hide and hope that someday the best sex he'd ever had would be enough to make someone stay. Because she couldn't be alone. Because she had nothing else to give.

10

Pete called Devlin, asked if he could buy him lunch. They met at Tony's, the same as before. Everything was the same: Devlin was late and made no apology for it, and when they began talking, he was as sure and as certain of himself as anyone Pete had ever met. Pete mentioned that he'd spoken to Frank: Devlin merely grunted around a mouthful of pork chop.

"He seems like a nice guy. Upset about his family and all. We talked about his movements in the days before the kids were…"

Devlin barked a laugh. "His movements? You been watching reruns of *Dragnet*, kid?"

He took a gulp of soda. "You don't think we already looked into him? You're wasting your time, Wonicke. Leave the alibis and the *movements*"—his fingers made quote marks in the air—"to us, and get back to your own job."

Then his eyes raked over Pete and he looked as if he found him wanting.

He went on, "Frank Malone is just a guy who lost his wife and kids. He was a father. Take it from another father—he wouldn't hurt those kids. He don't have it in him."

He pushed his plate away, wiped his mouth. "Anyway, he was suing for custody. He wanted the kids to live with him. And he probably would have gotten it—he had a steady job, a quiet life. Unlike their mother. Why would he kill them when he wanted them living with him? No, it's her. I know it."

Pete changed the subject. "When we met before, you mentioned you had a witness who called Mrs. Malone at two a.m. the day the kids went missing—and no one answered."

Devlin sat back, reached for a toothpick.

"That's right."

"You mind if I get his name?"

"Yeah, I do mind. This don't go in the newspaper. We're saving it for the trial."

"I won't print it. Just curious."

Devlin looked at him for a long moment. "His name's Salcito. But he won't talk to you." He went on before Pete could speak, "I do have one other piece of information for you."

Pete uncapped his pen. Waited.

"Mrs. Malone is looking for a new job."

Devlin unwrapped the toothpick and dug around in his back teeth, his voice wet and distorted by his stretched lips.

"Whaddya think of that? Not six weeks since her kids were murdered."

He dropped the toothpick on the table. Pete tried not to look at it.

"She ain't even applying for waitressing jobs. She wants to be a secretary. Receptionist. Some fancy job like that. She thinks she's moving up in the world, now she ain't got no kids holding her back."

He grinned. "She ain't going nowhere."

Pete looked at him, at his satisfaction, his sense of righteousness.

"What do you mean?"

His grin broadened. "Every time she gets an offer—of an interview, or a job—her new employer's gonna get a call, or maybe a visit. Make sure they know the truth about the trash they're taking in."

At the end of August, Ruth applied for a job as an executive secretary at an advertising agency in Long Island City. Pete trailed her out there one morning, noting the way she hung her head as she walked from her car. He sat in the parking lot and watched her go in. Later, she came out and lit a cigarette and drove away.

Then he went inside. Just to see.

It was a nice office: light, flowers in the reception area. He went in to ask for directions, pretended he was lost. Looked around, played the dumb tourist, asked what they did there. A guy came out to give the girl some typing: she said, "Here's Mr. Beckman, ask him yourself," and they exchanged a smile. Friendly. The man shook Pete's hand and introduced himself as Paul Beckman. He told Pete about some of the products they worked on, joked about a slogan he was writing for a new toothpaste brand, then pointed him back to the highway. He seemed like a nice guy.

As Pete got back in his car, he saw the cops pull in. Quinn was driving, Devlin sitting in the passenger seat, his elbow on the sill of the open window, his jaw set.

When Pete got to McGuire's that night, Devlin's encounter with Beckman had already become a story. Quinn was holding court in a booth, telling it to a skinny redheaded guy named Henriksen and a cop with blond hair and acne whose name Pete didn't know. They nodded at Pete as he sat down.

"So we walked right in, just like we always do. The guy was real polite, offered us coffee. And the sergeant gave him the usual speech: you had a girl in for an interview today, right?"

"Guy says, sure I did. And now he's starting to look puzzled. Devlin says, 'Were you planning on offering her the job?' The guy frowns. Pours himself a fresh cup of coffee. Takes his time. And he says, 'Can I ask what business this is of yours?' Can you believe it? I mean, seriously?"

Henriksen laughed, a high laugh like a girl's. "What'd the boss say to that?"

"What did he say? Well, he didn't know what to say. Bet no one talked to him like that in a while."

"He gave the guy a minute, waited to see if he'd answer. Nothing. So he said, 'She probably told you her name is Ruth Kelly. That was her name before she was married. Her married name, her *real* name, is Ruth Malone.'

"The guy is absolutely silent. So we wait another minute and then I say to him, 'That name sound familiar? Maybe you heard of her.' Still nothing. The guy just sat there, sipping his coffee. Like he was waiting for us to get to the point.

"So then the boss kinda sighs and sits up—you know, like, 'Okay, I gotta spell this out for you' and he looks the guy in the face and he says, 'Sir, the woman you met this morning is under suspicion of killing her children.' And the guy just fucking sat there! Like we just told him it was raining outside.

"Finally—*finally*—he spoke. You know what he said? He said, 'Why are you telling me this?'"

Henriksen looked around the booth, eyes wide. "Can you fucking believe that?"

The blond cop shook his head. "The thing about people—they never behave the way you think a sane person would."

He turned to Henriksen. "Like that crazy broad in Forest Hills last month, right?"

Henriksen nodded, grinned. "Ain't gonna forget that one in a hurry."

He turned to Quinn. "We got a call about a domestic disturbance. Neighbor could hear a woman screaming, furniture smashing against the wall, all that. So we head down there, we bang on the door—no one in there gonna hear shit, so we break it down. The place was a mess—blood everywhere, broken glass, chairs all smashed up. Turns out the guy came home from 'Nam, heard a rumor his wife was fucking around when he was away, decided to teach her a lesson. He punched out two of her teeth and I think he broke her arm—I had to pull him off her, and then the bastard takes a swing at me."

The blond took up the story. "So we cuff him and the wife's hollering at me, *What ya doing, what ya doing, don't take him in!* I tell her he ain't going in the wagon for what he did to her—this is just a domestic incident, no witnesses—he's going in for what he did to Henriksen. Crazy bitch jumped me and when I tried to push her off, she fucking bit me!"

A swell of laughter. The blond rolled up his shirtsleeve, Pete craned his neck, saw a circular purple mark on his forearm.

"Had to have a goddamn rabies shot—the doc told me human bites are worse than any animal ones. So the guy gets a fine for taking a swing, and she goes down on a six-month stretch. And I hope he finds another piece of ass by the time she comes home. Teach her a real lesson for what she done to me—and to him!"

More laughter. Then, as it quieted down, Quinn spoke again.

"Anyway, so the guy this morning? He says, 'Why are you telling me this?' I could tell the boss didn't know what to say. I didn't either. Then the guy asks, was there anything else? Like telling him he just had a child killer in his office ain't enough!"

"Jesus H. What'd the boss say then?"

"He said, 'We thought you should know, sir.'"

The blond cop laughed. "I like that. *Sir.*"

"I know, right? Then the guy said, 'What do you expect me to do about it?' Like we told him there was a rat in his fucking garbage. Like this wasn't nothing to do with him.

"So the boss leaned in real close. Said, 'Maybe you don't understand what kind of person she is. Maybe we haven't made it clear.'

"The guy finished his coffee, stood up, and said, 'You've made yourselves perfectly clear. Thank you for coming in. And now, if you'll excuse me, gentlemen, I have another meeting.'"

"Holy shit."

Henriksen nodded. "Un-fucking-believable."

"And that was that. Before we can get another word in, we're out on the sidewalk like a coupla clowns, just looking at each other. Know what the boss said? He said, 'That guy thinks he's done his good deed for the year. Thinks he's got the moral high ground. But every man has his limit, and I'm going to find his. When I do, Quinn, they'll both be sorry, him and that whore.'"

Pete looked at their hard faces, their narrowed eyes. Watched as they straightened their shoulders against her.

*   *   *

The next day, he got Janine to call Beckman's firm, to tell them
that the paper was writing profiles on executives working for com-
panies in growth areas. She rolled her eyes but Pete smiled at her
and promised to take her to lunch.

When she hung up, she read her shorthand back to him. Beckman was in his early forties, had been with the company nine
years. He'd left his wife and kids in Delaware when he transferred
to New York six months earlier.

Over the next few weeks, Pete went back to Long Island City several times. Beckman took Ruth out to lunch once or twice a week,
seemed to like her. They always went to the same restaurant, always
ate at twelve-fifteen. One afternoon, Pete came in behind them,
asked to be seated around the corner from their table. She couldn't
see him from her seat, but Pete was close enough to hear how she
was with Beckman. They talked mostly about work, once about a
movie they'd both seen. He seemed to rely on her. To trust her.

Pete watched them leaving together, watched how her hips
moved beneath her skirt. How the sun caught her hair and burned
it golden as she turned. And how her face changed completely as
she gazed up at him. She looked lighter somehow, the lines and
shadows smoothed out, and her eyes bright.

Pete had other assignments, but he made sure he was in the restaurant by noon most days, always within earshot of their table
but out of sight. He told himself he was following developments in
the case, but after a week or so he knew it had become something
more. He missed her on the days he couldn't get out there.

In mid-September, Beckman told Ruth that his contract had
been confirmed for two years and he was going to move out of the
temporary apartment the company had found for him. He said he
needed more space.

A few days later, she told him she had something for him. Pete could hear her fumbling in her bag and, curious, risked walking past them to the restroom. She was handing over a furniture catalog. When he returned to his seat, Beckman was leafing through it.

He said, "I don't know where to start with this stuff. Helen usually does all of this. Whatever I choose, it won't look right, and I'll be left staring at drapes and a sofa that I hate."

There was a pause, and Pete thought of Beckman's tired eyes, the way he frowned when he spoke. He never knew what Ruth saw, what passed between them during that pause, but he heard the warmth in her voice when she replied.

"I could help. If you'd like me to."

Pete thought it was just a way of filling another day. But it went further than that. The following week they went shopping together. Then Paul Beckman took her out for dinner to thank her, and afterward, he invited her up. Pete parked behind the cop car and watched Beckman's apartment for an hour, trying not to imagine what was going on up there. Unable to tear himself away until the lights went out and it was clear she wasn't leaving that night.

Sure, he'd heard all the rumors at the station house, all the jokes—and he had the memory of her parted lips, her wide eyes, as she looked at him on the day her son was put in the ground—but this was something else. This was a bereaved mother and a married man. Devlin was right about her. There was something rotten underneath the sweetness.

He didn't know what the cops did after that, but he drove home and opened one beer and then another, and wrote until his head ached.

MALONE CASE: MOTHER MAINTAINS SILENCE
By Staff Reporter Peter Wonicke

QUEENS, Sept. 20–The strawberry blonde at the center of a Queens double murder case today refused to comment on rumors that she is conducting a relationship with a married man.

Mrs. Malone, who is separated from her husband, reported her two children missing on July 14. Some hours later the body of little Cindy, age 4, was found lying in a weed-strewn lot not far from the apartment where Mrs. Malone has chosen to remain.

Two weeks later the body of Cindy's brother, Frank Jr., age 5, was found in a clump of bushes on an embankment above the Van Wyck Expressway, near to the World's Fair.

Mrs. Malone, neat in a white jacket over a pale knit dress, her hair teased into a bouffant to give her five-foot-four-inch frame the impression of extra height, was seen entering the apartment of Paul Beckman, a senior executive at advertising firm Schiller and Klein, just before midnight.

A source stated that Mrs. Malone has several close male friends. The police have learned that she is a "swinger" who frequents a number of popular nightspots in Flushing and Corona.

The Malone children were taken from a bedroom that was later found to be locked while their mother remained in her own bedroom next door. There were no sightings of strangers near the apartment building and Mrs. Malone's neighbors reported no unusual disturbances that night.

No arrest has yet been made in the case.

The next morning, he turned in the article and headed out to Long Island City. The waitress started to lead him to his usual table, but he stopped her, chose a different seat. He wanted to see them together now.

It was only when they arrived that Pete realized they might notice him, recognize him.

But in the event, they only had eyes for each other. Beckman seemed softer, somehow. A little shy. He saw Ruth basking in Beckman's gratitude, like a cat stretching in a pool of sunlight. Her skin and hair were sleek as satin.

"You're so lovely. Beautiful. You could have your pick of men. A guy would be a fool not to want you."

After they'd gone back to the office, Pete sat in his car a while, looking out at the East River, watching the light on the water. He pictured Beckman resting his head on her breasts and Ruth holding him until he fell asleep. Pete saw her lying there, listening to his gentle snores and feeling the weight of his body on hers, the solidness of him in her arms, his need for her like a balm.

Writing the article had released something in him. The anger was gone and for the first time, he was seeing Ruth not as a suspect, not as Frank's estranged wife or as Frankie and Cindy's mother, but as someone's lover.

Pete had seen her frustrated, furious, bored, flirtatious: this was Ruth satisfied. This was Ruth desired and desiring.

He laid his head back against the seat and closed his eyes and thought about her. About what made her different. He'd met other girls in New York: the sisters and cousins of guys he knew, or their friends and roommates. Compared to his hometown, it sometimes seemed like there were pretty girls everywhere: in every store and on every sidewalk, in every diner and movie theater.

The girls at home were mostly married now, frowsy and chapped by motherhood. A few were sliding with desperate resignation into spinsterous routines. City girls were different. They'd come to New York to get away from the narrowness of those options. They'd made a decision to be different. To take a chance on life.

And yet, for all that Pete thrilled to the brittle glamour of the office girls in Manhattan or the studied nonchalance of the black-clad beatniks in the East Village, he'd always felt, when he thought about it at all, that he'd end up marrying someone like him. Someone from a small town with the polish of a decent college, but someone with values and ambitions he could understand. Someone rosy and fresh who maybe wore her skirts a little shorter than they wore them back home, but who could otherwise have gone to high school with him. That was the kind of girl he understood.

And here was Ruth Malone, who wasn't like that at all. Who wasn't like any woman he'd ever met before.

He couldn't stop thinking about her. It wasn't just about the case: she was stuck in his head like a toothache, and that scared and excited him.

His mind drifted over her slow smile, the sound of her laugh.

He said her name out loud and it tasted like chocolate on his lips. Chocolate with something sharp and hot beneath, like a dessert with a good slug of brandy.

He imagined his own name on her lips. He saw her neat white teeth flash as she formed the long-ee sound, and then heard the noise of her tongue tuck in against the roof of her mouth. Like the smallest, softest kiss.

Friedmann called Pete into his office again. The piece about Ruth and Paul Beckman was lying on his desk. Friedmann poked it with a stubby finger.

"What the fuck is this?"

"Uh. It's..."

"I know what it is, it's a goddamn Cholly Knickerbocker item. Since when do we publish a gossip column, Wonicke?"

"I don't..."

"Damn right you don't. What the fuck were you thinking?"

"Mr. Friedmann, she's still news. Mrs. Malone. She's..."

"Sure she is. And if the cops had arrested her or this...Paul Beckman for murder, or if you had a confession on tape, I'd be the first to shake your hand. But *this*...This ain't news. This is like Eugenia Sheppard and the goddamned *National Enquirer* rolled into one!"

He looked disgusted.

"You even got any proof she's screwing this guy?"

"I saw them together."

"Doing what?"

"I saw them having dinner, I saw her going back to his apartment."

"That's what I pay you for now, to watch Mrs. Malone eating dinner?"

"I did it on my own time."

"You sat outside Beckman's apartment while they were screwing, *on your own time*. You think that makes it sound any better?"

"I just..."

Friedmann held up his hand. "Shut up, Wonicke."

He took off his glasses, massaged the bridge of his nose. Replaced them and looked hard at Pete.

"You won't leave this damn case alone. Well, I'm telling you now, you drop it until I say otherwise. Is that understood?"

"I..."

"Is that understood?"

"Yes sir."

"You are skating on some very thin ice right now, kid. Don't push it. You come in, you do as you're told, and you don't fuck up. And that's it. No getting your rocks off on Mrs. Malone's sex life. No playing detective. And no more of this bullshit."

He screwed the article into a ball, and aimed the wad of paper at the trash can.

"Now get the hell out of my office."

But Pete couldn't stay away. He tried to focus on other stories, on other articles, and on deadlines, but every afternoon he found himself on the freeway, heading out to Long Island City to make sure he was at Beckman's office by five. He watched them leaving together and followed them to whichever restaurant they were having dinner in. Sat in dark parking lots gazing at their figures in bright windows and surrendered to the sensation of her, of how she made him feel. She'd come into his life and shaken it up and made him question everything he'd once taken for granted about himself.

A week later, Ruth moved some of her things into Beckman's apartment. Pete watched him carry her suitcase inside as the cops on the afternoon shift made a note, and that night, in McGuire's, he watched Devlin's reaction.

"If she was my wife, I'd kill her. I'd kill her myself."

For days, Devlin kept talking about finding Beckman's limit. What would make him crack and drop her from his life. It was becoming an obsession.

Then one night he came into the bar grinning broadly. He'd figured out Beckman's weak point.

"The guy hired her, he slept with her, but I bet he won't let her threaten his marriage, break up his family. So I made some calls, got hold of his home address in Delaware. And I sent his wife a letter. Express delivery. I'd bet money that Mrs. Beckman will be arriving in New York tonight. Let's see how those two deal with this."

He was in a celebratory mood. Tipped his soda glass toward Pete. "Got something for you, kid"—and he nodded to Quinn, who passed him a thick manila envelope.

Pete slid his finger under the flap and looked inside. A sheaf of paper, a smaller envelope, and a tape.

Devlin leaned forward. "You got a few photos of the inside of the Malone apartment there. Plus the autopsy report on the girl. And something to go with it." He winked. "Something that will explain the significance of what the doctor found."

The next day, Pete watched Beckman and Ruth in the restaurant. Watched him avoid her eyes.

Helen had arrived late the night before, he told her. Had gone crazy, cut up Ruth's clothes, thrown her makeup in the garbage.

"We fought," he said, sounding astonished. "She was like a crazy woman. I've never seen her like that before. We never fight."

He rubbed his hands across his tired, drawn face and told Ruth that he'd requested a transfer. That he was going back to Delaware. That he was sorry.

"It's for the best. The kids. You know."

He walked away and left her sitting in the booth, and Pete watched her take in the loss of her job, her lover, whatever comfort he'd given her. He watched her order a beer, then another, and he watched her swallow and refuse to cry.

And for the first time, seeing this vulnerable side that she showed to no one else, he wanted to take care of her. She began to pick at her cuticles, and then worried at the torn skin with her teeth. Blood smudged onto her lip and she wiped her mouth in disgust, hard and impatient with the back of her hand, and her eyes were fierce and desperate.

This was the image of her he carried with him for a while. Blood. Revulsion at herself. A complete absence of tenderness.

That night, he watched her walk back into Callaghan's in a defiantly short dress and tall heels, drinking Scotch Mists fast and hard and flirting with a kind of feverish wildness that he hadn't seen before.

She recognized the two guys by the door as cops before Pete did. She stalked over to their table and stood squarely in front of them, hands on her hips, shoulders back.

"Having fun, boys? Like what you see?"

Their eyes crawled over her like ants.

"Some job you guys have. Some fucking job you're doing."

They just laughed.

"I know you bugged my apartment. You get off on listening to me and my friends? You're a bunch of sickos. All of you."

They kept laughing.

Two bright spots appeared on her cheeks and she spat out, "You'll *never* find out who killed my kids. You'll never find out the truth."

Then she turned her back on their startled faces and made her way unsteadily to the dance floor, grabbing an arm on the way, pulling the man along with her, holding him tight.

*   *   *

Pete was at home, lying on the rug, a beer beside him, rain spattering against the windows. He got up, wrapped a blanket around his shoulders, and began to read the report Devlin had given him.

The body is that of a young Caucasian female, approximately 4 years old. Well-nourished, weighing 36 pounds and measuring 39 inches in length. Hair blond, eyes blue.

They were just words. Just numbers.

He closed his eyes. Swallowed hard. Imagined white tiled walls, a row of shining steel gurneys. The smell of chemicals overlaying a faint hint of decay.

Lividity.

Congestion.

Abrasions.

Ecchymosis.

Petechiae.

Hemorrhages.

They were just words. The reality was a little girl lying as flat and white as the tiles surrounding her; her hands and feet purple, her cheek scratched and her neck covered in a circle of bruises.

Both lungs are congested with edema, surface dark red with mottling. The tracheobronchial tree contains no aspirated material or blood. Multiple sections of the lungs show congestion and edematous fluid along the cut surface. No suppuration noted. The mucosa of the larynx is gray-white.

The last photographs of Cindy showed her forever flat-chested, smooth-skinned, wearing a pink undershirt, yellow panties, a patterned pajama top. Pete tried not to think about how she would never choose an outfit for her prom, would never have her nails painted or her hair done.

Esophagus empty, lined by gray-white mucosa. Stomach contains fragmented pieces of undigested food particles (identified as

green-leaved vegetables and pasta). Proximal portion of the small intes-
tine contains yellow to brown apparent vegetable or fruit material. No
hemorrhage identified. Remainder of small intestine is unremarkable.
Large intestine contains soft fecal material. The appendix is present.

For all its undignified slicing and probing and weighing and measuring, the autopsy hardly gave up any secrets at all. There was no
evidence of sexual assault. There was no skin found under her nails,
no foreign fibers, no bruises other than those on her neck indicating
that she had been strangled. She hadn't fought; she'd died helpless.

Pete knew from the cops' official statement that the autopsy on
Frankie had yielded even less information. He'd been out in the
open for over a week, and the animals had done their work.

There were no answers, no real clues. Cindy had died between
six and eighteen hours before she had been found at one-thirty
p.m. The assumption was that Frankie had been killed in the same
way and at roughly the same time.

All that the autopsy report said was that there was nothing
clear-cut to say. There was no way of proving exactly when they'd been
killed. And Pete could see no way of proving whether Ruth Malone
was lying about the time she said she fed the kids, the time she said
she checked on them, the last time she said she saw them.

He could see no clues in there at all about who had killed them,
or why.

Pete rolled onto his back, tucked his hands behind his head. Tried
to piece it together. But his head was a jumble of beer and tiredness
and medical jargon. He dozed off and woke up hours later, sweating through his clothes, a foul taste in his mouth.

He got up, drank some water, stared at his reflection in the dark
window. He had a feeling he wouldn't sleep again tonight.

He sat on his bed, put the autopsy report back into the envelope,
took out the photos of Ruth Malone's home. They didn't show
much: it was just an ordinary apartment where a mother and two

kids lived. In the kitchen, there were plates stacked in the dish rack, toys on the floor. Piles of folded laundry on a couple of the chairs.

Then he came to a photo of Ruth's bedroom, and stopped. It was neater than the other rooms: the surfaces were uncluttered, polished. The large bed dominated the room. It was covered in patterned throw pillows; a satin comforter hemmed with ribbon lay across the foot.

Why had Devlin given these to him? There was nothing relevant here.

He tucked them back into the envelope, slid the interview tape into his cassette player. He lay down and listened to it clicking around, and then to Devlin's low, deliberate voice filling the air. There was something different about him on this tape. That rasping voice, those thick vowels, were the same—but he sounded like he was hurrying to get where he wanted to go.

"Interview restarting...September seventeenth, nineteen sixty-five, eleven twenty-two a.m. Okay. Uh...Mrs. Malone. What did you feed your children on the evening of July thirteenth?"

"I already told you. Twice."

"Tell us again."

"I fried veal, I opened a can of beans. They drank milk, I had iced tea."

"Are you sure about that?"

"Of course I'm sure. You asked me for the first time just the day after. It was the last meal I..."

There was a pause. A cough.

"Did you give them pasta? Macaroni? Anything like that?"

"I *told* you. We ate meat. String beans. They had milk. That's it."

Her voice was measured, emphatic.

"So, no pasta."

"Jesus Christ! How many times? We didn't have any fucking pasta!"

Another pause.

"So who put the empty box of macaroni in your garbage?"

"*What?*"

"We found a box of macaroni in your garbage."

She gave a harsh half-laugh. "So? Maybe a neighbor used our garbage can if theirs was full. Maybe it was me, I don't know. It could have been there for days! I don't remember everything I fed them that week."

"You don't?" He made it sound like a crime. Paper rustled.

"No, I don't." Verging on insolent.

The click of a lighter. The drawing of breath.

"And what about the plate of leftover macaroni in your refrigerator? Did a neighbor put that there too?"

"What? What the hell is all this? I just told you, I don't remember what else I fed them that week. Maybe there was pasta left over from the day before or from the weekend. *I. Don't. Remember.* Why does all this matter? Why aren't you out there looking for the person who killed my kids? There's some crazy guy out there killing children and you're asking me questions about goddamn macaroni!"

"Because right now, Mrs. Malone, I'm talking to you." A pause. "You said..." More rustling: Devlin, flicking through his notes, although Pete had a feeling that Devlin remembered exactly what she had said.

"...uh-huh, here we are...you said in your initial statement that you stopped at Walsh's Deli on your way home on the thirteenth because—and I'm quoting here—'There was nothing in the apartment for dinner.' Why would you do that, Mrs. Malone, if there was a plate of macaroni in the refrigerator?"

She was silent.

"Why, Mrs. Malone?"

"I don't know, okay? I don't know what you want me to say. I must have forgotten the macaroni was there."

Devlin took a soft breath, almost imperceptible. There was a gentle click—perhaps he was laying down his pen before speaking.

Pete could almost see him, hunched over the table, leaning toward her. Getting closer. Circling and smelling her fear.

When he spoke, his voice was low and measured.

"You bought veal, a can of string beans, milk, the day your children disappeared. At Walsh's Deli on Main Street. And you fed those items to your children that evening for their last meal."

"I *told* you, I—"

"So what would you say, Mrs. Malone, if *I told you* that the autopsy on your daughter found undigested pasta in her stomach?"

And as Devlin pounced, Pete could hear him relishing the panic and confusion that was surely painting her face.

"What? I don't understand. I—"

"*Undigested* pasta, which you fed both your children on the evening they were killed. Very shortly before they were killed. The autopsy shows that your daughter was dead less than two hours after she ate. This story about feeding them veal, about checking on them at midnight—none of it's true, is it, Mrs. Malone?"

Pete could hear complacency in his tone.

"It was such a stupid lie to tell. Didn't you know we could prove what she ate, when she ate it?"

Pete saw her as she had been that night in Callaghan's, facing down the two detectives by the bar. Wide-eyed and white-faced, other than two spots of angry color high on her cheekbones.

There was a pause: he imagined her eyes skittering across the desk, frantic, looking for a way out.

And then suddenly she seemed to collect herself. Her voice was firm.

"I fed my children veal on the evening of July thirteenth. Veal and canned beans and milk. And I checked on them at midnight and they were asleep. That's the last time I saw them and they were alive. They were fine. Just like I said, *Detective*."

11

The tape stopped and Pete turned on the lamp. Devlin was right: the lie about the food was a stupid one.

And from everything he'd seen and heard, Ruth Malone was not a stupid woman.

He could almost hear Friedmann's voice in his head, leading him. *And? Where does that take you? She's not a stupid woman. She wouldn't tell a stupid lie.*

Of all the things to lie about, why had she chosen this? The autopsy report said that Cindy had eaten pasta for her last meal. Devlin had found a box of macaroni in the garbage and a plate of pasta in the fridge. Confronted with this evidence, why was she so insistent that she'd fed them something else?

As with her made-up face and her lack of grief, the lie gave Pete the feeling there was something below the surface that he didn't understand. Something that Devlin wasn't aware of.

Just before dawn, Pete drifted into an uneasy doze and woke again at eight. He dressed quickly and tiptoed along the hall to the bathroom he shared with the guy in 5A. Quentin—Pete never knew if it was a first name or a last name—was a retired professor of theology from England. He sounded like James Mason and played crackling recordings of Churchill's wartime speeches on a tinny gramophone, and sometimes he yelled out in the night. In the mornings Pete had to step around the empty gin bottles lined up by his door.

He washed and shaved, then gathered his notes and photographs together, got in his car and drove for a while, trying to clear his head. His mind kept returning to the same questions: *What if she's telling the truth?* And then: *What if Devlin's wrong about her?*

He drove toward Ruth's apartment, pulled onto 72nd Drive, and parked behind a single police cruiser. Although the crowds were gone, there were still a couple of reporters sniffing around. Over two months since the murders and it was still news. She was still news. He leaned back and smoked two cigarettes while he tried to figure out what to do.

And then came what he'd been waiting for, without knowing it.

A cab pulled up and Gina Eissen emerged. She was wearing a wrinkled dress a size too small and dark circles under her eyes. As she reached back inside for her coat and then fumbled in her purse to pay, Pete got out of his car. Gina flinched at the sound of his door slamming, but she didn't look up. He leaned past her and handed the driver a five-dollar bill.

"That cover it?"

The driver nodded, tapped a finger to his forehead, and pulled away.

When Pete turned to Gina, she was still rummaging in her purse. Came up with a cigarette and a lighter that she clicked uselessly. He gave her a light and finally she looked up and met his eyes. Her skin was dry and her lips chapped.

"What do you want?"

"I need to talk to you."

She shook her head, backed away. "Uh-uh. I seen the things you wrote. The way you talked about her. I got nothing to say to you."

"Wait. Listen."

She kept walking.

"Please. I'm sorry."

She stopped.

"I'm sorry."

She turned and stared at him. "What about?"

He took a step toward her. Then a second. She didn't move.

"I've been doing a lot of thinking, and..." He didn't know how to keep going.

She just stood there, weight on one hip, blowing smoke at him.

"Maybe I was wrong."

"About?"

"About Mrs. Malone. About everything."

She almost spat her words out. "You got that right. You were wrong. You *are* wrong. About everything."

"I need your help to fix it."

She frowned. "Why should I help you?"

"I guess... I'm all you've got right now. I'm all Mrs. Malone's got."

She raised an eyebrow. "That's it?"

He nodded toward the nearest building, asked her, "Mind if we sit a while?"

She shrugged and they made their way over, sat on the stoop. The weak sun felt good on his skin. It felt good to take a moment. One of the reporters approached the police car, engaged the cops in conversation. Pete guessed he was looking for a new angle, something to fill a column on page five. Two women walked past, slowed as they went by the Malone building. They drew closer together, as if the weather had suddenly turned colder, and then they were out of the building's shadow and everything was bright again.

A woman came into view, walking stiffly, as though her joints were painful. She was plump, with dyed red hair and lipstick that didn't quite fit the shape of her mouth. She wore a shapeless flowered dress and low heels, her feet spilling over the sides. She looked familiar.

Pete nodded toward her and asked Gina, "Who's that?"

"Huh? Oh, that's Mrs. Gobek. She's an odd one."

"Odd, how?"

"Oh, you know. She's just a lonely old lady. She makes up stories. Likes to be the center of attention, I guess."

Then a man appeared, walking with his head down, gaze averted.

There was something off about him: he was tall and walked with a shambling gait as though he wasn't used to his long legs.

"That another Looney Tunes?"

"That's Gus Frederickson. He lives over there." She jerked her head toward the next building.

Pete kept watching him and Gina sighed. "Jesus. You're just like the cops. They hauled him in for two days before they found Frankie. Questioned him till he damn near fell apart. He's a weird guy, sure, but he ain't no killer."

"How do you know?"

"He's . . . there's something wrong with him. He had an accident when he was a little kid. Something went wrong inside his head after that. He lived with his mom till she died. He's gentle as a kitten. He likes kids . . . no, not like *that*—he likes to play with them, little kids, because he's like a kid himself. I've known him for years and he's not . . . he wouldn't hurt anyone."

Frederickson shuffled out of view and Gina took a last drag on her cigarette, flicked it onto the sidewalk below them, then wrapped her coat tighter around herself, stuck her hands deep in the pockets.

He saw she was looking at the cop car, the press men, and he said softly, "They think she's guilty."

"You think I don't know that? You think *she* don't know that?"

He nodded, watching her face. "I don't know what happened that night. But if she didn't do it . . ."

"She didn't."

"Well, then she needs to build a defense. The cops need another suspect. They need to be asking questions instead of just focusing on her."

He could see her thinking about that, and he pressed on.

"She needs to start fighting back."

Gina looked down, rubbed her hands over her face as though she was washing it. When she looked up again, her skin and her eyes were red. She sighed. Then she raised her chin defiantly.

"I want to show you something. Come on."

The cops and the guys by the car fell silent as they approached her building and four pairs of eyes watched them climb the steps. Watched Gina fumble with her key, watched Pete take it from her and unlock the door, watched him push her gently into the hallway and shut out their hostile stares.

She ran a hand through her hair.

"Jesus Christ. I hate this. I hate it. It's been months. When are they going to stop?"

"They're still hungry. They need a break."

She looked at him almost fearfully, and for a moment he thought she was going to change her mind. But she nodded toward a white door across the hallway. Pete stared at a polished brass number plate, at scuff marks on the paintwork made by small feet.

"Is that...?"

"Yes. You need to see this."

She knocked and the door opened and the old woman from the funeral was standing there. She looked at Pete with blank indifference and shifted her gaze to Gina. Just for a second, there was a sneer of disgust: then she shouted her daughter's name at them and behind her at the same time. A moment later, Ruth Malone was there.

She was tiny. She seemed to have gotten even smaller in the days since he'd last seen her. Even under her makeup he could see how pale she was, how fragile and afraid. This was not the glowing, golden woman he had seen in those bars. This woman was consumed by something bigger than she was. Her eyes were huge and dark and lost and she blinked and had to swallow before she could speak.

"Gina," is all she said, and she reached out a hand, and the other woman moved to take her in her arms. For a moment he almost thought that everything would be okay. That Gina would hold her and rock her until the pain had gone and she could stand up straight. As though a little kindness was all she needed to turn her back into that girl with the glossy hair and shining lips and eyes.

But she pulled her arm back and swallowed again and Pete saw something come down hard in her eyes. And then she looked over at him: there was a flicker of recognition and then of anger. Color came bright into her cheeks.

But before she could speak, Gina said, "Ruth, honey, this is Mr. Wonicke. He's a reporter. He's ... well, he's okay. I figured you keep getting bothered by them, you may as well give them something."

Ruth stared at her for a long moment, and looked at Pete again. Then she turned to Gina and said in a strange high voice, "Won't you both come inside? My mother is visiting. Go on into the kitchen. I won't be long."

He watched her heels click-clacking along the hallway until she turned the corner and disappeared. He heard a door close, and he followed Gina into the kitchen.

The two women had been sitting around the kitchen table, a pot of coffee in the middle. Someone had scrubbed the table—fading Formica, chipped and wearing the scars of crayon scribbles and fork scratches—and laid out a trivet for the pot and a placemat for two matching mugs. The floor gleamed and the room smelled of bleach and synthetic lemon. The tiles above the stove, yellow with a fading pattern of cherries, had recently been cleaned, the smears still visible in the too-bright light. There were dishes drying on a towel on the countertop, waiting to be put away.

It took Pete a moment before he realized what was wrong with the room. The photographs of this apartment that Devlin had given him had shown the kitchen as cluttered and untidy: toys littering the floor, laundry piled on the chairs, cereal bowls by the sink, scribbled drawings pinned to the wall. Now everything personal was gone. Every trace of the children, every indication that this had been the home of a family, rather than a single woman: gone.

Ruth's mother sat upright at the table. She didn't say a word, even to invite them to sit, but Gina sat anyway, nodded at Pete to do the same.

When he looked up, the mother was staring at him: her eyes cold, her lips thin. Pete met her gaze, cleared his throat.

"Ma'am? I'm..."

He heard footsteps behind him and the mother spoke over him. "Fetch two more cups, Ruth. Can't you see we've got company?"

Her voice was as hard as the rest of her. He thought suddenly of his own mother, of the way her anxious eyes would search his for reassurance and her shy, gradual smile, and there was a lump of selfish longing in his throat.

Ruth came into the kitchen, set out two more cups. He saw that she had powdered her face, combed her hair, applied fresh lipstick.

Her mother poured coffee and they sipped in silence, until eventually Gina cleared her throat. They all looked at her and she reached out, put her hand over Ruth's.

"I figured...I wondered if it might do you some good to talk. Maybe once you give them an interview, they'll go away."

They wouldn't go away, not until there was a trial and a conviction, or until something worse came along and took the place of two dead kids, but he didn't say so. Instead he put down his cup and got out his pen, and asked the questions that he knew he should ask.

"Tell me about the children, Mrs. Malone. Tell me about the last day you spent together."

"We went for a picnic in Kissena Park."

Her voice was hoarse.

"We left at four. I had to speak to my lawyer later. About the custody case."

As she told the story she'd told dozens of times before, as she took frequent gulps of hot coffee to ease the lump in her throat, he tried to sound professional. Sympathetic.

"I made dinner. Veal and string beans."

But his thoughts were steeped in her rather than the story. Skewed from his continual awareness of her. Of her every movement. Of the shape of her mouth.

He asked her: "What do you think happened, Mrs. Malone?" and watched her blink back tears. She lit another cigarette and tried to keep her voice steady.

"I think it must have been a crazy person. A man who was looking for an opportunity to hurt kids. Some kind of... *animal.*"

"And what do the police think? Have they said?"

"They... they don't know. They don't seem to have any real leads."

He looked at the shadows under her eyes, not quite hidden by her makeup. Her hollow cheeks, her bitten nails, the way she couldn't look at him when she talked about the kids.

He felt like he was seeing her in a different light today. However this played out—whether Devlin made an arrest or not, whether they got a conviction or not—how could this ever end for her? Surely she'd never be the same woman again. She'd never be able to sit in the sun for the sheer pleasure of it, or walk into a store and pick out a dress just because it was pretty. No one would ever be able to look at her and not remember.

She'd never escape this.

Half an hour later they were back in the hallway, the door shut firmly behind them.

Pete took a deep breath, raised his head to find Gina looking at him, her arms folded.

"Tough, wasn't it? Seeing her like that. Seeing what grief has done to her. That's what you and others like you, men who don't know her, don't see. I wanted you to see. I wanted you to feel it for yourself."

He took another breath. "I'm sorry."

She nodded, expressionless. "I know. If I didn't believe you, I wouldn't have taken you in there. But just saying sorry wasn't enough. You had to feel it. And now you do."

She nodded at the stairs. Said, "Come on." Began to climb.

When she opened the door of her own apartment, she surprised him again. He didn't know what he'd expected—garish colors, maybe? A mess? Bottles everywhere? But it wasn't like that at all. It was a little bare and the couch was sagging, but it was homey. The surfaces shone and there were plants on the shelves, a few pictures. Two tiny china figurines.

He turned and she was watching him, arms folded.

"Expecting something else?"

"I just...I'm sorry. I don't even know you and I guess I assumed..."

She cocked her head to one side and waited for him to finish. He felt like even more of an asshole.

"I had no right to assume anything. I'm sorry."

Something changed in her then: her brow cleared and her mouth twitched. She nodded and went into the kitchen.

She made coffee and brought a bottle of Scotch and two glasses over to the couch. Pete badly wanted a drink, but he shook his head when she offered him a glass, then shrugged when she held the bottle over his coffee cup. He had a feeling he might need something more than caffeine when he listened to what she had to say.

She splashed a measure into his cup, poured herself a large drink, and slumped back onto the couch.

"Christ. What a fucking mess this is."

He looked down at the cup he was cradling and wished he could think of something to say.

"Had you been friends with Ruth for a long time?"

"Have."

He looked at her.

"She's still my friend."

He nodded. "Well, have you? Known her long?"

She stared down into her glass.

"I met her—met all of them—the week they moved here. Two years ago."

And all at once he was curious, the way he should have been

from the beginning. He wanted to know what she was like, what kind of woman this terrible thing could happen to. He knew that logically Ruth Malone was the same person she had been three months ago, just with a layer of grief and horror laid over the top— but when tragedy strikes, there's a tendency to assume that someone is different. Special. That there's something about them that makes them the kind of person bad things happen to. Because the alternative—that bad things can happen to anyone, at any time— is unthinkable.

He wanted to know what made Ruth Malone the kind of person whose children could be murdered.

So he asked Gina, "What was she like—Mrs. Malone—before this happened? What was she like?"

She sighed. "Why? You finally want to write something about her that's real? You going to write the truth this time?"

And now he saw himself clearly through her eyes, and he was ashamed of how he'd let himself be used by Friedmann and by Devlin, to write the story they wanted.

He lifted his chin and met her gaze. "That's what I'm here for. To write the truth."

12

Gina refilled their cups, lit a cigarette, and began. And as she talked, gradually she unbent, and her voice softened and slowed. It was almost as though she was talking to herself.

It was maybe a week or so after Labor Day. I was in here, sitting on the windowsill, smoking, watching the street. Just killing time before my shift started.

It was quiet, I remember that. Warm. And I saw the car turn onto the street. It had a U-Haul trailer attached.

It pulled up, and they all got out. Frank and another guy—I think his name was Ed, or Eddie, maybe—Ruth, the kids.

They all got out and the guys went to the back, set to unpacking. Ruth just stood for a minute. I remember the kids were pulling at her, yelling, and she just ignored them. She was . . . sometimes she goes into a place where no one can follow. It's like she can't hear you or see you. She's alone.

Anyway, Frank and his buddy started taking stuff inside: boxes, a couple of tables. Little Frankie looked just like his daddy—dark hair, long legs, that serious frown. Could tell he was going to be well-built. Maybe a football player.

Christ.

Cindy was following him, like she always was. She was just toddling then. One hand on the railing, pulling herself up the steps. I remember Frankie shouted something from the top—"Slowpoke!"—something like that, and she looked at him and her face scrunched up. Remember thinking, "Uh-oh, there's gonna be tears"—but he didn't let that happen, Frankie didn't. He ran down and took her hand and helped her up, and five seconds later she was laughing.

They weren't like any kids I'd seen before. Most boys that age, they can't be bothered with girls, 'specially younger girls. But Frankie was real good with her.

Then I heard them run down the hall and into the apartment. Heard them shouting when their daddy told them which room was theirs. Frankie yelling that he wanted to sleep by the window.

They were nice kids, but they were overexcited that first day. Noise was beginning to bug me, so I decided to go out for a while. I remember I couldn't find my keys, and I came back into the living room to see if they were in here—and that's when I heard the voices.

I looked out and Ruth—I didn't know she was Ruth then, of course—was sitting on the steps of the next building. She had a cigarette in her hand and she was leaning back and shading her eyes and right in front of her were Maria Burke and Carla. Carla Bonelli.

Carla was smiling and pointing up at her own window, then Ruth spoke. She had a husky voice, sorta throaty. I thought she was faking it at first, but she wasn't. That's how she spoke. It drives guys crazy.

She said, "Ruth Malone. We're on the first floor. My husband and kids are inside."

I swear Maria Burke's the nosiest bitch in Queens. She actually turned around to stare at their car, then took a step to the side to see if she could see Frank. I looked at Ruth and saw her watching Maria—she had this little half-smile on her face, like she had her number—and I remember thinking, "Ah, this one ain't gonna make it easy." Made me smile too.

Then Maria seemed to realize how it must look, and she stepped forward again and held out her hand like she was Jackie Kennedy and they were at a White House reception.

She said, "I'm Maria Burke. I live at number thirty-eight with my husband and my daughter."

I don't know how she does it, but she somehow manages to get a whole bunch of stuff into the way she talks. Like she can be telling you the weather forecast, but what you hear is *I'm Maria Burke and my husband earns more than yours.* Or *We drive a more expensive car than you* or *My daughter attends a better school than yours.* Poor kid. Sally Burke's a sweetheart—she don't deserve to have Maria for a mother. Mrs. B's either hollering at her to finish her homework or boasting about her grades and her damn piano lessons.

Anyway, Ruth just looked at her and took a drag on her cigarette. You could tell Maria didn't know what to do with that. She looked at Carla, and Carla looked back at her and they both seemed like they didn't know what to do next.

Ruth sat there smoking, looking like she'd been on that stoop her whole life. She was wearing Capri pants and a shirt, I think. Heels. Her hair was done and I could tell all the way from my window that she was wearing makeup. And Maria and Carla were just in old housedresses. You met Maria? She has her hair in curlers overnight, then she pins it up in the same style she probably wore in high school. She told me once that she thinks too much makeup makes women look cheap. I just laughed. She was the prom queen in high school—she tells us that often enough—and she thinks that means she's the expert on beauty advice. I want to tell her, "Maria, sweetheart, that was fifteen years ago!" but I'd never hear the end of it.

Carla was just doing what she always does—following Maria's lead. Same kind of dress, same pattern on her apron, same damn lipstick color, probably. She's nothing like Maria: she's short and maybe carrying a little too much weight, and she's got beautiful thick dark hair that won't hold a curl, and thick eyebrows and a mole that she hates—but she don't really care that much about how she looks. She just wants people to like her. When Ruth dropped her cigarette butt, Carla was right there with her pack, offering her another one.

And when she did that, Maria took a Kleenex out of her pocket and used it to pick up the damn butt off the ground. Wouldn't have believed it if I hadn't seen it myself. She looked down her nose at Ruth like she was the queen of England and Ruth was some servant who didn't know any better, and she said, "We like to keep the neighborhood tidy. Take a little pride."

Ruth blushed but she still didn't say anything. I saw her hand creep down to smooth her pants, but she stopped herself, and I wanted to cheer her on. She didn't say a word, just smoked Carla's cigarette and looked at the two of them. Maria Burke probably thought she was rude or ignorant and, knowing Ruth as I do now, that would've stung. But she sat there like she didn't give a damn.

Eventually Carla said, "Well, we just wanted to say hello. Do you know this part of Queens?" And when Ruth shook her head, Carla chattered on about the grocery store and the children's bookmobile. She mentioned the church and she stopped then because she didn't know where to go. Ruth looked down and I could see that little smile again, as if she was wondering whether to help her out.

Then she softened a little and said, "We're Catholic," and you could see the relief on Carla's face.

She said, "Oh, then the church is just five blocks. St. Theresa's is a very..."

Maybe Ruth thought she'd given up enough. She interrupted her and said, "We're not big churchgoers."

They didn't know what to do with that either. They looked at each other again, and then Maria gave her this big fake smile and said, "Well, anyway, welcome! This is a lovely neighborhood. Very quiet. Very safe. I'm sure you and your family will be very happy here."

And Ruth smiled right back and said, "I'm sure we will. And

now I better get inside and see what kind of mess Frank's made."
And to Carla, "Thanks for the smoke."

As she got up, I left my apartment and she found me at the front
door. I nodded at her and she nodded back. Slid past me and inside.

And that was my first impression of her: that she knew how to
handle herself. That she didn't care what people thought of her. I
was wrong on both counts.

A few days later, she was outside again, sitting on the stoop when
I came home. Frank was on the late shift that night, so they'd eaten
early. He was inside reading the kids a bedtime story.

I sat down next to her and took out my smokes. She gave me a
light and I said thanks, but we didn't really speak for a while. Just
listened to their voices—Frank's rising and falling as he told the
story, the kids laughing at the funny parts. I could smell something
cooking: garlic, spices, and the sound of someone's radio. I could
hear Nina Lombardo on the telephone. It was still warm, although
the light was starting to fade a little.

It's strange, remembering this now, but I thought about my dad
that day. Hadn't thought of him in years. I remembered him telling me once that it would be an Indian summer, remembered asking him why Indians get two summers.

After a while, I asked her, "Just moved in?" Breaking the ice.
You know. And she said, "Yeah. On the first floor."

I asked if they'd moved here because her husband worked
nearby, and she said no, he worked at the airport, but she wait-
ressed at Callaghan's, over on Union and 164th. I think she said
that their old landlord was selling, so they had to get out. It was
just small talk. Just getting to know her a little.

I told her my name and she told me hers, and she asked if I lived
alone, if I had kids. Normally I get antsy when people ask me too
many personal questions, but with her...somehow I didn't mind.
She was the kind of person who made you feel like she was asking
because she was interested, not because she was prying or making
conversation.

Then she asked if I'd lived here long, and I said almost five years. Told her that some of the neighbors could be—I think I said they gossiped. She nodded—I guess she knew I meant Maria and Carla. When I got to know her better, I realized she hated people poking their noses into her life as well. Hated those "friendly" questions about how she brought her kids up, how much money her husband earned.

She wasn't...she isn't a typical *woman*. She used to make fun of the women around here. She wasn't interested in the things that made them different: who was having an affair with who, whose kid was in trouble at school. She used to talk about the stuff that made them alike. How they mostly wore their hair in identical styles, how they wore their clothes like a uniform. She called them the Barbie Dolls. She made fun of the big events in their lives— you know, the trips to the beauty parlor on Friday afternoons, the Saturday nights in the same restaurant, week after week, with their husbands and their in-laws. She didn't understand how they could be...*satisfied* with that, I guess. She hates routine. Hates cheapness, smallness.

One time she told me that Carla had redecorated and that she said she'd have to choose between buying new drapes and reupholstering the couch. I remember Ruth's face as she said, "She could have both, if she knew how." And she laughed. I guess she meant men. Guys used to give her money—ten bucks to get a couple of drinks and a cab home, or five for the powder room—and she'd keep the rest.

She said once, "Most people are afraid to take risks." I can see her now, lying back on her couch, stretching her arms above her head, laughing as she said, "They're afraid to take a bite out of life and see how it tastes."

She had two lives, really: the daytime one—the kids and laundry and tuna sandwiches and comic books and all that—and her own nighttime world. Bars. Cocktails. The men who paid for them.

There were a lot of men, always. But I guess since she separated from Frank, it was mainly Lou—Lou Gallagher. And Johnny Salcito.

Johnny I know by sight. He used to drink at Callaghan's. He's
a cop. Weird, huh? Short guy. Flashy. I think when they first got
together, maybe a year ago, she was impressed. She'd split up with
Frank a few months before, and Johnny was making good money
then, so he could afford to take her out and treat her nice. But it was
all on the surface. About six, seven months ago, things started to
go bad for him. He got into debt, owed money to people. The kind
of people you don't want to owe money to. He started drinking too
much. He was a good-looking guy, but he don't look so good these
days. He looks like he don't take care of himself. He's bigger. Put
on weight around his belly. And he's jealous. Of the other guys she
saw, her friends. Of Frank, even now they're separated.

He's angry too. The last few times I saw him, he was so angry.
Just raving—about people watching him, about being followed.
He wasn't making any sense. He sounded crazy. Maybe it was the
booze.

Lou is pretty much the opposite of Johnny. He's on the
up-and-up. His business is doing well and it seems like things just
keep getting better for him. It was like he was always making more
money, taking Ruth to fancier places. Since things started to go
bad for Johnny, she was seeing less of him, and then it got more
serious with Lou. He got himself a boat and took her away for a
weekend a couple of times. She'd only go if she could get a sitter. I
told her she should leave the kids with Frank, get him to take care
of them, but she said he'd make her life hell if he thought she was
going away with another guy.

You seen Lou? He's not a looker, but he's got this way about
him. Confident. He's a charmer. He looks like he's got money. And
he knows how to dress: nice suits, nice shoes.

He's pretty quiet: you'd think a guy with his money would be
loud, pushy—he's not like that. And even though Ruth would
come home at four or five in the morning, she told me he was
always in his office by eight. Always.

But there's something about him. Something...when you get to know him a little, you get this feeling that what's going on inside, underneath, don't match the nice shirts or the twenty-dollar haircuts. And when you realize ... it's like the feeling you get when you find a worm in a nice red apple.

One time I was at a bar out in Williamsburg with Ruth, Lou, a bunch of other people. Back in the spring. It was Lou's birthday and she made a big effort. Saved up for a while to buy him something fancy. Maybe cuff links, I don't remember. And she bought herself a new dress, had her hair and her nails done. The whole nine yards.

The dress was a little shorter than she usually wore. She kept asking if it was okay, if she looked okay, if it wasn't too tight. Tugging at it, you know? I told her she looked great. She was a fucking knockout. Guys were staring at her all night. But nobody touched her, nobody even asked her to dance, because she's Lou's girl, right? She belongs to him.

Then it happened. I was talking to one of the girlfriends, Lou wasn't around. Maybe he was in the bathroom. So Ruth was alone for a minute. Then I heard something and when I turned around, Lou was back. Standing over to one side with another guy. This one was skinny, drunk. Red in the face, hands in the air. A dope. And he was saying, "I didn't know, man. I didn't know she was your girl." And then Lou said something to him, real low. I couldn't hear. The guy tried to walk away and, as he turned, Lou punched him in the gut. I heard the thwack as he hit him and I watched the dope double over. I thought: Jesus Christ, that was too much. The guy apologized—what more did he want? But Lou was staring at him. Just staring—like he didn't even remember the rest of us were there, you know? Two of his men picked the poor guy up off the floor—he was groaning, he couldn't stand up—and one of them pulled his head up by the hair. And then Lou stepped up and beat the shit out of him.

I grew up in a rough neighborhood, I've seen some fights, but nothing like this. The guy couldn't move, let alone fight back. I still think about the noises Lou's fist made. Bone on bone. He broke the guy's jaw. And his cheekbone. It must've lasted minutes but it felt longer. The guy was spitting blood, teeth, his eye swelled up. And then Lou stopped and they let him fall and he threw up and then he just lay there, not moving. Lou turned around and stuck his fist in the ice bucket and said something and all his guys laughed. Like fucking apes. The guy just lay there. In the end the waiters had to carry him out. Lou just left fifty bucks on the table.

"For the inconvenience," he said.

He meant for the cleaning bill. He meant for not calling the cops.

Soon as I could get her alone, I asked Ruth, What the fuck was that? She didn't want to talk about it at first but I kept pushing it and finally she kind of shrugged and said yeah, maybe he overreacted, but he was jealous. And that was it. I told her it wasn't right. That he wasn't a nice guy. She wouldn't listen.

You know what? I think she liked it. She told me once that Lou was her happily-ever-after, and I think she liked he was that jealous. She said he was the only guy who made her feel really wanted. The only guy she felt could really take care of her.

It had been over an hour and Pete had hardly said a word. Gina fell silent and looked at him.

"I don't know why I'm talking so much, Mr. Wonicke."

He tried to sound reassuring.

"Call me Pete, please. I'm interested. I want to know about her."

She gave a nervous laugh, groped for her pack of cigarettes on the table.

"I guess... no one asked me anything before. Not really. Not about Ruth. Just did I hear anything that night? Did I have any idea who did it? No one wanted to know her, to know what she was like. Is like."

She bent to light a cigarette. Threw her head back. Exhaled.

"You going to use any of this? You going to write it down?"

"I don't know. I don't know what will help."

He sighed, stared down at his empty cup.

"I guess I don't even know what to ask you. I want you to keep talking because I keep hoping you'll say something and that'll be it, the clue I'm looking for."

He looked up.

"Only it doesn't happen like that, does it? That's just in the movies. So . . . to answer your question, no. I won't use anything you say unless you say it's okay."

She nodded. Reached over and patted his hand. Then she got up, made more coffee, brought out a box of cookies.

She said, "They're probably stale," and he took one to show her he didn't mind.

The name Johnny Salcito was bothering Pete. He couldn't figure out why it sounded familiar.

Then he thought of something. He took out the bundle of photographs, flicked through them until he found the one he'd taken on that first day, of Ruth walking to Devlin's car, her head turned toward the line of cops.

Pete gave Gina the photo and asked her, "You recognize anyone in that line?"

She studied it for a moment then she pointed at a guy in the middle, the one Ruth seemed to be looking at.

"Yeah, that's him. That's Johnny. You took that on the first day, right? Poor Ruth. That sonofabitch is taking her to see her dead baby girl and suddenly, she sees a guy she knows, a guy who tells her he loves her. Only instead of taking care of her, he turns out to be working for that bastard."

She shook her head and handed the photo back like it was dirty.

Pete took it, slid it back into the bundle, still thinking. There was something else about Johnny Salcito, something important. Then he remembered what Devlin had told him: Salcito was the guy who'd called Ruth at two a.m. the day the kids went missing.

There was a sudden flare of music from outside. Gina got up and pulled the drapes, shut the noise out. Turned the radio on.

Without looking at Pete, she said, "It's the World's Fair. That's the carousel. It's there every day. Been there all through the summer. I sat in here, that day, the day the kids ... and it kept playing. Over and over. I can't listen to it now."

She took another cigarette with trembling fingers and Pete lit it for her.

"The kids were always talking about the World's Fair, see. They wanted to go, and Ruth said she would take them in the fall. It would be cooler for them to be outside all day then, walking around, and it was going to be ... their birthdays are ... were both in October. It was going to be their birthday treat. And they never got to go. They never got to ..."

Her eyes filled with tears and she let them sit. Stared through them at nothing, just remembering.

"Christ. Ruth has to listen to that every day. And Christmas. I keep worrying about fucking Christmas. The stores and the decorations, the lights. Kids in the street and in the stores talking about Santa Claus and presents. Jesus. Imagine that. I keep picturing it—all those reminders that it's coming and they're ... they'll never have Christmas again."

She sniffed and shook her head and looked at him, and Pete blurted out the first question that came to mind.

"How did you and Ruth become friends?"

Gina got up to fetch a tissue, blew her nose hard. "It happened that first night, really. The first night we talked. She asked if I wanted to come in for a drink. I think she surprised both of us when she said that, she seemed like kind of a private person. But I thought, you know, she asked, I should go in."

"The kids were in bed by then—I didn't meet them that night. But Frank was there for a little while. He didn't like me."

"How could you tell?"

"He sat in the kitchen until his shift started, and he turned up the game on the radio when we were laughing. I asked Ruth if I should go, if we were bothering him. She said not to mind him, that he was a rude asshole and he had no manners. She said he only liked women who were like his mother."

"His mother?"

"Yeah. She said, 'Frank's ideal woman is his damned mother. Pastel suits, always watching her weight, and spending every afternoon at St. Joseph's, polishing candlesticks and waiting on Father Michael.' Ruth hated her. Hated her spending time with the kids, hated Frank visiting her."

"Why?"

"Competition. Competition for Frank, for the kids. She knew his mother would always come first for him. It drove her crazy."

"She really trusted you, huh? She told you everything."

Gina shrugged but smiled like she was pleased, and Pete knew he could ask the questions he wouldn't have dared ask before.

"Was she a jealous person?"

"No. Not really. She just had a problem with Frank's mother. I mean, Johnny's married. And Lou. She didn't care about that, long as they made her feel good. But she didn't have a lot of girlfriends. No one she was really close to. I think she found men more straightforward."

"But she liked you?"

"Yeah. Yeah, she did. We had some good times. She used to say that when she was with me, she felt like she hadn't felt in years. Before the kids. Before Frank."

She fell silent and Pete drank his cooling coffee. He imagined Ruth as a teenager: coming home in the early hours, climbing through her bedroom window. He saw her leaning out into the blue night air, her heart still beating to a distant music. Waiting for her life to start.

And then he thought of himself at fifteen, sixteen, sitting at his desk by the window, homework discarded, gazing out at endless summer evenings and neat sun-bleached lawns, wondering about other small towns, cities, places he'd never go, people he'd never meet. He remembered the overwhelming need to escape. And the fear that he wouldn't make it, that he'd wake up at forty and find himself with a job at the mill and a wife he couldn't talk to.

He'd kindled that fear until it burst into a flame that led him through extra-credit classes, through dozens of rejection letters, through a scene with his parents: his mother's tears, his father's disappointment, anger concealing his pain. Finally it led him onto a Greyhound out of Iowa.

Maybe he and Ruth weren't so different.

A voice on the radio announced the one o'clock news. Gina got up, turned it off, and put a record on. Something soft with guitars. Turned it down low. Came and sat back down and lit a cigarette. Poured another drink. Nodded her head in time to the music.

Then she said, "One day, when we'd known each other a while, Ruth asked me, 'What did you want to be when you grew up?' "

She smiled.

"It had been a long time since anyone had asked me that. Since anyone thought I had a choice. Anyway, I told her, "I just wanted to get married and have babies. Like everyone else. Like you." She looked at me, and I could tell what she was thinking. Me, with my cheap clothes and my cheap dye job, and my fat ass. It's what everyone sees."

Pete opened his mouth and she waved him away.

"Don't worry. You don't got to be polite, Pete. I know who I am. I pretend I don't give a damn, and most of the time it's true. But I used to want what all little girls want. Prince Charming, the fairy-tale wedding, the happy ending."

She drained her glass, set it down, and poured another.

"I know better now. Men don't want to marry me or have kids with me. Sure, they want to drink with me. Have a little fun with me. But I'm not the kind of woman that men marry. They have their fun, then they go back to their wives. Or they leave me for someone a little younger, a little skinnier.

"Anyone ever asks me, I say that love is for fools. That I don't believe in happy endings. But I got a box under my bed full of romance stories. I'm telling you this because you're here and I'm halfway to being more drunk than I've been in years. And because I don't feel like lying, not today.

"Once a month or so, I go and see a movie at the Dominion—one of those Bette Davis numbers where the ugly duckling turns into a swan and gets the guy and they live happily ever after. Deep down I always wanted that."

She blinked. "Didn't exactly get what I hoped for, did I?"

Her honesty made him reckless. "You mind?"

She shrugged.

"Truth be told…yeah. Sometimes. Sometimes I mind. At night, when I'm alone. When I know Mick's with his wife, when Paulie isn't returning my calls.

"I'm going to tell you something, something I never told no one. Even Ruth. I walked by her window one day last spring. Frank was still living there. It was about six. Ruth was dishing up supper and I was on my way to meet some guy at a bar. I was broke that week. Remember hoping he'd at least give me the cab fare to get home. I stopped to light a cigarette and I heard her talking about something normal—Frankie's new shoes or the linen sale at Gertz—just *normal*, you know? Frank was watching her—and there was something about the way he looked at her. Like he couldn't get enough of her.

"Then she gave the kids their plates and she kissed Cindy's head and I saw her press her nose into her hair. Just for a moment. And breathe her in."

Her eyes were wet, and this time she didn't blink the tears away.

"Ruth never knew how lucky she was. To her, that was just a regular Tuesday. To me, it was everything she got that I don't: a guy who worshipped her, two beautiful kids. A family."

Gina blew her cheeks out and picked up the bottle again.

"Jeez. Sure you don't want a drink?"

This time he shrugged, picked up the other glass, waited for her to pour, and then clinked it against hers.

"Did you ever ask Ruth the same question?"

"Huh?"

"Did you ever ask her what she wanted to be?"

Gina smiled. "Oh yeah. Know what she said? She said, 'I never wanted what you do—marriage and kids and all that. I just wanted to be special.'"

She emptied her glass, ran her finger around the rim.

"Guess she's got that now, huh? Everyone in Queens knows who she is."

Time passed. They talked about the kids, and then Pete asked, "Why did Ruth and Frank split up?"

Gina shrugged. Lit another cigarette.

"For Ruth, Frank was looking back. He was the best she thought she could do when they were in school. And I guess getting married so young meant she could get away from home. Away from her mother. Her father died when she was sixteen—did you know that? She loved him. The way she talks about him, she was a real daddy's girl. But after that...well, she and her mother never got along. She wanted out and Frank was her ticket. But she was past that by the time I met her.

"The thing is, Pete, Ruth's different. She's pretty, sure, but she's got something else. Men want her. Some men will do anything for her. She could've had any guy she wanted, and she didn't know it till it was too late, till she was married to a mechanic with two kids and a shitty job in a shitty bar."

She rubbed her eyes. "I'm not sure Frank understood any of that. Or maybe he did. He was always jealous of other guys."

Then: "I asked her one night, 'You ever think of just letting him have the kids? Just dropping the whole custody thing?'"

Pete put his glass down carefully. "What did she say?"

"She was all over me like gravy on mashed potatoes. How could I even ask that. Furious. I said, 'Hey, I'm just asking. I'm not saying you should. I'm asking if you ever thought about it.' She calmed down a little then, and she just said, 'They're my kids. I'm their mother.' And that was it. Subject closed.

"I think she couldn't bear the idea of letting Frank win. She'd fought every little battle so hard, she felt sorta...she'd be damned if she'd let him win the war. She used to say he was a deadbeat father anyway. Could barely take care of himself. She said a few times that if he had the kids for a few weeks, he'd feed 'em pizza for three days straight when he got his paycheck, then watery creamed corn until the next one came in.

"And there's something else. She never said so, not directly, but I think she worried about what people would say if she let Frank have the kids. If she just walked away. She knew that every woman in Queens would judge her for it. Would hate her for it. Under it all she really cares what people think of her. I used to tell her she cared too much."

Pete waited. He thought there had to be a reason she was telling him this.

"Just the same, I know she thought about it. The kids were all that was standing between her and the life she wanted. She'd never have given up the kids, but she sure as hell thought about it. She would get talking to a guy at work, a customer who'd pay her some attention—or she'd come back from those weekends away with Lou, and she'd talk about what it would be like to have a rich husband. Someone with gold lighters and cuff links, a big shiny car, someone who could fly you to California when he felt like it. She told me once—Cindy was sick with the stomach flu, Frank hadn't sent a check that month, she was on a real downer—and she said her dream was just to wake up to a closet filled with new clothes and to sit down every night to a dinner served by someone else. She'd never have gotten back with Frank, not once she'd had a taste of what was out there.

"I think she wanted those things real bad. I hope she gets them one day. I hope she does."

How strong was the pull of that other life, Pete wondered. *How tempting?*

She would have gotten a glimpse of it when the kids were asleep and Gina came over with a bottle. Or when she'd made enough in tips that week to leave them with a sitter and go to an afternoon movie, sit back in the dark and watch women just like her make men fall in love with them.

But then she'd have had to go home, park the kids in front of the TV, find something for dinner.

He thought about the photographs of the apartment that Devlin had given him. The dirty plates in the kitchen, the crayon marks on the walls. The kids' clothes on the sofa, their toys on the floor, the attempt to keep the living room neat by piling things in corners: the kids' drawings, their books, odd socks.

And then he thought of the photographs he'd seen of her own bedroom. The open closet where her clothes hung in an ironed, pastel-colored line. The drawers where her underwear and night-gowns were carefully folded. The gleaming surfaces, the vacuumed carpet. Everything tucked neatly away.

13

Ruth was lying on the couch, one-third-friendly with a bottle of Scotch. Gene Pitney was on the record player, set to repeat. She couldn't bear silence anymore. She sang along softly as she filled her glass, raised her head and swallowed, filled it again.

She was drinking to get drunk. It was almost the end of October, and the kids' birthdays were behind her. She had planned to pretend the seventeenth and the twenty-fourth were just regular days, and to fill them with bars and bourbon and men and not a single minute spent thinking about the dates. Then her mother had called and insisted they observe them together. That's what she said: *observe.* Like these were religious holidays for worship or devotion.

Ruth had given in, but she never wanted to spend another week like that. Just the two of them and the ticking clock. Daily visits to church, overcooked meals that no one wanted to eat, and everything unsaid heavy as lead in the overheated room.

Never again.

The phone rang, and she held her full glass out in front of her and reached back over her head to answer it. Knocked the whole thing onto the floor and rolled off the couch, spilling her drink on her shirt.

Frank's voice came faintly from the floor, "Ruth? You there, honey?"

He sounded so funny. Like he was a long way away. Ruth fumbled for the receiver. But as soon as she heard his voice clearly, heard the nervous edge to his tone, she knew why he was calling and she sobered up fast.

She'd thought about it, of course she had. Not so much that side of it—Frank was nothing special in the bedroom, but he was considerate and…well, she was comfortable with him and that counted for something—but more the rest of it. Eating dinner together every evening before Frank went off to his shift or out for a few beers with the boys. Saturday nights on the couch, smoking, watching TV. Or seats at the Trylon, and a hot dog apiece if it was after payday.

At one time, the thought of those routines, Frank's habits—his way of folding his pants before piling his change in neat stacks on the bureau, his way of turning to her in the night and saying real low, "Hey there, baby"—all of that had pushed her back and back against a wall until she felt trapped.

Now, though, since the kids were gone, things were different. Everything had changed. Including her. Maybe a little routine, a little kindness, was what she needed.

So when Frank suggested dinner the following evening, she said yes. And when he pulled up outside the apartment afterward and turned to her, his face backlit by the amber glow of the streetlight, she felt the reciprocal glow of the wine and the brandy she'd had with dinner, and she touched his face lightly and invited him in. She even played along with the fantasy of the demure wife, the one he'd made it clear he wanted: she sat with her legs crossed, back straight, eyes wide rather than heavy-lidded, lips in a sweet smile rather than pouting, inviting.

She knew Frank: she was still his wife in every way that mattered. She would always be his wife and she didn't need to invite him.

And so she looked into his eyes for half a second longer than was necessary, and he leaned toward her. And she felt the familiar texture of his mouth, smelled his cigarettes and the soap he used, felt the familiar strength of his arms around her, and felt something like relief as he picked her up and carried her to bed.

He was as gentle as he'd always been, and she clutched him to her and made the breathy moans that worked for him, and afterward they slept.

After Frank had left the next morning, she dozed a little longer and then lay on the couch. This is what he wanted. What her mother wanted. This is what Frankie and Cindy would have wanted: Mommy and Daddy together again. She tried to think about what she wanted, but it made tears come and her head ache, so she lit another cigarette and picked up a magazine and stopped thinking.

Later, the sky quickening toward dusk, she heard kids yelling in the street. She opened a bottle and drank four glasses in quick succession until she didn't notice the noise outside anymore, then she turned the radio on. Two more drinks and she turned the music up and began to dance.

She threw her head back and watched herself in the darkening window: slim shoulders, white arms, long fingers like grass under water, her hair a flying wind of red and gold. She spun and stretched and moved her hips and ignored the banging on the door, the ringing telephone. Drank harder and danced until the world was a glorious blur of color dancing with her. The colors and the light and the narrow band of sky above the dark buildings whirled faster and faster until Ruth fell, exhausted, across the back of the sofa and lay there laughing, legs in the air, while the beat played on through her whole body.

And it was while she lay there, head turned to watch the sun sink behind the rooftops across the street and the first stars peek out, that she noticed the lights and the cars and the shadows outside. And even as she watched, another car pulled up, long and sleek and shining. The door opened and Devlin stepped out, his profile lit neon by a streetlamp.

And Ruth just lay there, panting, her skirt around her hips and her hair across her face. She was surely invisible in there, in that secret darkness, but it seemed to her that their eyes met across that twilit distance. It seemed that, for a moment, they were as close as lovers.

Pete thought about his conversation with Gina for days. Then one morning he woke early, and he knew what he had to do. He splashed water on his face, avoiding his eyes in the mirror. He'd learned that if he didn't look inside himself, fear couldn't creep in. If he didn't look, he couldn't see the things he was most afraid of: that he didn't belong in New York, that he wasn't good enough, that one day he'd have to admit defeat and go back to Iowa with his tail between his legs and take a job at the local paper and pretend to his mother every day that he was happy to be home.

Normally when this feeling threatened, he'd grab his jacket, run downstairs, close the door behind him, and walk fast into the morning. And by the time he'd reached the diner on the corner of 2nd Avenue and ordered his usual pancakes and maple syrup, the feeling would have subsided and been replaced by astonishment. That he was here at all. That New York really was like every movie he'd seen, every commercial: yellow cabs driven by angry Italians changed lanes without signaling; white-tipped old men drank from brown paper bags on street corners. The Empire State Building was lit up at night like an angel on high and neon BAR signs were spread out below like glitter.

But he had a feeling that pancakes and the skyline wouldn't be enough today. As he lifted his razor toward his face, he saw that his hands were shaking. He put the razor down and took a breath, forced himself to meet his eyes in the mirror. This was the right thing to do. The moral thing.

He finished shaving and dressed and drove to the office, and all the time he was afraid.

But the taste of certainty was iron-sharp in his mouth and carried him all the way to his desk. He sat down and began to type.

. . . Mrs. Malone was visibly upset when this reporter visited her. She stated several times that she has no idea who would want to harm

her or her children. As she has maintained from the very beginning, she put them to bed at their usual time, she checked on them at midnight and she found they were gone in the morning. She heard nothing in between. She misses them terribly, as any loving mother would. The apartment is spic-and-span but oddly quiet, and she's finding it difficult to sleep. And she is still afraid that the person who took them may be out there, and that other children may be at risk.

When he finished, he pulled the pages from his typewriter, skimmed them, and took them through to Friedmann's office. Friedmann was on the phone and held up a finger, signaling him to wait, but Pete just put the article on his desk and walked down to the drugstore. He ordered an ice-cream soda and as he sat at the counter and watched the girl pour out the Coke and drop the ice cream in the glass, he realized he was calmer than he'd been in weeks. Whatever happened next, he could live with what he'd done.

Pete was in the newsroom by seven the next morning. He took the overnight bulletins out of the tray and started leafing through them. Then out of the corner of his eye, he saw Friedmann arrive. He'd never seen him in the office this early.

Friedmann looked over at him and jerked his head.

Pete straightened his tie and stood up. Took a breath and walked into Friedmann's office, head high.

His article was on the desk, a red line scratched through it. Friedmann gestured to it.

"What the fuck is this? I told you to leave this alone."

He removed his glasses, pinched the bridge of his nose.

When he spoke again, he sounded almost sad. "What's happened to you, Wonicke? You used to have fire in your belly. You had the makings of a damn good reporter. And now you're coming out with this crap!"

He sat heavily behind his desk. "The woman's a suspect in the murders of her own kids. And all you can think to write is that she's sad?"

"I don't think she killed them."

"Where's your evidence?"

"It's...complicated."

"It always is. Your job is...was...to make it simple for readers."

"Are you firing me, Mr. Friedmann?"

"I don't have a choice. You did this to yourself."

He looked Pete in the eye. "Nothing to say?"

Pete looked right back. "Just that I did the right thing. That's all, Mr. Friedmann."

And he turned and left. Picked up his jacket and walked out of the office just as the day shift was coming in.

The following morning, Pete sat in a diner with a plate of pancakes and a glass of milk, the HELP WANTED pages open in front of him. He had no idea what to do next. Being a reporter in New York City was all he'd ever wanted.

And yet, even as he circled ads for store assistants and filing clerks, his mind was still on Ruth Malone. He felt as though he was halfway through a book, and he wanted to know the ending.

He asked the waitress for a copy of the Yellow Pages and change for the phone, then looked up the names Gina had mentioned, and made some calls. Neither of them would talk: Johnny Salcito hung up on him; he didn't get past Lou Gallagher's secretary.

He decided to try a different tack. He sat in his car outside the station house and waited until he saw the guy Gina had identified as Salcito. Pete followed him for nine or ten blocks, to a rundown dive where there were no other cops. He sat at the end of the bar, and watched him drink.

Salcito drank like a man who wanted to get drunk: he never looked at the television screen, never lifted his head when someone made a joke or raised their voice. He drank blended Scotch, steadily, without ice or soda or apparent enjoyment. He stared dully down at the bar or the coasters; occasionally at a newspaper someone had left behind. He loosened his tie, ran his finger around his collar, dabbed his forehead with a dirty handkerchief. Then he pushed his glass forward half an inch and waited for the bartender to pour.

Pete looked at the purple veins on his nose, at his frayed cuffs. His hands shook and Pete thought about what Gina had said, that this was a man who owed money to the wrong kind of people.

For two nights, Pete watched Salcito arrive straight from his shift and leave around eleven. On the third evening Pete kept an eye on the clock, paid his check, and went out into the parking lot ahead of him. Saw Salcito stumble toward his car, his breath white smoke signals in the night air. Saw him fumble for his keys and drop them on the icy ground and bend and take a while to stand up straight and get his balance.

Finally they were on the highway, Salcito occasionally weaving over the center line. Pete thought about Frank's statement, about how he'd gone out to Huntington to find Salcito. It looked like they were headed in the same direction now.

Pete tried at first to stay two or three cars back but the darkness made it difficult, and he figured Salcito was too far gone to notice him. So he stayed close and took the exit when Salcito did and rolled through the dark suburban streets with him.

There was something strangely intimate about that drive that haunted Pete for a while afterward; something about the silence and the empty streets, about the familiarity of silver frost–tipped lawns, gleaming moonlit fences, black windows. It was the midnight land-scape of every small town in America. It felt like a homecoming and Pete and Johnny Salcito were the only men alive that night to feel it.

Pete let the car drift across an empty intersection and saw Sal-cito pull into a driveway ahead. He drove by with one hand on the wheel and his eyes on the road; an ordinary guy heading home to his wife and kids at the end of a late shift, noting the number on the mailbox and the shape of the tree at the end of the driveway, and the street name on the corner.

Good night, buddy. Good night.

He stopped at the next corner and wrote down the details and found his fingers itching to describe Salcito's heavy walk, his lost expression. But he told himself he would not do that because it was unnecessary. It was unprofessional. When, in fact, he did not want to make this man human. He was not a character in a story to be identified with: he was a possible witness, a possible accessory, a possible killer.

So just the facts. The address. The tree. The tilt of the mailbox. The Realtor's sign on the lawn next door.

And the next morning Pete drove back to the neighborhood while Salcito was working a shift, taking the facts with him in order to identify the house. But when he reached the street, he thought he might have been able to find it anyway. The overgrown lawn and the damage to the mailbox, the smears on the windows and the missing fence posts—all of that was probably enough of a clue to the kind of man who lived here that he could have found the house from the street name alone.

Pete thought again about Frank's statement, about how he'd said that Huntington was the kind of place you'd want to bring up kids. He called the Realtor's number on the sign next door and found that the houses were large. Four or five bedrooms, built with families in mind. But while the other houses on the street had bikes in the yards and swings hanging from trees and basketball hoops over the garage doors, this house was empty. Gina had said that Salcito was married, but Pete felt sure that if he were to walk inside, the master closet would be half-empty, the carpets marked with the feet of ghostly furniture and the walls checkered with the faded echoes of vanished pictures.

That night, Pete took the stool next to Salcito, ordered a beer, looked over at him.

"Hey."

And again: *"Hey."*

Salcito raised his head. His eyes met Pete's in the mirror over the bar. He looked exhausted. Defeated.

"You talking to me?"

"Who else would I be talking to?"

"Wha'...whaddya want?"

"To talk."

Salcito frowned at him, shook his head. Picked up his glass.

"I don't know you."

"You're Salcito, right?"

The glass was set down slowly. Salcito put his hands on the edge of the bar. Turned to face Pete.

"Who wants to know?"

"My name's Wonicke."

"I told you, I don't know you."

A pause.

"Who sent you?"

"No one."

"Who was it? Johanssen? Who?"

"No one sent me."

"Get the fuck away from me."

Pete looked at his red eyes, his clenched fists. Swallowed. "Mr. Salcito, I'm a reporter."

Salcito's shoulders dropped a little. His hands uncurled.

"And? I ain't news."

"I'm covering the Malone murders. I want to talk about Ruth Malone."

"Yeah? You and the rest of the world, kid. I don't talk to reporters."

He turned away, picked up the glass again.

"Look, I know you're a cop. And I know you had a relationship with Mrs. Malone."

This time he moved fast. The glass was slammed on the bar, and Salcito was close up in Pete's face.

"You threatening me?"

Pete raised his hands, slid off the stool, backed away. "*No*. Jesus Christ. Do I look like a threat?"

Salcito shook his head, muttered something. Sat down again, picked up his drink.

Pete exhaled. Said, "Mr. Salcito, maybe you want to talk to someone. Give your side of things."

No response.

"Okay. How about I just tell you what I know, and you can tell me what I got wrong?"

There was a pause, and then Salcito said quietly, "Not here."

Pete looked at him. Waited.

"I don't want my business known here. You know Ricky's, on 57th Street?"

"Sure." He'd find it.

"I'll see you there in an hour. There's a room in back—the owner knows me. Tell him you're meeting Sal."

When Pete arrived, Salcito was already there, seated at a rickety table with a bottle and two glasses.

He waved at Pete to sit. Frowned as he moved aside the glasses to make space for his tape recorder and notebooks.

"You ain't drinking with me?"

"I'm working."

Salcito opened his mouth, then shrugged.

"Okay. Well, let's start at the beginning. I know you were in a relationship with Ruth for several months, maybe longer."

"Rusty. We called her Rusty, on account of her hair."

"I'm guessing you met her on the job."

Salcito laughed.

"What's funny?"

"You're right, and you're wrong. Mostly wrong." He sighed. "I got a call. Two years ago, maybe a little less. Guy I know was in a bar one night with a few girls. I was on the late shift. He called the station house about eleven, told me to come on over."

His eyes were on the table, his mind in another room.

"I was in the squad room when the call came in. Paperwork and coffee. That's mostly what my job is. Fucking paperwork and coffee."

His speech was beginning to slur.

"Anyway, the phone rang and it was Meyer. He quit the force in the winter of sixty-two when his father died and . . . well, I guess you don't want to know 'bout that. But he still came out with us once in a while, still drank in cop bars."

He fell silent.

Pete asked, "And he called that night?"

Salcito nodded.

"Just occurred to me that he wasn't even calling me. He was calling to see who was around. He was looking for someone to meet him for a drink at the end of their shift. He didn't care who came, he just wanted someone to see the kind of girls he could get. Meyer, he came into some money when his father passed. It changed him. He liked to flash it around. Liked you to see he could afford nice things. He was calling for anyone—it wasn't me. It wasn't about me. Christ, if I hadn't . . ."

He took a long gulp of Scotch.

"Anyway, I did."

He paused, shrugged. Took another mouthful.

"He was drunk. Told me he had a party going on at McGuire's. Wanted me to come down. I told him I was working—he was so drunk he didn't know who he'd called. I had to tell him he'd called me at work. He said to come down when my shift ended. Wouldn't take no for an answer.

"When I got there, Meyer was on one of the big curved sofas near the door. He had a girl on either side and when he saw me, he put an arm around each of them. Leaned back and winked at me. There was champagne in the ice bucket, two empty bottles on the table and a ten in the tip tray, right by the keys to his Caddy. Like he'd just dropped them there casually.

"He always dresses nice, Meyer. Expensive suits, matching ties, pressed shirts. But I remember thinking there was something seedy about him that night. His suit was wrinkled and his shirt was stretched over his stomach, like he'd put on weight.

"He shook my hand and he introduced me to the blonde next to him. Donna. Or Dana, I don't really remember. It was the other girl, Donna's friend. She was the one I was interested in.

"She was something else. Really, something else. Meyer and the blonde were draped all over each other, she was shrieking and giggling and he was feeling her up under the table. But Rusty was... she was different. Quiet. We just talked, that night. Talked and drank Meyer's champagne, and danced."

He emptied his glass again.

"Rusty... She even danced different from most women—she let her hands lead, then her shoulders and her hips. She was like white ribbons in the dark."

He fell silent again, and Pete couldn't think of how to break it. Finally Salcito sighed and said, "That was it, that first night. I was... I don't know, it was like I was bewitched."

He laughed. "Jesus Christ, listen to me. Course I wanted to fuck her, but somehow... I just wanted to watch her move. Watch her laugh. Took me four days to work up the nerve to call her. I remember thinking she might not even remember me.

"But she did. She sounded like she was happy I called. I took her to dinner—someplace nice. Fancy."

He poured and drank. His eyes and his imagination were somewhere else.

"We flirted. She would lean forward, touch me on the arm when she was talking. I remember... I could smell her perfume. She was wearing stockings and I could hear the silk rustling whenever she moved. This tiny soft noise. It was driving me crazy. And she knew it."

Pete imagined the scent of her skin. That subtle whisper whenever she crossed her legs. The arch of her tiny foot.

"We went back to her place for a drink, and I was...well, I was respectful. I took it slow. I've been with married girls before and I guess I thought...even though she flirted, I thought she might be a little shy. When it came down to it."

He shook his head. "But she wasn't like that at all. She was incredible, the way she responded. The way she moved, the words she used. She was like an animal. And the difference between the way she was in public, all neat and controlled, and the way she was in bed...she was like a different woman. Incredible."

The bottle was two-thirds empty.

"But there were things that bothered me."

Pete waited.

"The way she would only fuck in the dark. Even when we'd been together a while. She never wanted me to see her. Soon as we'd finished, she'd slide away and she'd be in the bathroom before I could turn on the light. She'd come out fully dressed, makeup perfect, and pour us another drink."

"And when we went out for dinner or to a bar, we'd walk down the street afterward and I'd take her hand but she'd never let me kiss her outside of her apartment. She'd dance with me, tease me, touch me—but she'd never kiss me in public. I never understood that."

He poured and drank. There were tears in his eyes.

"There were so many things about her that I never understood."

Pete leaned forward.

"What about the kids?"

Salcito looked up.

"You think she did it? You think she killed 'em?" Pete held his breath, waiting for the answer.

Salcito shook his head. "I don't know. She hardly mentioned them. They weren't...I saw them a few times—went to pick her up and they'd be there. Read 'em a story once while I waited for her to finish getting ready. She yelled at 'em for spilling something, for not hurrying along to bed. But it was just normal mom stuff."

He shook his head again. "Shit, I don't know. Like I said, there were things about her that I never understood."

"You called her that night, right? The night the kids went missing. You called her at, what, around midnight, and then again at two a.m.? That right?"

Salcito half-laughed, shook his head again. "Jesus, I was drunk that night. I thought Ruth wanted to finish things with me and I got drunker than I ever been before."

"But you did call her? You told the cops you called her, that you spoke to her the first time, that there was no reply when you called the second time."

He shook his head again. "I could have talked to the pope and St. Francis that night an' I wouldn't have remembered. Who the fuck knows what I did?"

Pete leaned back in his chair. So Ruth could have been home that night after all. They couldn't prove she wasn't there.

And Johnny Salcito had no alibi either. He couldn't prove what he was doing at two a.m. any more than she could.

Pete waited a moment and then he asked, "Did you tell Devlin about all this? How you met her, how long you'd known her?"

Salcito looked at him through bloodshot eyes. Then he laughed. "Did I tell Devlin? That's funny."

He poured another drink. Took a gulp.

"The day the kids went missing—that same fucking *day*—I went to him. Told him I knew her. That I really knew her."

Another gulp.

"Know what he did? He took me into the men's room, pulled out a couple of notes I'd written to her. Guess they found 'em in her apartment. I was pissed at first. You know, embarrassed he'd read them. They were private between me and her. But then he tore out the page in her address book with my name on it. Showed it to me. Then he ripped all of it into confetti and flushed the pieces down the john. And he said to me, 'There. That's done. Forget about her.'"

He coughed. Drank again.

"I offered to talk to him, to tell him about her. He didn't want to know. He wrote down that I called her. He asked if I could have called her again, later, and I said sure. I said Lord knows what I did later. So he wrote down that I called Ruth again that night, that the second time there was no reply. And that was it. He didn't want to hear any more about her, and the next week I got a call telling me I was being transferred to Traffic. He told me if I opened my mouth about her again I wouldn't even have a job in Traffic anymore."

"He just didn't want to know. But I wanted to tell someone. I needed to tell someone what she was like. What she was really like. And he didn't want to know."

It was midnight in Queens and Ruth could not sleep despite the bourbon she had drunk. Frank had been back for two weeks and she couldn't bear the sound of his steady breathing. His occasional snores. The snores of Bill Lombardo through the wall. Gina's bed creaking above them as she turned in her sleep.

She felt the tension in her eyelids as she tried to keep her eyes closed. She couldn't bear the *fact* of these people. Couldn't bear that they should be able to sleep. Couldn't bear the weight of their peaceful dreaming.

Teeth clenched, she slid out of bed. Pulled on her thick coat and boots. Felt her way down the hallway. Held her breath. Held her mind on the idea of escape.

Then she opened the front door and the silvery light was bright around her. The frost and ice high and clear.

And she was outside in the November night and she breathed in the cold, clear air, and she breathed out slow like fog, welcoming the stillness.

She stood on the snow-covered grass in front of the building and the quiet seeped through her clothes, seeped through her skin until she was drunk with it. She wanted to run and leap and dance against the whiteness until she was silver-bright with cold and with silence.

She turned and spun, arms outstretched to the space, arms resting on the rich, clear currents of air. And when she was dizzy she let herself fall and lay calm and still in a thick blanket of snow. She felt her breath coming fast and her blood singing in her veins.

Then she opened her eyes and looked up at the rows of bricks, the rows of windows like empty eyes. The dozens of judgments shut in behind those walls.

For months, trapped in the apartment by the crowds and the reporters and the weight of all those stares, she had looked down from those windows and imagined there would be a time she'd be able to sit out here again like anyone else. Alone and unnoticed. She had wanted it so much she'd almost been able to feel the scrubby yellow grass scratching her arms and legs.

She had thought about long golden evenings out here with Frank or Gina, lazy conversations on battered lawn chairs, a bottle of beer apiece. Afternoons kneeling on faded blankets with Frankie and Cindy as they made an island or a city from a mound of dirt. And now, although she lay alone and in silence, she still felt like she was being watched. She lay flat, wrapped in warm damp wool, her hair sweating beneath Frank's old hunting cap, spread out beneath the night instead of the sun, beneath diamond-spattered blackness instead of hot blue skies.

She spread her legs and arms wide, and the snow fell gently on her flushed skin. She opened her mouth and let the soft snowflakes come, and she tasted each one as it melted in a cold kiss.

She held her breath and felt her stomach tighten, breathed out and watched the swaddled curve of her breasts fall. She looked up and saw the flat silvery gleam of each window, and felt their gaze on her. Knew that everything was noticed here and that nothing was missed.

But she closed her eyes and ignored them as the night continued around and within her and she lay in the shape of an angel and swallowed the thin black air. And she thought that if anyone were to ask what she was doing out here, she would tell them: *I am breathing.*

Pete took a job at a bookstore in Greenwich Village. The pay was lousy but it would just about keep him afloat for a while.

At the interview, he told them he could only work part time. When they asked why, he said he had family responsibilities. A sick relative. Maybe he only got the job because they felt sorry for him. He didn't care.

The first couple of days on the job, he couldn't get his encounter with Johnny Salcito out of his head. That first flare of anger. His sadness when he talked about Ruth.

He called Gina, asked her to meet him for a drink, told her what had happened. She drank two brandies, ordered a third. She listened, smoked, shrugged.

"Why are you so bothered about it anyway? You don't think it's Johnny? Tell me you don't. That poor schmuck. Why would he hurt her kids?"

Pete sighed. "Why would anyone?"

Then Gina looked away. "Well, sure. But it's more likely to be some people than others."

"Like who?"

Her eyes met his and she put her head on one side. "You don't remember what I told you?"

"About Ruth?"

"About Ruth and Lou."

"You think Lou Gallagher had something to do with this? With the kids?"

She stared at him for a long moment. Looked away again.

"You told me he beat up some guy in a bar because he was jealous over Ruth. There's a hell of a leap between knocking another man cold to killing two kids."

"That guy couldn't fight back. He was as helpless as a baby. And you weren't there. You didn't see Lou. He was...it was like he was possessed. It was brutal. Bloody."

"You really think it's him, don't you?"

She nodded slowly.

"You said anything about this to Ruth?"

"Christ, no! You've seen her, the way she is now. Imagine what it would do to her if I told her that I thought her boyfriend killed her kids. It would finish her."

She took another drag on her cigarette.

"And she'd tell him. I ain't under no illusion—she'd tell him right away. She'd want him to laugh and reassure her, tell her it's garbage. Or she'd want to warn him. She wouldn't believe it, but she might think the cops would."

"You've thought this through."

"Yeah, I have."

"What do you think Lou would do if she warned him?"

She shook her head. "I don't know."

Pete waited. Saw how her eyes flickered. How she licked her dry lips.

"You're afraid of him."

She nodded again. "Think I'd be dumb not to be."

"Why are you telling me this?"

"You said the cops needed another suspect."

"They do. I thought you were telling me you suspected Salcito."

"Christ, no. It wasn't Johnny. He's a drunk, and he's a little crazy, but he worships Ruth."

"So you want me to take Lou to the cops as a suspect? Why didn't you go to Devlin yourself? Tell him what you're afraid of?"

"You think I didn't try? I'd walk barefoot to Jersey if I thought it would put the guy who killed Frankie and Cin away. I was at the station house two days after Cin—after they went missing. He didn't want to know."

"What did he say?"

"Told me I'd been watching too many movies. Told me to go back to Ruth and tell her to send someone more... *credible* next time she wanted to give the police an alternative suspect. Told me I wasn't so dumb I gotta be doing her dirty work for her. I tried to explain and he told me to get out or he'd arrest me for wasting police time."

She swallowed the last of her drink.

"You're the someone credible, Pete."

14

Pete called Lou Gallagher's office and again the polite, neutral-voiced secretary told him that Mr. Gallagher wasn't available, that she couldn't say when he'd be free. So he took a chance and headed to Santini's. It took four nights before his efforts and his dollars paid off, and one of the waiters told him that yes, tonight Mr. Gallagher was in a booth in back. Pete found him with two girls and two bottles, took a breath, and, before he could lose his nerve, slipped into the seat opposite them.

Gallagher looked over at him with an air of inquiry. Not the irritation or the open hostility that Pete had expected. He was no threat, just a curiosity. And if he became a problem, there was presumably someone nearby who would find a solution.

"Good evening, Mr. Gallagher. My name's Pete Wonicke. I'm a reporter."

His hair was slick and shone dark against his scalp. Pete could smell his hair oil. His cologne. Gina was right—he did look like he had money. He looked well-fed. He looked satisfied with life.

Pete felt his inexperience seeping from every pore, dampening his armpits, beading his forehead.

Gallagher's voice was low and rich.

"If you'd like to talk to me about my business, Mr. Wonicke, you can make an appointment with my secretary. We're in the book."

He gave a wide, white smile, relaxed into his seat.

He reminded Pete a little of a mallard duck he'd seen while

fishing with his father. It had spent hours gliding between banks, sleek and complacent in the small pond. The gleaming emerald and sapphire feathers were oiled and slippery, the water sliding off it as it squatted low in the murky water.

"It's not about your business, Mr. Gallagher."

The wide smile returned.

"Then how can I help you?"

"I'm covering the Malone case."

One eyebrow went up. "I don't believe you mentioned which paper you work for."

A moment went by, and then: "I'm not sure how you believe I might have any involvement with that . . . tragedy. It was some time ago now."

"Four months. And your name came up, Mr. Gallagher."

The eyebrow crept higher. "How interesting. Then I think perhaps I should refer you to my lawyer. Martin Sherman at Kasen, Sherman, and Bower. They're also in the book."

The girls either side of him took their cue and giggled.

Gallagher stood, reached out a hand. His skin was soft and supple, his knuckles dimpled like those of a baby.

"Thanks for coming in, Mr. Wonicke. Have a drink before you leave. On me. James will take care of you."

And before he could reply, Pete felt a firm arm around his shoulders and was taken to the bar area. He guessed he'd been about to become a problem.

As he nursed a double Scotch—a good single malt, since it was on Gallagher's tab—and thought about his next move, Pete became aware of a commotion at the entrance. The doorman was struggling with a woman who was trying to get inside. He watched for a moment, and then heard her say Gallagher's name.

He threw back the last of his drink, went to the door, and took the woman's arm. Nodded to the frowning doorman, led her away. She was drunk, or partway there, stumbling and reaching back to try and get inside.

Pete half-dragged her around a corner, leaned her against a wall. As he took a step back, she stared at him, trying to focus. Her face was lined, her hair lank. She could have been any age from forty to sixty.

Suddenly she bent over and vomited. He jumped back and looked at her in disgust as she spat a couple of times, wiped her mouth with the back of her hand. She straightened up.

"Jesus Christ. That's better."

She raised red eyes to Pete. "What the fuck are you looking at?"

She broke into a fit of coughing, spat again. "You wanna have some fun, mister? That it?"

"Did I hear you say you wanted to speak to Lou Gallagher?"

She peered at him. "Christ alive. Did that sonofabitch send you out here to deal with me? Lou can't afford decent muscle these days or somethin'?"

"I don't work for Lou Gallagher. My name's Pete Wonicke. I'm a reporter."

He took out his pack of cigarettes, angled it toward her. She took two, stuck one behind her ear and the other in her mouth, and waited impatiently while he lit it for her.

She inhaled deeply, blew out a long stream of smoke, and then broke into another hacking cough.

"So why you talking to me?"

"I need information on Gallagher."

She paused to pick a flake of tobacco off her tongue.

"What kind of information?"

"About Ruth Malone. About her kids. You know her?"

The woman shrugged and took another drag.

"Never heard of her. But I know *him*."

"What can you tell me about him?"

Suddenly her expression was calculating. She shook her head and wagged her finger coyly. "Uh-uh, Mr. Reporter. You wanna know about Lou, it's gonna cost you."

He hesitated.

"You want to know about Louie? You want me to tell you what he's like? I got stories about him. About the things he done."

Her eyes were wet and desperate, but the anger in her voice was raw and real. He bit.

"Twenty bucks."

"Fifty. And I want the money up front."

"Thirty. After I hear what you got to say."

"Thirty bucks? Come on, mister. I got bills to pay! I got debts..."

He thought about his dwindling funds, and shook his head.

"Okay, okay. Jesus Christ. You men are all the same, out for what you can get. Thirty, and you can buy me a drink and I'll tell you."

He looked at her, sighed and said, "Don't you think you've had enough already?"

She drew herself up. "I think that's my business, kid."

She took him to a basement dive several blocks away. When they walked in, the guy behind the bar shook his head at her and opened his mouth to speak. She raised a hand.

"It's okay, Sam. I won't cause no trouble. And I got money—my friend here is paying."

Sam shook his head again, pointed a fat finger at her.

"One more night like Saturday and I'm calling the cops, Bee. Final warning."

"Yeah, yeah. Just pour, will ya?" And to Pete: "Show him some green, for Chrissakes."

He brought the drinks over to a dim corner where she was removing her shoes and rubbing her swollen feet. She swallowed half of hers in one gulp and sighed.

"So whaddya want to know, Mr. Reporter?"

"I want to know about Lou Gallagher. Whatever you can tell me."

"Give me a cigarette and let me see that thirty, and you can have whatever the hell you want."

He slid the pack over to her, opened his wallet, and showed her his money. Then he took out his notebook, and waited.

She said her name was Bette.

"It used to be regular Betty with a 'y' but I decided to change it when I moved to New York. I put an 'e' on the end. You know, like Bette Davis. More glamorous."

She saw his expression and shrugged.

"Yeah, well, that was a long time ago."

Then she half-smiled at him, showing uneven brown teeth.

"You know, I used to be a real looker. Soft skin, curls, the works. I wanted to be a model. Louie fell for me soon as he saw me."

She saw Pete's disbelief and smiled wider.

"Oh yeah. Hook, line, and sinker."

"How did you meet him?"

"I was working as a waitress. Waiting for my big break. Lou came in one night and that was it. He kept talking to me, kept asking me to sit with him, join him for a drink. I told him I was working and he called my boss over, said he'd give him fifty bucks if he'd give me the night off."

She sighed. "I thought that was the most romantic thing I'd ever heard."

Then she said, "I need another drink before I tell you any more. Ain't much romance in the rest of it."

"What are you having?"

She nodded toward the bartender. "Ask him for an Orange Blossom."

She smiled. "I drink 'em because they sound so pretty."

He brought it over and she started talking again. She'd fallen for Lou. Hard.

"He was real good to me at the start. Bought me presents, took me out. Told me he loved me, that he wanted us to get engaged. Only he told me he wanted to make it big first. He said he wanted to make enough money to support me, to buy us a nice house."

She threw back her second drink and Pete waved to the bartender to keep them coming.

"It was all bullshit. I found out later he was already married. But I was just a kid. I was young and in love and I wanted to believe him.

"The good times lasted a year. A year of nice dinners and afternoons on the lake and bouquets and expensive presents. We would go to his apartment in the Bronx, the one his wife didn't know about. And then . . . well, what always happens, happened. I found out I was having a baby."

She lifted a cigarette to her mouth with a trembling hand.

"I told Louie. I thought he'd be happy. We were having dinner at his favorite steakhouse and I held his hand and said, 'It's okay, it just means we'll have to get married sooner. I don't mind about the house and everything. I just want us to be a family.' His face closed up and he just got up and walked out. He left me sitting in that restaurant like an idiot. Crying and feeling sick and wondering what I'd done wrong."

Pete didn't want to hear this detail but something about her story fascinated him. He let her talk.

"I called and called. For weeks. I went to his office and he wouldn't see me. Then one day I went there and I was desperate. Hollering at the poor secretary. Louie came out and took me into his office. I was crying, begging him to help. He listened and then he slapped my face. Then he held me while I cried and told me a kid would ruin everything. Told me I'd have to get rid of it and that if I did, everything would be okay again."

"I stood there, holding my mouth, looking at him. I loved him and I hated him—you ever had that? He was the first guy I loved and he was telling me to kill our baby."

Bette looked at Pete.

"You know something? This is the first time I ever talked about this. No one ever wanted to listen before. Even the girls I know—well, everyone got their own story. Ain't nobody got time for someone else's sadness."

There was a fresh drink in front of her and she took a long swallow.

"Anyway, I went home after that, and I wrote to him. By then I'd guessed he was married and I said I'd tell his wife. If he ever read that letter, he ignored it. He knew I didn't know where to find her. That I didn't have the guts to do it. Maybe he knew I couldn't hurt someone else the way he hurt me."

She wiped her eyes, almost savagely.

"In the end, he got one of his men—his associates, he called 'em—to deal with it. The guy took me to a house in the Bronx. I never knew his real name but everyone called him Hop, on account of his limp. He was an older guy. Married. He drove me there and he kept looking sideways at me on the way, like he wanted to talk. I closed my eyes. Pretended I was asleep. I didn't want no judgment on me.

"The place was okay, I guess. Clean enough. But the woman who ran it was . . . there was no kindness in her. She never looked me in the eye. Not once. Just told me to take off my things and lie down."

She sighed again.

"Only . . . only I couldn't do it. She had a mask, a black rubber thing with a tube, and she brought it toward me and I felt like it was going to smother me. I pushed her away and I jumped off the bed and grabbed my underwear and my shoes, and I ran. The room where I left Hop was empty—maybe he was waiting nearby, maybe he just left, I don't know. I ran until I got to a main road and I waved down the first cab I saw. I remember staring out the back window all the way. Felt like I was being chased. Hunted down. I knew Lou would be angry, because I didn't do what he wanted. I was so afraid."

She scrabbled for another cigarette, but her hands were shaking and Pete had to light it for her.

"I went back to the place I was staying, and I told the cab to wait for me. It was a boardinghouse—very strict. No men, no noise after ten, all of that. Kinda funny when you think about it. Guess nobody told my landlady you can get into all kinds of trouble before ten, huh? She was an Irish woman. Widow. Christ alone knows what she thought that day. I ran up the stairs, threw everything I could carry into a suitcase, and ran out again. She tried to stop me—thought I was skipping on the rent, I guess. I told her I'd left a month's worth in my room, thinking she'd go on up, but when she still wouldn't get out of the way, I pushed her and she fell. Landed on the floor. Hard. And I didn't...I didn't stop. The cab was waiting, and I just told him to drive."

She looked at Pete.

"For weeks, I was worried I hurt her. She was old. It's strange—everything that was going on, and that's what worried me. I thought...I was afraid it made me like *him*."

He smiled gently at her and asked, "Where did you go?"

"Jersey. I had a friend there. Lou didn't know about her. I knew she'd let me stay a while till I figured out what to do. I slept on the couch and she got me a job. Waitressing. And she took me to the pawn shop to buy a ring. We decided I'd say I was a widow.

"Sometimes I'd catch sight of the ring—while I was serving coffee or gathering up dishes—and I'd forget I wasn't married. I made up stories about him: his name, where he came from. About the accident that killed him. At first it was just because I had to have some answers, but later...well, I wanted to give the baby a father. Even lies were better than the reality: a married guy, a naive kid, and a mean-eyed broad with ether and a knitting needle."

"What were you going to do? Did you have a plan? For the baby?"

She shook her head. "I was nineteen years old and green as grass. I had no savings. No future. But you know something? I was real happy. Maybe happier than I ever been. I used to come home from work and sit by the window in my room. Put my feet up on a stool to keep my ankles from swelling and stroke my belly. I'd tell her stories. I was so sure it was a girl. I made a list of names and I sewed her little dresses. I was . . . I was okay, you know?"

There were tears in her eyes, and Pete did the only thing he could think of to do: signaled to Sam for another drink.

Bette took a mouthful and sniffed.

"Is this what you want? Feels like I'm talking more about me than about Lou."

He looked at her, and tried to imagine her as a smooth-skinned girl with a pregnant belly and a drawer of baby clothes.

"It's okay. It's . . . well, it's okay."

He took a mouthful of his beer and asked her, "So what happened?"

She sighed. "I was lucky. I didn't really show until the last three months, so I could keep working. I didn't have a plan but I knew that whatever I did, I'd need money. So I just kept going, kept putting aside as much as I could.

"And then the baby came. It all happened in the middle of the night. It was December. I woke up and it was so damn cold. And the bed was wet, so I knew. I was scared, but I was excited too. I went down to the phone in the hallway and I called my friend and she took a cab and came over and waited with me until it was time to go to the hospital. Then she called another cab and took me there and helped me inside. She couldn't stay—her husband was home and she had to work the next day. Anyway, I was alone but I was okay. They got me a bed and the nurses fussed over me, helped me get undressed. For a few hours, everything was fine. And then something changed. The pains just stopped. I remember lying on my back looking up at the lights, this great round belly above me, and they called a doctor. His hands were like ice. He said to one of the nurses they'd have to give me something—I didn't understand the word. I tried to ask what was wrong, but they were so busy and it all happened so fast. There was a needle in my arm and then this feeling like I was drunk. Then I remember hearing screams and I remember the pain—like I was being ripped apart."

She was nodding, eyes unfocused, lost in her memories.

"And I remember a baby crying"—and her hand shot out and her nails were digging into Pete's skin and she was close against him so he could smell her sour breath, and she said again, "There *was* a baby. I heard my baby crying."

Tears came into her eyes, then her grip loosened and she leaned back and her voice was flat.

"And when I woke up, Lou was sitting by my bed with flowers."

"How did he find you?"

"Oh, he probably got one of his guys to call all the hospitals in the state. He knew when I was due. Or maybe he paid someone in each hospital to call him if I came in. When you have money, anything's possible. But whatever he did, he found me."

"You know, when I saw him, I wasn't even scared anymore. All I could think about was the baby.

"He smiled at me and I said, 'Have you seen her? Where is she?' I was so sure I'd had a girl, you see.

"And then he took my hand, and he looked at me and I knew something was wrong and I started to cry. Before he even said a word I was crying. Then he told me what he'd done. He said, 'Honey, we don't need no baby spoiling what we have. Don't worry about it. I found her a nice family to take care of her.'

"It took me a minute to understand what he was saying. Then I threw myself at him—hitting and scratching and yelling. He just held my wrists until the nurse came. I was trying to get to him and she kept pushing me back, holding me down. Then she called for a doctor, and they gave me an injection, and when I woke up, I was alone."

Pete let the silence sit for a moment and then he asked her softly, "So what happened to you? Afterward?"

She shook her head. "I sat in that hospital bed for days. Just crying. Waiting for Lou to visit. To call. To tell me it wasn't true. To tell me where the baby was. Nothing.

"I asked the nurses—begged them—to help me. To find out

where my baby was. Most of them ignored me. One of them, pretty little Mexican thing, she whispered to me that it would be better if I just forgot I had a baby. That there was no record of her. I asked her what she meant and she just shook her head and that was the only thing anyone ever told me.

"After that, I stopped eating. Couldn't eat. They told me if I didn't eat they'd have to take me into the psych ward. I didn't care. They could have thrown me off the Brooklyn Bridge for all I cared by then.

"In the end, I stopped talking and they took me to the madhouse. I was in there five months."

She saw Pete's shocked face and nodded.

"Yeah, once you're in, it's easier just to let the crazy wash over you than fight to get out. I guess I just gave up. I sat in a chair and stared at the wall. They pumped me full of drugs. Had to put a tube down my throat to feed me. I didn't know where I was, what day it was. I just wanted to forget."

"What happened? I mean, how did you get out?"

"One of the nurses... she was kind to me. The radio was on one day and there was a song playing. 'Love Letters in the Sand.' You know that song? Ah, you're too young. Pat Boone sang it. He had a beautiful voice. It was my favorite song to slow-dance to, once upon a time. And I heard it that day and I just closed my eyes and I was right back at the Roseland, humming along without even thinking about it. When the song was over, the nurse came and sat down. I opened my eyes. I was crying. I hadn't even realized I was crying. And this nurse, she looked right at me. I'll never forget her face. She said, 'You shouldn't be in here.'

"I was so shocked—it was the first time anyone had spoken to me, like directly to me, in weeks and weeks. I looked right back at her and she smiled and she said, "Yeah, you're still in there. You're no more crazy than I am. You're depressed, is what you are.

"And then it got easier. She would come and talk to me and when she was there, I could eat. She spoke to the doctors and they eased up on the meds, and I started to feel...well, like me again. I cried more, but I wasn't numb anymore. It felt good to just feel again, you know?

"And eventually I was eating and showering and combing my hair, and I guess they didn't have no reason to keep me in there. So they let me go.

"Only I lost my apartment and my job and my family didn't want to know me. My mother came to visit while I was in the hospital and they told her about the baby. She said I was a sinner and I wasn't her daughter no more.

"I got another job and a room but...well, I was drinking a lot and not sleeping much and I got fired. I got another job and the same thing happened again. Finally my money ran out. I guess I was desperate. I went out and watched the whores around Times Square and I practiced walking and talking like them. Then I got an eighth of rum inside me and I went out and got me my first john. And here I am.

"You know, sometimes I think about my mother. I want to call her up and say to her: you think I was a sinner then? You should see me now. You should see what happens to girls like me. Only she's dead. Car accident in sixty-two. There ain't no one left now."

Pete asked her, "Did you try to find your baby? Find out if there was a record of her adoption?"

She sighed. "There ain't no record."

"But there..."

"Whatever happened in that hospital, it wasn't official. I never signed nothing. Either they put me down as unfit to sign, or they said I died giving birth, or they put fake names on the papers. My baby don't exist no more. What I think—Lou just sold her to some rich couple who couldn't have kids. I think that's what the Mexican girl was trying to tell me."

She threw back the last of her drink. "Whatever happened, it was a lie and I don't know how to untangle it. It was almost twenty years ago. She could be anywhere. I can't go through every family in New York looking for her.

"You know what? Maybe it's for the best anyway. Look at me. What do I have to give a kid?"

She shook her head.

"So...what now? Why are you telling me all this?"

"Because Lou didn't just take my kid away. He took the choice away too. I think we could have been okay, me and my baby, but he decided that wasn't up to me."

Her face was wet and he heard the anger rising in her voice.

"I know what you think of me. What men like you think of me. I'm a drunk. I'm a whore."

She raised a finger, jabbed him in the chest.

"But you don't judge me, mister. I don't need no more judgment on me. You're a reporter? You write my story. You write what I told you. People need to know. They need to know about that man. What he's capable of."

She turned away and waved at Sam to pour another drink. Pete couldn't think of a single thing to say that seemed adequate, so he put her thirty on the scarred and sticky table, and then put down another ten. He walked away, her face and her tears etched on his memory, thinking about what Lou had done to her.

And then he thought of Ruth. She'd been a waitress when she'd met Lou. Just like Bette.

Pete thought about the bars he'd drunk in himself. About the women who'd waited on him, and the men who watched them.

The after-work crowd always peaked around seven p.m. A man like Lou Gallagher, a man with deals to do and money to make, wouldn't notice a woman like Ruth Malone in the hot press of bodies. His eyes would skim over her, he'd dismiss her as just another waitress. He'd shout his order over the throb of voices and she'd nod and write it on her pad and he wouldn't even notice her walk away.

But when the crowd had thinned a little, he might notice her then. He might let his eyes rest on her a moment: on the tits in the no-longer-crisp white blouse, on the ass in the tight black skirt, on the muscular legs and the cheap heels. Then he'd move on, looking for someone who could buy him a drink instead of serving him one.

By nine, when the bar was quiet and he'd had more than enough for a weeknight, he might come back to her. Let his eyes linger on her red-gold hair, the way she laughed and moved, the husky way she spoke.

He might tip her more than he normally would. Smile at her. Offer to buy her a drink that he knew she wasn't allowed to accept.

And by ten-thirty, the room a blur of color and light, he'd be sliding her number into his wallet. Slowly, letting her see the wad of notes in there. He'd get up to leave and he'd take her hand in his. Let her see the signet ring on his little finger, raise her hand to his mouth and kiss it. Gently. Letting her know he'd like to be kissing her somewhere else. He'd treat her like a lady, like she was something special.

Bye, baby. I'll call you.

He'd wink at her; he'd walk away knowing she was watching.

A man like that, a man like Gallagher, knew that guys like him were Ruth's only hope of getting out.

Some nights Ruth would sit with Frank and drink until she couldn't feel anymore: four fingers of bourbon to every one of his bottles of Bud. The voice of Johnny Carson or Ed Sullivan boomed over laughter and applause, the picture on the screen blurred into a haze of red and green, and she sank down into the couch and let the mess of color rub at her eyes. When she woke, hours later, tears drying on her cheeks and her throat sore, he was sometimes still snoring beside her. Despite herself, she was oddly touched, as though this was loyalty. She lay back again, let her eyes rest on his heavy familiar face, leaned into his warm familiar smell and found something like comfort.

Other nights she couldn't stand it and had to leave the apartment after dinner, had to get out. She pretended she was just going to buy cigarettes, knowing that she wouldn't come back for hours. Frank just nodded to her over his glass and turned back to the TV. He didn't worry that she was going to meet other men, not these days. She'd let him back in: he thought she was his now.

Sometimes she noticed the cops following her as she left; other nights she didn't bother to look and pretended she was alone, just as she tried to pretend it was all happening to someone else: the endless questions, the probing and pushing, the same questions again and again until she thought she would go mad. The sly hints and insinuations and her constant fear that *this* would be the day they would come out with it and accuse her of killing her kids.

Once outside, she did not walk the streets; she crept. Close to walls, in the shadows, hugging dark doorways as she held herself together tightly, as she held inside the seeping black knowledge of who and what she was. Mother. No longer a mother. Wife. Not-wife.

She stole past neon-lit bars that spilled pools of light and noise onto the wet sidewalks so that she had to step around them. These were the same bars she used to work in, used to sit and drink in with Gina, the two of them laughing with their heads thrown back, while her kids slept locked in a room with a plate of stale cookies, a toy rabbit for comfort.

She took her shame and her grief, held them close, and crept in the dark so that normal people, clean people, wouldn't have to see them.

She saw lighted rooms, glimpsed in the detail of a film still from the sidewalk. The silhouette of a guy leaning over a table in semi-darkness. Two women sitting side by side playing a piano, faces shining, mouths open. A girl talking on the telephone, leaning against the wall, the cord wrapped around her splayed fingers, her face serious.

Ruth looked at each snapshot of a life: at the warm, bright kitchens of strangers, at the tangled phone cord of someone else's drama. Her heart recognized these as different stories, different rooms, and longed to set down its own burdens while she watched these stories play out. Just for a little while.

When she was tired of walking, she sought out the dark corners of bars and watched men like the ones she used to wait on: men who sat hunched over a single glass, who used a raised finger to keep the bottle coming. Men who knew the names of every other man like them in the bar, but who rarely spoke. She was like those men now.

There was a place she went to once, when things were very bad. A dank black archway under a rail bridge, a dim place where men lived and died. They wore filthy mismatched gloves and coats tied with twine, and they huddled around a metal garbage can where a fire burned. She wrapped her scarf around her bright hair and stood in the shadows, needing the closeness of others who were just as wretched.

Somewhere back in the darkness, on a piece of wood nailed to a sheet of corrugated metal, someone had painted a picture of a girl. From her lank unstyled hair and her red lips, Ruth thought at first that she was young, but as she moved closer, she saw the darkness around the girl's eyes. She looked at Ruth with something approaching pity, and Ruth turned and fled.

The day after his encounter with Bette, Pete went down to McGuire's and found Devlin and Horowitz in a corner booth. As he walked toward them, he thought about what he'd learned in the New York Public Library. He looked at Horowitz and thought about the lies he must have had to tell. Wondered how he'd reconciled himself to being that kind of man.

As he reached the booth, they noticed him and stopped talking. Devlin said, "You want something?"

"I need to talk to you. You want a drink?"

They exchanged a glance, and then Horowitz leaned forward. "Wonicke, this...this ain't right. You ain't working no more. You can't just come down here and..."

"I'm not looking for information. I got something to tell you."

To Devlin: "I've been talking to someone about Lou Gallagher."

And to Horowitz: "He's one of Mrs. Malone's boyfriends."

Devlin took a handful of peanuts from the dish on the table, threw them into his mouth.

"And?"

Pete slipped into the booth opposite them.

"This woman told me he got rid of their kid. Newborn. He told her he'd had it adopted, but she never signed anything, and she was told there's no record. Baby just disappeared."

He leaned forward.

"Look, he got rid of her kid because it was in the way. If he did that to one woman, got rid of a child, you don't think he could do it again? You don't think he'd be capable of getting rid of two? Maybe the Malone kids were in the way of his relationship with the mother? Maybe they were..."

"Maybe, maybe, maybe." Devlin tipped his head on one side. "You got any proof of this? What's this woman's name? Where can I find her? She never came forward at the time—or if she did, nothing stuck. Gallagher's squeaky-clean."

"She's...she doesn't have a fixed address."

"She a bum?"

"No, she's a...well, she's..."

"She's a *whore*? Jesus, Wonicke. Come *on*! I'd be laughed right outta the DA's office!"

He took a mouthful of soda and said, "Listen, kid, I know you're caught up in this. You spent a lot of time on it, you're invested. I get that. But there ain't no big complicated story for you here. I *know* the Malone woman did it. She's as guilty as sin. Yeah, we know she had help. Someone helped her get the kids out of the apartment, kept them quiet. Someone helped her hide the bodies. And maybe this Gallagher was the guy who helped her.

"But we'll never get him to court. He's got everyone in his pocket. Plays golf with the chief, his wife is on a couple of charity boards with Judge Ames's wife. He don't matter. We gotta focus on Mrs. Malone. She was there. And even if she didn't kill 'em, she was involved. She was their mother; it's a mother's job to take care of her children. This happened on her watch."

He leaned forward and his face was close to Pete's.

"And she's the one going down for this, make no mistake. We got a letter today that might be the final link in the chain. Another week or two and we'll have everything we need to charge her."

15

Ruth woke in the chair by the window. There was no traffic noise, but weak daylight was already filtering through the slats in the blinds. She stood and stretched out the ache in her neck and shoulders, rubbed her jaw where she'd been grinding her teeth, decided to take a hot bath. Down the hallway, past closed doors, past Minnie, whimpering in her sleep. She made coffee, added two fingers of vodka.

The noise woke Minnie and she padded into the kitchen, circled her empty bowl, whining gently. Ruth ignored her, took her cup into the bathroom and locked the door behind her. She put the coffee on the floor and sat on the john. Breathed out for a long moment.

Frank was gone again. The distance and the silence between them had grown and deepened and she hadn't cared enough to try to breach it.

He would come home to find her sitting in the dark, a cigarette burned down between her fingers, staring at nothing. Would whisper to her while she ignored him, and then he would leave her alone, and for that she was grateful.

Until one night when he switched on the light and asked if she was okay, and she still said nothing. He tried to hold her, and she lay limp against him until he got angry and shook her. Nothing.

He began to cry—and then she did look at him because she had never seen him cry before. She stared at his red face and his wet cheeks, and he came toward her, fast, and slapped her hard, and she stared at the spit in the corners of his mouth as he shouted.

"This isn't just about you!"

She didn't know what to say so she said nothing and continued to stare, and he asked why the fuck was she looking at him like that and he hit her again and again until she tasted blood. And then after a while he stopped hitting and he stopped crying and went into the bedroom. She heard drawers opening and shutting, muffled swearing, a series of thuds. Then he stood in the doorway holding a suitcase and she gazed at his forehead while his face moved and he said things to her and she wanted him out of the apartment more than she'd ever wanted anything from him before. She closed her eyes and eventually his voice stopped and it was quiet. She held her breath until the door closed behind him and then she got off the couch and went into the kitchen, opened the cupboard and found his mug with the chip in the rim that he'd forgotten to take. She threw it against the wall and watched it shatter.

So Frank was gone again, but her mother was back. Her mother, who couldn't understand why Ruth was just throwing away her marriage. Who had never understood how Ruth could want more than a handsome husband and two children. And Frank was calling every day because they were *awfully worried* and she *shouldn't be alone.* And now she was behind a locked door with her hands in her hair, silent tears running down her face and the relief of being alone was so great she felt sick with it. She peed and cried and felt herself emptying until the lump in her throat was gone. She stood, turned the faucet on full, blew her nose, and flushed pee and tissue and grief away. As she waited for the bathtub to fill, she tensed against the possibility of the dog whining again, needing to be fed, needing to be taken out, needing, needing, needing. Against the possibility of the running water waking her mother, against the expectation of a knock on the door and that insistent voice asking what she thought she was doing, taking a bath at a time like this, so much to be done, what would people think—and she dropped her shoulders and let her breath out.

"Fuck you," she whispered to the door, teeth set in fury. Spitting out the syllables. "Fuck you and leave me alone and let me get through this *in my own way.*"

She closed her eyes and clenched her fists and dug her nails in until she was aware of the pain and until the wave of anger had passed. Picked up the bottle of Avon bath foam that Gina had given her for her birthday, and upended half of it into the running water. Breathed in roses and geraniums and imagined her mother sucking in air through her teeth and making shocked comments about waste.

As the bathtub filled, she stood at the mirror and stared at her white face. Squinted until the shape was just a blur. Refocused. The harsh bathroom light meant there was nowhere to hide. Her skin was oily and flushed from sleep, the pores dark. Every blemish, every bump, every scar: they were all there.

She'd known a guy once, a guy who'd gone from beer to bourbon to something worse, who had an urge, an itch, to pick and squeeze at his skin for hours. He'd sit slumped in a chair, unaware of conversation around him, picking at his scalp, his arms, his neck, his lips, until the scars bled. She knew she had that same need.

Just under her bottom lip was a tiny blackhead. Almost invisible. She squeezed and for a moment, nothing happened. Harder, and her nail broke the skin. A bubble of blood, followed by a trickle of clear liquid. She breathed in the sting. Exhaled, long and slow.

She turned her head to highlight the other side of her face, pulled her skin tight up to her ear. Stared at the old acne scars over her cheekbone. Sometimes she found ugliness oddly comforting.

A half-hour later, still lying in the warm water, still sipping on her vodka-laced coffee, she heard the bedroom door open and her mother pad down the hallway. She took a large swallow, prepared herself.

Then she heard a knock at the front door: Minnie barking, her mother's footsteps changing direction, the door opening and the low murmur of Devlin's voice. Heard her mother's nightgown-flustered "I think she's in the bathroom. I'll just fetch her. Do come in"—as though these were guests, for Christ's sake—her voice growing louder as she walked back toward the bathroom, and then the expected knock and a hissed "Ruthie, it's the police."

Ruth was silent, holding onto the sensation of power. Let her wait. Let her feel helpless and unsure. Let her feel that she had no control.

But the knock came again and the hiss was louder.

"Ruth! The police are here. They want to talk to you."

Ruth sank down in the foam and closed her eyes.

"I'm in the bath."

Knowing what response that would bring. Holding onto the power of that locked door.

"Well get out of the bath! Now! What are you doing lying around in a bath in the daytime when your children . . . when all of this is going on?"

Ruth leaned her head back and lifted her cup.

"And when there are men in the house waiting to speak to you!"

Ah, there was the heart of it.

She took another gulp, felt the warmth curl around her.

"Tell them they'll have to wait. Or tell them to go away and come back later. I'm busy."

A shocked beat and then: "I'll tell them no such thing! Get out of that bath *now*! You can't keep them waiting, they're . . ."

"I can, and I will. This is my apartment. I didn't invite them in. They're here all the time, asking their questions, the same damn questions, over and over, and I can't . . . I want to be left alone."

And she reached up to the shelf over the bath and turned the dial on the radio and Elvis's rich, rolling voice blasted out, blocking out her mother's thin disgusted one.

She felt something rush through her. Realized it was strength.

She didn't understand that they would make her pay for this later. That this was the day that everything would change again.

Ruth was in her bedroom putting the final touches to her hair when they came back. She called to her mother to show them in. Lit a cigarette and walked slowly down the hallway, trying to hold onto that earlier feeling.

She entered the living room and fear prickled under her arms, at her hairline. Devlin stood at the window, looking out, hands clasped behind him. It might be her apartment, but this was his interview.

He turned as she came in, nodded at her—"Mrs. Malone"—and then at another man on the sofa. Fat. Smiling. Sweating in his suit and tie. "This is Sergeant Mackay."

"Officers."

She sat gracefully, leaned forward to tap her cigarette in the ashtray. When she looked up, both men were watching her. She focused on Devlin.

"I apologize if we disturbed you earlier, Mrs. Malone. If we disturbed your morning routine. You seem to have had enough time to get ready now"—and his eyes raked over her.

She had to force herself not to cross her arms over her body, not to hide her face with her hands.

Instead, she took a breath and then exhaled a long plume of smoke toward him. One tiny, hopeless act of defiance.

"How can I help you?"

More questions, of course. They went on for hours, circling the details of that night like dogs. Maybe she hadn't bolted the door after all. Maybe she'd mistaken some of the times she'd given them. They poked and prodded, trying to goad her, trying to make her angry. The fear built in her stomach like hunger. Then they changed tactics.

"Ruth—may I call you Ruth?" Mackay didn't wait for an answer. "Is there anything you want to tell us? Anything on your mind?"

She stared at him. Shook her head.

"Are you sure? We have some new evidence, you see. It casts some...doubt on your story. Are you sure there's nothing you want to tell us?"

She shook her head again. Forced herself to maintain eye contact. Mackay's voice was soft, persuasive. Devlin retreated to the window to watch, took out his cigarettes and let the other man talk.

"We know that sometimes accidents can happen. The kids are misbehaving, not listening. You just mean to spank them. Things get out of hand. Accidentally. It can happen to anyone."

A new wave of fear like freezing water on the nape of her neck. But with it, a little relief.

Finally. This was it. This accusation was the thing she had been afraid of, and now that it was here, she found it in her to fight.

"You think I hurt my kids? You think I killed them?"

There was a pause and she felt them looking at each other. Then that soft voice again.

"Ruth, this thing...whatever happened, you can tell us. We've seen it all before. We know how these things can happen."

She said nothing.

"It'll go better for you if you tell us now. What do you say? Ruth?"

It was four days since his conversation in McGuire's with Devlin, and Pete had to talk to Ruth again. He couldn't think about Salcito, about Gallagher, about Devlin—without knocking up against her animal eyes, her soft mouth. He had to talk to her because he couldn't bear not to talk to her any longer.

By now he knew her habits. She'd be in Gloria's because it was Thursday. Alone except for Jim Beam—but there would be a couple of shadows in the background watching her and he'd have to make a move before they did.

He pictured the scene: him sliding along the bar, Ruth taking her cue from this shapeless figure who was just like all the other figures, pulling out her cigarettes so he could offer her a light.

Maybe she wouldn't recognize him. Maybe they'd just make small talk at first. The bar. The weather. The Giants.

All as natural as if nothing had been planned, and maybe he'd start to feel less like a dog with an eye on a butcher shop across a busy street, wondering if hunger and raw luck were enough to get him safely through the traffic. But then she'd narrow her eyes and stub out her half-smoked Lucky.

"I remember you." Unsteady on her barstool, ice in her voice. "What do you want?"

He wouldn't know how to answer her. He was afraid of her and she'd feel it, just as he'd feel the moment she took hold of that power, when she lifted her chin and stared and he would try to look composed. Try to think of her husband. Of Devlin.

But he was entirely lost in her smoky glitter, and she would know that too.

So she'd drain her glass and slam it on the bar and push upright like a skater moving out onto thin ice.

"C'mon then, Mr. Mystery."

"What?"

"Let's go. Liquor's cheaper at my place"—a filthy look to Hud, who would just scratch his cheek and smile and go on calmly polishing glasses—"and you can tell me all about it."

She would laugh. He'd never seen her laugh before. "If you can find your tongue."

But back at her place, wrapped in the harsh, husky voice of a jazz singer, the music low and yearning, and dizzy in the colorful spin of five Scotches, Ruth would stop the playful taunting. Would pour drinks in silence and swallow hers in one defiant gulp. And then she would stop talking altogether, and he'd be helpless as she came toward him, and he would have to close his eyes to stop himself from seeing his reflection in her hungry black pupils.

He imagined the warmth of her, the smell of her powder, her hair, and then the touch of her lips on his.

He would kiss her gently, the way he'd always kissed girls, but her mouth would come down hard and hot and needy and he wouldn't know how to respond. He'd feel his skin flush and move to kiss her neck with soft pink pecks.

But she would take his face in her two hands and claim his mouth again and speak against his lips.

"Don't think."

"Huh? I..." Startled, he might pull away, but she would pursue him, her voice harsher this time.

"Stop thinking. Just feel."

Before he could ask her what she meant, before he could admit that he didn't know how, her mouth would be on him, her tongue against his, and he would feel her hot breath and her sharp teeth against his lips, and he would feel fear and a growing desire. Let them come, let them swell in him like a great rush of breath so that he felt. He felt.

And at that point his imagination moved beyond conscious thought to a series of images and pure sensations. The soft suck of her lips. The silky whisper of her voice, of her hair. The white expanse of her throat. The long curve of her closed eyelids. The heat of her. The jagged line of pain as she gripped him with her red-tipped fingers. Her moans. The salt taste of her. And then the cresting of a great wave and a sense that there was no way back.

And afterward. How would it be, afterward?

Would he wake up with her in a tangle of sheets, damp with their mingled sweat, the scent of her in his head and her eyes on him? Or would he wake up alone, his muscles aching, water running in the background and then Ruth there in the doorway, the light behind her, and the shape of her all wrong and fully dressed.

"Here are your clothes. You can pick up a cab on Main Street."

His brain would reach for the memory of her warmth, for the smell of her skin beneath the powders and the creams. But the powders and creams would have been reapplied and the woman he'd touched would be hidden away, beneath arched brows and the slow drag on a cigarette. And when he tried to kiss her, his lips would meet her cool cheek.

How would it be?

The night was cold and the street silent and full of pre-dawn calm. He walked for over an hour, thinking of her. Pushing the image of her husband from his mind, the image of his mother's face, the faces of Ruth's children. Pushing away his own shame, his own guilt.

He tried to focus only on her. On her tired, beautiful face. On how she would taste. The sounds she would make. The softness of her under his fingerprints. And he found that it was easy to think only of her.

He felt his heart pound and imagined it attuning itself to her heart. He thought of the connection between them stretching across the city: elastic, taut with possibility. With promise.

He thought of her voice. Of how she looked, and the different textures of her hair and her skin and her mouth. He thought of the things he wanted to say to her, the letters he wanted to write and knew he would never send.

He felt an ache of longing in the pit of his stomach, in the back of his throat. And he felt the space where she ought to be.

Frank came by and said he needed to talk to her.

Ruth's mother smiled at him, gave him her cheek to kiss, said that she would leave them alone, that she had planned to go to church that morning anyway.

They went into the living room and Ruth sat by the window, smoking. She watched her mother walk down the path, stiff-legged, back bent. She let Frank's words wash over her, let the warmth of the winter sun through the glass relax her.

Then he said something that shook her awake. She turned to him. "Devlin said what?"

"He told me a lie detector test would make all the questions stop. He said if we both took the test, they'd leave us alone."

Ruth lit another cigarette, blew out smoke, looked at him through narrowed eyes.

"And you believed him?"

Frank spread his arms in a gesture she knew well. It was his I-forgot-the-time pose. His they-didn't-tell-me-you-called, I-couldn't-get-the-money-today stance.

"Ruth, he's a cop. He just wants to find out who did it. That's his job."

She took another drag, stared at the floor. Thought about Devlin and that other cop—Mackay. Telling her he understood. Telling her he knew how things could get out of hand. That low voice, insinuating he knew she'd killed her children. They'd been pushing and pushing her for months. She needed to find a way to make them stop.

Two days later, Ruth sat in the chair in the dark room.

She'd told Devlin that she would do the test, but she wanted Frank to do it as well. And she wanted assurances that she would be alone in the room with the technicians, that no one would be watching her. She'd had enough of being watched.

"Fine. That's fine, Mrs. Malone. Sure. If that's what you want."

"And Frank will be doing it at the same time?"

"That's right. Both of you. He'll be just in the room next door."

As the technician checked the wires and tested that the machine was working, she smoked one cigarette after another.

"This isn't legal, you know. I read that they don't accept it in court."

The man kept his head down, turned dials, flicked switches.

"There must be something wrong with it. Otherwise they'd accept it in court."

He stayed silent, but glanced toward the door.

Then they began:

"Is your name Ruth Marie Malone?"

"Yes."

"How old are you?"

"Twenty-six."

"Are you married?"

"Not anymore."

"On the night of July thirteenth, nineteen sixty-five, were you alone at your apartment with your children?"

"Yes."

"Have you ever hurt your children?"

"No."

"When did you last see your children alive?"

"I've been through this. Over and over."

"When did you last see your children alive?"

"Are you asking Frank the same questions?"

The technician looked toward the mirror along the wall.

"Are you?"

"I'm sorry, ma'am, I don't..."

"Frank Malone. My ex-husband. He's taking the test next door right now."

"There's...we only have one machine."

Ruth pulled the wires from her arm and threw them at the bemused technician as though they were radioactive. Then she walked to the mirror on the wall and spoke into it.

"You bastard. You lied to me!"

And then: "I can hear you laughing at me, you piece of shit! This isn't fair. It isn't *fair*!"

She spat her words at the men in the mirror. "You're not interested in finding out the truth about my kids—you just want to twist everything against me!"

MALONE MOTHER REFUSES TO TAKE LIE DETECTOR TEST
By Staff Reporter Tom O'Connor

QUEENS, Nov. 9–The mother of two murdered children has refused to take a lie detector test to answer questions about the mystery surrounding their deaths, it was revealed yesterday.

Frank Malone Jr., 5, and his sister Cindy, 4, disappeared on the night of July 13, 1965 from their first-floor apartment in Kew Gardens Hills, and were later found dead nearby. They lived with their mother, 26-year-old Ruth Malone, who was estranged from their father, Frank Malone Sr. Mr. and Mrs. Malone were briefly reunited by the tragedy.

Despite a thorough investigation, the police have not yet been able to obtain enough information to make an arrest.

Mrs. Malone originally said she was willing to help the police investigation by undergoing a polygraph examination. It has now emerged that she refused to take the test because the results are not admissible as evidence in a court of law.

A police spokesman told this newspaper: "Mrs. Malone said she would take the lie detector test to prove her innocence, but in reality, she had no intention of ever doing it. She knew all along that polygraphs cannot be used in court."

Lie detectors work by measuring physiological responses, such as blood pressure levels, pulse rate and sweat gland activity during questioning. Any significant variation in these rates may indicate that the subject is lying.

Mrs. Malone left her apartment this morning, and refused to comment on her failure to take the test or on rumors that an arrest in the case is imminent.

Another call. This time they wanted Ruth to come into the station house.

"Just a few questions."

She went in with her head high, asked to call a lawyer. Devlin said she didn't need one. She asked again and he said she must have something to hide. She kept asking and he took her to a phone and she called Arnold Green.

When he answered, he sounded distracted. When he realized who was calling, his tone became guarded.

"Mrs. Malone. How can I help?"

"I'm at the police station. I think...I need a lawyer."

There was a moment of silence and then, "I'm a divorce attorney, Mrs. Malone. I deal with family law. Civil matters."

"I don't...I don't know what to do."

"I'm sorry. I can't help with your current situation."

She opened her mouth to reply, but the phone was dead.

She turned to Devlin, standing behind her and, without looking at him, told him she needed a lawyer.

"You mean you need us to appoint someone for you?"

She stared at a mark on the wall somewhere to the left of his head. "Yes. That's what I mean."

"I'll see what I can do. Keep in mind,"—and she heard the smile in his voice—"It might take a while. I can't imagine what lawyer would take the case."

They put her in a locked room with no windows and the heat turned up, and a door that only opened from the outside. Quinn came in to tell her they were trying to get hold of someone from the public defender's office. She didn't look around, just waited for the door to close.

Hours later, the door opened again and she heard Quinn say, "She's in here."

She glanced up and saw a stranger. A man in his fifties, with silver hair and bright blue eyes. He was wearing a beautiful suit, a tie pin, an immaculate white shirt. She was suddenly aware of how hot the room was, of how she must look. She pushed her hair back, half-stood, and he waved her to sit down, held out his hand.

"I'm Henry Scott. I'm your lawyer."

His skin was dry. She could smell his cologne: something woody. Fresh.

She blurted out, "You're not from the public defender's office."

He smiled at her, reminding her of someone.

"No, I'm not."

Then he turned to Quinn and his voice was sharp.

"This room is stifling. Get the temperature fixed, or find us another room. Bring us some water. And some coffee and sandwiches—and make sure my office has copies of all of my client's interview tapes and the transcripts by tomorrow morning."

Quinn blushed and nodded. Once he'd left, Scott turned back to her.

"I've been retained by Mr. Gallagher. I believe he's a friend of yours."

She realized then that it was Lou he reminded her of. She had the same feeling with them both: here was a guy who knew what he was doing. Who could take care of her.

Scott put his briefcase down, shook his head.

"Pathetic."

She looked at him. He smiled again, nodded toward the door.

"Clearly they've got nothing on you. They're subjecting you to these conditions to try and break you. If they had any real evidence, they'd come out with it. This"—he gestured around the small room—"this tells me they have nothing and they're trying to put pressure on you to confess."

She had a sudden, dizzying sensation of being able to hand over responsibility to someone whose job it was to take care of her. She tested the feeling cautiously. Sat up, looked him in the eye, and waited for him to begin.

Scott was in the chair next to her. She could just make out the smell of his expensive cigars beneath the cigarettes that the rest of them were chain-smoking. Across from her was Devlin and, next to him, a thin-faced guy she had never seen before. Carey, Caruso—something like that. He had a furtive look, like a rat.

There were four people in the room, but it was just her and Devlin as far as she was concerned.

He leaned forward, his eyes drilling into hers, pressing deeper until she felt him inside her head. She struggled to push back. To keep him out. To keep her thoughts her own.

Without taking his eyes off her, he held out his hand so that the rat-faced man could place a manila folder in it. He laid the folder on the table between them and opened it. Spread out the photographs that were bundled inside like a dealer at a card table. And all without taking his eyes off hers.

"Look at them, Mrs. Malone."

She couldn't look away from his face. If she looked away, he would see it as a sign of weakness.

"Look at them, please."

She heard Scott's voice, as though from a distance. "I really must object to this. My client..."

She blocked him out, kept her eyes on Devlin's.

"LOOK AT THEM!"

His voice, his fist on the table, made her jump: shock made her pull back, look down.

At first, her mind couldn't make sense of what her eyes were seeing. There were leaves, shadows, twigs. Then she made out a shoe. And a foot inside it. What she had taken for a slender branch was a leg. What she had thought was a knot in the wood was a bruise.

She reached out and stroked it gently. She'd seen that bruise when it was a raw scrape, still bleeding. She'd bathed it with warm salty water, she'd dabbed iodine on it. She'd held it firm as it wriggled to escape from the stinging. She'd kissed it better.

She kissed her fingertip now, pressed her mouth to the warm pink skin and felt the heat of herself and the blood pulsing beneath, and then she pressed her kiss into that flat cold leg.

She closed her eyes for a brief moment and then looked at the next picture. At an arm that was dark with something that was not shadow. At a fall of hair, white against the grays of the grass it was spread over. At the torn fabric of a pale gray shirt that should have been neither pale nor gray but the bright blue of a summer sky.

Her eyes moved faster, skittering over the pictures to the background rhythm of Devlin's voice, the noise of it rising as her gaze floated from photograph to photograph, and falling as her eyes fell on another shoe. On a pattern of leaves. On a close-up of something white and soft. On the blurred image of curled fingers.

She reached the end, kept her head bowed, felt Scott's hand on her arm, heard his gentle voice breaking into Devlin's harsh one. She could not hear their words. Could not speak.

She pressed her lips together, shook her head to clear it of noise. The voices fell silent and then, in the space that followed, she heard Scott say clearly, "My client needs a break."

And she shook her head again, because a break would mean standing. It would mean leaving this room for another one much like it. It would mean deciding whether or not she wanted coffee, or needed to visit a cold tiled bathroom under the hard eyes of a female officer.

While staying still would mean she could keep her arms wrapped around herself. Could stay inside herself. Quiet. Safe.

Until Devlin leaned forward and jabbed with his words so that they broke through—and then his voice was pushing, pushing, and there was nowhere to hide.

"What happened to your children was a tragedy, Mrs. Malone. We're very close to making an arrest. Very close."

His breath on her skin like a lover.

"We know you didn't do this without help. No one heard a car at your apartment that night, so whoever he was, we know he parked a distance away. It would have taken two people, or a strong man, to get the children out of your apartment and carry them that distance. We want to get that man, Mrs. Malone. And we need you to help us put him away. We can give you immunity if you help us put him away."

A pause.

"Or would you rather go to prison for him? Think about it, Mrs. Malone. Think about being locked up for years for a crime that someone else committed."

She listened to the rise and fall of breath in the room, to the rise and fall of the tape as it clicked around, and she thought about being shut away. About not being able to walk outside. Not being able to dance. To drink. To laugh. About not being able to breathe.

"Don't you want to help us, Mrs. Malone? If you say nothing, we'll be forced to conclude that you're not interested in getting justice for your children."

She tasted the word and it was bitter. Justice wouldn't bring Cindy and Frankie back. A conviction for murder couldn't raise the dead. So what did any of this matter?

Devlin's voice broke into her thoughts, as he went on telling the story of this man.

"Maybe you stayed in the other room while he did it. While he silenced them. While he took them outside. Maybe all you're guilty of is taking another hit from the bottle and turning the radio up. Is that how it was, Mrs. Malone?"

She bowed her head. He knew nothing about guilt.

He knew nothing about leaving your kids home alone or with a teenage sitter while you went out to work eight hours on your feet in a pair of heels that rubbed, serving drinks to assholes who thought they were buying the right to paw you with every round. He knew nothing about leaving your sleeping children while you went to meet a man who would pay you for your company because your daughter needed shoes. He knew nothing about sending your kids to bed on half-empty stomachs, trying to fill them up with water, adding a drop of whisky to make them sleep—because if you let them eat, there'd be nothing for breakfast and your deadbeat husband's checks kept bouncing.

He knew nothing about coming home from a twelve-hour shift, having held the image of their faces in front of you the whole time, holding onto the sweet smell of their skin as you wiped vomit from your shoes, as you picked cigarette butts out of a half-full glass. And then stepping through the door and hearing the noise of them: the screams and shrieks and the endless demands, for food and for attention, and feeling that just the fact of them—their spilling, their pulling and grabbing and *needing*—made you want to hand the sitter all the money you had in your purse and beg her to stay. Or if there was no money, or no sitter, just walking out anyway because you were so damn tired, and you just needed a little time alone. A little peace.

This man had no idea about any of this. None of these men did. They got paid men's wages and they had wives to deal with the noise and the mess, with Jimmy's problems at school, with little Susie who wouldn't eat her vegetables, with the baby who just wouldn't stop crying.

They knew nothing of guilt. They were not mothers.

16

Ruth click-clacked along the sidewalk, heading for her car. She was showered, dressed, made up. She had rubbed lotion into her hands, hooked her earrings into place. She had drunk coffee, walked the dog, tucked a spare sanitary napkin into her handbag.

It was the week before Thanksgiving, a cold shining day. She lifted her head to feel the sun on her skin. She hadn't heard from the cops in three days. No phone calls, no visits.

Then she heard a car door slam, footsteps behind her.

As she started her engine and reached out to close the door, a car appeared from nowhere to block her in. A hand appeared on top of her door. She looked up but the sun had turned the figure into a silhouette with no face. She focused on the hand. Clean clipped nails, a short thumb, a white scar on the forefinger. It was a very ordinary hand. It could have belonged to anyone.

"What do you want?"

"You have to come with us," said Devlin.

"I don't *have* to do a damn thing."

"You have to come with us, Mrs. Malone. The grand jury has indicted you. You're under arrest for the murder of your son and the manslaughter of your daughter."

"I don't believe this. I don't believe it."

"Mrs. Malone…"

"I'm not going anywhere with you."

Hands on the steering wheel. Tight.

"I suggest you don't make a fuss, Mrs. Malone. People are watching."

She let out her breath and then got out of the car, made to hand her keys to Quinn, who stood stolidly next to Devlin like a dummy. She dropped them and looked at him scrabbling in the road. It was all she had.

Ruth sat in the backseat of Devlin's car, stared straight ahead at the morning going on without her.

Devlin shifted in his seat, making the car rock. She lifted her eyes to the mirror, saw him watching her.

"What?"

"You know, it would have gone much easier for you if you'd only told the truth from the beginning."

She raised her head. Looked him in the eye and then let her gaze drift past him. She would not give him anything.

They didn't speak again until they reached the precinct. Ruth stepped out and through the glass doors ahead of her she saw that the lobby was full. Cops in uniform, men in suits, secretaries: they all turned to watch her approach. They were all waiting for her.

She stopped. Took a long breath. Turned to Devlin.

"I want my phone call."

He shrugged. "Sure. There's no one who can help you, but why not?"

"Frank, it's me."

"Huh? Ruth? What time is it?"

"I've . . . I'm at the precinct. They've arrested me."

A pause. "What? What for? What the fuck's going on?"

"Yeah, I know. Christ, Frank. That bastard was waiting for me outside the apartment this morning. Brought me in with everyone staring."

"Jesus . . . Ruthie. I don't . . . Are you okay?"

"Listen, I don't have much time. You need to call Scott for me. Tell him what happened."

"Sure. Scott. Okay."

"You got his number? You got it, Frank?"

"Yeah, I got it. Okay, I'll call him now. I'll meet him outside the precinct."

"Okay."

"You need anything?"

"No. Just Scott."

"Okay. Hang in there. I love you, baby. I'll be there soon."

"Okay."

Pete was standing in line at Mario's, waiting to order breakfast before work. A bulletin came over the radio. *Ruth Malone has been indicted and arrested for the murder of her son and the manslaughter of her daughter.*

He dropped his newspaper and just stared at the radio until the guy behind him nudged him and nodded toward the girl at the counter, who was looking at him with raised eyebrows, tapping her pen on her pad.

"Sorry," he said. "Changed my mind."

He pushed his way out the door. Disbelieving. It had taken over four months, but Devlin must finally have what he'd been looking for. He'd mentioned a letter. Whatever had been in that letter was enough to charge her.

Pete drove to the station house. The lobby was crammed with reporters. Two hookers were leaning against the desk while a sergeant booked them. They kept yelling at the photographers, "How d'ya want me, honey?" and "Ten bucks for a close-up!" and then collapsing into laughter.

He stared around wildly, desperate for a familiar face, for some idea of what to do. The sergeant behind the desk was shouting, trying to bring some order to the chaos, but Pete could hardly hear him above the clamor of voices.

A door opened and Devlin's bulky figure emerged. He raised a hand and the room fell silent. Just like that.

"Gentlemen. I know why you're here, but we got nothing more for you today. She's been arrested, she'll probably get bail, we don't have a date for the hearing yet. That's it."

He turned and went back inside and the noise broke out again, louder still. Reporters pushed toward the door.

Pete wandered outside, stupid with confusion. What had happened? What had changed between yesterday and today to make the cops feel confident enough to go ahead and bring her in?

The parking lot was deserted: everyone had a lead to follow. He could hear Friedmann in his head: *Stick close to the cops, get the reaction in her neighborhood.*

He stopped to light a cigarette, noticed a guy leaving the station house with a leather briefcase. He had silver hair, a well-cut suit, an air of money. He looked like Pete's idea of a lawyer and, judging by his suit and his shoes, he was a good one. There was surely only one person in the station who needed an expensive lawyer today.

Pete dropped his cigarette and broke into a run, skidding to a halt in front of the guy with the briefcase. He merely raised a curious eyebrow, as though Pete were something interesting that he'd come across in a book.

"Sorry, sir. I didn't mean to startle you. I'm . . . My name's Peter Wonicke. Are you representing Mrs. Malone?"

He said, not unkindly, "Well now, son, I'm afraid I'm not at liberty to talk about my clients."

"No, of course."

"Then . . ."

"It's just . . . I know her. I might have information that could help."

He raised his eyebrow again and studied Pete for a long moment.

"I'm not in the habit of falling into conversations about my clients on the street either. But I am in the habit of making snap judgments about people. Have to be, in my line of work."

He fell silent again and looked at Pete.

"I'm a little busy today, as you can imagine. But why don't we meet tomorrow? Somewhere quieter. Have a cup of coffee together, and you can tell me...well, whatever it is you want to tell me. I'm Henry Scott, by the way."

He gave Pete an address, and they agreed on a time the following afternoon.

The address turned out to be an old-fashioned café, the kind of place frequented by women having morning coffee or treating grandchildren.

Scott was there before him, stood when Pete arrived, shook his hand. They ordered, and Scott asked the waitress if they had any walnut loaf. When she said they did, he beamed like the small boy at the next table who had just been served a slice of pie and a mound of whipped cream.

When she'd gone, he looked after her, still smiling.

"This place used to serve a wonderful walnut loaf. My mother used to bring me here when we had to come into the city to buy me new shoes for school. Of course, the frequency of our visits and that ritual declined at the same rate as the growth of my feet. A strange link, don't you think, Mr. Wonicke?"

His smile broadened, and Pete smiled back uncertainly.

"However, we're not here to talk about walnut loaf or, indeed, my feet. Is there something you'd like to tell me? Something about Mrs. Malone?"

"Yes sir. It's not...I don't really know where to begin."

"Why don't you start by telling me how long you've known Mrs. Malone."

"I met her after her children were killed."

"And how would you define your relationship with her?"

"I know her pretty well. We're...close."

"All right. How did you get to know her?"

"Well, I was a reporter."

Scott's face twitched then and his manner became more formal.

"I see. In that case, Mr. Wonicke, I'm going to have to ask you..."

"No! No, please. I'm not a reporter anymore. And I'm not here because of that. I'm just telling you how I met her."

Scott nodded, but his manner was guarded.

"So you met her. You interviewed her?"

"Yes. Her and some of her neighbors. And her mother."

Their coffee arrived, together with a slice of walnut cake that would have defeated even a hungry schoolboy. Scott picked up his cup and eyed Pete over the rim.

"So far, you haven't told me anything that sets you apart from the rest of your profession, Mr. Wonicke."

"I guess... well, I believe her. I think she's innocent."

Scott put his cup down, folded his hands on the table.

"Why?"

"Because I don't think she's capable of murder. Especially the murder of her children."

"Based on?"

"Excuse me?"

"Have you met many murderers? I met a woman a few years ago who drowned her grandson because she believed he was possessed by Satan. I assure you, she was far more personable and charming than most people in this room."

Scott's smile never faltered and his eyes continued to twinkle at Pete above his coffee cup.

"So what makes you so sure that Mrs. Malone is innocent?"

Pete flushed, realized he was clenching his jaw. Maybe Scott intended to needle him, to get something out of him. If so, it was working. He tried to stay calm. To focus on Ruth.

"Okay, I see your point, Mr. Scott. Maybe it would be more accurate to say that I don't think she's guilty based on the evidence the police seem to have on her."

Scott put down his cup and nodded.

"Now you've got me interested, Mr. Wonicke. Because now you may be offering me something I don't currently know. I assume you got this information in a way that's completely legal and aboveboard?"

"Some of it I got through interviews. Some of it I overheard."

"Hearsay, I'm afraid. But potentially useful, depending on what was said."

Pete gave him the gist of the conversations he'd had with Quinn and with Devlin, their view of Ruth. Scott ate a forkful of cake and listened in silence.

"Mr. Scott, I think they're going to attack her morals on the stand. Make her out to be a . . . to be the kind of woman who's capable of killing her kids."

Scott nodded. "So I would assume."

Pete flushed and looked down. Ran his finger around the edge of his saucer and wondered what he was doing there. Why he was wasting his time on a guy who seemed to get a kick out of patronizing him.

And then Scott said quietly, "But you've confirmed what I needed to know. You've met Devlin in a social setting. And you know more about my client than I do right now. All of which is helpful."

Pete looked at him and he was smiling again, but this was a real smile with warmth in it. Suddenly Pete wanted to help him, and not just for Ruth's sake.

"Mr. Scott, I think . . . She's not the only person the police should be looking at."

He told Scott about Lou Gallagher. What he'd learned from Bette. What he suspected.

"He's done this before—made a woman he was involved with get rid of a kid. He has a history of violence. The cops should at least be talking to him."

Scott frowned at him. Stroked his chin as though he was

thinking. There was a long pause and then he said, "That's interesting, Mr. Wonicke, but the state's case is all about Mrs. Malone. The police think she's guilty. So it's Mrs. Malone I must concentrate on."

He stood and excused himself to make a phone call and Pete leaned back in his chair, glanced idly around the room and noticed a copy of the *Herald* discarded on a nearby table.

MALONE MOTHER SHOPS FOR DRESSES AS KIDS LIE DEAD
By Staff Reporter Tom O'Connor

QUEENS, Nov. 17—Mrs. Ruth Malone, who was arrested yesterday on charges of strangling her son Frank Jr. and her daughter Cindy, was shopping for clothes just hours after her children were killed, it was revealed today.

The day after reporting her children missing, and less than 24 hours after little Cindy's body was removed from the weed-strewn lot where it was found, her mother was seen by witnesses at a local clothing store.

A police source said, "We thought that Mrs. Malone had gone shopping for groceries or perhaps personal items—although with family and neighbors rallying around, there was no real need. But we were shocked when she was seen entering a ladies' dress shop."

The source went on to say that the attractive cocktail waitress had purchased items from Debonair Doll, a small boutique on Main Street that opened three years ago.

The owner of the store told this reporter that Mrs. Malone bought two dresses, pantyhose and a new hat.

"She seemed absolutely normal. I remember she had on lot of makeup, lipstick. Her hair was done. She didn't look as if she'd been crying."

A witness, who prefers to remain anonymous, saw the striking redhead cross the street to a car which is believed to have been driven by her estranged husband. As she approached the car, he leaned out and beckoned to her to hurry up. In response, the witness clearly heard her say,

"If we're late, we're late. This is important. I have to look right."

Mrs. Malone's thoughts were surely more with her own outfit than with her daughter, lying cold and alone on a morgue slab. And she was apparently focusing more on her appearance than on the continued disappearance of her son, aged just five years old.

Police and volunteer searchers spent hour after hour combing the neighborhood for the boy over the course of a long and difficult week. Most of those involved were parents themselves, and the moment when the child's body was discovered was "a terrible blow" to all, according to one officer.

From the outset, the police suspected Mrs. Malone, who is expected to be released on bail in the next couple of days.

The piece was accompanied by a photograph of Ruth in a short dress and heels. Her head was bowed but her eye makeup was as clear and dark as the ink on the page.

Scott returned, took his seat, picked up his cup. Pete threw the paper on the table in disgust.

"Have you seen this?"

Scott nodded, his face expressionless.

"That's bullshit. I don't know what the real story is, but that's just..."

But even as he spoke, Pete was aware that, until recently, he'd been part of that. That he'd written what he'd been told to write, that he'd portrayed shades of gray as black and white.

He felt a hot rush of shame and then, underneath, cool relief that his life was different now.

Scott was holding the paper, skimming the article.

"I hope so, Mr. Wonicke. Because this is the kind of thing the jury will be reading every day until the trial. That's what I've got to work with."

"But she's . . . she didn't do it. These people don't know her. They don't know her at all."

Scott looked at him, and Pete had the strange feeling that the other man was seeing him for the first time.

"This is going to be a tough case, Mr. Wonicke. An ugly case. I don't underestimate the sizable task ahead. My first opponent is Mrs. Malone herself."

He saw Pete's frown and nodded. "Oh yes. My first hurdles are Mrs. Malone's appearance and her manner. The way she chooses to dress and the image she chooses to project are not those of a grieving mother. She is the very picture of a scandalous woman."

"Christ. You sound just like . . ."

He raised his hand. "Please. I am on her side. My job is to think the way a typical jury will. Twelve average men and women who will have never met anyone like Ruth Malone. Who won't be able to imagine the mind-set it might take to kill two children. Who will have condemned her out of hand just for being in this position.

"I've filed a motion that Mrs. Malone should not be questioned on the stand about her extramarital relationships. But it's probable the motion will be rejected, and that will mean that Mrs. Malone cannot give evidence."

"Why would it be rejected?"

"They think it's relevant, Mr. Wonicke. They think her relationships are relevant to this crime."

He sighed. "And the coverage in the press is driving that idea. That said, as much as your ex-colleagues are giving her a rough time, what people are saying in the street is far worse."

"What do you mean, worse?"

Scott took a breath. "I had dinner last night with an old friend, in a restaurant not far from here. A nice place. Nice people. I heard two women behind me talking about the case and about Mrs. Malone.

One of them said—please excuse the expression—'I'm going to the trial. I want to see that bitch get what she deserves.' And the other said, 'I know just what you mean. I don't like to prejudge but in this case it's difficult not to. A tramp like that is capable of anything.'"

He put down his fork then and wrinkled his nose.

"This cake's stale."

Scott told Ruth that the court appearance was a formality, that she would be granted bail that afternoon. He asked who would post it and she said, "My mother."

She thought of her mother's lined red face, her rough red hands. Her mother's prayers at her father's bedside. Her anger. Her shame.

"My mother will post bail."

Then they talked about the trial in general terms: who would be there, who would be allowed to speak. He told her that she would not be called as a witness, would not have to take the stand. That she would not have a voice.

And when she asked why, he only said, "It's best this way, trust me."

She was trying to trust him, but she felt his reluctance to trust her. He didn't trust her to remain calm. Didn't trust her not to get angry, not to get emotional, not to show the court her defiance. He didn't trust that she would not be tripped and tricked into revealing that the stories about her—the men, the drinking, the sex—were true.

So he thought it was best that she sit quietly with her eyes downcast and her lips pressed together behind a white lace handkerchief.

When they were done talking, he began to pack up his papers. But he spent so long shuffling and stacking them to make the edges neat that she knew he had something else to say, so she folded her hands and waited. And eventually his eyes rose to meet hers and he closed his briefcase and cleared his throat.

"Mrs. Malone. We need to talk about your appearance."

His voice was gentle. He was trying to be kind.

Ruth looked at his expensive suit, at his neatly pressed shirt. Smelled his woody cologne and wondered if his wife bought him a bottle for Christmas every year. She imagined the wife: ironing his shirts, sponging his tie, starching his collars. She imagined neat gray hair, a light dusting of face powder, fresh pink blouses, a discreet string of pearls. The smells of clean laundry, of lavender skin cream.

"I'm sorry to be so personal. But it is relevant. The more conservative you appear, the more chance you have of appealing to the jury. The prosecution will do their best to make sure the jurors are as conventional as possible."

She thought: he is doing his job the best way he knows how.

But every word he spoke was a judgment on how she looked. On every blemish, every pore, every line.

"Perhaps if you just toned down the color of your hair a little? Or wore a more subdued style? And perhaps dressed a little more modestly?"

His words were like fishhooks, ripping into her skin, showing the soft and vulnerable underpart of her. The part that was weak. Ugly. Wrong.

She scrabbled for the scent of lavender again but all she could smell was sweat, bleach, old food. The stink of fear and despair.

A month later, Scott arranged a meeting at his office for Ruth and Salcito. She dressed carefully in a neat pink suit, low heels, her hair freshly washed and set, and she drove downtown, her face pale from lack of sleep.

She still didn't know if she was doing the right thing. Scott had talked to her, told her that she had to be seen to be with Frank, that their marriage had to appear solid—but she couldn't help feeling the pity of what she was about to do. This seemed cold.

Although she was early, Johnny was there already, talking to

Scott in the lobby. He was leaning unsteadily against the wall, his voice slurred. He looked like he hadn't been to bed.

Scott offered them coffee and when they declined, gestured toward his office, said he would leave them to it.

Ruth walked in and sat in one of the high-backed chairs that faced the desk. She crossed her legs, folded her hands, took a breath. But it was useless: as soon as Scott had closed the door on them, Johnny was on the floor at her feet, embracing her legs, crying, telling her he loved her, how much he'd missed her. She fought down irritation, frustration, pity, raised him up and sat him in a chair, let him hold her hand. Tried for a brisk but serious tone.

"I'm sorry, Johnny, but I won't be able to see you for a while. Mr. Scott says it wouldn't look right before the trial."

"What about after the trial?"

"Well, we'll see."

"Once you're free, we can get back to how things were, huh, baby? Maybe take a trip, whaddya say?"

"I don't know, Johnny. I can't think about that right now."

She held his hand tight, squeezing as she spoke, but she could hear the desperation in his voice. His eyes filled with tears.

"Ruth. Ruthie. Please. I love you. You know I love you. I want to marry you, baby. We could have more kids. Together. I could give you more kids. I love you, baby. Please."

She held tight to his hand, watched his face as he cried, marveled at the disgust that rose in her: this was a man she'd admired once. She tried to shush him, to tell him that everything would be okay, but he kept shaking his head.

"Not without you, baby. Nothing's okay without you. I need you, baby...please. Say you need me too. The way you used to. You told me that you needed me to make you feel good...that no one else could make you feel the way I did. We can have that again, baby..."

As he spoke, he sank to the floor again, began to run his hands up her legs, over her thighs. She pushed them down, pushed her skirt down, tried to take hold of his hands, but he kept moving them back, sliding them higher.

"This isn't... it's not you, Ruthie. I know you. It's Frank or this lawyer, this Scott, they're making you do this. But you want me, you want me as much as I want you..."

"Johnny, this isn't helping either of us. Please try to understand. This is for the best. The trial's coming up and..."

"Fuck the trial. This is about me and you. When the trial's over, what then? What then?"

She raised her hands, started to speak, saw Scott in the doorway and sagged with relief. She smoothed her skirt again, sat up.

Scott took his time closing the door and walking to the far side of his desk, giving Johnny a few moments to pull himself up into the chair. He sat with his head in his hands, sobbing. Ruth looked helplessly at Scott.

"Mr. Salcito? We really need to talk about the trial. I'm going to get Louise to bring us in some nice strong coffee, okay?"

Scott came out from his side of the desk, took a crisp white handkerchief out of his breast pocket, held it out. At last, Johnny reached up and took it. His sobs slowed; he blew his nose.

Scott returned to his seat, picked up his telephone receiver.

"Coffee for three, Louise. And could you bring in some of the lemon cake that my wife made? Thank you, dear."

He waited until Johnny had finished wiping and blowing, and then said firmly, "Mr. Salcito, the prosecution will call you to give evidence. I need to know what you're going to say. We need to plan for it."

Johnny tore his blurred gaze from Ruth.

"What will you say when they ask you about the events of that night? The night the children disappeared?"

He sniffed. "Well, just what I've always said."

"Good. So let's recap: you called Ruth the night the children went missing, everything seemed as usual, yes?"

"Yeah. Sure."

He looked over at Ruth and she gave him her hand. He kissed it, rubbed it against his face. She felt a sick shudder deep in her rib cage. Clenched her other hand so hard that her nails dug into her palm. Smiled at him.

"And since that night, Ruth has never said anything to you regarding the children?"

"Just that she missed them. Just that the police weren't doing nothing to find the guy."

"That's fine. That's very good, Mr. Salcito."

17

Ruth stood between two guards in the hallway. She tried to breathe deep, tried to hold onto herself.

She was the same person she had always been. Nothing they could do to her in this room would change that.

The heavy wooden doors opened. She took a breath. Bit the inside of her cheek. In front of her: a flight of worn steps. A smell of polish and the dry dusty scent of old paper. Then a sudden sense of space and light as she reached the top. A room full of murmuring voices and hard eyes.

And somehow she was sitting at a table between Scott and his assistant with the horn-rimmed glasses, whose name she kept forgetting. The murmuring had swollen so that she could make out individual voices. She could feel the weight of those stares.

She risked a glance behind her and saw that the public benches were full. Rows of strangers. Mostly women. Their mouths moved but they never took their eyes off her.

She looked to the side, and the first figure she saw was Devlin. The cop who looked like an actor was rehearsing his lines from a notebook. Now and then his head came up and his stern, steady gaze swept the room. As she watched him, his eyes met hers. She almost smiled at him—she knew him so well, and here they were, playing opposite each other—but she remembered in time and let her gaze fall and her lips settle back into a somber line.

In the second row: the bit parts. That journalist Gina had brought around—he was there, pushing his hair off his forehead, leaning forward so as not to miss a single moment. And Johnny Salcito in his sad suit, with his shaking hands and the Scotch veins on his cheeks.

And there was Frank, frowning, looking around him as though he wasn't quite sure how he'd come to end up here, nodding sadly at her when their eyes met.

Three years ago, she thought. Three years ago we were just another married couple with two kids. How did we get here?

Tears pricked her eyes at that, so she moved her gaze on, searching for something to distract her. And there, at the end of a row, was Lou. Her heart sped up as she looked at him sitting there, one elbow on the back of his seat, as calm and as confident as though he was in his own office. She thought of what it could cost him to be here for her, showing his belief in her, and she felt a great rush of gratitude.

There was a series of thuds and the audience stood in a swish of fabric. Scott's hand was under her arm, pulling her up and into position as the judge swept in. Her surroundings faded into the background and she gripped the edge of the table, focusing on the tall figure at the center of the room. On the black gown. On the white hair, the sober face. His voice was deep and measured as he spoke to open the trial.

She pressed her hands into fists and willed herself to remain silent as fear washed over her. This was real.

A movement to her right made her turn, as one of the men at the next table rose to speak. An expensive suit. Thick oiled hair. A flashy diamond on his little finger.

He began to speak, walking toward the jury box, leaning casually against it and letting his eyes rake over her. Ruth felt an urge to wrap her arms around herself. To hide her body from him.

He opened with a brief account of the children's disappearance. The locked door, the empty room. Finding Cindy in the weed-strewn lot. The search for Frankie. Ruth swallowed down tears, kept her head high and her eyes on his.

"Gentlemen of the jury, the prosecution will demonstrate that the defendant in this case, an attractive redheaded cocktail waitress, found her role as a mother to be incompatible with her chosen lifestyle. Ultimately this led her to murder her own children, and to a succession of lies in an attempt to cover up her crime."

Saliva flooded her mouth and her head snapped up. She turned to Scott, wanting to see her fury reflected in him, wanting him to stand up and stop this, but he merely flapped his hand and shushed her.

She took a breath, gripped the table, kept listening. The man with the ring went on to make several statements about her: she was defiant; she had refused to take a lie detector test; she had had relations with several men.

Ruth could not see what any of this had to do with her guilt or innocence. She could feel the anger rising, threatening to overwhelm her. She began to make notes on the yellow pad in front of her, trying to control it, to contain it in words. After a few moments, she gave up and wrote: *SEX???* She underlined it heavily, pushing her pencil into the page, scoring the paper, almost ripping it.

Then two pictures of her children were tacked to a board by a bailiff, and the mood of the courtroom changed. The voice of the man with the ring slowed and deepened further and he half-turned so that his body was angled toward the images.

"The lives of these little angels were ended cruelly and prematurely by the one person who should have protected and cared for them. For this reason, the murder of children has been condemned down the centuries as the most heinous crime there is: it breaks not only the laws of every civilized society, but the natural law that mankind lives by.

"And so we the prosecution will therefore ask you to find the defendant guilty as charged."

The silence that followed his words resonated around the wood-paneled walls of the room, and then a rustle of hushed whispers rose to fill it.

As Scott stood to speak, Ruth dropped her eyes and thought about Frankie and Cindy. About the pink and tender softness of them. The loudness of them: their laughter, their screams, their shouts for attention. Their fat scarred knees, their hands tugging at her. Their dimpled knuckles. Their sweet-tasting kisses.

She kept her head bowed and her eyes fixed on a knot of wood in the tabletop until she heard a name that made her feel something. And there was Devlin, on the stand, looking at her. She looked right back until he turned away.

The district attorney was on his feet again. Polite, deferential. He asked Devlin a series of questions about his experience, about notable cases he had worked before. And then:

"Would you tell us please, Sergeant Devlin, what you found in the Malones' apartment on the morning of July fourteenth, nineteen sixty-five. In your own words."

Devlin took them through the details of that first day. His impressions of Ruth. "She was calm. Very calm. She wasn't crying at all. She was wearing makeup. A lot of makeup. Uh... revealing clothes. And she had her hair all fixed."

"Did your men search the apartment?"

"We did."

"And did you find anything of significance?"

"We found an empty box of pasta in the garbage, and..."

Scott was on his feet. "Objection, Your Honor. Pasta is not mentioned in the list of evidence found in the apartment."

The judge looked startled and turned to the district attorney, who frowned. There was a beat of silence, when no one seemed to know what to say.

"Approach the bench, please, counselors."

Ruth watched the men talking, Scott gesticulating at Devlin, still in the witness stand. Something had clearly gone wrong for the prosecution. Perhaps Devlin's evidence would be discredited. Perhaps this even meant that the charges would be dismissed.

But then the judge leaned forward and said something and both men nodded, Scott expressionless, the other reluctant. As they returned to their tables, the judge addressed the jury.

"Please disregard the prosecution's last question. The list of evidence removed from the apartment is . . . it seems to be incomplete."

She could feel the heat of Devlin's discomfort, had to force herself not to look at him.

"Continue, Mr. Hirsch."

"Thank you, Your Honor. Returning to my earlier question, Sergeant, did you find anything else of significance in the apartment on the morning of July fourteenth?"

"We found a number of empty liquor bottles in the trash."

Scott was on his feet again. "Objection! That has no bearing on the case."

"Overruled. Members of the jury, please disregard that interruption. Witness will answer. However, please make sure your line of questioning has a point, Mr. Hirsch."

"Of course. Thank you, Your Honor. Sergeant, other than the empty bottles, what state was the apartment in? Was it clean?"

"It was untidy. There was dust on some of the surfaces."

"I'd like to draw your attention to page four of your statement where you specifically mention the dust on the bureau in the children's bedroom."

"Yes, we found a film of dust on the bureau."

Ruth scribbled furiously and pushed the paper toward Scott. *I cleaned apt & BUREAU the day before!!*

He patted her arm, kept his eyes on Devlin.

"Gentlemen of the jury, there was a film of dust on the bureau. Please turn to Exhibit 18, the floor plan of the children's room, and note that the bureau was pushed up against the window. What was the significance of this, Sergeant? In your opinion?"

She remembered the silence and the thin, tired-looking man with the crumpled suit and the camera. She remembered the sprinkling of white dust on the bureau and Devlin's focused expression.

She heard Devlin's voice from that day. Low. Harsh.

"Make sure you get it all."

He said now: "The dust eliminated the possibility that the children left the room through the window. It would have been impossible for them to do so without touching the bureau and leaving marks in the dust."

"Objection! Witness is speculating." Scott again.

The judge removed his glasses and rubbed the bridge of his nose. "Overruled. Mr. Hirsch has asked the witness what his opinion is, and the witness has provided it."

"Thank you, Your Honor." She could hear the smirk in the DA's voice. "And what, in your opinion, Sergeant, was the implication of this?"

"That the children must have been taken out of their bedroom through the door. By someone who was inside the apartment. They cannot have left the room by themselves as the door was latched from the outside."

Ruth saw the white dust dancing, Devlin's eyes like embers in smoke. She saw the camera shutter clicking, again and again.

And suddenly she was struggling to get air into her lungs. As though a rope had been slipped around her neck.

On the second day, the photographs seemed even larger when she entered the courtroom. She couldn't stop looking at them, even when the judge arrived and the men around her began to talk about her children. About her.

The real Frankie and Cindy no longer existed; only these black-and-white cherubs with their bright frozen smiles. And even they didn't belong to her anymore—they belonged to the court, to the newspapers, to anyone with an opinion. They weren't Frankie and Cindy now—they were "the deceased," they were those to whom "death has occurred." As though death were just an idea that had come to them.

She closed her eyes for a moment against the tears that had risen, and then opened them and looked over at Frank, who was watching her. She imagined that something passed between them at that point. A shared memory of their babies.

Just before lunch, a Dr. Dunn was sworn in. He had gray hair, half-moon glasses, kind eyes. Hirsch took him through his credentials and experience, and then brought him to the findings of the autopsy he had carried out on Cindy. The doctor glanced at Ruth and she tried to swallow.

"From the temperature taken at the scene, it is possible to determine that she was killed approximately six to twelve hours before she was found."

Ruth felt a sudden splintering pain at her temples. The room was too hot.

"She was dressed in a cotton undershirt, a pair of yellow panties…"

She heard a low keening sound, ragged breathing.

"The cause of death was strangulation…"

She saw a length of cord. A strip of cloth. A pair of hands, fingers tightening.

She saw Cindy, purple-faced, terrified, struggling to breathe.

"Dr. Dunn, please tell the court what your findings were regarding the child's last meal."

"We found pasta, fruit, and vegetables in her stomach. Green vegetables. And oranges."

Hirsch gave Scott a flushed triumphant glance, and then turned to the jury.

"As you'll hear, gentlemen, this is inconsistent with the testimony of Mrs. Malone herself, who claims that she fed the children veal on the night they died."

"Dr. Dunn, how soon after the child digested the food was she killed?"

"Our findings in this case were consistent with a post-ingestion period of two hours, maximum."

Hirsch was still facing the jury.

"Two hours, gentlemen. *At the most.*"

He let those words sink in for a moment, then spun around and addressed the courtroom.

"And yet the accused said in her statement that she fed Frank Jr. and Cindy at seven p.m., that their meal was over by seven-thirty, and that she checked on them around midnight. According to Mrs. Malone, the children were alive and well almost five hours after they finished dinner."

There was another pause and it seemed to Ruth that the whole courtroom was holding its breath, waiting for his next line.

"If Mrs. Malone lied about the time at which she said she fed them dinner and the last time at which she said she saw them— and the evidence of Dr. Dunn here says that she *did* lie about one or both of these facts—we must ask ourselves: what other lies has she told?"

Ruth felt the rope around her own neck. Tightening.

After Dr. Dunn, Devlin was recalled. Hirsch held up a number of pages stapled together and turned to the judge.

"Let the record show that I am handing Sergeant Devlin a copy of Exhibit 34b. Sergeant, please identify this for the court."

Devlin flicked through the papers, bent to the microphone.

"It's a shift report written by Officer George Bresnick, dated July fifteenth, nineteen sixty-five."

"And why was Officer Bresnick asked to write this report?"

"He was on duty that day with his partner, Officer Johnson. They were instructed to follow Mr. and Mrs. Malone and to report on their observations."

"Thank you. Please read aloud the marked passages on pages three and four of the report."

"One fifty-one p.m.—Mr. and Mrs. Malone left their apartment. Mrs. Malone wore white dress and shoes, sunglasses, carried purse. Three reporters attempted to get her attention (*Daily News*, *Tribune*,

third unknown). Neither Mr. nor Mrs. Malone spoke to or acknowl-
edged them. Mr. and Mrs. Malone entered vehicle parked directly
in front of building, identified as Mr. Malone's car. Mr. Malone in
driver's seat. Drove east along 72nd Drive, north on 150th Street, and
then proceeded west along 72nd Road and turned onto Main Street.

"Two oh nine p.m.—vehicle parked on Main Street. Mrs.
Malone exited vehicle and entered store. Mr. Malone remained in
car and lit cigarette."

Scott: "Objection. These details are irrelevant."

Hirsch, quickly, smoothly: "I'm coming to the crux of it, Your
Honor."

The judge waved at Devlin to continue.

"Officers made decision not to pursue Mrs. Malone. Mr. Malone
waiting in car indicated her intention to return.

"At two forty-one p.m., Mrs. Malone emerged from store wearing a black dress and carrying bag with DEBONAIR DOLL on it in
silver lettering."

Devlin paused and raised his eyes.

"There's a note here—shall I read that?"

"Please do, Sergeant."

"Inquiry by Officer Bresnick July fifteenth established Debonair
Doll is a dress shop at sixty-one Main Street, Queens, New York,
one one three six seven. Proprietor Miss Dorothea Lister."

Devlin looked up again and Hirsch nodded at him to continue.

"Officer Johnson exited the patrol vehicle and proceeded in the
direction of Mr. Malone's car. His statement is attached."

Hirsch interrupted. "Officer Johnson's statement is Exhibit 34c.
Please read that to the court."

There was a soft rustle of paper as the jury scrambled to find the
next part of the story in their own copies.

"Mrs. Malone approached her husband's car at approximately
two forty-two p.m. on the afternoon of July fifteenth. As she drew
near, he leaned out of the window and called to her, 'Come on
honey, we need to hurry now.'

"I was near enough to hear her response which was given in a lower voice.

" 'I know that, Frank. You think I don't know that? If we're late, we're late. This was important. I have to look right, I have to—'

"At this point, the suspect stopped speaking and bent her head. I was unable to see her face clearly due to the dark glasses she was wearing.

"Mr. Malone opened his car door but she waved him away and got into the car on the passenger side. Mr. Malone started the engine and the car exited the parking lot and headed north. The car arrived at St. Michael's Church at approximately two fifty-four p.m., at which point surveillance of Officers Bresnick and Johnson ceased and that of Officers Schwartz and Goldstein at the funeral home took over."

"Thank you, Sergeant Devlin. To confirm, this report details the observed activities of Mrs. Malone on July fifteenth—that is, the day after the children disappeared and the day after the body of her daughter was found strangled?"

"Yes sir. That's correct."

"No further questions, Your Honor."

But none of that told how it was.

She stood in the hall, looking at her white dress in the mirror. Smoothing the skirt again and again, focusing on the cleanness of it, the unspoiled evenness. Smoothing away the memory of the day before: the dirt on her daughter's face. The stink. The terror.

Frank watched her from the doorway of the living room.

"Come on, honey. You look fine. We should go to church. It'll help."

A glimpse of her frightened face in the glass as she turned. Then she walked deliberately back down the hall, away from the front door, past Frank, past the closed door of the kids' room, into her own room. Her hands sweating, her heart pounding as she rummaged through her closet, pushing dress after dress aside, as she realized that she had nothing black to wear. That she would look all wrong. That she would look as wrong on the outside as she felt on the inside.

She hated black, has always hated black—it made her look tired, washed-out—but she had to look right for Cindy. She had to show her grief in the right way.

Pete had taken unpaid leave from the bookstore to be in court. He sat at the front of the public benches and watched Ruth watching the jury. She was very pale, with dark circles under her eyes. She was wearing a yellow dress and jacket, but the dress was tight and cut low in front. That sensuality was still there—restrained, muted, but apparent.

The jury was all male, all middle-aged, probably blue collar. Ruth looked at them and they looked right back at her. A row of hard faces. She wrote something on her notepad and pushed it toward Scott.

Pete wondered if she was asking the same question he had asked. *Why are there no women on the jury?*

Scott had told him that all the women who could have sat on this jury had been excused. This could have been for any number of reasons: maybe they were too busy. Maybe they just didn't want to get involved. Maybe they had children and homes to take care of, while their husbands sat here, judging Ruth.

Scott scrawled something back, his eyes on Hirsch, who was speaking to the jury. He sounded fierce now, staccato, like a bulldog barking.

"There's no room for sympathy in a case like this."

Ruth leaned in to Scott and whispered something. He bent to listen, still focusing on Hirsch, and her smallness next to him made her seem even more fragile.

Pete hoped she wouldn't guess the real reason, or worm it out of Scott. Every woman on the prospective jury panel had been released after they had stated they believed she was guilty.

He didn't want her to learn how it had been that morning in the packed hallways of the courthouse. The swiveling heads, the curious eyes, the pointing fingers. He didn't want her to know about the harsh voices, bristling with righteous anger, with condemnation.

"I heard she put her face on before she even called the cops."

"She's never shed a single tear for those poor children. Not a single one, and that's a fact."

"My sister's husband, his cousin knew them, she said they were the most beautiful kids you ever saw."

There were women on the public benches who were obsessed with the case, or with her. Women who'd taken three buses to be here, who'd slept in the corridor to ensure their place in line. Who were willing to miss meals, to sit for hours on hard benches and listen to legal arguments, who were willing to abandon their own children to neighbors and friends—all to bear witness to Ruth.

As Scott had told Pete earlier, Ruth had already been judged and pronounced guilty in the beauty parlors, the backyards, and the kitchens of Queens. Everything depended on whether the jury would feel the same way.

The next few days were taken up with cross-examination of the medical experts. By the end of the second afternoon, Pete's head was aching from trying to make sense of long scientific words he'd never heard before. When the court adjourned for the day, he walked outside and took a long sweet breath of fresh air. Instead of heading straight home, he looked over to the far side of the parking lot, shading his eyes, trying to see if there was somewhere nearby he could get a soda or a sandwich.

And then he noticed them: four men walking in a tight line toward an unremarkable car. Hirsch, his assistant, and a short paunchy guy he'd seen around the courthouse—and between them, stumbling like a man too drunk or too tired to hold himself up: Johnny Salcito.

He watched them for a moment as Salcito climbed unsteadily into the back of the car, Hirsch's assistant with him. Hirsch shut the door behind them and walked to the back of the car to speak to the short guy. They shook hands, the man got into the driver's seat, and the car pulled away. Hirsch lit a cigarette and walked back toward the courthouse.

Pete stared after the car, pursed his lips, then shrugged and turned away. It would be another twenty-four hours before he understood the significance of Salcito being driven away by the prosecution team.

The witness stand was fifty paces from where Johnny was sitting, down the center aisle of the courtroom, past the defense table, left past the judge.

He kept his eyes fixed straight ahead. Ruth kept a smile pasted on her face, kept looking at him, kept hoping he'd turn around and wink.

Scott had told her that Johnny's evidence could save her. So she needed him to do this right. She needed him to look at her and reassure her that it was going to be okay.

He reached the witness stand, took the oath. He answered Scott's questions as he'd said he would. He'd spoken to Ruth on the night of July thirteenth. She had seemed normal. Everything was as usual.

She had expected to feel relief when he said that, but his voice was too quiet, his demeanor subdued. He looked like a condemned man. As Hirsch rose to cross-examine, she saw the smirk on his face and clutched Scott's arm. Whispered: "What's wrong? What's happening?"

Scott didn't answer, just shook his head. A tic started up in his eyelid.

It'll be okay. Johnny loves me. He needs me.

Hirsch smiled at Johnny as though they were old friends, and began to ask him about his relationship with her.

"How many nights would you say you spent with the defendant? In total."

"Well, it's difficult to say."

"Fifty? A hundred?"

"More than fifty."

"And where did you meet with her?"

"I'm not sure what…"

"You took her to dinner? You went to shows together?"

"Yes."

"And you stayed in motels?"

"Yes."

"Mr. Salcito, did the defendant ever visit your home?"

"She…yes."

"And where was your wife on these occasions, Mr. Salcito? When Mrs. Malone came to your home?"

Johnny asked for a glass of water, and a bailiff poured one, reached up to hand it to him. He took a sip, wiped his mouth and then his brow.

"My wife was…she was away."

"And the defendant, was she still living with her husband at the time?"

"Yes. At first."

Murmured voices behind her, rising and falling. Red heat in her face. The line of pain in her palms where her nails pushed into the skin.

She was suddenly aware of Frank on the other side of the room. He didn't need to hear this.

Hirsch led Johnny through events in the weeks leading up to the children's disappearance.

"One night, maybe two months before, we went to a steak restaurant on Main Street and Jewel. She was mad that night. Real mad."

"The defendant was angry?"

"Yeah. Real angry. Frank wanted custody of the kids. She kept saying she wouldn't let him have them. She said she wasn't going to let anyone take her kids."

Johnny took another drink of water.

"What else did the defendant say, Mr. Salcito?"

"Um...she said..."

"Can you speak up, please? For the jury."

"Sorry. She—Ruth—she said that she didn't want Frank to have the children. Then she said she would rather see the children dead than let Frank have them."

Ruth straightened up, her eyes wide. Shook her head, hard.

Muttered, "No. I didn't mean...*No*."

Scott patted her arm. Whispered, "It's okay. It's okay. We can deal with this."

But Hirsch wasn't done.

"Let's move to the night the children disappeared. You spoke to the defendant that night, is that correct?"

"Yes sir."

"You've given testimony that you spoke to her at around midnight. That you asked her to join you at the bar you were in."

"That's right."

"Is that the only time you called the defendant that night?"

"No. I called her again a couple of hours later."

"What time would that have been?"

"Uh...around two a.m."

"And what did you say to her then?"

"Well, nothing. I didn't speak to her. I called and there was no answer."

"You called her at two a.m. and"—here Hirsch fixed the jury with a stare—"and she didn't answer."

Ruth was scribbling furiously. *Took dog for walk, fell asleep. In my statement!* Scott nodded, patted her arm again.

Hirsch continued.

"Let's turn now to the night of April fifth, nineteen sixty-six. Where were you that night, Mr. Salcito?"

Johnny bent his head.

"I was at the Kings Motel. On the Van Wyck Expressway."

Ruth felt an ache in her chest. That had been private. It had meant something, at the time. It had been for the two of them, not for an entire courtroom to hear.

"Nice and loud, please. Were you there alone?"

"No sir."

"Will you tell the court who you were with?"

He lifted his head and Ruth had a moment of hope—if he would only look at her!—but he raised his gaze to Hirsch.

"I was with the defendant, Mrs. Malone."

"And will you tell the court, in your own words, what happened that night?"

Johnny took a breath, dropped his gaze again.

"We had dinner. We had been drinking. And then she—Ruth—started crying. She kept crying. Then she said there was no reason for the kids to be dead. That there was no reason for them to be killed.

"I asked her what she meant, and she kept crying. Then she said 'They must understand. They know it's for the best.'"

The same words she'd used to him when he'd been crying and humiliated in Scott's office. When she'd told him that she wouldn't be able to see him for a while.

Why was he saying these things, using her own words against her? Was he punishing her for pushing him away?

"A little louder again, Mr. Salcito."

"Yes sir."

"The defendant said, 'They must understand. They know it's for the best.' And you understood her to be referring to the children."

"Yes sir."

"What did you say to that?"

"Uh . . . well, I said, 'Frankie and Cindy are dead. All we can do for them now is help the cops find who did it.'"

"And what did she say?"

"She kept repeating, 'They will understand, they will know it was for the best.' On and on, several times."

His voice grew in strength, as though the significance of what he was saying was giving him courage. She sat straight, shoulders tense and aching, mouth dry.

"And then...and then she said to me, "Johnny, forgive me. I killed them.""

The room exploded in gasps, shouts, the judge banging his gavel again and again.

And then, finally, Johnny looked at her, just for a moment, and his jaw was set and his eyes were dead.

Ruth stood with her fists clenched, her eyes fixed on the man on the witness stand, and she screamed as though they were the only two people in the room.

"Johnny! How could you? It isn't true! You know it isn't true! Johnny—you of all people! You said you loved me! How could you?"

18

The judge called for a recess and Pete made his unsteady way into the hallway. Paced the corridor. Picked at his cuticles. Wondered what the hell he could do for her.

His mouth was dry and there was a line for the water fountain, so he found another one down the hall. As he was drinking, he became aware of two men walking by, heads bent, voices low. One of them had Devlin's slow parade-ground tread.

Pete turned the water off and brought his handkerchief up to his face. Remained stooped over as though he was just wiping his mouth.

He heard "...just about finished. And by tomorrow she will be."

And Quinn's nervous tone. "Tomorrow, sir?"

"Tomorrow, Lena Gobek will be giving her testimony."

He waited until they'd turned a corner and then he stood and tried to think about where he'd heard that name before. It took him ten minutes and a walk around the block, but he got there. He left a note with the bailiff for Scott, asking him to call him that night, and then he got in his car.

At home, he pulled out his old files and dug through them until he found her. He read back through his notes and then played the beginning of the interview he'd recorded with her. Lena Gobek was just a neighbor. She was no one.

Then he began to remember, and let the tape play all the way through.

He remembered a small apartment, the curtains closed against the sun. Lace tablecloths, a china cabinet, a doll in an old-fashioned costume on a chair in the corner.

He remembered a well-built woman with a thick Polish accent. Dyed red hair, a shapeless dress, swollen feet in slippers. She'd offered him tea and pressed slices of dry seed cake on him, which had stuck to the roof of his mouth.

She'd talked about her husband a lot. How they'd met just after the war when he came into her father's restaurant.

"His dark wavy hair, his serious eyes. He was just like Gregory Peck."

She'd described how her husband had courted her and how romantic he was. Had smiled as she said this. Touched her throat and traced her fingers along her collarbone.

"The wedding was wonderful, Mr. Wonicke. Here is my album—see? My dress. The cake. That's Mama with my sister. And the meal at my father's restaurant after the church was beautiful. Perhaps not quite what it would have been before the war, but then nothing was the same. Everyone was making the best of things: that's what they said on the radio. Paul and I were no different from Joan Fontaine and William Dozier, not really. And we had champagne—oh, that was exciting! Papa managed that. I never had champagne before—I'd only seen it in movies. I felt like Myrna Loy.

"And then we moved here, to this apartment. That was in September. September, 1946. And Paul had his job, and I made us a home. And we waited for children, but God decided not to bless us with little ones, and we had to make our peace with His decision. It was not an easy time. Not easy.

"But we made the best of things. You have to. I went out and got a job. A sales position at Saks. You know Saks? On Fifth Avenue? Oh, a wonderful job. Elegant people, rich people. Ladies who bought beautiful clothes, jewelry. Luggage as soft as skin. They carried little dogs, little curly dogs with jeweled collars, and they had beautiful expensive handbags and shoes. They charged hundreds of dollars to their husbands' accounts the way I would buy milk at the corner store. No one believed me when I told them. Paul laughed and made jokes about having a charge account at the bodega, but no one believed me when I told them how much these ladies would spend.

"I would stand behind the counter and they would give me the things they wished to buy: lipsticks, bracelets, wallets. The bigger things would be delivered or they would send a car to fetch them. I would wrap their cosmetics and their jewelry in pretty tissue paper and they would reach out to take them from me, and I would think—I remember thinking—that even their arms were beautiful. Gold wristwatches and silk blouses. The wool—thick. Like silk. I have forgotten...ah yes, cashmere. The cashmere coats. So soft. Everything so soft. They all had long polished nails, diamond rings, emeralds, rubies. Beautiful. Their hands were...oh, the skin was like satin. They used hand cream and when I picked up the pen they had used to sign the receipts, I would smell it. Roses or violets. Lilies. Can you imagine a life that smells of roses and lilies, Mr. Wonicke?

"And it was funny, all the time that I was working there and helping these ladies to buy things, I knew I did not belong behind that counter. I came to this country when I was fourteen years old and I know well how it is here. This is the Land of the Free. Opportunities. Work hard, get ahead. I worked hard, and I know I could have been just like those women. But I had bad luck. Such bad luck. God called our babies to Him before they even opened their eyes. Five babies, in nine years. And so I lost my figure, of course. And if I had kept it, I could have been just like those ladies. People always tell me I could have been pretty.

"But I had to give up my job. All those pregnancies made me ill. And I would get terrible headaches. Terrible. So I left in 1960 and now I spend my afternoons with my family—my niece had twins last year, two boys and now another on the way—and at the movie theater. I like the old films best—Clark Gable and Lana Turner, or...I saw last week, Gene Tierney and George Sanders. Beautiful. Magical. And so sad.

"And living in New York, I sometimes see the movie stars in real life. When we came here, it wasn't like this—the film people all lived in California. In Los Angeles. But now they begin to move here, to New York. I saw a man on the subway last month— he looked familiar, I went closer—Gary Cooper! Gary Cooper, getting on at Canal Street on a Tuesday morning. But my sister wouldn't believe me when I told her!

"Oh, New York...things are always happening in New York. I write to my cousin Sonja in Frombork—a small town, very small— and I tell her all my news. I was in the bakery last month and a man came in and demanded all the money in the register! I was so frightened, I had to sit with my friend Mrs. Roberts who lives nearby before I could go home. Good neighbors are so important, are they not?

"Yes, I know Mrs. Malone. Of course. I know all my neighbors. But I know her well. We met when I was behind her in the checkout line. I remember Mrs. Malone because of her hair. She has beautiful hair—red with that golden shine. I told my friend about it afterward and she said it was called strawberry blond. Did you ever hear of such a thing! Everyone knows strawberries are not blond! I think that Edith is having a joke with me.

"So yes, she had red hair with gold. She was very small. Skinny. No meat on her! Men always prefer a woman with a real figure, do they not?

"I remember the day I first saw her, she was wearing a blouse and trousers with white heels. Tight trousers. She was humming to herself, tapping her foot.

"And the next week I saw her in the street and of course I nodded when I recognized her, but she kept walking. At first I was a little shocked—people can be rude—but then I saw her going into Dolly's Beauty Parlor and I realized she must be thinking about her appointment and so she did not see me. Then I remembered I need to get my own hair cut and so I went in, and there she was, with her hand flat on the table and her nails being filed and sharpened. She was laughing and talking with a fat lady who sat in the next chair.

"And so it was easy to ask Dolly, the owner, to make my hair the same color. I think she used the wrong dye because it is not quite the same, but it is pretty, yes? Cheerful.

"And then I noticed Mrs. Malone often. We passed on the street and I would smile and nod but she never spoke to me. We went to the same supermarket sometimes.

"I don't like to say it, but I began to notice other things. Not nice things. Her blouses—always open a little too far. Her trousers, very tight. A lot of makeup. And no ring on this finger. No husband.

"One morning I see the children, her children, playing on the grass in front of my building. I ask the little boy where his mother is and he tells me she is in bed. In bed! At nine in the morning! It is not right. Not right! I take the children by the hand and bring them inside, give them milk. And then I take them home and Mrs. Malone, she says not one word of thanks. Not one.

"I was so polite, always smiled, always said good morning. And from this lady, nothing. Nothing. To tell the truth, Mr. Wonicke, each time it was like a slap in the face."

Scott called and Pete told him what he'd overheard from Devlin: that Lena Gobek's statement would finish Ruth. And then he told him what he'd remembered about Mrs. Gobek herself.

There was a pause and Pete asked him, "Is this a problem? Is this Mrs. Gobek a problem?"

Scott sighed and when he spoke again, his voice sounded tired. A little cracked.

"Maybe. But let's wait and see what she says tomorrow. And how she comes across. What did you think of her when you interviewed her?"

"She was … she was just a neighbor. An old lady. A little lonely. She liked to talk. She liked telling stories."

Scott grunted. "A little old lady who tells stories. Let's hope that's all she is."

Pete watched Mrs. Gobek walk from her seat to the witness stand. It seemed to take forever. Finally she climbed the steps and took the oath, then settled herself into the small chair, her round softness emphasizing the stark corners of the wooden surround.

She held her handbag on her wide flowered lap, protecting herself from the men who were watching her. Her hands were curled around the handle, skin taut, as though she was ready for a fight.

Pete looked over at Ruth and saw only neutral interest. Maybe a little curiosity. She was more focused on Lou Gallagher. She kept glancing at Lou until he looked up, and then she smiled nervously. Only when he smiled back did she seem to relax.

Pete thought of her face in the diner when Beckman told her he was leaving. He thought of her desolate wails when Salcito betrayed her in this courtroom. Lou Gallagher was all she had left.

Hirsch adjusted his tie, stood up, cleared his throat. He let his eyes roam over the room before he turned to face the jury. He was enjoying this, Pete realized. He'd been waiting for this moment.

With his back to the witness stand, he began.

"Will you please state your name and address for the record?"

Mrs. Gobek frowned. Pressed her fingertips to her broad chest and looked around.

"Me?"

Hirsch turned to face her, half-hiding his impatience under a smooth smile. He nodded and her brow cleared. She smiled back at him.

"My name is Helena Elzbieta Gobek. My maiden name was Wachowiak. I was born in Elblag, in Poland, on the ninth of January, 1917. My address is forty-four 72nd Road, Queens, New York."

She spoke in a tight little rhythm, unconsciously tapping her hand on her knee. And as she listed the details of her life, a breath of laughter rippled through the courtroom. Pete noticed her raise her head to feel it, noticed her take pleasure in her audience, and smile around the room. Then she leaned forward over her handbag, waiting for the next question.

"How long have you lived at that address, Mrs. Gobek?"

"My husband and I have lived there since September 1946. Since we married. That will be twenty-one years this year."

"Would it be fair to say, then, that you know the neighborhood well?"

She cocked her head, said seriously, "I do not know if it would be fair, Mr. Hirsch. But it is true to say that. It is true that I know the neighborhood."

Another ripple of laughter, a little louder this time. Mrs. Gobek lifted her eyes to the public benches. Her face flushed and she beamed.

"And the defendant. How long have you known Mrs. Malone?"

Lena Gobek looked at Ruth for the first time that day and her face was suddenly hard.

"I have known Mrs. Malone for three or four years."

Ruth's whisper was loud enough to make the judge frown at her.

"I don't know that woman!"

Scott shushed her. Rested his hand on her wrist.

Hirsch turned to face the jury again and spoke slowly. Emphatically.

"Three or four years. Since well before the children were murdered."

He swung back to face Mrs. Gobek.

"How did you meet Mrs. Malone?"

"We met at the beauty parlor on the corner of Ascan and Queens Boulevard. Mrs. Malone goes there once a week for her hair, her nails. I began to go there too."

Pete looked at Ruth, who was staring at Lena Gobek.

"That would be Dolly's Parlor at three sixty-eight Queens Boulevard?"

Mrs. Gobek nodded.

"Please speak up for the court reporter, Mrs. Gobek."

She looked toward the thin blond girl at the side of the witness stand, fingers flying over the keys of her stenotype machine. Leaned forward and said carefully, "Yes, Dolly's Parlor."

"And when was that? When did you start going to Dolly's?"

"In nineteen sixty-three. At the end of October."

"How can you be so sure of the date, Mrs. Gobek?"

"I go every week. And I was there for the third or maybe fourth time when Mr. Kennedy was shot. Everyone remembers where they were that day. The whole place was talking about poor Mrs. Kennedy. The blood on her dress. About the man who shot the president from the window."

"Did you ever meet Mrs. Malone anywhere other than the beauty parlor?"

"Yes, we met in the grocery store. We both did our shopping on Tuesday and Friday afternoons. I often saw her there and said hello."

Ruth looked startled. She frowned and shook her head.

"Anywhere else?"

"Oh yes. All around the neighborhood. I would see her in the street, or sometimes in the park. Mostly with her children. Very pretty children. Polite."

"You recognized the children?"

Mrs. Gobek looked over at the blown-up photographs of the children on the wall, and the jury followed her gaze.

"Yes. I know little Frankie and his sister. Mrs. Malone always called her Cin."

Pete's eyes flickered to Ruth's white face.

Hirsch turned back to the jury.

"So you knew Mrs. Malone well, Mrs. Gobek? You got to know her over a period of years?"

"Oh yes. Certainly. I did."

"Good. Thank you. Let's turn now to the night of July thirteenth, nineteen sixty-five. Please tell the court what you remember about that night. In your own words."

Pete watched her settling herself in the chair. Surely she must have read so many words about this case in the newspapers by now, heard so many from the mouths of her family and neighbors, from strangers. How could she find her own?

Her gaze slid from Hirsch to the jury. The judge. Hirsch again.

He nodded, and she began, tentatively at first.

"It was hot that night. Very hot. I could not sleep so I got up to . . . to visit the bathroom. And to get some water."

"And then what happened?"

Hirsch was leading her gently but Pete could hear impatience in his voice. He wanted her to get to the meat of it. His mouth was almost watering.

"I took my glass into the living room and sat by the window. I was not tired. I thought that I would read until I was ready to sleep. Then I remembered that I left my book in the bedroom and I did not want to get it and wake Paul. He had a cold, he was tired."

It was the detail that made it real. Pete looked at the faces of the jury and saw that they were in that dark apartment with her.

"So what did you do, Mrs. Gobek?"

"I was in my chair by the window. The window was open and there was a breeze."

"Which way did your window face?"

"It looked out onto Main Street."

"What time was this?"

"I looked at the clock when I got up and it was almost two. At first it was quiet, and then I heard voices. So perhaps fifteen or twenty minutes after two."

"How many voices did you hear, Mrs. Gobek?"

"At first I could not tell. And then they came closer. There were two of them. A man and a woman."

"Could you hear what they were saying?"

"No. Not then. They were coming toward me. Under the street-light. I could not hear what they were saying, but I heard her heels."

Her eyes went to Ruth.

"She always wore heels."

Scott was on his feet. "Objection!"

The judge was shaking his head before Scott had even spoken.

"Sustained. The jury will ignore Mrs. Gobek's last remark. Mrs. Gobek, please confine your answers to what happened on that particular night."

She flushed. Bowed her head.

"Yes sir."

Looked up at Hirsch.

"I heard her heels that night. And I could hear voices."

"So you heard the voices of two people. Did they come into view? Did you see them?"

She nodded vigorously. "Oh yes. I saw them on the other side of the street. Under the streetlight. Very clear."

"Can you describe what you saw?"

"A woman. She was wearing trousers. Her hair was very bright under the streetlamp. And she was carrying the children."

"Both of them?"

Mrs. Gobek looked over at Ruth. At her slight frame.

"She was carrying the little girl who was...perhaps the child was asleep. And pulling the little boy by the hand. The man was walking ahead of her."

Pete thought again of the newspaper reports he'd read. The accounts he'd written himself. All of these details had been reported in the press.

Hirsch faced the jury.

"On the night of July thirteenth, you saw a woman walking down the street with a man and two children? Is that what you're saying, Mrs. Gobek?"

"Yes. Yes, it is what I am saying. It is what I saw."

"What did they do then?"

"She stopped and she..." She brought her arms up, cradling air. "She moved the child on her shoulder. As though the little girl was heavy. She let go of the little boy and he ran ahead to the man. Then the man came back and took the child from the woman. He walked to a car that was parked the wrong way on the street. He opened the back door of the car and he threw the child into the backseat.

"She ran over and she said, 'Don't do that to her.' And he looked at her and said, 'Now you're sorry?' And he said something else I could not hear. And she said, 'Don't say that. Don't say that.' Like that. Twice, like that."

Ruth's face was frozen. Her eyes wide, desperate. Pete glanced over at Frank Malone, who sat hunched over, staring down at his hands.

"The little boy got into the backseat of the car. I tried to close the window and it squeaked and she said something to the man. They both looked up so I moved behind the drape. I heard the engine start and when I looked out again, I saw the car turn around and drive away."

"Mrs. Gobek, I want you to think very carefully before you answer my next question."

He paused and the whole courtroom waited. The silence was absolute.

Hirsch said, "I'm sure you don't need me to explain that the balance of this entire proceeding may depend on your answer."

Pete realized he was holding his breath.

"Can you recognize either of the people you saw that night—either the man or the woman—in this court?"

This time there was no pause, no tense silence. She was nodding before Hirsch had even finished the question.

"It was that lady there. Her. Her," and the plump white hand rose from its grip on the handle of her bag. She pointed at Ruth.

Ruth's response was a howl.

"You liar! You liar! You swore to tell the truth! You don't know what the truth is!"

Her face was flushed and furious. She half-stood, Scott holding her arm, pulling her back into her seat.

A murmur arose around the courtroom and the judge banged his gavel two, three times. Gradually the room fell quiet and Hirsch asked again, "Was it Mrs. Malone that you saw that night?"

"Yes. Absolutely it was."

Ruth was out of her seat again, shrieking. "It wasn't me! It wasn't me!"

This time Pete could hear the terror beneath her anger, rising above Scott's shushing and the swelling wave of voices, and even above the judge's gavel as he called for order.

"I've never met this woman! I don't know her! She doesn't know me. *She doesn't know me!*"

Eventually Scott forced Ruth to sit back down and the judge made himself heard.

"One more outburst like that, Mrs. Malone, and I'll have you removed from the courtroom. Counselor, control your client."

Scott turned to her, put his arm around her. Pete saw shock in his face.

Hirsch smiled at the judge and said, "Just a few more questions, Your Honor."

He waited another moment, facing Ruth as though studying her. The members of the jury followed his gaze.

There was a bright spot of color on each cheek. Hirsch wanted the jury to see her anger, Pete realized. He wanted them to be able to imagine her raging and out of control.

"Mrs. Gobek, the events you've described took place on the night of July thirteenth, nineteen sixty-five, is that correct?"

She nodded, puzzled, and then remembered and leaned toward the stenographer again.

"That is correct."

"I believe the police interviewed you on August sixth, just over three weeks after the children went missing. Is that also correct?"

"Yes sir."

"And yet at that first interview, you didn't mention any of this. Not waking in the night, nor sitting at the window, nor what you saw on the street."

She looked flustered.

"Could you tell the court why that was? Why you didn't mention any of this until you wrote to the police a full four months after the crime took place?"

Pete stared at Mrs. Gobek. At her shapeless dress, her dyed hair. And realized: she was the final piece of the puzzle. It was her statement that had finally given Devlin what he needed to arrest Ruth.

Ruth was frowning, leaning forward in her chair, but Scott looked almost resigned, as he listened to Hirsch anticipate the defense's points before he could make them.

Mrs. Gobek threaded her fingers through the chain of the crucifix she wore around her neck and looked down.

"Well, it was my husband."

"Your husband told you not to talk to the police?"

"Yes. I said I wanted to speak up, but he said not to get involved. That the police knew their job and they didn't need me. And that if what I said was true, then someone else would have seen it too. He said, let them report it."

Hirsch leaned against the witness stand, almost casually, and grinned at the jury. A couple of them smiled back.

"Your husband was reluctant to let you come forward. Understandably so. But what happened, Mrs. Gobek, to make you change your mind?"

"I read in the newspaper about the case. About the police, about how they have made no arrest. I realize that they do not know. That no one else has seen what I have seen."

She lifted her chin.

"I realize—I tell my husband: I am the only one who has seen this lady, Mrs. Malone, with her children on the night they were murdered."

Her gaze swept the jury, the public benches, then came to rest on Ruth. Her lip curled.

Hirsch stood back and let her deliver her last line without interruption.

"I realize that I am the only one who can help them catch this killer."

Hirsch smiled at her.

"Thank you, Mrs. Gobek. Please remain seated."

He walked away from her, winked at Scott, and said clearly, "Your witness, Counselor."

Scott rose from the table. He looked exhausted.

"Mrs. Gobek, the people you saw from your window that night—were they speaking loudly? Were they shouting?"

"No, they were speaking in normal voices."

"And how far from your window were they? When they were under the streetlight, for example?"

She frowned. "Well, I do not know exactly."

He waved his hand. "Were they, for example, farther than I am from you now? Farther than you are from the jury? From that window?"

She looked around her for a long moment and pointed to the public door of the courtroom.

"I would say they were that far."

Scott followed her gaze. "Thank you, Mrs. Gobek. So about forty feet."

She shrugged.

"I would now like to show you Exhibit 16a, a plan of the block where Mrs. Malone's apartment is located."

The bailiff handed her a sheet of paper with a diagram printed on it, and the jury scrabbled to find their own copies.

"Mrs. Malone's apartment is marked with a cross. Can you see that on your copy, Mrs. Gobek?"

She studied the piece of paper and nodded. "Yes. I can see it."

"And your own apartment is marked with a blue cross. Would you confirm for us that this is your apartment?"

She nodded again. "Yes. Yes, that is our apartment."

Scott reached in his breast pocket for something and walked toward her, arm outstretched.

"And now I would like you to take this pen and mark where you think those people were on the night of July thirteenth."

He handed her the pen and waited. She looked at Hirsch, who nodded.

Perhaps encouraged by this, she uncapped the pen and made a mark on the card. Scott took the pen and paper from her, and held the latter up.

"Will the court note that Mrs. Gobek has placed a mark on the plan that is *almost two hundred feet* from her window, according to the scale given on the card."

He handed the piece of paper to the nearest member of the jury and they passed it down the row.

Scott turned back to his witness.

"Two hundred feet, Mrs. Gobek."

Pete leaned back in his seat. Surely this would unsettle her.

But she just looked at Scott and said nothing.

"That's quite a distance to recognize someone and to hear their conversation."

She remained silent.

"You have stated that they were speaking at a normal volume. You are claiming that from two hundred feet, you heard them talking in normal tones?"

Her face flushed. "I do not claim. I did hear. And that is normal: when my friend Mrs. Ciszek calls to me from her apartment and asks do I want anything from the store, I hear her from my apartment."

There was a low ripple of laughter, the tension easing a little.

Scott asked, "Where does your friend Mrs. Ciszek live?"

The bailiff passed back the paper and pen, and Mrs. Gobek made another mark.

"Will the record note that Mrs. Gobek has indicated an apartment approximately one hundred and eighty feet from hers."

Again, the piece of paper was handed to the jury. They seemed to have little interest in it this time: every gaze was fixed on Mrs. Gobek.

"If your friend speaks to you—in a normal voice..."

Mrs. Gobek nodded. "Yes. Yes. A normal voice."

"If your friend speaks to you in a normal voice, and you are in your apartment, you can hear her from one hundred and eighty feet away?"

He managed to make his tone incredulous, but this only seemed to provoke her. She leaned forward into the microphone, her eyes fixed on Scott.

"Of course I can hear her. My hearing is perfect. My eyesight, perfect."

Scott looked at her for a long moment while Pete leaned forward, silently urging him to keep going. There must be something he could do, another angle he could push.

But Scott simply walked back to his seat, saying quietly, "No further questions, Your Honor."

Hirsch was on his feet before Scott had reached the defense table. As Mrs. Gobek struggled with the gate to the witness stand, Hirsch was there to help her down.

"How was I? How did I do?"

He took her arm. "Beautiful. It was beautiful."

And for a moment, her flushed and triumphant face was indeed beautiful. As the judge adjourned for the day and Ruth was taken down, Mrs. Gobek's smile was like a wash of sunlight in the dim courtroom.

19

That night Pete sat on the floor of his room, surrounded by piles of notes and interview transcripts. Was this how defeat came: in the shape of a plump woman with badly dyed hair, in the memory of a dim room, curtains closed against the sun?

Pete dug the heel of his hand into his brow. There had to be something he could do. If only he could find another witness. Someone to counter Mrs. Gobek's testimony.

For twenty-nine hours, he didn't sleep. He listened to all his interview tapes again. Dug through his notes and reread the transcripts. He went out and knocked on doors. He scoured neighborhood bars, diners, Laundromats for someone he'd somehow missed two years before. He asked questions, took insults on the chin, kept going.

But the few people who agreed to talk to him gave him nothing new. No one was awake that night. No one saw anything, no one heard anything, to stand up to Mrs. Gobek's account.

He went back to his apartment, looked over his notes. And around four in the morning, his hands lost their grip on whatever he was reading and he lost consciousness. He woke up five hours later, unrefreshed and dehydrated, ran a hand over his chin. He badly needed a shave.

And then he realized. *No one was awake that night. No one saw anything. No one heard anything.* And he knew what he needed to do.

He called Horowitz at the office.

"Wonicke? Jesus. Been a long time. How you doing?"

"Listen, can we meet? I need to talk to you. I need your help."

There was a pause and then Horowitz said, "Sure. Tony's?"

"No. Not Tony's. Somewhere private. Somewhere we can't be overheard."

Another pause, longer this time.

"You know the old Regal Cinema off Park Drive East? The place they're knocking down? I'll see you in the parking lot in an hour."

Pete washed quickly, shaved, put on a shirt with a cleanish collar. When he arrived, Horowitz was already there, leaning against the hood of his car, holding two paper cups of take-out coffee.

Pete took one, swallowed half of it in a single gulp. Shuddered.

"Thanks. I needed that."

Horowitz eyeballed him.

"You look like shit. What you been doing?"

Pete sighed, ran a hand through his still-damp hair.

"I was in court last week. The Malone case...things aren't going well."

"What do you mean you were in court? You ain't a reporter anymore—what were you doing there?"

Horowitz stood squarely and forced Pete to meet his eyes.

"The case isn't going well for who? What the fuck have you been doing? What's going on?"

Pete told himself not to look away.

"I went to see Mrs. Malone's attorney."

His face went pink. "What the fuck? Jesus, Wonicke..."

"I know, I know. Spare me the lecture. I wanted to help."

"You wanted to help? Help who? You practically begged me to meet Devlin. The meet was on the basis you'd give him a decent write-up. Suddenly you're fired from the paper, and now you're... what the fuck are you doing?"

Then Horowitz paused and his face changed.

"Oh, I get it. You're following your dick."

"I'm not...It's not like that."

"It never is. Every single time, it's different. When it happens to you, it's always Romeo and goddamn Juliet."

He sighed, looked away for a moment.

Then: "So what did you tell him, this attorney?"

"Not much he didn't already know."

A gull filled the silence with a scream.

"Then what are we doing here? Why did you call me?"

So Pete told him. He told him what he needed and he watched Horowitz's face change again and his hand tighten around his coffee cup.

All the way up until the moment Horowitz tried to walk away, Pete didn't know if he could do it.

Then he thought of Ruth. "I read about the Kaufman case."

Horowitz's eyes widened in shock. Pete swallowed, then pulled out his copies of the newspaper articles he'd found in the New York Public Library, just a month after the Malone murders. Spread them out on the hood of his car and watched Horowitz's gaze drop to them, watched him take them in, and then shrug and try to dismiss them.

"And? That was, what, ten years ago? What does that have to do with anything?"

"Almost ten years. The fall of fifty-seven."

"Ancient history. Why are you bringing this up now? The Kaufman case was straight down the line. Two dead guys. Open and shut. It was nothing like this."

Horowitz was talking too much.

Pete took a deep breath. "Yeah, that's what I thought at first. Guy comes under suspicion of killing his business partner. Not much of a headline. No proof it was even murder—the dead guy could have shot himself. But a nice neat suicide doesn't make a good story."

Pete took his time, drawing it out, hoping he wouldn't have to keep going, hoping Horowitz would interrupt and tell him it was okay, that he'd help him, that Pete didn't need to do this.

But Horowitz was silent.

"I couldn't find any cases you'd reported on since then that Devlin had also worked. I figured that had to mean something. So I dug around a little."

There was a pause. Pete could hear distant traffic noise. A gull screamed.

Then Horowitz cleared his throat. "This is bullshit, Wonicke. You're…"

"I read the testimony you gave in court."

Pete dropped his eyes to the clippings and licked his dry lips. This had to work. This was the end of the line—after this, he was out of ideas to help her.

"You said Kaufman confessed to murder when you were interviewing him, the day before he was arrested. Two months before he was stabbed in a prison riot, while he was waiting for a trial date. Unfortunate for Mr. Kaufman. But not for you, right? Because now it's a real story. And what a fucking story. Two murders. A confession. Both victims are white, middle-class, wealthy. This is big. Must've opened a lot of doors for you."

He talked faster, hoping Horowitz couldn't hear the tremor in his voice.

"You testified, in court, that you gave the interview tapes to Devlin. Only they disappeared somewhere between the evidence locker and the courtroom."

Horowitz looked away.

"Devlin said in court that the tapes were lost. A missing link in the chain of evidence meant a black mark on his record. Maybe even a pass when it came to reviewing promotions that year. But I don't think there ever were any tapes. Just the transcripts. Transcripts that you wrote. And if that had come out, it would have been the end of your career. The end of you."

Pete badly wanted a cigarette. Didn't dare light one in case Horowitz saw his unsteady hands.

"Devlin took the fall for you. That's what he's got on you. That's what you owe him for. It has to be—you've never worked together since. Was that your choice? Or his?"

Now Horowitz raised his head. "This is all your imagination, kid. You got no evidence. Nada."

Pete forced himself to look the other man dead in the eye. He had to get this out fast.

"The day before Kaufman was arrested, the day you claimed you interviewed him, was September twenty-seventh, nineteen fifty-seven. The date..." He pushed on. "The date is my evidence."

He took a final piece of his paper from his pocket and unfolded it. It was an obituary column, dated September twenty-eighth, nineteen fifty-seven.

"I found this in the library files as well."

Horowitz stared at it, then turned his head away. "I don't need to see that. I wrote the damn thing."

He took out his cigarettes. It took him four matches to light one.

"You know, that obituary was the hardest thing I ever wrote. I wrote it sitting by Claire's bed the night she passed."

Pete cleared his throat. "That was the twenty-seventh."

"Yeah. The nurses kept coming in. I kept asking them not to take her away. Not yet."

"Horowitz...I'm...I'm sorry."

Horowitz looked at him and said, "You know something? I really think you are."

Then he sighed. "This came out, it would finish me. Devlin too, maybe, after all this time."

Pete thought back to the night in McGuire's when he'd wondered how Horowitz had come to accept himself as the kind of man who lied.

And now he saw that after all, this kind of moral choice was just a question of figuring out what was most important, and keeping that front and center in your mind. It wasn't any kind of choice at all.

So he swallowed his pity and just nodded. And then he told him again what he needed.

Horowitz scrubbed a hand over his face.

"Okay. Jesus Christ. Okay, I'll help you. And then we're done. We're done and you don't ask me for nothing, ever again. And you don't mention this to no one. This conversation never happened."

He turned away, kicked viciously at the rough floor of the construction site, raised a cloud of white dust.

Through his teeth, "Jesus Christ. This fucking job…"

He balled up his cup and flung it away from him. Stared at the ground for a moment, and then turned back.

"There's a guy I know—he was an actor for a while. He needs money. He'll do it."

"How do you know him? Do you trust him?"

"He's… he was my wife's nephew. Bad apple."

He shook his head, blew out his cheeks.

"This is gonna cost you. You know that."

Pete pushed away thoughts of his mother. Focused on the check she'd sent him for his future.

"I got money."

Horowitz looked at him a while.

"I can't believe this. You sure you want to do this?"

"I have to do it. I have to help her."

Horowitz shook his head slowly.

"You poor bastard."

Then he sighed.

"How do you even know she's innocent?"

Pete forced himself to meet Horowitz's eyes.

"I don't."

Horowitz opened his mouth but Pete rushed on.

"I think she is. I hope she is. But she's… I don't want her to go to prison."

And then he looked down so he didn't have to see what was in the other man's face.

"Jesus, Wonicke. I hope you know what the fuck you're doing."

There was a long pause, and then Horowitz said, "Take it from me, you do this, there's no coming back from it. You won't be the same person you are now. Lies change everything."

He looked at Pete for a long moment.

"But I guess you've already changed."

There was a strained silence.

Then Horowitz said, "One more thing. I covered a lot of trials. Juries are unpredictable. You do this, and you might still lose. You told me that Charlie Devlin's spent his time on the stand making Mrs. Malone into the Whore of Babylon. The drinking. The makeup. The men."

"And?"

"Just think about it, is all I'm saying. You do this, you put everything you have, everything you are, on the line—you're still up against a bunch of people who think it's their God-given duty to do the right thing. They've had hours of Devlin making her out to be a woman with no morals, and now hours of this Mrs. Gobek telling them that she practically saw Mrs. Malone do it. You really think they'll believe the right thing to do is let the bad lady walk?"

Pete hated him. He fucking hated him for saying this.

"They won't have a choice. The evidence."

"Yeah, yeah, the evidence. It's not all about evidence and witness statements. Just think about it."

But there wasn't time to think about it. Ruth needed him.

Pete took down the phone number Horowitz gave him. He made a couple of calls. And on Monday morning, Scott called a new witness to the stand.

Ruth sat with her head propped on one hand, letting the words of the men around her wash over her. She looked at the photographs of Frankie and Cindy pinned to the board, remembered Dr. Dunn standing in front of them, giving his evidence.

She glanced over at Frank and saw that he was staring at the photographs too. To everyone else in the room, her children were merely bodies. Their skin and teeth, their clothes, the very strands of their hair and the contents of their stomachs—these were just props used to make a point.

But once upon a time, they had been her babies. Their babies. No matter how bad things had gotten between them, she and Frank had that together, at least.

She looked up at those gap-toothed smiles and longed to feel their softness, their wriggling warmth, just one more time. She saw them playing in the park as they had on that last day. They had bickered and giggled and shrieked, had eaten cereal and oranges and meatball subs. They had dropped crumbs and peel and stained their shirts and skin.

And now all of those memories had been reduced to cold specimen dishes, to typed reports, to flat testimonies of long words. To this room.

She closed her eyes, pushing out those thoughts of the courtroom. She didn't want these to become her last memories associated with the children.

Pete watched the tall figure amble toward the witness stand, take his seat, swear the oath. He swallowed down his nausea, focused.

"Please state your name for the record."

"Clyde Harrison."

"Mr. Harrison, please tell the court where you were on the night of July thirteenth, nineteen sixty-five."

"I was in Queens. I was staying in the apartment of a friend on 72nd Road, just off Main Street. With my wife and our kids."

He nodded toward a woman with short auburn hair sitting in the second row of the public benches. She blushed prettily.

"How old were your children at the time?"

"Well...Robert would have been just five—his birthday is in April. And Mary would have turned three in March."

Harrison's slick blond hair shone under the bright lights of the courtroom, and he grinned affably at Scott. It was the same way he'd smiled at Pete when they'd met in Kissena Park two days earlier. The same smile he'd given when Pete had handed over a thousand bucks of his father's insurance money in twenty-dollar bills.

"What were you doing at your friend's apartment that night, Mr. Harrison?"

"Well sir, it's like this. My wife and I had been having some trouble that summer. We were living in Garden City and I was working at the Ford factory. Long and short of it is that they made some cutbacks and I lost my job in April. There were a lot of men out of work back then and I couldn't find nothing else, and by July money was pretty tight. I called everyone I could think of, but there was nothing doing."

He took a sip of water. Adjusted his tie.

"Then I got a call from a friend of a friend who said he might have something for me. We couldn't pay another month on our apartment anyway, so we packed up and headed over to his place in Kew Gardens Hills. That was July twelfth. Figured we'd spend a few days with him and see about this job, and then we'd find a new place to live. Seemed like things might be looking up for us."

Hirsch got to his feet with the air of a man who shouldn't have to call attention to this sort of thing.

"Objection, Your Honor. None of this is relevant to the case."

Scott slid in smoothly. "Your Honor, there is a point to all of this. I'm establishing context to explain what Mr. Harrison and his family were doing in the neighborhood on the night of July thirteenth, nineteen sixty-five."

The judge hesitated, then nodded. "Very well. But please get to the point, Mr. Scott."

"Thank you. Go on, Mr. Harrison."

"Well, it didn't work out like we'd hoped. The job fell through and the guy didn't want us all staying in his apartment. Kathy and me were arguing—we had no money, no place to live, didn't know what to do. She wanted us to take the kids to her parents' place in Wayne

County till we got on our feet again, and I took that hard. A man wants to feel he can provide for his family without relying on charity."

Pete glanced over at the jury. Most looked sympathetic; one or two were nodding.

"Anyway, the next night, things... things came to a head."

"This would be the night of July thirteenth?"

"Yes sir. Ron—the guy we were staying with—he told us over dinner that we'd have to be gone the next morning. Said he was going on a trip. Well, I didn't believe him—I thought it was a story to get rid of us. Told him I thought it was a lousy thing to do, turning away a guy who needed help. Putting a man and his family on the street."

He sighed, ran a hand through his hair.

"Things got a little heated and I wound up saying that we'd leave there and then, that we wouldn't sleep another night under his roof. I got my pride."

Pete looked over at the jury again. More of them were nodding now.

This is going to work, Pete thought. He looked at Ruth, willing her to turn to him. He wanted to see her face when she realized that things were beginning to go her way.

This is going to work and it will all be worth it.

"My wife was crying. She went into the guest bedroom where we were all sleeping, and lay down on the bed. She said I should go back out and make my peace with him. I told her it was too late and... well, we had words. With all the noise, the kids woke up and Mary started crying too, and I just... I had to get out. So I took a long walk. To cool down. Then I came back and told Kathy to call her parents. Said we'd go and stay there after all. Seemed like we were fresh out of options.

"Ron had gone out by then, so Kathy and I had coffee, talked things over some more. I took a shower and then we got packed up. I loaded up the car while she got the kids ready, and then I came back to help her with them, and we left."

"Was the car parked in front of the apartment?"

"We hadn't been able to get a space there. I parked it on Main Street, just around the corner."

Pete saw Devlin lean forward in his seat, his face tense.

"What time was it when you left Ron's house, Mr. Harrison?"

"Well, we didn't eat dinner till around nine, and with everything that was going on . . . I was out for an hour, maybe more, so it was a little after two when we left. I took a quick look around the room to make sure we hadn't left anything behind and I noticed the clock. I remember thinking it would be awful late to wake Kathy's folks."

"So you and your wife took the children outside: were you carrying them?"

"My wife was carrying Mary—she was fast asleep. I started out carrying Robert, but he wanted to be with his momma. Guess he was still upset at all the fighting earlier. I let him down and he ran back and held her hand till we were almost at the car, and then he came and caught up with me again."

Pete listened, afraid that Harrison would slip up, that he'd get something wrong. It had taken Pete hours to come up with all this detail, to type it all out. The man who called himself Clyde Harrison had looked over the closely typed pages, shaken his head.

"Going to take me a while to learn all of this. I'll be earning that money all right."

Now Scott turned to face the jury.

"You heard from the previous witness, Mrs. Gobek, that she saw a man and a woman with two children on Main Street in the early morning of July fourteenth, nineteen sixty-five. She identified that woman as the defendant."

He looked back at Harrison.

"Now, Mr. Harrison, can you confirm for the jury that at that time, shortly after two a.m. on the morning of July fourteenth, *you* were on Main Street with your wife and your two young children?"

"Yes sir, I was."

Scott nodded at him, took a moment, then turned to the judge. "No further questions, Your Honor."

Pete glanced at Frank, who was frowning, like he didn't understand the significance of what Harrison was saying, and then looked over at Ruth. She was leaning forward, her hands clasped as though in prayer. He gazed at her profile, at the way her cheekbones gleamed through her skin.

Hirsch leapt to his feet, launched straight into battle.

"Mr. Harrison, the events you've described took place over eighteen months ago, yet you've given us an uncommonly detailed account of that night. You must have an excellent memory. An exceptional memory, even."

Harrison ducked his head and said, "Thank you, sir."

Pete wanted to applaud. But Hirsch wasn't through.

"How is it that you are able to remember the events of that one night back in the summer of nineteen sixty-five in such extraordinary detail?"

"Well sir, that was a desperate time for us. Not a time that's easy to forget. And that night was the worst of it. When Ron told us we had to leave...well, I've never felt so bad, not before nor since. Kathy would tell you, we hardly ever argue."

"I see."

Hirsch left a short pause and then went on, "And how is it that you've come forward now, just in the nick of time?"

"Well, we drove straight up to her folks' place that night and I guess the...uh...the case wasn't in the newspapers up there. And we didn't have a lot of time for reading news stories anyhow—Kathy had the kids, and I was going after every job I could. Leaving before dawn some days to wait in the employment lines. And when I wasn't looking for work, I was helping Kathy's dad around the house to pay for our keep. Then about five weeks later, I had a call from a buddy—his brother had work in a factory in Cleveland, he told me they were expanding, taking men on. I got on the next Greyhound, got myself fixed up with a job, and found us an apartment, and then my wife followed on with the kids. And since then ... well, I guess there's not been too much in the newspapers all the way out in Ohio 'bout a murder case in Queens."

"So how did you come to hear about it, Mr. Harrison?"

"We came back for a few days to visit my wife's parents, and I read about the trial in the paper on Friday. About the lady's testimony, what she saw from the window that night. Soon as I saw the dates, I realized what must've happened."

"What a happy coincidence."

Hirsch's tone was sour but he nodded toward the judge and said, "No more questions."

As Harrison left the witness stand, Pete felt light-headed with relief. He studied the jury. They looked thoughtful; one or two were making notes.

Ruth leaned over in her seat, talking to Scott in a low voice. She pointed at something on the legal pad in front of her, underlined it twice, then turned to Scott's assistant, talking animatedly, her eyes bright. Pete glanced over at Frank, who was watching Ruth. He looked anxious.

Hirsch was frowning, conferring with his team, thumbing through his papers and stabbing passages with his fingers.

And on the other side of the courtroom, Devlin looked furious.

Scott's closing statement lasted a little under two hours. As always, he was reasonable. Measured.

He dismissed Johnny Salcito as a man bent on revenge; Lena Gobek as a fantasist who wanted to draw attention to herself.

"Her astonishing claims about her superhuman hearing tell us that she prefers to create drama, to entertain, rather than to tell the truth."

He focused on attacking the prosecution's case and on the

testimony of Clyde Harrison, but talked very little about Ruth herself. Looking over at the jury, Pete wondered if this might be a mistake. And by the time Hirsch had finished the prosecution's summation, he was sure of it.

Hirsch stood, walked over to the jury box, and waited a moment to let the tension build.

"Gentlemen of the jury, the prosecution has established the following facts beyond any reasonable doubt: firstly that on the evening of July thirteenth, nineteen sixty-five, the defendant did strangle her son, Frank Jr., and her daughter, Cindy Marie; secondly that the defendant then attempted to cover up her actions by dumping the bodies of her children some distance from her apartment; and thirdly that the defendant may have had an accomplice who helped her move the bodies, but she is solely and entirely responsible for their deaths.

"You have heard from Mrs. Lena Gobek that she saw Mrs. Malone with the two children on the night in question. This evidence directly contradicts Mrs. Malone's own statement. But Lena Gobek has nothing to gain from lying. She came forward when her natural reticence meant that she would have preferred to remain anonymous, just another ordinary Queens housewife. She came forward because she believed she had a duty to stand up and tell the truth to this courtroom.

"You have heard testimony from Mr. Salcito about Mrs. Malone's character, about her attitude toward her children and toward motherhood. You have heard his sworn statement that she confessed to him that she murdered her children because she would rather see them dead than lose custody to their father."

Hirsch's voice rose.

"Mr. Salcito does not claim to be a hero. He has never pretended to be something he's not. But what he did was get up on that stand and tell the truth. He had nothing to gain from it and everything to lose—but he told the truth about his relationship with Mrs. Malone: not only to you gentlemen and to everyone in this court, but he told his wife and the rest of the world what happened between them. Telling the truth in this way, openly and sincerely, may have damaged his marriage. But we in this courtroom cannot fail to admire his honesty and his regard for the truth."

And then he came to Ruth.

He dug up all the garbage again: the liquor bottles found in the apartment; the number of male friends she'd had; the way she'd shopped for a new dress the day after she discovered the children were missing. The day after Cindy's body was found.

As Pete listened to Hirsch's version of Ruth's story, he felt his face flush, felt the tension in his jaw. He glanced at her and saw her head was bowed, as though in supplication. He felt a fullness in his throat and swallowed, forced his attention back to Hirsch, who was winding down.

"Gentlemen of the jury, I say to you now that you must find the defendant guilty as charged. The murder of two young children, by the one person they should have been able to trust absolutely, is the most monstrous crime there is. Frankie and little Cindy"—here his gaze went to the blown-up photographs of the children that had presided over the courtroom since the first day, and he raised his arm to them—"are calling out for justice."

He let his arm fall slowly and his expression became earnest, almost noble, as he faced the jury.

"Please, gentlemen. Don't ignore the cries of those poor children."

Once the judge had turned the case over to the jury and they had filed out to begin their deliberations, Pete hung around the courtroom for another couple of hours. Eventually, the bailiff came back with the news that the jury wasn't going to reach a verdict anytime soon and was retiring for the night. He walked outside and stretched, working out the kinks in his shoulders, tasting the cool evening air.

He got in his car but didn't feel much like going home. He rolled down the windows and just drove for a while. Thinking about Ruth. Wondering how she was feeling. Thinking about Scott and his defeated expression.

Pete found himself turning toward the Malones' old neighborhood and decided he may as well go on to 72nd Drive. He parked—and then he noticed there was a light on in the Malones' apartment. A shadow moved behind the blind.

Adrenaline hit him like a wave of cold water and he felt his heart pounding. Then he made himself take a shuddering breath.

Stupid.

It was just a neighbor, checking everything was okay. Or maybe Frank had sublet it.

There were no ghosts.

Yet as he got out of the car and forced himself to walk up the path, fear crawled up his back and down his dry throat.

He took another breath and tried to steady his heart, straightened up and stuck his hands into his pockets, needing the hot comfort of his fists, knowing that any watching eyes wouldn't be able to see his hands shake.

The front door was unlocked, and the apartment door ajar. As though whatever was in there knew he was coming.

He tapped the door and watched it swing slowly away from him into a long black yawn. And then he heard the awful mechanical laughter of a children's wind-up toy.

He crept toward the noise and when he reached the doorway of the room and saw a hunched shape low against the wall, he heard a rushing in his ears and thought he would faint.

Then his eyes adjusted to the shadows and he realized who was sitting there. On the floor between the twin beds, leaning against the wall, turning the key in the back of a laughing doll over and over again, the neon streetlight outside giving his hair, his skin, an unholy glow.

"Mr. Malone."

Frank turned his head as coolly as though this was just a regular meeting in a bar. Squinted at him.

"Oh, hey. You're that reporter. Womack, is it?"

"Wonicke. Pete Wonicke."

He extended his hand and Frank shook it without getting up.

"I was passing by and I saw the light."

Pete took out his cigarettes, offered him one, sat down.

"Mr. Malone, I know this is none of my business, but what are you doing here? Are you okay?"

Frank turned to him and smiled, but it was a smile without humor or warmth.

"Wonicke, my kids are dead and my wife is facing life inside for killing 'em. Do I look like I'm okay?"

"Sorry, I..."

"It's okay. I know what you meant."

He sighed.

"It must seem weird, me being here."

"Well...a little."

"I guess it's as good a place as any to wait. I'm too wound up to sleep and whatever happens in court tomorrow, I got to wait somewhere, right?"

"Sure."

Frank looked around the empty room, his hands plucking at the rug.

"I knew it'd be empty, anyhow. They can't rent it. People take on the lease—families, with kids—then they find out what happened here, and they move on. Even though the police say nothing did happen in here, in the apartment.

"But, you know. They say there's an atmosphere. Ghosts. Bad feeling. All that. All the same thing, isn't it?"

Pete nodded. "I guess so."

Frank shrugged. "I don't seem to mind the ghosts."

Pete was back at the courthouse by seven the next morning. Drinking the strong coffee they served in the lobby. Pacing the halls.

Smoking endless cigarettes. He watched the hallway fill up: with cops, with reporters with the curious. Scott nodded to him and then looked over at Hirsch, who was talking in low, intense tones to his assistant.

It was after eleven when the call finally came. The bailiff who delivered it sounded composed but the news rippled through the waiting crowd like a bomb blast.

"Jury's back! They're back!"

As they took their seats, Pete looked around him. The jury had been out for a total of sixteen hours. He couldn't tell if this was a good sign and, from their faces, neither could Scott or Hirsch.

Ruth sat in her usual place. The photographs of the children had been taken down and she didn't seem to know where to look. She held her hands in her lap, clasped together. Her face was pale and there were dark circles around her eyes. He watched her turn to Scott and say something and try to smile.

Then the jury filed back in. Scott placed his hand on Ruth's arm, bent to whisper to her. She nodded, biting her lip, her eyes on the jury.

The judge called for order and then:

"On the charge of murder, are you all agreed upon a verdict?"

The foreman rose. He was short, plump, heading for fifty, with receding hair and bifocals with wire frames. The kind of man you wouldn't notice if you passed him in the street.

"We are, Your Honor."

"How do you find the defendant?"

Pete clasped his hands. Kept his eyes on Ruth.

"Guilty of murder in the first degree."

It must be a mistake.

This was a terrible mistake.

But Pete felt the reality in his body. His stomach dropped and the breath left him as though he'd been winded. He fell back in his seat, stunned, then heard a low moan from the defense table, turned to see Ruth burying her face in her hands.

"Oh God. Oh God, no."

"And on the charge of manslaughter, are you all agreed upon a verdict?"

"We are."

"How do you find the defendant?"

"Guilty of manslaughter in the first degree."

There was a moment where time seemed to stand still. And then he heard a high-pitched wail that grew in volume and intensity.

Ruth stood and faced the judge. "You don't give a damn who killed my kids! Nobody gives a damn!"

He banged his gavel and Ruth collapsed into Scott's arms, weeping. Pete could only stare helplessly as her face dissolved into a red wet mass, as that neat figure crumpled over, as she gave in completely to her grief.

A bubble of conversation rose in the courtroom. Doors were flung open, crashed against the walls. Reporters rushed out, heading for the phones.

Pete looked over at Frank, who was slumped in his seat, his head in his hands.

The judge banged his gavel again and raised his voice to be heard.

"This case is adjourned for sentencing. The jury is free to go. Court dismissed."

Two guards approached Ruth. They took hold of her upper arms and pulled her away from Scott, turning her toward the door.

Pete staggered to his feet, reached for her.

"Ruth. I'm here."

One arm outstretched as though he could touch her.

She swayed in their grip, her eyes unfocused.

"I'm here, Ruth. I'll get you out. I'll find a way, I swear."

The door closed behind them and he had no idea if she had even heard.

The court was emptying rapidly now that the entertainment was over. Pete made his way to the front of the public benches, against the tide of people, and sank into a seat, numb.

Then he heard laughter and looked up to see Hirsch over by a crowd of cops, clapping Devlin on the shoulder. Hirsch's face was shining with success. Pete dragged his unwilling gaze over to Devlin, expecting to see the same triumph reflected there. Instead, Devlin was staring up at the photographs of the children that had dominated the courtroom throughout the trial.

As Pete watched, he turned to Hirsch, then looked down at the other man's hand on his arm with something like distaste.

Devlin's face was expressionless and his voice subdued as he spoke.

"I can't take any pleasure from this, Mr. Hirsch. Two children are still dead, and a lot of lives have been ruined."

Then he nodded. "But we did at least get justice. And we got that bitch. We got her."

And he turned toward the door, Quinn scurrying behind him.

20

In a lot of ways, the obvious ways, Pete has moved on.

Two months after the trial, he'd applied to a master's program to study history, and then he took a job as a teacher in a private school. The bookstore wasn't enough—he needed to do something more than earn a living. And sometimes, showing the kids the mistakes of the past, he feels like he is making a small difference.

On his days off, he goes to the movies. He takes long walks at night and needs three or four fingers of Scotch before he can sleep.

But Ruth Malone is still the first thing he thinks of when he wakes every morning. He tried dating a few girls, but he felt like he was being unfaithful to everyone, so he stopped. Sometimes he sees a certain type of woman in a bar, with a certain way of moving, and although he knows it can't be her, he always has to make sure.

The date of her parole hearing is marked on his kitchen calendar, winking at him as he fixes dinner. Two weeks before, he cracks and writes her a letter, telling her he'll be there afterward.

The date of her parole hearing is circled on her calendar, hanging above her bed so it's the first thing she sees when she opens her eyes. She has tried not to get her hopes up, but hope is all she has. Hope and time to think.

She has tried not to imagine the outside world going on without her. For almost four years she has tried to think only of the day to day in here: the library, the cleaning rota, the line for the bathroom.

The feel of her mattress under her back at night and the lines crossed through each day on her calendar before she goes to sleep.

Only occasionally does she allow herself to think about the past. About the kids: the Christmases they had; the feel of Cindy's hair under her fingers as she braided it; the way Frankie stuck his tongue between his front teeth when he practiced writing his name in shaky letters.

And lately, prompted by thoughts of her parole hearing, snippets of the trial keep cutting in around the edges. Thinking about the trial gets her thinking about Devlin: the way he looked at her on that first morning in her apartment. His broad figure on the witness stand, that deep measured voice echoing across the courtroom. Most of all she thinks about his heavy-lidded eyes staring into hers across countless tables in countless bare and ugly rooms.

One interview with him keeps coming into sharp focus. And now, with time to puzzle it out, she keeps going back to one accusation. To one particular detail that doesn't add up.

She can't stop worrying at these loose threads—pulling and pulling and waiting for the whole thing to unravel. Until one morning she wakes—and there it is, clear as day. Suddenly, she knows.

So she writes a note and encloses a visiting order, and she waits.

She has been in this room, or one very like it, a hundred times before. Has sat on the same hard chairs and faced the same visitors across the same tables. Her lawyers. Her mother. Gina.

Lou only visited once, the week after the trial ended.

"I need to think of my business, baby," he told her. "You know that. I have to think how things might look to my clients."

She said nothing.

"Everything has to be squeaky-clean. You understand."

She said nothing, just watched his face as he fell silent. As he turned away. And then as he stood by the door and called for the guard and left without looking back, taking his money for Scott's retainer with him.

Gina was the only one who could shrug off the prison, take Ruth back into the world for a while. She didn't talk much about appeals or the courts or the sentence, but she made her laugh about the past.

It's the smell of this place Ruth hates most. At the beginning, she volunteered for cleaning duty, knowing she'd rather smell bleach and soap than be in the kitchens all day. And the library is better still: the quiet, the smell of old paper. But no matter how hard she tries, she can't get the oniony stink of too many people living too close together out of her head.

Gina helped block it all out. And then one day she told her that she wouldn't be able to come anymore either.

"Mick got a job. A good one."

"Yeah? That's great, G."

"It's in Orange County. It's a real good opportunity."

Her words rushed over one another like a river: her excitement, her need to get the news out. To purge herself.

"Well, Orange County's not so far."

Gina smiled sadly.

"It's Orange County in California, honey. I didn't even know there was more than one. Strange, huh? He got a job all the way out there and he asked me to go with him. He's even talking marriage."

She took Ruth's limp hand in her own strong one.

"I feel like it's my last chance. If I don't go . . . well, what am I going to do?"

Her eyes begged for understanding. Ruth tried to smile back. Told her to go. It's what she'd do herself if she could: run far away where no one knows her.

So now it's just her new attorney from the public defender's office and her mother, and her mother's mouth set in the same thin line, and her mother's hands raw with penance and prayers.

Every month Ruth looks past her visitors to the same white-tiled walls, scratched with initials and curses and promises. But Frank, sitting opposite her today, seems to suck everything out of the room. His size means that he fills the small space and somehow she can't see the tiles or the table or the guard—just his familiar, solid figure. And as she sits down opposite him, memories rise like bubbles: each one a complete story of their past. She remembers him singing along to Buddy Holly on the car radio. She doesn't know when or where they were headed, but she knows there was rain on the windows, that his fingers tapped the wheel and that he sang falsetto just to make her laugh.

She remembers the way he sprawled in his seat in class, legs stretched out, hands in his pockets. She sat behind him in study hall for two years and she can still conjure up a picture of how he looked at fifteen. The line of his jaw. The way his hair curled against his temple. The mole on his neck that was the first detail she noticed about him.

And she remembers their wedding night and how serious he was, how determined that this would be done right. The smell of him as she woke up next to him for the first time. The warmth and the solidness of him that she still reaches for, before she's fully awake. After all these years.

She adjusts her chair and gives herself a moment to get used to him again. Because she can now. She's grown into the habit of not caring what other people think or feel, because there's nothing left to lose. And so only when she's ready does she raise her eyes to his.

"Frank."

He smiles at her. The same slow smile that made her heart skip when she was seventeen and irritated the hell out of her by the time she was twenty-four.

"Ruthie. How you been?"

"Oh, you know."

He nods as though she's said something interesting. "You look good."

And now she smiles back because she knows she doesn't look good, even for thirty-two. She looks thin and tired and worn down. When she lets herself glance in a mirror, she can see the gray hairs, the lines around her eyes. She looks like someone who hasn't been able to take a long bath or choose her own bedtime for almost four years.

"You too."

And she sees that he does look good. He's lost the paunch he had during the trial. His skin is bright and flushed: she can almost smell the fresh air on him.

"Been a long time, huh?"

More than three years since he stopped visiting. Not such a long time on the outside but in here, where each sleepless night lasts thirteen hours and there isn't a whole lot to make the afternoons go by faster, three years feels like a lifetime.

She doesn't answer him because he'll never understand what time means to her. She just shrugs and lets him make of that what he will.

"Think the hearing'll go well?"

She wonders if he only answered her letter, if he only came today, because he wants to know where she's headed if she gets out. He wants to know she's not going to come asking for anything.

He needn't worry.

She lifts her head and forces a smile.

"My attorney says there's a very good chance I'll get parole. God bless prison overcrowding, huh?"

He nods but she sees from the shadow that crosses his face that he doesn't understand her last remark.

She lights a cigarette and thinks how odd it is; not just the fact of him in here, but this conversation. The mention of prison and parole between them as though those words have nothing to do with their children. The ordinary tone of this strange exchange.

But even as she thinks this, she can feel the fear building. She knows she needs to say it. She needs to tell him why she asked him to come today. She needs to put a question to him and she needs to hear his answer, and then she can close the door.

In the end, it's simple. She looks him in the eye and takes a breath and pushes the words out fast before she can stop them.

"It was you. All the time, it was you."

And he looks right back at her and nods, as though he's been expecting this. He brings his head close to hers so the guard can't hear and talks in a sigh, as though he's been waiting a long time to let it out.

He's lying on an old couch in the storage room below her apartment, a warm bottle of beer in one hand. His shoes sit neatly on the floor beside him, his head rests on a pile of old magazines.

Sometimes he flicks through one to make the time pass, but it's too hot tonight to read the same stories again, so his eyes are fixed on the ceiling. He's found that if he lets them roam along the damp stains, looking for patterns, the hours go by faster.

He shifts a little, peels his shirt away from his wet skin, wipes his forehead, taps out a beat on the bottle. Other than that: silence. It's been silent for—he looks at his watch—an hour and twenty-seven minutes.

He drains his beer and sets the empty bottle on the floor by his shoes. Looks back up at the ceiling, and links his hands behind his head. Stretches his legs as far down the couch as he can and inhales: laundry detergent and Marlboros and dust, and underneath it all, the smell of damp that never really goes away, even when it's as humid as all hell outside.

Chrissakes. This fucking damp will mess up his lungs and make him sick—and whose fault is that? He's not down here night after night for himself. He's here because of that bitch upstairs.

That whore up there, fucking other men, giving them what's his. His fucking wife.

He's not allowed to touch. He's never allowed to touch anymore. Everyone and the fucking garbage man is allowed to touch her—and not just touch her, but touch her there, *make her groan and cry out with her sticky red mouth, loud enough so you can hear her even down in the basement.*

She must know he's down here. She knows what it does to him, imagining her with other men. That's why she turns it up, moans so loud. All these years she's been a wife, a mother, and now she's reminding him that she's still a whore. She's waking up that part of him, the part of him that responds to her like this.

She needs to be reminded who she belongs to. She needs to be reminded what she's done to him. And she needs to be hit where it will hurt her most.

Jesus.

Look what she's making him do.

Look at the things he has to do for love.

"When I thought you were asleep, I walked to the nearest phone booth and I called you. I knew if you heard it ring, you'd answer, that you'd think it was one of your johns. Gallagher. That cop—Salcito. No answer would mean you were sleeping too deep to hear it. I thought then that maybe I'd be able to go through the front door. Into my house. Into my kids' room. Like a regular father."

His breathing quickens, and there is a thickness in his voice.

She's always thought of him as stupid. Just stupid slow Frank.

"So yeah, I called and when you answered, I picked a fight to get you to hang up. Then I crept back in and I heard you moving around, heard the dog whine and the door slam, and I knew that I could go in."

He clears his throat. "I just walked into the apartment. Easy as anything."

She'd thought she was ready to hear this. How could she have thought she'd be able to bear it?

"I unlatched their door and went in. They were asleep, both of them, lying on their sides, facing each other. Cin was muttering and sighing, and Frankie had his mouth open. Little soft snores like a puppy.

"I opened the window, thinking I might get them out that way in case you came back. Took off the screen and dropped it on the ground. But then I realized it was too difficult. Decided to carry them out through the apartment after all."

"Frankie half–woke up but I just said we were going for a ride and when he realized it was his daddy, he fell back asleep, quick as winking."

There's a roaring in her ears. It's her blood she can hear. Her own blood.

She stares at him, focusing on the dark bristles on his jaw that his razor missed. The wrinkle in his collar. The cracked tile above his head. Desperately reaching for the ordinary, the mundane.

"Cin never woke up at all. As I took them out, I relatched the bedroom door again. Figured if you checked, that'd prove you cared enough about them. That you deserved them. I would've brought them back then, told you it was just a joke, that we'd only been around the block."

"But you never checked, did you? When you came back with the dog, you never checked. I sat in the car and watched you sitting on the steps with a drink and a smoke like you didn't have a care in the world. So I knew you hadn't bothered to check they were okay, and I had to take 'em."

She realizes that her mouth is open and dry. Tries to swallow.

"As I took them out, I noticed a stroller near the next building. Just on the grass. And a box lying near it. So I put the box on the stroller and wheeled the whole thing under the window. Guess I thought it might look like they climbed out themselves. Maybe used the stroller to step down."

She focuses on the detail of his words. As though this will make the horror easier to bear.

"You didn't think people might wonder how they could've moved the stroller? How they could've taken the screen down? Two little kids couldn't have managed that."

She marvels at how calm her voice sounds. She could have sworn she was yelling. But her voice comes out tiny and level.

He shrugs. "I didn't think that far. I just wanted to mix things up a little."

In his story, they're still alive and she wants him to write her a new ending. "What were you going to do? With...with the kids?"

He shrugs again. "I'd have brought 'em back in the morning, I guess. I don't know, I didn't have a plan. Maybe I'd have said I was in the neighborhood and I found 'em wandering outside. That I took 'em home."

"But they'd say...they'd tell me. Frankie would have told me that wasn't true."

Even as she says it, she knows she's wrong. Frankie adored his daddy, would have said whatever Frank had told him to. And maybe they wouldn't even remember right, would think it was a dream—going to sleep in their own house, waking up at Frank's place.

All those interviews. Those statements. The police, looking for a careful, clever plan. Herself wanting to believe in a careful, clever stranger, in someone watching them all for days.

And all the time: just Frank.

"After you put...them...in the car, what then?"

"I put the kids in the back and got out the same way I got in—took the emergency brake off and pushed the car to the end of the street, then got in and just drove home. It was that easy. I carried 'em up to my room. Gave 'em some comics. Grape juice."

And now she has to look away. She can't look at his face and listen to the rest of it.

But he just says, "I never meant to hurt 'em."

And then, "How did you guess?"

Here it is: the thing she puzzled over for so long, the question she prodded like a sore, refusing to let the wound heal. Now the poison is coming out. The filthy truth.

"Someone fed them after I did. It had to be someone who..." She can't make herself say the word. "Someone fed them and took care of them. Why would anyone else feed them?"

He nods and his breath eases.

"It's funny, nobody even noticed what I did with the stroller. But the food, I didn't even think about it."

"People never notice what you think they will. I told the cops that I was in bed by midnight and that I never woke up till you called me in the morning. But you told 'em about the call I made to you at three a.m. I realized I slipped up. I got scared. Worried they'd check the phone records. But you know, they never picked up on it. Or if they did, they didn't care. They were so set on you being guilty, 'specially when you wouldn't take the lie detector test."

She blinks. Answers almost automatically, "You didn't take it either."

He nods. Says, "Yeah, but they never asked me. And after you walked out of the test, the cops hardly noticed me at all."

Clears his throat.

"Anyway, I fed 'em. I went upstairs to get them some juice and when I came back, Frankie was awake again. He needed to pee, then he said he was hungry. I asked him what they had for dinner—know what he said? He said, 'We haven't had nothing, Daddy.'"

"I fed them. I fed them! I gave them veal. Veal and canned beans and milk. Just like I told the cops. Only...only they wouldn't eat it. The meat was chewy and Frankie said he didn't like it."

She has no idea why it seems so important to make him understand this.

"I told them there was nothing else and they'd have to go hungry if they didn't eat it. Frankie threw his plate on the floor and I...I was so tired..."

Frankie's stubborn face, lip stuck out, his cheek glowing from her hand. Cindy crying but refusing to eat when her brother wouldn't. Wanting to be just like him.

"They were hungry, Ruth. And I didn't want them grousing and whining, so I made mac 'n' cheese and they ate some of it and went back to sleep for a while. But when they woke up, Cin started to cry.

"She said she wanted her mommy. Wanted to go home. I kept telling her to hush, to calm down, but the more I told her, the worse she got, until she was howling. Then Frank Jr. started up, yelling at me that he was going to tell his mommy, that she would be mad at me."

She feels as though her throat has closed up. Can't breathe.

"I was panicking, scared the guys down the hall would hear them, so I slapped Frankie and I picked Cin up and shook her. That just made it worse and she started screaming. She was red and screaming and her face was wet—I didn't know what to do. I put one hand over her mouth and the other on her neck. And then I don't remember much else, 'cept she was lying there, limp, and there was a sort of…foam coming out of her mouth. I shook her again, but there was…there was just nothing.

"And when I turned around, Frankie was huddled up on the couch, looking at me. I reached out a hand, but he wriggled back further right into the wall, and that made me real mad."

His eyes on her. Burning. "You made him afraid of me. My own son."

"I said, 'It's okay, Frankie, it's okay,' and he shook his head and he started rocking. He said, 'You hurt Cin. You hurt my Cin.' And he kept saying it, over and over, and I couldn't stand it, so I had to quiet him too."

His voice falters a little and for the first time he looks away.

"I had to make him quiet."

She stares at him, looking for a glimpse of the man she's known for more than half her life. She looks for the humor, the tenderness she knows is in him. And they're not there.

She loved this man, once. Carried his children.

She wants to vomit.

Their father.

Their own father.

The fact of it is like her own heartbeat. Her own blood, pounding in time with the horror of it.

She's trembling. "Why? Why did you ... why?

"Frank?"

He raises his head, and through the shock of it all, she sees that he's smiling at her. Like it's a sunny afternoon at Coney Island and he's just handed her a corn dog. But there's something in his smile ... something slithering behind his eyes.

And although his head is angled down and his breath is regular and even, the words come out sizzling.

"Ruth, honey, you were behaving like a bitch in heat. Running around with all those men. You'd spread your legs for any guy with a fat wallet and a fancy watch. You were a mother, but you wouldn't act like one. So you had to be taught a lesson. And I was ready to forgive you, but you had to ask for it. And I knew that if the kids were gone, you'd need me again. You'd need my help. I knew you'd want me to come back."

His eyes bore through her, all the way inside her, and his mouth twitches.

"And you did, didn't you, baby? I was the first person you called. You needed me again."

His smile is a red blur through her tears.

"You came back to me."

Somehow the ring of arrogance in his voice breaks the spell and she lets out the long breath she has been holding. She realizes that beneath the horror and the disgust, she is knotted with rage. She clenches her fists and feels the nails break her skin and for one white-hot moment she feels the depth of her hate.

She lifts her head. "But we broke up again, Frank. We broke up. I've been with other men since you."

His tongue flickers out, just for an instant, to wet his lips.

"Lots of men."

He smiles again.

"Yeah. Yeah, I knew that, Ruthie. I knew you'd leave again."

He sighs, tips his chair back, studies her with his head to one side.

"And I knew that when you got out of here, you'd disappear.

You'd go off with Gallagher or someone else, and you'd think you could move on. Without me."

Suddenly his chair lunges forward, the legs crashing against the floor, and she jumps and he's looking over at the guard and nodding like everything is fine, and then he's leaning toward her. She doesn't want to give him an inch but she can't help it, and even though she recoils he's close enough that she can smell his sour breath as he spits his words out.

"But no matter where you go or who you're with, no matter who you're whoring yourself out to, no matter which rich dupe you find to take care of you, you'll know what I did and why. I'll be in your head every day. You're going to get what you deserve."

He leans back and folds his arms and that smile is back in place.

"When we were waiting for the verdict, I was so afraid you'd get off. These past four years, I finally knew where you were. Knew you weren't with another guy. And now it doesn't matter what happens. You could walk out of here tomorrow and it wouldn't matter. After today, I'll always be right here"—and he reaches over and taps his finger against her temple. Twice.

That's the image that stays with her: his finger, tapping; his bright eyes; that broad grin.

She doesn't remember much after that: not Frank leaving or the walk to her cell. She doesn't remember the bell ringing for dinner or making the decision not to get up and eat, but when she comes back to herself, she's huddled on her bed and it's dark. The lights are off in her cell and there's just the pale glow from the hallway and the noise of hundreds of women falling asleep: low voices, coughing, someone sobbing quietly.

She closes her eyes and all she can see is his smile, and she thinks: *This is how it's going to be now.*

And this is how it is through the days that follow.

She eats and showers and gets into bed when they tell her to. She mops floors, scrubs toilets, pushes the library cart, and all the time Frank is there, like he promised.

The day of the parole hearing arrives and her attorney looks at her naked face, her red eyes, and nods.

She sits in a small stifling room facing another row of faces across another table. She speaks softly. She hears the words *remorse* and *guilt* and she bows her head in acknowledgment and weeps.

"Yes," she wants to say. "I am guilty. I did not protect them. I did not stop him. I did not recognize him for what he was.

"I admit it. I am guilty."

She lets their voices wash over her and thinks about telling them. She imagines the words in her mouth. How they would sound. She imagines the clear truth hanging in the close air of this room. How it would taste. And then she imagines them looking through it and seeing only her fury and her grief. She imagines their disbelieving expressions and their eyes slip-sliding away to their notes, the murmured shaking of their heads.

She imagines being sent back to her cell, knowing that Frank's words have won her more years behind bars. She imagines his triumphant smile.

And so instead she takes a Kleenex from the box they push toward her, and she presses it to her wet face. Presses it against her mouth to keep the truth contained.

All they see and hear are her tears, and they nod because, finally, she is broken.

Pete watches her emerge from the dark cocoon of the prison gateway and into the sunlight in a long smooth ripple of pink filmy scarf. The guard says something to her—he thinks it's Baker, although he's not sure. It's been almost three years since she told him to stop coming.

As she turns to listen, he lets his eyes rest on her tight skirt and bright blouse and on her careful glossy smile. For her, the sixties have not ended. Jim and Janis and Jimi and Altamont—none of that has touched her.

He comes out from his own shadows, one hopeful step and then another and another, breath thick in his dry mouth and his hands damp. He thinks of how long it's taken them to get here, of the lies he's told, the vows he's broken, and the money he's spent. He thinks of Clyde Harrison and of his mother and father, and of the things he's had to do for love.

She stands in the sun for a moment and closes her eyes, lifts her face to the light. As Pete walks toward her, his steps quickening, she opens her eyes and he stops.

There's a little distance between them and she looks uncertainly across it, shades her eyes with her hand.

"Ruth. I came to . . . I thought maybe we could have lunch."

She keeps looking at him, her eyes in shadow.

He pushes on. "And . . . I don't know if you have a place to stay, but I . . ."

He trails off into her silence.

"I thought you'd want to celebrate."

Her hand falls and she frowns, and now he sees what the years have done to her. The shadows underneath her eyes, the lines around her mouth. She looks old and tired and afraid.

"Celebrate?"

"Sure, why not? You're free now. You're a free woman."

But she shakes her head, slowly at first and then faster, as though she can't stop.

And she hears his voice as though from a great distance.

"Ruth?"

"How can I be free?"

"I don't understand. I want . . . I wanted to take care of you."

She stares at him and shakes her head again, and then the noise of a car horn breaks the silence. There is a streak of yellow and a cab opens up the space between them, and she is gone.

She feels his eyes on her all the way to the highway but she sits straight and tall on the worn vinyl seat, and she does not look back.

She has imagined this moment for a long time: driving away with a stranger, an empty road ahead of her. Anonymity. She wondered how she would feel, facing a life without Frankie and Cindy, without Lou, without the promise of endless gauzy nights.

Frank has changed everything. Since he left her with the truth, she has often thought she would not be able to bear the weight of her grief and her guilt. She has lain awake, imagining pills and vodka in a cheap motel room. She has fantasized about pure nothingness.

But now, looking ahead at the approaching city, feeling the half-forgotten rush and rhythm of a New York afternoon break over her, she realizes that she cannot give in. For their sake, for Frankie and Cindy, she will not let Frank win.

She sits a little straighter. Inhales gasoline and Juicy Fruit, the smell of warm doughnuts from a roadside stand, the sweet rich leather of the driver's jacket. And the road rises before them and the car begins to climb into the blue infinity of the summer sky.

Acknowledgments

Little Deaths is a work of fiction. Readers who are interested in the case that inspired it can find more details in *The Alice Crimmins Case* by Kenneth Gross, and *Ordeal by Trial* by George Carpozi Jr.

There are a lot of people who helped shape this book and make it possible for me to write it, and I'm exercising the prerogative of the debut author to thank them all.

Thank you to my family. To my mum and dad, for instilling in me a love of history; for the sacrifices you made so that I could go to university and read for four years; and for being so proud of me. To my brother Martin, for widening my taste in crime fiction, and for showing me that people like us could write novels. I can't wait to read yours. And to my grandma, Mary Cuthbert, for everything, with much love.

To my wonderful agent, Jo Unwin. Thank you for your unstinting and unwavering encouragement, support, and all-round cheerleading of me and of Ruth. Thank you for spotting our potential and hanging in there, for always knowing the right thing to say, and for your honesty and kindness and invaluable advice.

I'm very lucky to have such a wonderful team of people behind me in the publishing world. To everyone at Jo Unwin Literary Agency, at Rogers, Coleridge & White, at Picador, and at Gelfman Schneider, who has worked so hard to bring *Little Deaths* into the world, and to give it the best chance of succeeding: especially Deborah Schneider, Saba Ahmed, Isabel Adomakoh Young, and the hugely talented Francesca Main. And at Hachette, an enormous thank you to Paul Whitlatch and Lauren Hummel, Michelle Aielli and Emily Caldwell, Mauro DiPreta, Betsy Hulsebosch, to Amanda Kain for my astonishing and wonderful American cover, Diana Drew, Odette Fleming, Grace Hernandez, Marina Lowry, Mike Olivo, Anna Maria Piluso, and Erin Vandeveer.

To everyone who read and commented on early drafts of this book, especially Francesca Pagnacco, Carrie Plitt, Karen Campbell, Andrew Wille, and L. E. Yates. Your comments and suggestions made this a far better book.

To Clare Palmer, for your practical help and generosity. Without you and your retreat, your kitchen table and your Squeaks, writing this book would have been a far tougher and far lonelier experience.

And to the other Kings Place Writers, who continue to offer friendship, support, and tough critiquing: Andrea Terroni, Geraldine Terry, Harriet Sawyer, and Sydnee Blake.

To my North London Writers Group, who so generously read an entire draft of this novel, and provided immensely valuable and constructive feedback to a demanding and stressed writer on short notice: Adi Bloom, Alix Christie, Cathy de Freitas, Zoe Gilbert, Eva Holland, Adam Marek, Anna Mazzola, and Evie Miller. (Neil Blackmore, Lily Dunn, and Yojana Sharma—your input was missed!)

To my other writer friends: Rae Stoltenkamp, Raf Torrubia, Claire McTague, Deb Jess Kermode, Katja Sass, Sarah Steele, and Frances Pearce. Thank you for your support and camaraderie over the years, and for being so willing to share the ups and downs of the process of becoming a writer. And to Nichole Beauchamp, thank you for introducing me to the original writers' group, and for your continued and valued friendship.

To my oldest friends, especially Nicola Hill, Yvonne Rhodes-James, Helen Parr, Veronica Teall, Matthew Redhead and Libby Summers, Una and James Eve, and Candi Bloxham: this book has been a long time in the making, and you've all influenced it. And to Faye Emery and Bernardo Rodriguez-Gonzalez: thank you for providing a wonderful location for me to work on (almost) the last draft. Hilton Farm saved Five Writers Go(ing) Mad in Bude, and in dire need of a retreat at short notice.

To my fabulous fellow Faber students: thank you for your warmth, honesty, and encouragement. This has been an astonishing journey, and one I'm proud to be sharing with you.

To my teachers, particularly Sarah Fearon and Robin Hodnett, for teaching me to think critically and to be interested in the world around me. And to Adrian Beard: thank you for not giving up on me despite a disastrous beginning to my English A-level, and for teaching me to read critically. Without you, I wouldn't have fallen in love with language, and I wouldn't have started an English degree.

To Marie Larkin, who taught me that I could do it.

To Julia Bell, who was the first real writer I met, and who told me I was a writer too. Thank you for taking me seriously.

To all the people I've worked with who became friends instead of colleagues: thank you for keeping me sane for the past twenty years, and for all those nights in the pub. I owe you a pint. A special thanks to Christian Reichert and Laura Colclough, who helped make it possible for me to spend time on the last couple of drafts in 2016.

And finally, to all the dreadful managers and employers I've had: thank you for making my day job so awful that I rushed to escape into Ruth's world every night and every weekend. You made me **determined**.

35674056673669